About the Author

Sharon Kendrick started storytelling at the age of eleven and has never stopped. She likes to write fast-paced, feel-good romances with heroes who are so sexy they'll make your toes curl! She lives in the beautiful city of Winchester – where she can see the cathedral from her window (when standing on tip-toes!). She has two children, Celia and Patrick and her passions include music, books, cooking and eating – and drifting into daydreams while working out new plots.

The Tycoon's Affair

July 2025
Tempted by Desire

January 2026
Stealing his Heart

August 2025
Craving his Love

February 2026
Playing with Power

September 2025
Business with Pleasure

March 2026
After Hours Passion

The Tycoon's Affair: Craving his Love

SHARON KENDRICK

MILLS & BOON

All rights reserved including the right of reproduction in whole or in part in any form. This edition is published by arrangement with Harlequin Enterprises ULC.

This is a work of fiction. Names, characters, places, locations and incidents are purely fictional and bear no relationship to any real life individuals, living or dead, or to any actual places, business establishments, locations, events or incidents. Any resemblance is entirely coincidental.

Without limiting the author's and publisher's exclusive rights, any unauthorised use of this publication to train generative artificial intelligence (AI) technologies is expressly prohibited. HarperCollins also exercise their rights under Article 4(3) of the Digital Single Market Directive 2019/790 and expressly reserve this publication from the text and data mining exception.

® and ™ are trademarks owned and used by the trademark owner and/or its licensee. Trademarks marked with ® are registered with the United Kingdom Patent Office and/or the Office for Harmonisation in the Internal Market and in other countries.

First Published in Great Britain 2025
by Mills & Boon, an imprint of HarperCollins*Publishers* Ltd
1 London Bridge Street, London, SE1 9GF

www.harpercollins.co.uk

HarperCollins*Publishers*
Macken House, 39/40 Mayor Street Upper,
Dublin 1, D01 C9W8, Ireland

The Tycoon's Affair: Craving his Love © 2025 Harlequin Enterprises ULC.

The Billionaire's Defiant Acquisition © 2016 Sharon Kendrick
The Argentinian's Baby of Scandal © 2019 Sharon Kendrick
Di Sione's Virgin Mistress © 2016 Harlequin Books S.A.

Special thanks and acknowledgement are given to Sharon Kendrick for her contribution to *The Billionaire's Legacy* series.

ISBN: 978-0-263-41755-5

MIX
Paper | Supporting
responsible forestry
FSC
www.fsc.org
FSC™ C007454

This book contains FSC™ certified paper and other controlled sources to ensure responsible forest management.

For more information visit: www.harpercollins.co.uk/green

Printed and Bound in the UK using 100% Renewable Electricity
at CPI Group (UK) Ltd, Croydon, CR0 4YY

THE BILLIONAIRE'S DEFIANT ACQUISITION

With special thanks to fascinating Fredrik Ferrier,
for giving me an illuminating glimpse into
the world of art.

And to the fabulous Annie Macdonald Hall,
who taught me so much about horses – and made
me understand why people love them so much.

CHAPTER ONE

IN THE FLESH she looked more dangerous than beautiful. Conall's mouth hardened. She was exquisite, yes...but *faded*. Like a rose which had been plucked fresh for a man's buttonhole before a wild night of partying, but which now lay wilted and drooping across his chest.

Fast asleep, she lay sprawled on top of a white leather sofa. She was wearing a baggy T-shirt, which curved over her breasts and bottom, ending midway along amazingly tanned legs which seemed to go on for ever. Beside her lay an empty champagne glass—the finger-marked crystal upended and glinting in the spring sunshine. A faint breeze drifted in from the open windows leading onto the balcony, but it wasn't enough to disperse the faint fug of cigarette smoke, along with the musky scent of incense. Conall made a barely perceptible click of distaste. Cliché after cliché were all here—embodied in the magnificent body of Amber Carter as she lay with her head pillowed on her arm and her black hair spilling like ink over her golden skin.

If she'd been a man he would have shaken her awake with a contemptuous hand, but she was not a man. She was a woman. A spoilt and distractingly beautiful woman who was now his responsibility and for some reason he didn't want to touch her. He didn't dare.

Damn Ambrose Carter, he thought viciously, remembering the older man's plaintive appeal to him. *You've got to save her from herself, Conall. Someone has to show her she can't carry on like this.* And damn his own stupid conscience, which had made him agree to carry out this crazy deal.

He listened. The apartment was silent—but maybe he should check it was empty. That there were no other bodies sprawled in one of the many bedrooms and able to hear what he was about to say to her.

He prowled from room to room, but, among all the debris of cold pizza lying in greasy boxes and half-empty bottles of vintage champagne, he could find no one. Only once did he pause—when he pushed open a door of a spare bedroom, cluttered with books and clothes and a dusty-looking exercise bike. Half hidden behind a velvet sofa was a stack of paintings and Conall walked over to them, his natural collector's eye making him flick through them with interest. The canvases were raw and angry—with swirls and splodges of paint, some of which had been highlighted with a sharp edging of black ink. He studied them for several moments, until he was forced to remember that he was here for a purpose and he turned away from the pictures and returned to the sitting room, to find Amber Carter lying exactly where he'd left her.

'Wake up,' he growled. And then, when that received no response, he repeated it—more loudly this time. 'I said, wake up.'

She moved. A golden arm reached up to brush aside the thick sweep of ebony hair which obscured most of her face, offering him a sudden unimpeded view of her profile. Her cute little nose and the natural pout of her rosy lips. Thick lashes fluttered open and as she slowly turned her head to look at him he realised that her eyes were the most startling shade of green he'd ever seen. They made the breath dry in his throat, those eyes. They made him momentarily forget what he was doing there.

'What's going on?' she questioned, in a smoky voice. 'And who the hell are you?'

She sat up, blinking as she looked around—but not creating the kind of fuss he might have expected. As if she was used to being woken by strange men who had walked into her apartment at midday. He felt another shimmer of distaste. Maybe she was.

'My name is Conall Devlin,' he said, looking at her face for some kind of recognition, but seeing only a blank and shuttered boredom on her frozen features.

'Oh, yeah?' Those amazing eyes swept over him and then she yawned. 'And how did you get in, Conall Devlin?'

In many ways Conall was the most old-fashioned of men—an accusation levelled at him many times by disappointed women in the past—and in that precise moment he felt his temper begin to flare because it confirmed everything he'd heard about her. That she was careless. That she didn't care about anything or anyone, except herself. And anger was safer than desire. Than allowing himself to focus on the way her breasts jiggled as she moved. Or to acknowledge that as she rose to her feet and walked across the room she moved with a natural grace, which made him want to stare at her and keep staring. Which made his groin begin to harden with an unwilling kind of lust.

'The door was open,' he said, not bothering to hide his disapproval.

'Oh. Right. Someone must have left it open on their way out.' She looked at him and smiled the pretty kind of smile which probably had most men eating out of her hand. 'I had a party last night.'

He didn't smile back. 'Doesn't it worry you that someone could have walked right in and burgled you—or worse?'

She shrugged. 'Not really. Security on the main door is usually very tight. Though come to think of it—you seem to have got past them without too much difficulty. How did you manage that?'

'Because I have a key,' he said, holding it up between his thumb and forefinger so that it glinted in the bright spring sunshine.

She was walking across the room—the baggy T-shirt moving across her bottom to draw his unwilling attention to the pert swell of her buttocks. But his words made her jerk her head back in surprise and a faint frown appeared on her brow as she extracted a pack of cigarettes from a small beaded handbag which was lying on a coffee table.

'What are you talking about, you *have a key*?' she questioned, pulling out a filter tip and jamming it in between her lips.

'I'd rather you didn't light that,' said Conall tightly.

Her eyes narrowed. 'Oh, really?'

'Yes. *Really*,' he gritted back sarcastically. 'Discounting the obvious dangers of passive smoking, I happen to hate the smell.'

'Then leave. Nobody's stopping you.' She flicked the lighter with a manicured thumbnail so that a blue-gold flash of flame flared briefly into life, but she only got as far as inhaling the first drag when Conall crossed the room and removed the cigarette from her mouth, ignoring her look of shock.

'What the hell do you think you're playing at?' she spluttered indignantly. 'You can't do that!'

'No?' he questioned silkily. 'Watch me, baby.' He walked out to the balcony and crushed the glowing red tip between thumb and forefinger, before dropping it into another empty champagne glass, which was standing next to a large pot plant.

When he returned he could see a look of defiance on her face as she took out a second cigarette.

'There are plenty more where that came from,' she taunted.

'And you'll only be wasting your time,' he said flatly. 'Because every cigarette you light I'm going to take from you and extinguish, until eventually you have none left.'

'And if I call the police and have you arrested for trespass and harassment,' she challenged. 'What then?'

Conall shook his head. 'Sorry to disappoint you, but neither of those charges will stand up—since I think the law might find that you are the one who is actually guilty of trespass. Remember what I just told you? That I have a key.' He paused.

He saw her defiance briefly waver. He saw a shadow cross over her beautiful green eyes and he felt a wave of something which felt almost like empathy and he wasn't quite sure why. Until he reminded himself what kind of woman she was. The spoilt, manipulative kind who stood for everything he most despised.

'Yes I know but I'm asking why—and it had better be a good explanation,' she said in a tone of voice which nobody had dared use with him for years. 'Who are you, and why have you come barging in here, trying to take control?'

'I'm happy to tell you anything you want to know,' he said evenly. 'But first I think you need to put on some clothes.'

'Why?' A smile played at the corners of her lips as she put a hand on one angled hip and struck a catwalk pose. 'Does my appearance bother you, Mr Devlin?'

'Actually, no—at least, not in the way I think you're suggesting. I'm not turned on by women who smoke and flaunt their bodies to strangers,' he said, although the latter part of this statement wasn't quite true, as the continued aching in his body testified. He swallowed against the sudden unwanted dryness in his throat. 'And since I don't have all day to waste— why don't you do as I ask and then we can get down to business?'

For a moment Amber hesitated, tempted to tell him to go to hell. To carry through her threat and march over to the phone and call the police, despite the fact that she was enjoying the unexpected *drama* of the situation. Because wasn't it good to feel *something*— even if it was only anger, when for so long now all she had felt had been a terrifying kind of *numbness*? As if she were no longer made of flesh and blood, but was colourless and invisible—like water.

She narrowed her eyes as her mind flicked back through the previous evening. Had Conall Devlin been one of the many gatecrashers at the impromptu party she'd ended up hosting? No. Definitely not. She frowned. She would have remembered him. Definitely. Because he was the kind of man you would never forget, no matter how objectionable you found him.

Unwillingly, her gaze drifted over him. His rugged features would have been perfect were it not for the fact that his nose had obviously once been broken. His hair was dark—though not quite as dark as hers—and his eyes were the colour of midnight. His jaw was dark and shadowed—as if he hadn't bothered shaving that morning, as if he had more than his fair share of testosterone raging around his body. And what a body. Amber swallowed. He looked as if he would be perfectly at ease smashing a pickaxe into a tough piece of concrete—even though she could tell that his immaculate charcoal suit must have cost a fortune.

And meanwhile the inside of her mouth felt as if it had been turned into sandpaper and she was certain her breath must smell awful because she'd fallen asleep without brushing her teeth. Her fingers crept up surreptitiously to her face. Yesterday's make-up was still clogging her eyes and beneath the baggy T-shirt her skin felt warm and sticky. It wasn't how you wanted to look when you were presented with a man as spectacular as him.

'Okay,' she said carelessly. 'I'll go and get dressed.'
She enjoyed his brief look of surprise—as if he

hadn't been expecting her sudden capitulation—and that pleased her because she liked surprising people. She could feel his gaze on her as she padded out of the room towards her bedroom, which had a breathtaking view over some of London's most famous landmarks.

She stared at the perfect circle of the London Eye as she tried to gather her thoughts together. Some women might have been freaked out at having been woken in such a way by a total stranger, but all Amber could think was that it made an interesting start to the day, when lately her days all seemed to bleed into one meaningless blur. She wondered if *Conall Devlin* was used to getting everything he wanted. Probably. He had that unmistakable air of arrogance about him. Did he think she would be intimidated by his macho stance and bossy air? Well, he would soon realise that nothing intimidated *her*.

Nothing.

She didn't rush to get ready—although she took the precaution of locking the bathroom door first. A power shower woke her into life and after she'd dressed, she carefully applied her make-up. A quick blast of the hairdryer and she was done. Twenty minutes later she emerged in a pair of skinny jeans and a clingy white T-shirt to find him still there. Just not where she'd left him—dominating the large reception room with that faintly hostile glint in his midnight-blue eyes. Instead, he was sitting on one of the sofas, busy tapping something into a laptop, as if he had every right to make himself at home. He glanced up as she walked in and she saw a look in his eyes which made her feel faintly uncomfortable, before he closed the laptop and surveyed her coolly.

'Sit down,' he said.

'This is my home, not yours and therefore you don't start telling me what to do. I don't want to sit down.'

'I think it's better you do.'

'I don't care what you think.'

His eyes narrowed. 'You don't care about very much at all, do you, Amber?'

Amber stiffened. He said her name as if he had every right to. As if it were something he'd been rehearsing. And now she could make out the faint Irish burr in his deep voice. Her heart lurched because suddenly this had stopped feeling like a whacky alternative to a normal Sunday morning—whatever *normal* was—and had begun to feel rather...disturbing.

But she sat down on the sofa opposite his, because standing in front of him was making her feel like a naughty schoolgirl who had been summoned in front of the headmaster. And something about the way he was looking at her was making her knees wobble in a way which had nothing to do with anger.

She stared at him. 'Just who are you?'

'I told you. Conall Devlin.' He smiled. 'Name still not ringing any bells?'

She shrugged, as something drifted faintly into the distant recesses of her mind and then drifted out again. 'Maybe.'

'I know your brother, Rafe—'

'*Half*-brother,' she corrected with cold emphasis. 'I haven't seen Rafe in years. He lives in Australia.' She gave a brittle smile. 'We're a very fragmented family.'

'So I believe. I also used to work for your father.'

'My father?' She frowned. 'Oh, dear. Poor you.'

The look which greeted this remark showed that she'd irritated him and for some reason this pleased her. Amber reminded herself that he had no right to storm in and sit on one of her sofas, uninvited. Or to sit there barking out questions. The trouble was that he was exuding a disturbing air of confidence and certainty—like a magician who was saving his show-stopping trick right for the end of his act...

'Anyway,' she said, with an entirely unnecessary glance at the diamond watch which was glittering furiously at her wrist. 'I really don't have time for all this. I'll admit it was a novel way to be woken up but I'm getting bored now and I'm meeting friends for lunch. So cut to the chase and tell me why you're here, Mr Conall. Is my dear daddy having one of his occasional bouts of remorse and wondering how his children are getting on? Are you one of his heavies who he's sent to find out how I am? In which case, you can tell him I'm doing just fine.' She raised her eyebrows at him. 'Or has he grown bored with wife number...let me see, which number is he on now? Is it six? Or has he reached double figures? It's *so-o-o* difficult to keep up with his hectic love life.'

Conall listened as she spat out her spiky observations, telling himself that of *course* she was likely to be mixed up and angry and combative. That anyone with her troubled background was never going to end up taking the conventional path in life. Except he knew that adversity didn't necessarily have to make you spoilt and petulant. He thought about what his own mother had been forced to endure—the kind of hardship which would probably be beyond Amber Carter's wilful understanding.

His mouth tightened. He wouldn't be doing her any favours by patting her on her pretty, glossy head and telling her it was all going to be okay. Hadn't people been doing that all her life—with predictable results? Quite frankly, he was itching to lay her across his lap and spank a little sense into her. He felt an unwanted jerk of lust. Though maybe that wasn't such a good idea.

'I have just concluded a business deal with your father,' he said.

'Bully for you,' she said flippantly. 'No doubt he drove a hard bargain.'

'Indeed he did,' he agreed steadily, wondering if she had any idea of the irony of her words—and how much he secretly agreed with them. Because if anyone else had attempted to negotiate the kind of terms Ambrose Carter had demanded, then Conall would have given an emphatic no and walked away from the deal without looking back. But the acquisition of this imposing tower block in this part of London wasn't just something he'd set his heart on—a lifetime dream he'd never thought he'd achieve just shy of his thirty-fifth birthday. It was more than that. He owed the old man. He owed him big time. Because despite Ambrose's own car crash of an emotional life, he had shown Conall kindness at a time when his life had been short of kindness. He had given him the break he'd needed. Had believed in him when nobody else had.

'You owe me, Conall,' he'd said as he had outlined his outrageous demand. 'Do this one thing for me and we're quits.'

And even though Conall had inwardly objected to

the blatant emotional blackmail, how could he possibly have refused? If it weren't for Ambrose he could have ended up serving time in prison. His life could have been very different. Surely it wasn't beyond the realms of possibility that he could teach his mixed-up daughter a few fundamental lessons in manners and survival.

He stared into her emerald eyes and tried to ignore the sensual curve of her mouth, which was sending subliminal messages to his body and making a pulse at his temple begin to hammer. 'Yesterday, I made a significant purchase from your father.'

She wasn't really paying attention. She was too busy casting longing looks in the direction of her cigarettes. 'And your point is?'

'My point is that I now own this apartment block,' he said.

He had her attention now. All of it. Her green eyes were shocked—she looked like a cat which had had a bucket of icy water thrown over it. But it didn't take longer than a couple of seconds for her natural arrogance to assert itself. For her to narrow those amazing eyes and look down her haughty little nose at him.

'You? But...but it's been in his property portfolio for years. It's one of his key investments. Why would he sell it without telling me?' She wrinkled her brow in confusion. 'And to *you*?'

Conall gave a short laugh. The inference was as clear as the blue spring sky outside the penthouse windows. He wondered if she would have found the news less shocking if the purchase had been made by some rich aristocrat—someone who presumably she would have less trouble twisting around her little finger.

'Presumably because he likes doing business with me,' he said. 'And he wants to free up some of his money and commitments in order to enjoy his retirement.'

Another frown pleated her perfect brow. 'I had no idea he was thinking about retirement.'

Conall was tempted to suggest that if she communicated with her father a little more often, then she might know what was going on in his life, but he wasn't here to judge her. He was here to offer her a solution to her current appalling lifestyle, even if it went against his every instinct.

'Well, he is. He's winding down and as of now I am the new owner of this development.' He drew in a deep breath. 'Which means, of course, that there are going to be a number of changes. The main one being that you can no longer continue to live here rent-free as you have been doing.'

'Excuse me?'

'You are currently occupying a luxury apartment in a prime location,' he continued, 'which I can rent out for an astronomical monthly sum. At the moment you are paying precisely nothing and I'm afraid that the arrangement is about to come to an end.'

Her haughty expression became even haughtier and she shuddered, as if the very mention of money was in some way vulgar, and Conall felt a flicker of pleasure as he realised he was enjoying himself. Because it was a long time since a woman had shown him anything except an eager green light.

'I don't think you understand, Mr...*Devlin*,' she

continued, spitting his name out as if it were poison, 'that you will get your money. I'm quite happy to pay the current market value as rent. I just need to speak to my bank,' she concluded.

He gave a smile. 'Good luck with that.'

She was getting angry now. He could see it in the sudden glitter of her eyes and the way she curled her scarlet fingernails so that they looked like talons against the faded denim of her skinny jeans. And he felt a corresponding flicker of something he didn't recognise. Something he tried to push away as he stared into the furious tremble of her lips.

'You may know my father and my brother,' she said, 'but that certainly doesn't give you the authority to make pronouncements about things which are none of your business. Things about which you know nothing. Like my finances.'

'Oh, I know more about those than you might realise,' he said. 'More than you would probably be comfortable with.'

'I don't believe you.'

'Believe what you like, baby,' he said softly. 'Because you'll soon find out what's true. But it doesn't have to get acrimonious. I'm going to be very magnanimous, Amber, because your father and I go back a long way. And I'm going to make you an offer.'

Her magnificent eyes narrowed suspiciously. 'What kind of offer?'

'I'm going to offer you a job and the chance to redeem yourself. And if you accept, we'll see about giving you an apartment more suited to a woman on a working wage, rather than this—' He gave an expansive wave of his hand. 'Which you have to admit is more suited to someone on a millionaire's salary.'

She was staring at him incredulously, as if she couldn't believe what he'd just said. As if he were suddenly going to smile and tell her that he'd simply been teasing and she could have whatever it was she wanted. Was that how men usually behaved towards her? he wondered. Of course it was. When you looked the way she looked, men would fall over themselves whenever she clicked her beautifully manicured fingers.

'And if I don't accept?'

He shrugged. 'That will make things a little more difficult. I will be forced to give you a month's notice and after that to change the locks, and I'm afraid you'll be on your own.'

She jumped to her feet, her eyes spitting green fire—looking as if she'd like to rush across the room and rake those scarlet talons all over him. And wasn't there a primitive side of him which wished she would go right ahead? Take them right down his chest to his groin. Curve those red nails around his balls and gently scrape them, before replacing them with the lick of her tongue.

But she didn't. She just stood there sucking in a deep breath and trying to compose herself...while his erotic little fantasies meant that he was having to do exactly the same.

'I may not know much about the law, Mr Devlin,' she said, biting out the words like splinters of ice, 'but even I know that you aren't allowed to throw a sitting tenant out onto the streets.'

'But you're not a tenant, Amber, and you never

have been,' he said, trying not to show the sudden triumph which rushed through him. Because although she might be spoilt and thoroughly objectionable, she was going to learn enough of life's harsher lessons in the coming weeks, without him rubbing salt into the wound. He picked his next words carefully. 'Your father has been letting you live here as a favour, nothing more. You didn't sign any agreements—'

'Of course I didn't—because he's my *father*!'

'Which means that your occupancy was simply an act of kindness. And now he has sold it to me, I'm afraid he no longer has any interest or claims on the property. And as a consequence, neither do you.'

Wildly, she shook her head and ebony tendrils of hair flew around it. 'He wouldn't just have sprung it on me like this! He would have told me!' she said, her voice rising.

'He said he'd sent you a letter to inform you what was happening, and so had the bank.'

Amber shot an anguished glance over at the pile of mail which lay unopened on the desk. She had a terrible habit of putting letters to one side and ignoring them. She'd done it for longer than she could remember. Letters only ever contained bad news and all her bills were paid by direct debit and if people wanted her that badly, they could always send an email. Because that was what people did, wasn't it?

But in the meantime, she wasn't going to take any notice of this shadowed-jawed man with the mocking voice and a presence which was strangely unsettling. All she had to do was to speak to her father. There had to be some kind of mistake. There *had to*. Either that, or Daddy's brain wasn't as sharp as it had once been. Why else would he choose to sell one of the jewels in his property crown to this...this *thug*?

'I'd like you to leave now, Mr Devlin.'

He raised dark and mocking brows. 'So you're not interested in my offer? A proper job for the first time in your privileged life? The chance to show the world that you're more than just a vapid socialite who flits from party to party?'

'I'd sooner work for the devil than work for you,' she retorted, watching as he rose from the sofa and moved across the room until he was towering over her, with a grim expression on his dark face.

'Make an appointment to see me when you're ready to see sense,' he said, putting a business card down on the coffee table.

'That just isn't going to happen—be very sure about that,' she said, pulling a cigarette from the pack and glaring at him defiantly, as if daring him to stop her again. 'Now go to hell, will you?'

'Oh, believe me, baby,' he said softly. 'Hell would be a preferable alternative to a minute more spent in *your* company.'

And didn't it only add outrage to Amber's growing sense of panic to realise that he actually *meant* it?

CHAPTER TWO

AMBER'S FINGERS WERE trembling as she left the bank and little rivulets of sweat were trickling down over her hot cheeks. Impatiently brushing them aside, she stood stock-still outside the gleaming building while all around her busy City types made little tutting noises of irritation as they were forced to weave their way around her.

There had to be some kind of mistake. There had to be. She couldn't believe that her father would be so cruel. Or so dictatorial. That he would have instructed that tight-lipped bank manager to inform her that all funds in her account had been frozen, and no more would be forthcoming. But her rather hysterical request that the bank manager stop *freaking her out* had been met with nothing but an ominous silence and now that she was outside, the truth hit her like a sledgehammer coming at her out of nowhere.

She was broke.

Her heart slammed against her ribcage. Part of her still didn't want to believe it. Had the bank manager been secretly laughing at her when he'd handed over the formal-looking letter? She'd ripped it open and stared in horror as the words written by her father's lawyer had wobbled before her eyes and a key phrase had jumped out at her, like a spectre.

Conall Devlin has been instructed to provide any assistance you may need.

Conall Devlin? She had literally *shaken* with rage. Conall Devlin, the brute who had stormed into her apartment yesterday and who was responsible for her current state of homelessness? She would sooner starve than ask *him* for assistance. She would talk her father round and he would listen to her. He always did.

But in the middle of her defiance came an overwhelming wave of panic and fear, which washed over her and made her feel as if she were drowning. It was the same feeling she used to get when her mother would suddenly announce that they were leaving a city, and all Amber's hard-fought-for friends would soon become distant and then forgotten memories.

She mustn't panic. She mustn't.

Her fingers still shaking, Amber sheltered in a shop doorway and took out her cell phone. She rang her father's number, but it went straight through to his personal assistant, Mary-Ellen, a woman who had never been her biggest fan and who didn't bother hiding her disapproval when she heard Amber's voice.

'Amber. This *is* a surprise,' she said archly.

'Hello, Mary-Ellen.' Amber drew in a deep breath. 'I need to speak to my father—urgently. Is he there?'

'I'm afraid he's not.'

'Do you know when he'll be back or where I can get hold of him?'

There was a pause and Amber wondered if she was

being paranoid, or whether it sounded like a very deliberate pause.

'I'm afraid it isn't quite as easy as that. He's gone to an ashram in India.'

Amber gave a snort of disbelief and a passing businessman shot her a funny look. 'My father? Gone to an ashram? To do yoga and eat vegan food? Is this some kind of joke, Mary-Ellen?'

'No, it is not a joke,' said Mary-Ellen crisply. 'He's been trying to get hold of you for weeks. He's left a lawyer's letter with the bank—did you get it?'

Amber thought about the screwed-up piece of paper currently reposing with several sticks of chewing gum and various lipsticks at the bottom of her handbag. 'Yes, I got it.'

'Then I suggest you follow his advice and speak to Conall Devlin. All his contact details are there. Conall is the man who'll be able to help you in your father's absence. He's—'

With a howl of rage, Amber cut the connection and slung her phone back into her bag, before starting to walk—not knowing nor caring which direction she was taking. She didn't want *Conall Devlin* to help her! What was it with him that suddenly his name was on everyone's lips as if he were some kind of god? And what was it with her that she was behaving like some kind of helpless *victim*, just because a few obstacles had been put in her way?

Worse things than this had happened to her, she reminded herself. She'd survived a nightmare childhood, hadn't she? And even when she'd got through that, the problems hadn't stopped coming. She wiped a trickle of sweat away from her forehead. But those kinds of thoughts wouldn't help her now. She needed to think clearly. She needed to go back to the apartment to work out some kind of coping strategy until she could get hold of her father. And she *would* get hold of him. Somehow she would track him down—even if she had to hitchhike to the wretched ashram in order to do so. She would appeal to his better judgement and the sense of guilt which had never quite left him for kicking her and her mother out onto the street. Surely he wasn't planning to do that for a second time? And surely he hadn't *really* frozen her funds? But in the meantime...

She caught the Tube and got out near her apartment, stopping off at the nearest shop to buy some provisions since her rumbling stomach was reminding her that she'd had nothing to eat that morning. But after putting a whole stack of shopping and a pack of cigarettes through the till, she had the humiliation of seeing the machine decline her card. There was an audible sigh of irritation from the man in the queue behind her and she saw one woman nudging her friend as they moved closer as if anticipating some sort of scene.

'There must be some kind of mistake,' Amber mumbled, her face growing scarlet. 'I shop in here all the time—you must remember me? I can bring the money along later.'

But as the embarrassed shop assistant shook her head, she told Amber that it was company policy never to accept credit. And as she rang the bell underneath her till deep down Amber knew there had been no mistake. Her father really had done it. He'd *frozen her funds* just as the bank manager had told her.

She thought about her refrigerator at home and its meagre contents. There was plenty of champagne but little else—a tub of Greek yoghurt, which was probably growing a forest of mould by now, a bag of oranges and those soggy chocolate biscuits which were past their sell-by date. Her cheeks growing even hotter, Amber scrabbled around in her purse for some spare change and found nothing but a solitary, crumpled note.

'I'll just take the cigarettes,' she croaked, handing over the note but not quite daring to meet the eyes of the assistant as she scuttled from the shop.

The trouble was that these days everyone *glared* at you if you dared smoke a cigarette and Amber was forced to wait until she reached home before she could light up. Whatever happened to personal freedom? she wondered as she slammed the front door behind her and fumbled around for her lighter with shaking hands. She thought about the way Conall Devlin had snatched the cigarette from her lips yesterday and a feeling of fury washed over her.

On a whim, she tapped out a text to her half-brother, Rafe, as she tried to remember what time it was in Australia.

What do you know about a man called Conall Devlin?

Considering they hadn't been in contact for well over a year, Amber was surprised and pleased when Rafe's reply came winging back almost immediately.

Best mate at school. Why?

So *that* was why the name had rung a distant bell and why Conall's midnight-blue eyes had bored into her when he'd said it. Rafe was eleven years older than her and had left home by the time she'd moved back into their father's house as a mixed-up fourteen-year-old. But—come to think of it—hadn't her father mentioned some Irish whizz-kid on the payroll who'd dragged himself up from the gutter? Was Conall Devlin the one he'd been talking about?

She wanted to ask him more, but Rafe was probably lying on some golden beach somewhere, sipping champagne and surrounded by gorgeous women. Did she inform him she was soon to be homeless and that the Irishman had threatened to have the locks changed? Would he even believe her version of the story if he and Conall Devlin had been *best mates*?

There was a ping as another text arrived.

And why are you texting me at midnight?

Amber bit her lip. Was there really any point in grumbling to a man who was thousands of miles away? What was she expecting him to do—transfer money to her account? Because something told her he wouldn't do it, despite the fortune Rafe had built up for himself on the other side of the world. Her half-brother had been one of the people who were always nagging her to get a proper job. Wasn't that one of the reasons why she'd allowed herself to lose touch with him—because he told her things she preferred not hear?

Her fingers wavered over the touchpad.

Just wanted to say hi.

Hi to you, too! Nice to hear from you. Let's talk soon. X

Amber's eyes inexplicably began to fill with tears as she tapped out her reply: Okay. X.

It was the only good thing which had happened to her all day but the momentary glow of contentment it gave her didn't last long. Amber sat on the floor disconsolately finishing her cigarette and then began to shiver. How *could* her father have gone away to India and left her in this predicament?

She thought about what everyone was saying and the different alternatives which lay open to her, realising there weren't actually that many. She could throw herself on people's mercy and ask to sleep on their sofas, but for how long? And she couldn't even do *that* without enough money to offer towards household expenses. Everyone would start to look at her in a funny way if she didn't contribute to food and stuff. And if she couldn't buy her very expensive round in the nightclubs they tended to frequent, then everyone would start to gossip—because in the kind of circles she mixed in, being broke was social death.

She stared down at the diamond watch glittering at her wrist, an eighteenth-birthday present intended to console her during a particularly low point in her life. It hadn't, of course. It had been one of many lessons she'd learnt along the way. It didn't matter how many jewels you wore, their cold beauty was powerless to fill the empty holes which punctured your soul…

She thought about going to a pawnbroker and wondered if such places still existed, but something told her she would get a desultory price for the watch.

Because people who tried to raise money against jewellery were vulnerable and she knew better than anyone that the vulnerable were there to be taken advantage of.

The sweat of earlier had dried on her skin and her teeth began to chatter loudly. Amber remembered her father's letter and the words of Mary-Ellen, his assistant. *Speak to Conall Devlin.* And even though every instinct she possessed was warning her to steer clear of the trumped-up Irishman, she suspected she had no choice but to turn to him.

She stared down at her creased clothes.

She licked her lips with a feeling of instinctive fear. She didn't like men. She didn't trust them, and with good reason. But she knew their weaknesses. Her mother hadn't taught her much, but she'd drummed in the fact that men were always susceptible to a woman who looked at them helplessly.

Fired up by a sudden sense of purpose, Amber went into her en-suite bathroom and took a long shower. And then she dressed with more care than she'd used in a long time.

She remembered the disdainful look on Conall Devlin's face when he'd told her that he didn't get turned on by women who smoked and flaunted their bodies. And she remembered the contemptuous expression in his navy-blue eyes as he'd said that. So she fished out a navy-blue dress which she'd only ever worn to failed job interviews, put on minimal make-up and twisted her black hair back into a smooth and demure chignon. Stepping back from the mirror, Amber hardly recognised the image which stared back at her. Why, she could almost pose as a body double for Julie Andrews in *The Sound of Music*!

Conall Devlin's offices were tucked away in a surprisingly picturesque and quiet street in Kensington, which was lined with cherry trees. She didn't know what she'd expected to find, but it certainly hadn't been a restored period building whose outward serenity belied the unmistakable buzz of success she encountered the moment she stepped inside.

The entrance hall had a soaringly high ceiling, with quirky chandeliers and a curving staircase which swept up from the chequered marble floor. A transparent desk sat in front of a modern painting of a woman caressing the neck of a goat. Beside it was a huge canvas with a glittery image of Marilyn Monroe, which Amber recognised instantly. She felt a little stab at her heart. Everything in the place seemed achingly cool and trendy, and suddenly she felt like a fish out of water in her frumpy navy dress and stark hairstyle. A fact which wasn't helped by the lofty blonde receptionist in a monochrome minidress who looked up from behind the Perspex desk and smiled at Amber in a friendly way.

'Hi! Can I help you?'

'I want to see Conall Devlin.' The words came out more clumsily than Amber had intended and the blonde looked a little taken aback.

'I'm afraid Conall is tied up for most of the day,' she said, her smile a little less bright than before. 'You don't have an appointment?'

Amber could feel a rush of emotions flooding through her, but the most prominent of them all was a sensation of being *less than*. As if she had no right to be here. *As if she had no right to be anywhere.* She found herself wondering what on earth she was doing in her frumpy dress when this sunny-looking creature looked as if she'd just strayed in from a land of milk and honey, but it was too late to do anything about it now. She put her bag down on one of the modern chairs which looked more like works of art than objects designed for sitting on, and shot the receptionist a defiant look.

'Not a formal appointment, no. But I need to see him—urgently—so I'll just sit here and wait, if you don't mind.'

The smile now nothing but a memory, a faint frown creased the blonde's brow. 'It might be better if you came back later,' she said carefully.

Amber thought of Conall walking into her apartment without knocking. About the smug look on his face as he'd held up the key and warned her that she had four weeks to get out. She was the sister of his best friend from school, for heaven's sake—surely he could find it in his hard heart to show her a modicum of kindness?

She sat down heavily on one of the chairs.

'I'm not going anywhere. I need to see him and it's urgent, so I'll wait. But please don't worry—I've got all day.' And with that she picked up one of the glossy magazines which were adorning the low table and pretended to read it.

She was aware that the blonde had begun tapping away on her computer, probably sending Conall an email, since she could hardly call him and tell him that a strange woman was currently occupying the reception area and refusing to move—not when she was within earshot.

Sure enough, she heard the sound of a door opening on the floor above and then someone walking down the sweeping staircase. Amber heard his steps grow closer and closer but she didn't glance up from the magazine until she was aware that someone was coming towards her. And when she could no longer restrain herself, she looked up.

The breath dried in her throat and there wasn't a thing she could do about it, because yesterday she hadn't been expecting him and today she was. And surely that meant she should have been primed not to react—she was busy telling herself *not* to react—but somehow it didn't work like that. Her heart began to pound and her mouth dried to dust and feelings which were completely alien to her began to fizz through her body. On his own territory he looked even more intimidating than he had done yesterday—and that was saying something.

The urbane business suit had gone and he was dressed entirely in black. A black cashmere sweater and a pair of black jeans, which hugged his narrow hips and emphasised his long, muscular legs. His shadowy presence only seemed to emphasise the sense of power which radiated from him like a dark aura. Against the sombre shade, his skin seemed more golden than she remembered—but his midnight eyes were shuttered and his unsmiling face gave nothing away.

'I thought I told you to make an appointment—although I can't remember if that was before or after you told me to go to hell.' His lips flattened into an odd kind of smile. 'And since you can see for yourself that this place is as far from hell as you can imagine—I'm wondering exactly what it is you're doing here, Amber.'

Amber stared into his eyes and tried to think about something other than the realisation that they gleamed like sapphires. Or that his features were so rugged and strong. He looked so powerful and unyielding, she thought. As if he held all the cards and she held none. She wanted to demand that he listen to her and stop trying to impose his will on her. Until she reminded herself that she was supposed to be appealing to his better nature—in which case it would make sense to adopt a more conciliatory tone, rather than blurting out her demands.

'I've been to the bank,' she said.

He smiled, but it wasn't a particularly friendly smile. 'And the nasty man there informed you that your father has finally pulled the plug on all the freebies you've survived on until now—is that what you were going to say, Amber?'

'That's exactly what I was going to say,' she whispered.

'And?'

He shot the word out like a bullet and Amber began to wonder if she should have worn something different. Something shorter, which might have shown a bit of leg instead of her knees being completely covered by the frumpy dress.

Well, if you're going to dress like a poor orphan from the storm—then at least start behaving like one.

Her voice gave a little wobble, which wasn't entirely fabricated. 'And I don't know what I'm going to do,' she said.

His lips twisted. 'You could try going out to work, like the rest of the human race.'

'But I...' Amber kept the hovering triumph in her voice at bay and replaced it with a gloomy air of resignation. 'I'm almost impossible to employ, that's the trouble. It's a fierce job market out there and I don't have many of the qualities which employers are seeking.'

'Agreed,' he said unexpectedly. 'An overwhelming sense of entitlement never goes down well with the boss.'

She cleared her throat. 'Things are really bad, Conall. I can't get hold of my father, my credit cards have all been frozen and I can't...I can't even *eat*,' she finished dramatically.

'But presumably you can still smoke?'

Her head jerked back and her eyes narrowed...

'And don't bother denying it,' he ground out. 'Because I can smell it on you and it makes me sick to the stomach. It's a disgusting habit—and one you're going to have to kick.'

Amber could feel her blood pressure rising, but she forced herself to stay calm. Be docile, she told herself. Let him believe what he wants to believe.

'Of course I'll give it up if you help me,' she said meekly.

'You mean that?'

Chewing on her bottom lip and making her eyes grow very big, Amber nodded. 'Of course I do.'

He gave a brief nod. 'I'm not sure I believe you, but if you're just playing games, then let me warn you right now that it's a bad idea and you might as well turn around and walk out again. However, if you're really in a receptive place and serious about wanting to change, then I will help you. Do you want my help, Amber?'

It nearly killed her to do so but she gave a sulky nod. 'I suppose so.'

'Good. Then come upstairs to my office and we'll decide what we're going to do with you.' He glanced over at the blonde and Amber was almost certain that he *winked* at her. 'Hold all my calls, will you, Serena?'

CHAPTER THREE

CONALL DEVLIN'S OFFICE was nothing like Amber would have imagined, either. She had expected something brash, or slightly tacky—something which would fit well with his brutish exterior. But she was momentarily lost for words as he took her into a beautifully decorated first-floor room which overlooked the street at the front and a beautiful garden at the back.

The walls were grey—the subtle colour of an oyster shell—and it provided the perfect backdrop for many paintings which hung there. Amber blinked as she looked around. It was like being in an art gallery. He was obviously into modern art and he had a superb eye, she conceded reluctantly. His curved desk looked like a work of art itself and in one corner of the room was a modern sculpture of a naked woman made out of some sort of resin. Amber glanced over at it before quickly looking away, because there was something uncomfortably *sensual* about the woman's stance and the way she was cupping her breast with lazy fingers.

She looked up to find Conall watching her, his midnight eyes shuttered as he indicated the chair in front of his desk, but Amber was much too wired to be able to sit still while facing him. Something told her that being subjected to that mocking stare would be unendurable.

So start clawing some power back, she told herself fiercely. *Be sweet. Make him* want *to help you.*

He was rich enough to give her a temporary stay of execution until her father got back from his ashram and everything could be cleared up. She walked over to one of the windows and stared down onto the street as two teenage girls strolled past, chewing gum and giggling—and she felt a momentary pang of wistfulness for the apparent ease of their lives and a sense of being carefree which had always eluded her.

'I haven't got all day,' he warned. 'So let's cut to the chase. And before you start fluttering those long eyelashes at me, or trying to work the convent-schoolgirl look—which, let me tell you, isn't doing it for me—let me spell out a few things. I'm not giving you money without something in return and I'm not letting you have an apartment which is way too big for you. So if the sole purpose of this unscheduled visit is to throw yourself on my mercy asking for funds—then you're wasting your time.'

For a moment Amber was struck dumb because she couldn't ever remember anyone speaking to her like that. Up until the age of four she'd been a princess living in a palace, and then she'd been catapulted straight into a nightmare when her parents had split up. The next ten years had been several degrees of horrible and she hadn't known which way to turn. And when she'd been brought back to live in her father's house after her mother's accident—seriously cramping his style with wife number whatever it had been—everyone had tiptoed round her.

Nobody had known how to deal with a grieving and angry teenager and neither had she. Her confidence had been completely punctured and so had her self-esteem. Her moods had been wild and unpredictable and she'd quickly realised that she could get people to do what she wanted them to do. Amber had learnt that if her lips wobbled in a certain way, then people fell over themselves to help her. She'd also realised that rubbing your toe rather obsessively over the carpet and staring at it as if it contained the secret of the universe was pretty effective, too, because it made people want to draw you out of yourself.

But there was something about Conall Devlin which made her realise he would see right through any play-acting or attempts at manipulation. His eyes were much too keen and bright and intelligent. They were fixed on her now in question so that, for one bizarre moment, she felt as if he might actually be able to read her thoughts, and that he certainly wouldn't like them if he could.

'Then how am I expected to survive?' she questioned. Defiantly she held up her wrist so that her diamond watch glittered, like bright sunlight on water. 'Do you want me to start pawning the few valuable items I have?'

His eyes gleamed as he plucked an imaginary violin from the empty air and proceeded to play it, but then he put his big hands down on the surface of his desk and stared at her, his face sombre.

'Why don't you spare me the sob story, Amber?' he said. 'And start explaining some of *these*.'

Suddenly he upended a large manila envelope and spread the contents out over his desk and Amber stared at the collection of photos and magazine clippings with a feeling of trepidation.

'Where did you get these?'

He made an expression of distaste, as if they were harbouring some form of contamination. 'Your father gave them to me.'

Amber knew she'd made it into various gossip columns and some of those 'celebrity' magazines which adorned the shelves of supermarket checkouts. Some of the articles she'd seen and some she hadn't—but she'd never seen them all together like this, like a pictorial history of her life. Fanned across his desk like a giant pack of cards, there were countless pictures of her. Pictures of her leaving nightclubs and pictures of her attending gallery and restaurant openings. In every single shot her dress looked too short and her expression seemed wild. But then the flash of the camera was something that she loved and loathed in equal measure. Wasn't she stupidly grateful that someone cared enough to want to take her photo—as if to reassure her that she wasn't invisible? Yet the downside was that it always made her feel like a butterfly who had fluttered into the collector's room by mistake—who'd had her fragile wings pierced by the sharp pins which then fettered her to a piece of card...

She looked up from the photos and straight into his eyes and nobody could have failed to see the condemnation in their midnight depths. *Don't let him see the chink in your armour*, she told herself fiercely. *Don't give him that power.*

'Quite good, aren't they?' she said carelessly as she pulled out the chair and sat down at last.

At that point, Conall could have slammed his fist onto the desk in sheer frustration, because she was shameless. Completely shameless. Worse even than he'd imagined. Did she think he was stupid—or was the effect of her dressing up today like some off-duty nun supposed to have him eating out of her hand?

But the crazy thing was that—no matter how contrived it was—on some subliminal level, the look actually worked. No matter what he'd said and no matter how much he tried to convince himself otherwise, he couldn't seem to take his eyes off her. With her thick black hair scraped back from her face like that, you could see the perfect oval of her face and get the full impact of those long-lashed emerald eyes. Was she aware that she had the kind of looks which would make men want to fight wars for her? Conall's mouth twisted. Of course she was. And she had been manipulating that beauty, probably since she first hit puberty.

He remembered his reaction when Ambrose had asked him for his help and then shown him all the photos. There had been a moment of stunned silence as Conall had looked at them and felt a powerful hit of lust which had been almost visceral. It had been like a punch to the guts. Or the groin. There had been one in particular of her wearing some wispy little white dress, managing to look both intensely pure and intensely provocative at the same time. Guilt had rushed through him as he'd stared at her father and shaken his head.

'Get someone else to do the job,' he'd said gruffly.

'I can't think of anyone else who would be capable of handling her,' had been Ambrose's candid reply. 'Nor anyone I would trust as much as I do you.'

And wasn't that the worst thing of all? That Ambrose *trusted* him to do right by his daughter? So that, not only had Conall agreed, but he was now bound by a deep sense of honour to do the decent thing by the man who had saved him from a life of crime.

It would have been easier if he could just have signed her a cheque and told her to go away and sort herself out, but Ambrose had been adamant that she needed grounding, and he knew the old man's determination of old.

'She needs to discover how to live a decent life and to stop sponging off other people,' he said. 'And you are going to help her, Conall.'

And how the hell was he supposed to do that when all he could think about was what it would be like to unpin her hair and kiss her until she was gasping for breath? About what it would be like to cradle those hips within the palms of his hands as he drove into her until they were both crying out their pleasure?

He stared into the glitter of her eyes, unable to blot out the unmistakable acknowledgement that her defiance was turning him on even more, because women rarely defied him. So what was he going to do about it—give up or carry on? The question was academic really, because giving up had never been an option for him. Maybe he could turn this into an exercise in self-restraint. Unless his standards had really sunk so low that he could imagine being intimate with someone who stood for everything he most despised.

He thought back to the question she'd just asked

and his gaze slid over the pile of photos—alighting on one where she was sitting astride a man's shoulders, a champagne bottle held aloft while a silky green dress clung to her shapely thighs.

'They're good if you want to portray yourself as a vacuous airhead,' he said slowly. 'But then again, that's not something which is going to look good on your CV.'

'Your own CV being whiter than white, I suppose?' she questioned acidly.

For a moment, Conall fixed her with an enquiring look. Had Ambrose told her about the dark blots on his own particular copybook? In which case she would realise that he knew what he was talking about. He'd had his own share of demons; his own wake-up call to deal with. But she said nothing—just continued to regard him with a look of foxy challenge which was making his blood boil.

'This is supposed to be about you,' he said. 'Not me.'

'So go on, then,' she said sarcastically. 'I'm all ears.'

'That's probably the first sensible thing you've said all day.' He leaned back in his chair and studied her. 'This is what I propose you do, Amber. Obviously, you need a job in order to pay the rent but, as you have yourself recognised, your CV makes you unemployable. So you had better come and work for me. Simple.'

Amber went very still because when he put it like that it actually *sounded* simple. She blinked at him as she felt the first faint stirring of hope. Cautiously, she looked around the beautifully proportioned room, with its windows which looked out onto the iconic London street. Outside the trees were frothing with pink blossom, as if someone had daubed them with candyfloss. There was a bunch of flowers on his desk—the tiny, highly scented blooms they called paper-whites, which sent a beguiling drift of perfume through the air. She wondered if the blonde in the minidress had put them there. Just as she wondered who had sent him that postcard of the Taj Mahal, or that little glass dish in the shape of a pair of lips, which was currently home to a gleaming pile of paperclips.

And suddenly she was hit by that feeling which always used to come over her at school, when she was invited to a friend's house for the weekend and the friend's parents were still together. The feeling that she was on the outside looking in at a perfectly ordered world where everything worked the way it was supposed to. She swallowed. Because Conall Devlin was offering her a—temporary—place in that sort of world, wasn't he? Didn't that count for something?

'I'm not exactly sure what your line of business is,' she said, asking the competent kind of question he would no doubt expect.

He regarded her from between those shuttered lashes. 'I deal in property—that's my bread-and-butter stuff. I sell houses and apartments all over London and I have subsidiary offices in Paris and New York. But my enduring love is for art, as you might have gathered.'

'Yes,' she said politely, unable to keep the slight note of amazement from her voice but he picked up on it immediately because his midnight eyes glinted.

'You sound surprised, Amber.'

She shrugged. 'I suppose I am.'

'Because I don't fit the stereotype?' He raised a pair of mocking eyebrows. 'Because my suit isn't pinstriped and I don't have a title?'

'Careful, Mr Devlin—that chip on your shoulder seems like it's getting awfully heavy.'

He laughed at this and Amber was angry with herself for the burst of pleasure which rushed through her. Why the hell feel *thrilled* just because she'd managed to make the overbearing Irishman laugh?

'I deal solely in twentieth-century pieces and buy mainly for my own pleasure,' he said. 'But occasionally I procure pieces for clients or friends or for business acquaintances. I act as a middle man.'

'Why do they need *you* as a middle man?'

He stared briefly at the postcard of the Taj Mahal. 'Because buying art is not just about negotiation—it's about being able to close the deal. And that's something I'm good at. Some of the people I buy for are very wealthy, with vast amounts of money at their disposal. Sometimes they prefer to buy anonymously—in order to avoid being ripped off by unscrupulous sellers who want to charge them an astronomical amount.' He smiled. 'Or sometimes people want to sell anonymously and they come to me to help them get the highest possible price.'

Amber's eyes narrowed as she tried not to react to the undeniable impact of that smile. Somehow he had managed to make himself sound incredibly *fascinating*. As if powerful people were keen to do business with him. Had that been his intention, to show her there was more to him than met the eye?

She folded her hands together on her lap. How hard could it be to work for him? The only disadvantage would be having to deal with *him*, but the property side would be a piece of cake. Presumably you just took a prospective buyer along to a house and told them a famous actress had just moved in along the road and prices had rocketed as a result, and they'd be signing on the dotted line quicker than you could say bingo.

'I can do that,' she said confidently.

His eyes narrowed. 'Do what?'

'Sell houses. Or apartments. Whatever you want.'

He sat up very straight. 'Just like that?' he said silkily.

'Sure. How hard can it be?'

'You think I'm going to let someone like you loose in a business I've spent the last fifteen years building up?' he questioned, raking his fingers back through his thick black hair with an unmistakable gesture of irritation. 'You think that selling the most expensive commodity a person will ever buy should be entrusted to someone who hasn't ever held down a proper job, and has spent most of her adult life falling out of nightclubs?'

Amber bristled at his damning assessment and a flare of fury fizzed through her as she listened to his disparaging words. She wanted to do a number of things in retaliation, starting with taking that jug of water from his desk and upending the contents all over his now ruffled dark hair. And then she would have liked to have marched out of his office and slammed the door very firmly behind her and never set eyes on his handsome face ever again. But that wouldn't exactly help foster the brand-new image she was trying to convey, would it? She wanted him to believe she could be calm and unruffled. She would give him a glimpse of the new and efficient Amber who wasn't going to rise to the insults of a man who meant nothing to her, other than as a means to an end.

'I can always learn,' she said. 'But if you think I'd be better suited to shifting a few paintings, I'll happily give that a go. I...I like art.'

He made a small sound at the back of his throat, which sounded almost like a growl, and seemed to be having difficulty holding on to his temper—she could tell that by the way he had suddenly started drumming his fingertips against the desk, as if he were sending out an urgent message in Morse code.

But when he looked up at her again, she thought she saw the glint of something in his dark blue eyes which made her feel slightly nervous. Was it anticipation she could read there, or simply sheer devilment?

'I think you'll find that selling art involves slightly more of a skill set than one described as *shifting a few paintings*,' he said drily. 'And besides, my plans for you are very different.' He glanced down at the sheet of paper which lay on the desk before him. 'I understand that you speak several languages.'

'Now it's your turn to sound surprised, Mr Devlin.'

He shrugged his broad shoulders and sat back in his seat. 'I guess I am. I didn't have you down as a linguist, with all the hours of study that must have involved.'

Amber's lips flattened. 'There is more than one way to learn a language,' she said. 'My skill comes not from hours sitting at a desk—but from the fact that my mother had a penchant for Mediterranean men. And as a child I often found myself living in whichever new country was the home of her latest love interest.' She gave a bitter laugh. 'And, believe me, there were plenty of those. Consequently, I learnt to speak the local language. It was a question of survival.'

His eyes narrowed as he looked at her thoughtfully. 'That must have been...hard.'

Amber shook her head, more out of habit than anything else. Because sympathy or compassion—or whatever you wanted to call it—made her feel uncomfortable. It started making her remember people like Marco or Stavros or Pierre—all those men who had broken her mother's heart so conclusively and left Amber to deal with the mess they'd left behind. It made her wish for the impossible—that she'd been like other people and lived a normal, quiet life without a mother who seemed to think that the answer to all their problems was *being in love*. And remembering all that stuff ran the risk of making you feel vulnerable. It left you open to pain—and she'd had more than her fair share of pain.

'It was okay,' she said, in a bored tone which came easily after so many years of practice. 'I certainly know how to say "my darling" in Italian, Greek and French. And I can do plenty of variations on the line "You complete and utter bastard".'

Had her flippant tone shocked him? Was that why a faintly disapproving note had entered his voice?

'Well, you certainly won't be needed to relay any of those sentiments, be very clear about that.' He glanced down at the sheet of paper again. 'But before I lay down the terms of any job I might be prepared to offer—I need some assurances from you.'

'What kind of assurances?'

'Just that I don't have any room in my organisation for loose cannons, or petulant princesses who say the first thing which comes into their head. I deal with people who need careful handling and I need to know that you can demonstrate judgement and tact before I put my proposition to you.' His midnight eyes grew shadowed. 'Because frankly, right now, I'm finding it hard to imagine you being anything other than... difficult.'

His words hurt. More than they should have done. More than she'd expected them to—or perhaps that had something to do with the way he was looking at her. As if he couldn't quite believe the person she was. As if someone like her had no right to exist. And yet all this was complicated by the fact that he looked so spectacular, with his black sweater hugging his magnificent body and his sensual lips making all kinds of complicated thoughts that began to nudge themselves into her mind. Because her body was reacting to him in a way she wasn't used to. A way she couldn't seem to control. She could feel herself growing restless beneath that searing sapphire stare—and yet she didn't even *like* him.

He was like some kind of modern-day *jailer*. Strutting around in his Kensington mansion with all his skinny, miniskirted minions scurrying around and looking at her as if she were something the cat had dragged in. But she had only herself to blame. He had backed her into a corner and she had let him. She had come crawling here today to ask for his help and he had taken this as permission to give her yet another piece of his mind. Imagine *working* for a man like Conall Devlin.

A familiar sense of rebellion began to well up inside her, accompanied by the liberating realisation that she was under no obligation to accept his dictatorial attitude. Why not show him—and everyone else—that she was a survivor? She might not have a wall covered with degrees, but she wasn't stupid. How hard could it be to find herself a job and a place to live? What about tapping into some of the resilience she'd relied on when she'd been dragged from city to city by her mother?

Rising to her feet, she picked up her handbag, acutely aware of those eyes burning into her as if they were scorching their way through her frumpy navy-blue dress and able to see beneath. And wasn't there something about that scrutiny which excited her as much as terrified her? 'I may be underqualified,' she said, 'but I'm not desperate. I'm resourceful enough to find myself some sort of employment which doesn't involve working for a man with an overinflated sense of his own importance.'

He gave a soft laugh. 'So your answer is no?'

'My answer is more along the lines of *in your dreams*,' she retorted. 'And it's not going to happen. I'm perfectly capable of being independent and that's what I'm going to do.'

'Oh, Amber,' he said slowly. 'You are magnificent. That kind of spirit in a woman is quite something—and if you didn't reek of cigarette smoke and feel that the world owed you some sort of living, you'd be quite worryingly attractive.'

For a moment Amber was confused. Was he insulting her or complimenting her—or was it a mixture of both? She glowered at him before walking over to the door and slamming her way out—to the sound of his soft laughter behind her. But the stupid thing was that she felt like someone who'd jumped out of an aeroplane and forgotten to pull the cord on their parachute. As if she were in free fall. As if the world were rushing up towards her and she didn't know when she was going to hit it.

I'll show them, she told herself fiercely. *I'll show them all.*

CHAPTER FOUR

'I'M SO SORRY!' Quickly, Amber mopped up the spilled champagne and edged away from the table as the customer looked at her with those piggy little eyes which had been trailing her movements all evening. 'I'll get you another drink right away.'

'Why don't you sit down and join me instead?' He leered, patting the seat beside him with a podgy hand. 'And we'll forget about the drink.'

Amber shook her head and tried to hide her ever-present sense of revulsion. 'I'm not supposed to mix with the customers,' she said, grabbing her tray and heading towards the bar on feet which were far from steady. She was used to wearing high heels, but these stilt-like red shoes were so gravity defying that walking in them took every ounce of concentration and it wasn't helped by the rest of the club 'uniform'. Her black satin dress was so tight she could scarcely breathe and meanwhile the heavy throb of the background music was giving her a headache.

And judging by the look on her manager's face, the drink spillage hadn't gone unnoticed. Behind her smile Amber gritted her teeth, wondering if she'd taken leave of her senses when she'd stormed out of Conall's office telling him she didn't want his job. Had she really thought the world would be at her feet, waiting to dole out wonderful opportunities by way of compensation? Because life wasn't like that. She'd quickly discovered that a CV riddled with holes and zero qualifications brought you few opportunities and the only work available was in places like this—an underlit hotel nightclub where nobody looked happy.

'That's the third drink you've spilled this week!' The manager's voice quivered indignantly as Amber grew closer. 'Where did you learn to be so clumsy?'

'I...I moved a bit too quickly. I thought he was going to pinch my bottom,' babbled Amber.

'And? What's the matter with that?' The manager glared. 'Isn't it nice to have a man show his appreciation towards an attractive woman? Why else do you think we dress you up like that? Well, you'll have the cost of the drink taken from your wages, Amber. Now go and fetch him another one and, for goodness' sake, try and be a bit friendlier this time.'

Amber could feel her heart thudding as the bartender put a fresh glass of fizzy wine masquerading as champagne on her tray and she began to walk back towards the man with piggy eyes. *Just put the drink down carefully and then leave*, she told herself. But as she bent down in front of him, he reached out to curve his fat fingers around her fishnet-covered thigh and she froze.

'What...what are you doing?' she croaked.

'Oh, come on.' He leered at her again. 'No need to be like that. With legs like that it's a crime not to touch them—and you look like you could do with a square meal. So how about we go up to my room after you finish? You can order something from room service and we can—'

'How about you get your filthy hand off her right now, before I knock you into kingdom come?' came a low and furious voice from behind her, which Amber recognised instantly.

The podgy hand fell away and Amber turned around to see Conall standing there—his rugged face a study in fury and his powerful body radiating adrenaline as he dominated the space around him. The lurch of trepidation she felt at his unexpected appearance was quickly overridden by the disturbing realisation that she'd never been so glad to see someone in her whole life. He looked so strong. So powerful. He made every other man in the room look weak and insubstantial. Her heart began to pound and she felt her mouth grow dry.

'Conall!' she whispered. 'What are you doing here?'

'Well, I certainly haven't come here for a quiet drink. I tend to be a little more discerning in my choice of venue.' Raising his voice against the loud throb of music, he glanced around at the other cocktail waitresses with a shudder of distaste he didn't bother to hide. 'Get your coat, Amber. We're leaving.'

'I can't leave. I'm working.'

'Not here, you aren't. Not any more. And the subject isn't up for discussion, so save your breath. Either you come willingly, or I pick you up and carry you out of here in a fireman's lift. The choice,' he finished grimly, 'is yours.'

Amber wondered if there was something wrong

with her—there must be—because why else would the thought of the Irishman putting her over his shoulder make her heart race even harder than it was already? She could see her manager saying something to a burly-looking man who was standing beside the bar, and as the music continued its relentless beat she began to dread some awful scene. What if Conall got into a fight with Security—with fists and glasses flying?

'I'll get my coat,' she said.

'Do it,' he bit out impatiently. 'And hurry up. This place is making my skin crawl.'

She headed for the changing room—relieved to strip off the minuscule satin dress and fishnet tights and kick the scarlet shoes from her aching feet. Her skin was clammy and briefly she splashed her face with cold water, dabbing herself dry with a paper towel before slithering into jeans and a sweater. Her heart was racing when she reappeared in the club—thankful to find Conall still standing there, with the bar manager handing over what looked like a wad of cash, with a sour expression on her face.

'Let's go,' he said as she approached.

'Conall—'

'Not now, Amber,' he snapped. 'I really don't want to have a conversation with you here, in earshot of all this low life.'

His expression was resolute and his determination undeniable—so what choice did she have but to follow him through the weaving basement corridors of the hotel until they found the elevator which took them to the main lobby?

They emerged into the dark crispness of a clear

spring night and Amber sucked in a lungful of clean air as a chauffeur-driven car purred to a halt beside the kerb.

'Get in,' said Conall and she wondered if he'd spent his whole life barking out orders like that.

But she did as he asked and a feeling of being cocooned washed over her the moment she climbed onto the back seat, because this level of luxury was reassuringly familiar. A luxury she'd been able to count on before Conall and her father had conspired to take it away from her. She glanced over at his hard profile as he got into the car beside her, and her temporary gratitude began to dissolve into a feeling of resentment.

'How did you find me?' she demanded as the powerful engine began to purr into life.

He turned to look at her and, despite the dim light of the car's interior, the angry glitter in his eyes was unmistakable. 'I had one of my people keep track of you.'

'Why?'

'Why do you think? Because you're so damned irresistible I couldn't keep away from you? I hoped I might be able to tell your father how well you were doing following your dramatic exit from my office.' He gave a short laugh. 'Some hope. I should have guessed that you'd head for the tackiest venue in town in search of some easy money.'

'So why bother coming to look for me if you'd already written me off as useless?' she flared.

Conall didn't answer straight away, because his own motives were still giving him cause for concern. He'd been worried about her ability to adapt to a hard world without the cushion of her wealth—yes. And he'd heard stuff about the club where she was working which made him feel uneasy. Yes. That, too. But there had been something more—something which wasn't quite so easy to quantify—which had nothing to do with his moral debt to her father. Hadn't there been a part of him which had admired the way she'd flounced out of his office? And he didn't just mean the pleasure of watching the magnificent sway of her curvy bottom as she'd done so. The way she'd turned down his offer of a job with a flash of defiance in those emerald eyes had made him think that maybe there was a strong streak of pride hidden beneath her wilful surface. He'd imagined her scrubbing floors, doing anything rather than having to work for him, and he couldn't deny that the idea had appealed to him.

He had been wrong, of course. She had gone for the easy solution. The quick fix. She'd seized the first opportunity to shoehorn her magnificent body into a dress which left very little to the imagination and work in a place which attracted nothing but low life. Clearing his throat, he tried to wipe from his mind the memory of those magnificent breasts spilling over the top of the tight satin gown, but the hard aching in his groin was proving more stubborn to control.

'I felt a certain responsibility towards you.'

'Because of my father?'

'Of course. Why else?'

'Another of Daddy's yes-men,' she said tonelessly.

'Oh, I'm nobody's yes-man, Amber. Be very clear about that.' His voice sounded steely. 'And ask yourself what would have happened if I hadn't turned up when I had. Or have I got it all wrong? Maybe you liked that creep pawing your thigh like that? Maybe you couldn't wait to get back to his room for him to give you a "square meal".'

'Of course I didn't! He was a complete creep. They all were.'

He shook his head in exasperation. 'So why the hell couldn't you have taken a normal job? Worked in a shop? Or a café?'

'Because shops and cafés don't provide accommodation! And the club said if I worked a successful month's trial, then I could have one of the staff rooms in the hotel! Which would have coincided neatly with me being evicted from my apartment.' She glared at him. 'And I don't know why you're suddenly trying to sound like the voice of concern when it's *your* fault I'm going to be homeless.'

He gave an impatient sigh. 'I can't believe you'd be so naïve. You must realise how these places operate.'

'I've been to more nightclubs than you've had hot dinners!' she retorted.

'I don't doubt it—but you went there as a rich and valued customer, not a member of staff! Places like that exploit beautiful women. They expect you to *earn* your bonuses—in a way which is usually some variation of lying flat on your back. Haven't you ever heard the expression that there's no such thing as a free lunch?'

The way she was biting on her lip told him that maybe she wasn't as sophisticated as her foxy appearance suggested, or maybe her wealth had always ensured that she'd frequented a classier kind of club, up until now. Unwillingly, he let his gaze drift over her and once he had started, he couldn't seem to stop. Her black hair was spilling down over the shoulders of her raincoat and her green eyes were heavy with make-up. The fading scarlet streak of her lipstick matched those killer heels she'd been wearing when he'd watched her sashaying across the bar, making him have the sort of unwanted erotic thoughts which involved having her ankles wrapped very tightly around his neck. Hell, it would be easy to have those kinds of thoughts even now—even when she was bundled up in an all-concealing raincoat.

He tapped his fingers against one taut thigh. It would be better to wash his hands of her. To tell Ambrose that she was pretty much a lost cause and maybe he would just have to accept that and let her carry on with an open chequebook and a life of pure indulgence.

But as the car passed a lamp post and the light splashed over her face, he noticed for the first time the dark shadows beneath her long-lashed eyes. She looked as if she hadn't had a lot of sleep lately—and she'd lost weight. Her cheekbones were shockingly prominent in her porcelain skin and the belted raincoat drew definition to the narrowness of her waist. She looked as if a puff of wind might blow her away. As if on cue, her stomach began to rumble and he frowned.

'When did you last eat?'

Her expression was mulish. 'What do you care?'

'Stop being so damned stubborn and just answer the question, Amber,' he growled.

She shrugged. 'At the club they advised you not to

eat for at least four hours before your shift. Actually, it was pretty sound advice because it seemed to be club policy to give you a uniform dress which was at least one size too small.'

'And do you have food back in your apartment?'

'Not much,' she admitted.

'Spent it all on cigarettes, I suppose?' he accused.

She didn't correct him as he leaned forward to tap the glass panel which divided them from the chauffeur and the panel slid open.

'Take us to my club,' he commanded.

'Conall, I'm tired,' she objected. 'And I want to go home.'

'Tough. You can sleep afterwards. You need to eat something.'

He didn't say anything more until the car drew up outside the floodlit classical building a short distance from Piccadilly Circus. A uniformed porter sprang forward to open the car door to let her get out and Conall felt a stab of something he couldn't decipher as he followed her sexy sway as she made her way up the marble steps. As she handed over her raincoat he thought he saw her shiver and he took his own cashmere scarf and wound it around her neck, leaving the ends to dangle concealingly in front of her magnificent breasts.

'Better wear this,' he said drily. But it was more for his benefit than any attempt to conform to the club's rather outdated dress code. This way he wouldn't have to look at the pinpoint tips of her nipples thrusting their way towards him from beneath her sweater and making him imagine what it would be like to lock his lips around each one in turn.

It was very late, but they were shown into the long room known as the North Library which overlooked Pall Mall, where a table was quickly laid up for them. Conall ordered soup and sandwiches for Amber and a brandy for himself. He watched in silence as she devoured the comfort food with the undivided attention of someone who was genuinely hungry and, for the first time that evening, he began to relax.

He sipped his drink. Outside the busy city was slowing down. He could see the yellow lights of vacant cabs and the unsteady weave of people making their way home, while in here all was ordered and calm. It always was. It was one of the main reasons why he'd joined, because it had an air of stability which had always attracted him.

Antique chandeliers hung from the corniced ceiling and at one end of the room was a polished grand piano. Despite its traditional air, it was a club for movers and shakers—the kind of place to which few were granted entry because the membership requirements were so high. But there had been no shortage of proposers keen to get him onto the members' list and Conall had defied the odds brought about by youthful misdemeanour. He'd been proposed by a government minister and seconded by a peer of the realm and that fact in itself still had the ability to make him smile wryly. Whoever would have thought that the boy who had been born with so little would end up here, with the great and the good?

He signalled for a fire to be lit and then watched as Amber dabbed at her lips with a heavy linen napkin. Now that the edge had been taken off her hunger, she relaxed back into the leather armchair and began to look around—like a rescued kitten which had been brought from the cold into the warmth. He wondered what the waiter who came to remove her plate must think, because he didn't usually bring women here, to this essentially male enclave—where deals were done over dinner and alliances formed over summer drinks taken outside on the pretty terrace. On the rare occasions he'd brought a date, they hadn't been dressed in skinny jeans and a sweater, like Amber Carter. They had worn subtle silk, with shoes the same colour as their handbags and make-up which was soft and discreet—not laden on so thickly that from a distance she appeared to have two black eyes.

And yet not one of them had made him feel a fraction of the desire which was currently pulsing through his blood and making him achingly aware of his erection.

'So,' he said heavily, putting his glass down on the table and raising his eyebrows in what he hoped was a stern expression. 'I think you've just proved fairly conclusively that independence is not an option—unless you want to take another job like that. The question is whether or not you're finally ready to knuckle down and see sense.'

Amber didn't answer straight away, even though he was firing that impatient look at her. She felt much better after the food she'd just eaten, no doubt about it—but just as one hunger had been satisfied, so another had been awoken and she wasn't sure how to deal with it.

It wasn't just the unexpectedness of seeing Conall Devlin in this famous London club—which, quite frankly, was the last place she'd ever imagined finding someone like him. And it wasn't just the fact that he currently resembled the human equivalent of a jungle cat—a dark and potentially dangerous predator who had temporarily taken refuge in one of the beautifully worn leather chairs. No, it was more than that. It was the subtly pervasive scent of him invading her nostrils, which was coming from the soft scarf he'd draped around her neck. And hadn't she felt a whisper of pleasure when his fingertips had brushed against her skin, even though it had been the most innocent of touches? Hadn't it made her want more, even though experience had taught her that she always froze into a block of ice whenever a man came close?

She looked into the gleam of his eyes. 'By seeing sense, I presume you mean I should do exactly what *you* say?'

'Well, you could give it a try,' he said drily. 'Since we've seen what happens when you do the opposite.'

'But I don't know exactly what it is you're offering me, Conall.'

Conall stiffened. Was he imagining the provocative flash of her eyes—or was that just wishful thinking on his part? Was she aware that when she looked at him that way, his veins were pulsing with a hot, hard hunger and he could think of only one way of relieving it? She must be. Women like her ate men like him for breakfast.

He needed to pull himself together, before she got an inkling of the erotic thoughts which were clogging up his mind and started using her sexual power to manipulate him. 'I'm offering you a role as an interpreter.'

'Not interested,' she said instantly, with an emphatic shake of her head. 'I'm not sitting in some claustrophobic booth all day with a pair of headphones on, while someone jabbers on and on in my ear about something boring—like grain quotas in the European Union.'

Conall failed to hide his smile. 'I think you'll find my proposal is a little more glamorous than that,' he said.

'Oh?'

She had perked up now and his smile died. Of course she had. Glamour was her lifeblood, wasn't it?

'I'm having a party,' he said.

'What kind of party?'

He picked up his brandy glass and took a sip. 'A party ostensibly to celebrate the completion of my country house. There will be music, and dancing—but I'm also hoping to use the opportunity to sell a painting for someone who badly needs the money.'

'I thought you'd decided that, with my lack of experience, I would be useless when it came to selling paintings.'

'I'm not expecting you to *sell* the paintings,' he said. 'I just want you to be there as a sort of linguistic arm candy.'

'What do you mean?'

He hesitated, wondering if her father would approve of the offer he was about to make to her. It would probably be more sensible to give her a lowly back-room job somewhere in his organisation—preferably as far away from him as possible. But Conall could see now that it would be as ineffective as trying to pass fish paste off as caviar, because Amber Carter wasn't a back-room kind of woman.

No way could someone like her ever fade into the background. So why not capitalise on the gifts she *did* have?

'The painting in question is one of a pair,' he said. 'Two studies of the same woman by a man called Kristjan Wheeler—a contemporary of Picasso and an artist whose worth has increased enormously over the last decade. Both pictures went missing in the middle of the last century and only one has ever been found. That is the one I am trying to sell on behalf of my client, and…'

She looked at him as his words tailed away. 'And?'

'I believe the man who wants to buy the painting is in possession of the missing picture. Which means that the one I'm selling is part of a set, and naturally that makes it much more valuable.'

'Can't you just ask him outright whether he's got it?'

He gave the flicker of a smile. 'That's not how negotiation works, Amber—and especially not with a man like this.' He watched her closely. 'You see, the prospective buyer is a prince.'

'A *prince*?'

Conall watched as she sat bolt upright, her fingers tightening around her glass. Her lips had parted and he could see the moist gleam of her tongue. He thought she looked like a starving dog which had been allowed to roam freely around a kitchen and a quiver of distaste ran through him. He took another sip of his brandy. Had he really thought that the chemistry which sizzled between them was unique? Or was he naïvely pretending that she wasn't like this with every man she came across, and the higher that man's status and the fatter his wallet, the better?

And yet surely that would make her perfect for what he had in mind—didn't they say that Luciano of Mardovia had a roving eye where women were concerned?

'That's right,' he said, his eyes narrowing. 'I want you to come to the party and be nice to him.'

Her eyes narrowed. 'How nice?'

The inference behind her question was clear and Conall felt a wave of disgust wash over him. 'I'm not expecting you to have sex with him,' he snapped. 'Just chat to him. Dance with him. Charm him. I shouldn't imagine you would find any of that difficult, given your track record. He will be accompanied by at least two of his aides and he will converse with them in any language except English. Just like you he speaks Italian, Greek and French and he certainly won't be expecting a woman like you to be fluent in all three.'

A woman like you.

It was odd how hurtful Amber found his throwaway comment, especially when for a minute back then she had been lulled into a false sense of security. Secretly, she had *enjoyed* the way he'd turned up and taken her away so masterfully. He'd brought her here—to this club, which was the epitome of elegance and comfort—and she couldn't deny that she was enjoying watching him sitting bathed in flickering firelight, while he sipped at his brandy. He was very easy on the eye.

But she needed to remember that for him she was just a burden. A problem to be dealt with and then disposed of. No point in starting to have fantasies about Conall Devlin.

'So what you're saying, in effect, is that you want me to spy on this Prince?'

He didn't seem particularly bothered by her accusation, for he responded with nothing more than a faintly impatient sigh.

'Don't be so melodramatic, Amber. If I asked you to have a business meeting with a competitor, I would expect you to find out as much information as possible. So if the Prince should happen to comment to one of his aides in, say, Greek that the wine is atrocious, then it would be helpful to know that.'

A smile flickered over her lips. 'You're in the habit of serving atrocious wine, are you, Conall?'

'What do you think?'

'I'm thinking…no.'

'Look, I'm not asking you to lie about your language skills, but there's no need to advertise them. This is business. All I want is to get the best price possible for my client—and Luciano can certainly afford to pay the best price. So…' His midnight gaze swept over her. 'Do you think you can do it? Play hostess for me for an evening and stick to the Prince's side like glue?'

Amber met his eyes. The food and the fire and the brandy had made her feel sleepy and safe and part of her wished she could hold on to this moment and not have to go and face the chill of the outside world. But Conall was clearly waiting for an answer to his question and the expression on his face suggested he wasn't a man who enjoyed being kept waiting. And deep down she knew she could do something like this in her sleep. Go to some upmarket party and be charming? Child's play.

'Yes,' she said. 'I can do it.'

'Good.' He nodded as his cell phone gave a discreet little buzz and he flicked it a brief glance. 'You'll need to get down to my country house early on Saturday afternoon. Oh, and bring some party dresses with you.' His eyes glittered. 'I don't imagine you'll have too much trouble finding any of those in your wardrobe?'

'No. Party dresses I have in abundance—and plenty of shoes to match.'

'Just wear something halfway decent, will you?'

'What *do* you mean?'

'You know damned well what I mean.' There was a pause. 'I don't want you flaunting your body and looking like a tramp.'

Amber swallowed, knowing that she should be outraged by such a statement, and yet something about the way he said it made her feel all...shivery. She forced her mind back to the practical. 'So what time will I expect the car?'

'The car?' he repeated blankly.

'The car which will be collecting me,' she said, as if she were explaining the rules of a simple card game to a five-year-old.

There was a short silence before he tipped back his dark head and laughed, but when he looked at her again his eyes weren't amused, they were stone cold. 'You still don't get it, do you, Amber?' he said. 'You may be about to deal with a prince, but you're going to have to stop behaving like a princess. Because you're not. You will catch the train like any other mortal.

Speak to Serena and she'll give you details of how to find the house. Oh, and I've got your wages from the nightclub in my pocket. I'll give them to you in the car. I didn't want to hand them over in here.' His eyes glittered. 'It could be a gesture open to misinterpretation.'

CHAPTER FIVE

AMBER HADN'T BEEN on a train for years. Not since that time in Rome when her mother's lover had confessed to having a pregnant wife who had just discovered their affair and was on the warpath. It had been bad enough having to flee the city leaving behind half their possessions, but the journey had been made worse by Sophie Carter's increasingly hysterical sobs as she'd exclaimed loudly that she would be unable to live without Marco. It had been left to her daughter to try to placate her, to the accompaniment of tutting sounds from the other people in the carriage.

Amber sat back against the hard train seat and thought about the bizarre twists and turns of life which had brought her to this bumpy carriage which was hurtling through the English countryside towards Conall's country home. She had been corralled into working for the Irish tycoon—the most infuriating and high-handed man she'd ever met.

And the fact that there didn't seem any credible alternative had made her examine her lifestyle in a way which had left her feeling distinctly uncomfortable.

Yesterday she'd gone to the Devlin headquarters in Kensington for a briefing which hadn't been brief at all. Serena had spent ages telling her boring things like making sure she kept her receipts so that she could submit a travel expenses form. Amber remembered blinking at Conall's assistant with a mixture of amusement and irritation. Receipts! She had wanted to tell the lofty blonde that she didn't *do* receipts, but at that moment the great man himself had walked into the building—a distracting image dressed in all black. Cue an infuriating rocketing of Amber's pulse and the spectacle of various female members of staff cooing around him. And cue the uncomfortable realisation that she *didn't like* seeing him surrounded by all those women.

His gaze had met hers.

'I hope you're behaving yourself, Amber?'

'I'm doing my best,' she'd replied from between gritted teeth.

'I'm just talking Amber through the expenses procedure,' Serena had explained.

'And I'm sure she has been nothing but completely cooperative,' Conall had murmured in response, but there had been a definite flicker of warning in the sapphire depths of his eyes.

She'd wanted to defy him then, because defiance was her default mechanism, yet for the first time in her life she had come up against someone who would not be swayed by her. And wasn't that in some crazy way—*reassuring*?

Amber stared out of the train window, realising there was only an hour to go before her journey's end and that she had better be prepared for her meeting with the Prince. Conall had suggested she find out as much about the royal as possible and so she had downloaded as much as she could find on the Internet and had printed it out. No harm in looking at it again. She pulled out the information sheets and began to doodle little drawings around the edge of one of the pages as she reread it.

She had been unprepared for the impact of Prince 'Luc' and his gorgeous Mediterranean island, when his photograph had first popped up on the screen. With his olive skin, bright blue eyes and thick tumble of black hair, he was as handsome as any Hollywood actor, but his looks left her completely cold. That in itself wasn't unusual, because she'd met enough manipulating hunks through her mother to put her off handsome men for ever. What *was* infuriating was that she kept unfavourably comparing the Prince to Conall—and yet Conall wasn't what you'd call *good-looking*. His jaw was dark and his nose had been broken at one point. And he had a hard, cold stare, which proved distractingly at odds with the way his fingers had brushed her skin as he'd wound his scarf around her neck at his club the other night…

The train juddered to a halt at Crewhurst station and Amber climbed out onto the platform, clutching her case, which contained some of her less-revealing dresses. Blinking, she looked around her and breathed in the fresh air, the bright spring day making her feel like an animal who'd spent the winter in hibernation and was emerging into sunshine for the first time. She sniffed at the air and the scent of something sweet. She couldn't remember the last time she'd been out of the city and in the middle of the countryside like this. Cotton-wool clouds scudded across an eggshell-blue sky and frilly yellow daffodils waved their trumpets in the light breeze.

She had been told to take a taxi, but the rank was empty and when she asked the old man in the ticket office when one might be available, he shook his head with the expression of someone who had just been asked to provide the whereabouts of the Holy Grail.

'Can't say. Driver's gone off to take his wife shopping. It isn't far to walk,' he added helpfully, when she told him where she was headed.

Under normal circumstances Amber would have tapped her foot impatiently and demanded that someone find her a taxi—and quickly. But there was something about the scent of spring which felt keen and raw on her senses. She couldn't remember the last time she'd felt this *alive* and a sudden feeling of adventure washed over her. Her bag wasn't particularly heavy. She was wearing sneakers with her skinny jeans, wasn't she? And a soft silk shirt beneath her denim jacket.

After taking directions, she set off along a sun-dappled country road, walking past acid-green hedges which were bursting with new life. Overhead the sound of birdsong was almost deafening and London seemed an awfully long way away. She found herself thinking that Conall seemed to have his life pretty much sorted, with his successful business and his homes in London and the country. And she found herself wondering whether or not he had a girlfriend. Probably. Men like him always had girlfriends. Or wives. A wife who presumably could only speak English.

This thought produced an inexplicably painful

punch to her heart and she glanced at her watch, calculating she must be about halfway there when she noticed that the sky had grown dark. Looking up, she saw a bank of pewter clouds massing overhead and increased her speed, but she hadn't got much further down the lane when the first large splash of rain hit her and she wondered why she hadn't stopped to consider the April showers which came out of nowhere this time of year.

Because usually you're never far from a shop doorway and completely protected from the elements, that's why.

Well, she certainly wasn't protected now.

She was alone in the middle of a country lane while the rain had started lashing down with increasing intensity, until it was almost like walking through a tropical storm. She thought about ringing someone. Conall? No. She didn't want another lecture on her general incompetence. And it was hardly the end of the world to get caught in an April shower, was it? Sometimes you had to accept what fate threw at you, and just suck it up.

Thoroughly soaked now, she increased her pace, her shirt clinging to her breasts like wet tissue paper and her jeans feeling heavy and uncomfortable as the wet denim rubbed against her legs. She didn't hear the car at first and it wasn't until she heard a loud beep that she turned around to see a low black car coming to a halt on the wet lane with a soft screech of tyres. The muscular silhouette behind the wheel was disturbingly familiar and as the electric window floated down she was confronted by the sight of Conall's face and her heart missed a beat.

'Conall—'

'Get in,' he said.

For a moment she was tempted to tell him that she'd rather walk in the pouring rain than get in a car driven by *him*. But that would be stupid—and wasn't she trying her best to be a bit more sensible? She was cold and she was wet and she was headed for his house and the grown-up thing to do would be to thank him for stopping. Pulling open the passenger door, she threw her bag on the floor, beginning to shiver violently as she slid onto the passenger seat and slammed the car door shut.

'This is getting to be something of a habit,' he said grimly. 'Do you think I have the words "rescue mission" permanently stamped on my forehead?'

His rudeness made her polite response disintegrate. 'I didn't ask you to rescue me.'

'But you accepted my help soon enough, didn't you?'

'Because even I'm not stubborn enough to throw up the chance of getting into a warm car! And now I s-suppose you're going to ch-chastise me for getting wet.' She began to shiver. 'As if I have any control over the weather!'

'I was going to chastise you for walking in the middle of the damned road and not paying any attention!' he retorted. 'If I'd been going any faster I could have run you over.'

Her teeth had started to chatter loudly and the way he was looking at her was making her feel… Beneath her sopping silk shirt, Amber's heart began to hammer. She didn't want to think about the way he was making her feel. How could that cold blue stare make her body spring into life like this? How could it make her feel as if her breasts were being pierced by tiny little needles and make a slow melting heat unfurl deep in her belly?

But he was tugging off his leather jacket and draping it impatiently over her shoulders and as his shadow fell over her Amber was suddenly aware of just how close he was. Coal-black lashes framed the gleaming sapphire eyes and his deeply shadowed jaw seemed to emphasise his own very potent brand of masculinity. An unfamiliar sense of longing began to bubble up inside her and she held her breath as she looked up into his face. For a split second she thought he might be about to kiss her. A second when his mouth was so close that all she needed to do was reach up and hook her hand behind his neck, and bring those lips down to meet hers. And in that same second she saw his eyes narrow. She thought… thought…

Did he read the longing in her eyes? Was that why he suddenly pulled away with a hard smile, as if he'd known exactly what was going through her head? Maybe he was able to make women desire him, even if they didn't want to, just by giving them that intense and rather smouldering look. Instinctively, she hugged the coat closer, the leather feeling unbearably soft against her erect and sensitised nipples.

'Do up your seat belt,' he ordered, turning up the car's heater full blast and glancing in his rear mirror before pulling away. 'And talk me through the reason why you decided to walk from the station. It's miles.'

'Why do you think? Because there was no taxi and the man at the ticket office said it wasn't far.'

'You should have rung me.'

'Make your mind up, Conall. You can't criticise me for not behaving like a normal person and then moan at me when I do. I thought it would be good for me to make my way to the house independently. I thought you might even award me a special gold star for good behaviour.' She glanced at him, a smile playing around her lips. 'And to be honest, I didn't know you were already there.'

Conall said nothing as the car made its way through the downpour, the rhythmical swishing of the wiper blades the only sound he could hear above his suddenly erratic breathing. Of course she hadn't known he'd be at the house—he hadn't known himself. He'd planned to arrive later when everything was in place but something had compelled him to get here earlier, and that something was making him uncomfortable because it was all to do with her.

He'd tried telling himself that he needed to oversee the massive security detail which the Prince of Mardovia's bodyguards had demanded prior to the royal visit. That he needed to check on the painting he was hoping to sell and to ensure it was properly lit. But although both those reasons were valid, they weren't the real reason why he was desperately trying to avert his gaze from the damp denim which outlined the slenderness of her thighs.

Admit it, he thought grimly. *You want her. Despite everything you know about her, you haven't been able to get her out of your head since you saw her lying on a white leather sofa wearing that baggy T-shirt.* Only now the image searing into his brain was the way her wet silk shirt had been clinging to her peaking breasts before he'd hastily covered them up with his jacket. Was it shocking to admit that he wanted to rip the delicate fabric aside and lick her on each hard nub until she squirmed with pleasure? To slide the damp denim from her thighs and put his heated hands all over her chilled flesh?

Of course it was shocking. He had been entrusted to look after her, not seduce her. If it was sex he wanted then Eleanor was only a phone call away. Their grown-up and civilised 'friends with benefits' relationship suited them both—even if the physical stimulation it gave him wasn't matched by a mental one.

But for once the thought of Eleanor's blonde beauty paled in the face of the fiery, green-eyed temptress on the seat next to him and he was relieved when the sudden shower began to lessen. The sun broke through the clouds as the car made its way up the long drive, just in time to illuminate his house in a radiant display which emphasised its stately proportions. Golden light washed over the tall chimneys and glinted off the mullioned windows. The emerald lawns surrounding the building looked vivid in the bright sunshine and, on a tranquil pond, several ducks quacked happily. Beside him he felt Amber stiffen.

'But this is...this is *beautiful*,' she breathed as the car drew up outside.

He heard the note of wonder in her voice and his mouth hardened. He wondered if she would have been quite so gushing if she'd known the truth about his background. About the hardship and pain and the sense of being an outsider which had never quite left him.

'Isn't it?' he agreed evenly as he stared at the house. With its acres of parkland and sense of history, places like this didn't come on the market very often and Conall still couldn't quite believe it was his. Coming hot on the heels of his London deal, it had been a heady time in terms of recent property acquisitions. Had he ever imagined being a major landowner, when he was eighteen and mad with rage and injustice? When the walls of the detention centre had threatened to close in on him and he had been looking down the barrel of an extended jail sentence?

He turned off the ignition, his glance straying to Amber's large handbag, and it wasn't the sight of the printout about Prince Luciano which caught his eye—although he was pleased to see she'd been doing her homework—but the intricate doodles on the edge of one of the pages which stirred a faint but enduring memory.

He frowned. 'I remember seeing some drawings like this in your apartment that first day.'

She stiffened. 'What, you mean you were snooping around?'

'They were half hidden behind a sofa. Were they yours?'

'Of course they were mine—why?'

Ignoring the defensive note in her voice, he narrowed his eyes. 'I thought some of them showed real promise and a few were really very good.'

'You don't have to say that. Anyway, I know they're rubbish.'

'I don't say things I don't mean, Amber. And why are they rubbish?'

She shrugged, but the words seemed to take a long

time coming. 'I used to paint a lot when we were in Europe and my mother was otherwise *occupied*. But when I went to live with my father, he made it very clear he thought they were no good—that a kid of six could throw some paint at the canvas and get the same effect, and that I was wasting my time.' She flashed a brittle kind of smile. 'So I stopped trying to be an *artist* and became the society girl that everyone expected. Those paintings you saw were years old. I just…just couldn't bear to throw them away.'

Conall experienced a moment of real, silent rage as he read the brief flash of hurt and helplessness in her eyes. Were adults deliberately cruel to troubled teenagers, or was it simply that they didn't know how to handle them?

But maybe she'd always been difficult to handle—in so many ways. Right now she looked like every teenage boy's fantasy in her wet shirt, with his bulky jacket draped around her slender shoulders, making far too many lustful thoughts crowd his mind. 'I'll show you around the house so you have plenty of time to acclimatise yourself before the party, but the guided tour can wait until later. First you need to get out of those wet clothes.'

As soon as the words had left his lips he wanted to take them back, because they sounded like the words a man would say to a woman just before he began touching her. Silently chastising himself for his own foolishness, he got out of the car and opened the door for her.

Still hugging his jacket to her, Amber followed him inside the house into a huge oak-panelled hallway from which curved a majestic staircase. Enormous bucketfuls of white flowers stood on the floor, obviously waiting to be transplanted into vases, and she could hear the sound of female voices coming from a room somewhere and a radio playing in the distance.

'Last-minute party prep,' he said, in reply to a question she hadn't asked. 'You'll meet the team later. Now come with me and I'll show you to your room.'

Her clothes were still clinging damply to her body and Amber guessed she should have been cold—but cold was the last thing she felt right now. Her blood felt heavy and warm as she followed Conall upstairs and her heart was beating painfully against her ribcage. She barely noticed the beautifully restored woodwork or the walls covered with paintings, so fixated was she on the hard thrust of his buttocks against the black denim of his jeans. She could feel her throat growing dry as she stared at the back of his neck, unable to tear her gaze away. With his black hair curling over the collar of his cashmere sweater and his muscular physique rippling with health and strength, he looked in total command of the situation, which she guessed he was. But the weird thing was that she didn't *do* this. She didn't drool over men who treated her as if she were a naughty schoolgirl. Truth was, she didn't drool over anyone. She bit her lip as she remembered the accusations which had been levelled at her in the past. *Cold. Frigid. Ice queen.* Valid accusations, every one of them. Yet when Conall looked at her, he made her want to melt, not freeze.

Pushing open the door of a second-floor bedroom overlooking the parkland at the back of the house, he put her case down. 'You should be comfortable enough in here,' he said abruptly.

Amber glanced around, suddenly shy to find herself alone in a bedroom with him. Comfortable was an understatement for such a lavish room and she was grateful he'd given her somewhere so lovely to sleep, with its heavy velvet drapes and enormous four-poster bed. She looked up into his face, knowing she ought to be asking intelligent questions about the forthcoming party but it was difficult when all she could think about was the curve of his lips and the shadowed roughness of his jaw.

'What time do you need me?' she said, her words sounding jerky as she moistened the roof of her mouth with her tongue.

'Come downstairs at around seven and I'll show you the painting. The Prince is arriving at eight-fifteen and his timetable is worked out to the nearest second. I'd better warn you that lateness won't be tolerated when you're dealing with royals.'

'I won't be late, Conall.' Amber took off his jacket and handed it to him, feeling chilled as the leather left her skin and missing the subtle scent which was all his. 'And thanks for lending me this.'

But he didn't take the jacket from her. He just stood there as if someone had turned him to stone. His brilliant eyes gleamed from between the dark lashes and his golden skin suddenly seemed taut over his cheekbones. 'You know, you're really going to have to stop doing this, Amber,' he said softly. 'I've given you several chances but my patience is wearing thin and, in the end, I'm only made out of flesh and blood—the same as any other man.'

'What are you talking about?'

'Oh, come on.' His voice was edged with a note

of irritation. 'There are many parts you play exceedingly well, but innocence isn't one of them. Much more of those big green eyes gazing at me like that and licking at your lips like a cat which has just seen a mouse—and I'll be forced to kiss you, whether I want to or not.'

Amber looked at him, genuinely confused. 'Why would you even consider kissing me if you didn't want to?'

He laughed, but his laugh contained something dark and unknown and Amber felt as if she were a non-swimmer paddling on the edge of the shore, not noticing the powerful tug of the undercurrent edging towards her.

'Because you're not my kind of woman and because I am, in effect, your employer.' His voice dipped to a silken whisper. 'But that doesn't mean I don't want to.'

His unmistakable passion mixed with the complexity of her own feelings filled Amber with a sudden sense of power and she tilted her chin to look at him defiantly. 'Well, if you really want to kiss me that badly, why don't you just go ahead and do it?'

'I don't kiss women who smoke.'

There was a pause. 'But I haven't had a cigarette since that day I came to your office.'

'You haven't?' His eyes narrowed. 'Why not?'

Should she tell him the truth? Because he'd told her she smelt disgusting and had made her feel *dirty*. But mainly because she'd wanted to show him she could. Somehow Conall Devlin had succeeded where two very expensive hypnotherapy courses had failed, and she'd quit smoking without a single craving.

'Because I am at heart a very obedient woman.' Shamelessly she batted her eyelashes at him. 'Didn't you know that?'

It was provocation pure and simple and Conall felt something inside him snap, like a piece of elastic which had been stretched beyond endurance. He heard the roar of blood in his ears and felt the jerk of an erection pushing hard against his jeans as he found himself pulling her into his arms and breathing in her warmth.

'The only thing I know is that you are a stubborn and defiant woman who has tested me beyond endurance,' he said, his voice rough. 'And maybe this has been inevitable all along.'

She stared into his eyes. 'You're going to put me across your lap and smack my bottom?'

'Is that what you'd like? Maybe later. But not right now. Right now I'm going to kiss you—but be warned that this is going to spoil you for anyone else. Are you prepared for that, Amber? That every man who kisses you after this is going to make you remember me and ache for me?'

'You are *so* arrogant,' she accused.

But her lips were parting and Conall knew she wanted this just as much as him. Maybe more—for he caught a flash of hunger in her darkening eyes. Sliding one hand around her waist while the other cushioned her still-damp hair, he lowered his mouth onto hers. And didn't part of him *want* her to have lied to him—to discover the stale odour of tobacco on those soft lips so that he could pull away in disgust?

But she hadn't lied. She tasted of peppermint and she smelt of daisies and the way she melted into his body was like throwing a match onto a pile of bone-dry timber. He groaned as he felt the stony stud of her nipples pressing against him and he reached down to cup one between his thumb and forefinger, enjoying the way she squirmed beneath his touch and whispered his name. He was so hard that he was afraid that his jeans might rip open all by themselves and, with something which sounded like a roar, he pushed her against the open door, so that it rocked crazily beneath the sudden urgent force of their bodies.

They kissed as if they'd just discovered how to kiss. Her arms were reaching up to his shoulders, as if she was trying to stop herself from sliding to the ground, and as Conall nudged his thigh between hers he was tempted to do just that. To lay her down on the hard floorboards and rip off their clothes and just *take* her, as he had been wanting to for days. Because if he did that—wouldn't he rid his blood of this fever so that he could just *forget* her? His hand cupped her breast and she gasped, drawing in a shuddering breath as he bent his head and grazed his teeth against the nipple which was hard against her damp silk shirt.

'C-Conall,' she gasped.

'I know,' he ground out as desire shot through him in a potent stream. 'Good, isn't it?' With his middle finger, he rubbed along the seam of her jeans at the crotch and he could feel her heat searing through the thick denim as she wriggled her hips in silent invitation.

The scent of sex and of desire was as potent as any perfume and he groped his hand downwards, reaching for his belt. He tugged it open and was just about to undo the top button of his jeans when some sharp splinter of sanity lanced into his thoughts and reality hit him like a slug to the jaw. He dragged his lips away, his eyes focusing and then refocusing as he stared at her and took a step back. Her shirt was half-open and her magnificent breasts were rising and falling as she struggled to control her breathing. Her black hair was plastered to her head, her eyes streaked with mascara from the rain and her lips were rosy-pink and trembling. He wondered what part of teaching her how to try to be a better person this fell under and a wave of self-disgust shot through him as he thought of what he'd just done. And what he'd been tempted to do...

Since when did he violate another man's trust in him, when he knew all too well how painful the consequences of shattered trust could be?

And since when did he lose control like that?

'Is something...wrong?' she questioned.

But he didn't answer. He was too angry with himself to even try. Did she put out like that for everyone? he wondered furiously. Was he just one in a long line of men she indiscriminately chose to satisfy her sexual needs? He took another step away from her, even though every sinew of his body was screaming out its protest. And yes, at that moment he would have traded his entire fortune to slide her panties down her legs and unzip himself and take her, but some last shred of reason stopped him as he reminded himself of the stark reality. That she was everything he'd spent his life trying to avoid and that wasn't about to change any time soon.

It was difficult to speak when all he could think about was thrusting deep into her and losing himself inside her. Difficult to regain control when his heart was racing so hard that it hurt, but Conall had learnt many lessons in his life and masking his temper had been right at the top of the list. He hid it now, replacing it with a silky reason which was always effective.

'Oh, Amber.' Slowly he shook his head. 'Where did you learn to look at a man like that and make him want to go against everything he believes in?'

Her expression was dazed but for once she wasn't flying back at him with one of her smart comments and that pleased him, for it gave him back the power which had momentarily deserted him.

'Judging by the look on your face and your body language, I imagine you must be greedily anticipating the next time,' he continued, struggling to control his ragged breathing. 'But I'm afraid there isn't going to be one. Because that was something which should never have happened. Do you understand what I'm saying, Amber? From now on we're going to stick to business and only business—so be downstairs at the time I told you so that I can brief you before the Prince arrives.' His mouth hardened into a grim and resolute line. 'And we'll both forget this ever happened.'

CHAPTER SIX

AMBER'S HANDS WERE trembling as she shut the door on Conall and tried to block out the sounds of his retreating footsteps—but it wasn't so easy to blot out the mocking words which still echoed around her head.

Forget it had ever happened?

Was he out of his *mind*?

Her fingers strayed to lips which felt as if they were on fire—as if he'd branded them with that hot and hungry kiss. Leaning back against the door, she closed her eyes. He'd done things to her she shouldn't have allowed him to do. He'd touched her breasts and put his hand in between her legs but instead of feeling outrage or disgust—or even her habitual freezing fear—she had embraced every moment of it. It had been the most erotic thing which had ever happened to her until he had ended it so abruptly. His belt undone, he had pulled away from her with disgust darkening his eyes, his accusatory words making her sound like some sort of predator—as if she were using all her wiles to lure him into her bed. Oh, the irony.

Walking over to the window, she stared out over the beautiful green parkland and thought about the way she'd responded to him. How *infuriating* that a desire which had eluded her all these years had been awoken by a man who made no secret of despising her. Who had looked at her as if she were something he'd discovered in a dark corner of a room and wished he hadn't. And his rejection had hurt. Of course it had—especially coming so fast on the heels of the nice things he'd said about her painting.

What mattered now was how she reacted to it. Why take all the responsibility for something *he* had started? Why not show Conall Devlin just what she was capable of? Show him that she was not going to become some simpering fangirl, but do what she had been brought down here to do.

Quickly she unpacked her case and took a shower—and afterwards studied the couple of dresses she'd brought with her, realising that Conall had only ever seen her in a series of unflattering outfits. She brushed her fingertips over the soft fabrics, unsure which one to pick. The scarlet was more showstopping and did wonders for her silhouette—but something stopped her from choosing it. Instead she pulled the ivory silk chiffon from one of the hangers and gave a small smile. She might have rejected most of the rules of her upbringing, but she could still remember what they were. That less was more and quality counted—especially if you were dealing with a royal prince.

By six-thirty, and feeling more confident, she was swishing her way down the sweeping staircase into the entrance hall, where the buckets of flowers had been transformed into lavish displays. She could see Conall deep in conversation on his cell phone, but he raised his bent head as Amber reached the bottom of the stairs. His eyes narrowed and she felt a beat of satisfaction as she registered his expression. He looked *amazed*. As if she'd grown a pair of wings in the time it had taken her to get ready and come downstairs. Suddenly she was glad that she'd opted for no jewellery other than a discreet pair of pearl studs at her ears and that her newly washed hair fell simply down over her shoulders.

'Hi, Conall,' she said. 'I do hope I'm appropriately dressed to meet this royal guest of yours.'

Conall didn't often find himself lost for words but right now it was a struggle to know what to say. A raw and visceral reaction began to pound its way through his body as Amber came downstairs. He stared at her with a mixture of anger and desire, feeling his groin begin to inevitably harden beneath the material of his suit trousers. How the hell did she manage to make him *feel* this way—every damned time? As if he would die if he didn't touch her. Unwillingly his gaze drifted over her, lingering in a way he couldn't seem to help. Her dress fell in creamy folds to the ground, beneath which you could just see the peep of a silver shoe. With her black hair a sleek curtain of ebony and her eyes as green as a cat's, she looked...

He swallowed. She looked as if butter wouldn't melt in that hot mouth of hers. Like those girls he used to see when he was growing up and his mother was working at the big house. The kind you were encouraged to look at because they always wanted you to look at them, but were forbidden to touch.

But he was no longer the servant's son who had to accept what he was told, he reminded himself grimly.

He was more than Amber Carter's equal—he was her *boss*—and he was the one calling the shots.

'Very presentable,' he answered coolly. 'And certainly an improvement on anything I've seen you wear before.'

She cocked her head to one side. 'Do you always end a compliment with a criticism?'

He shrugged. 'Depends who I'm talking to. I don't think a little criticism would go amiss in your case. But if the point of you coming down here looking like some kind of goddess is to try to snare the Prince, let me save you the trouble by telling you that he has a bona fide princess in the wings who's waiting for him to marry her.'

She shot him an unfriendly look. 'I'm not interested in "snaring" anyone.'

'Even though acquiring a wealthy husband would be a convenient way out of your current financial predicament?'

'Oh, come on! Which century are you living in, Conall? Women don't have to *sell* themselves through marriage any more. They take jobs like this—working for men whose default mechanism is to be moody and more than a little difficult.'

'Or they get Daddy to support them,' he mocked.

'Not any more, it seems,' she said sweetly. 'So why don't we get the show on the road? You're supposed to be giving me a guided tour of the house and showing me this painting the Prince wants to buy.'

Conall nodded as he gestured her to follow him, but he could feel the growing tension in his body as she walked beside him, aware of the filmy material which drifted enticingly against her body and whispered against every luscious curve. Her arms and her neck were the only skin visible and it was difficult to reconcile this almost ethereal image with the earthy woman who had kissed him so fervently in the bedroom earlier.

Tonight his country house looked perfect, like something you might see in the pages of one of those glossy magazines—but hadn't that always been his intention? Wasn't this the pinnacle of a long-held dream—to acquire a stately home even bigger than the one his mother had worked in during his childhood? A way of redressing some sort of balance which had always felt fundamentally skewed.

He led Amber through the ground floor—furnished and recently decorated in the traditional style—showing her the drawing rooms, the library and the grand conservatory. In the ballroom where the party was being held, a string quartet was tuning up and bottles of pink champagne were being put on ice. Everywhere he looked he could see candlelight and the air was scented with the fragrance of cut flowers and the sweet smell of success.

But Conall felt as if he was just going through the motions of showing Amber his home. As though all this lavish wealth suddenly meant nothing. Was that because the beautiful antiques just looked like bog-standard pieces of furniture when compared to the black-haired beauty by his side? Or because all he wanted to do was to drag her off to some dark corner to finish off what he had begun earlier?

He took her to a galleried room at the far end of the house, outside which a burly guard stood. The velvet drapes were drawn against the night outside and on one bare wall—beautifully lit—hung a painting.

'Here it is,' he said.

Amber was glad to have something to concentrate on other than the man at her side, or the remark he'd made earlier about her looking like a goddess. Had he meant it? A wave of impatience swept over her. *Stop reading into his words. Stop imagining he feels anything for you other than lust.*

Stepping back, she began to study the canvas—a luminous portrait of a young woman executed in oils. The woman was wearing a silver headband in her pale bobbed hair and a silver nineteen-twenties flapper dress. It was painted so finely that the subject seemed to be sending out an unspoken message to the onlooker and there was a trace of sadness in her lustrous dark eyes.

'It's exquisite,' Amber said softly.

'I know it is. Utterly exquisite.' He turned to her. 'And you're clear what you need to do? Stay by the Prince's side all evening and speak only when spoken to. Try to refrain from being controversial and please let me know if he communicates any concerns to one of his aides. Think you can manage that?'

'I can try.'

'Good. Then let's go and wait for the guest of honour.'

They walked towards the ballroom, where Amber could hear the string quartet playing a lively piece which floated out to greet them. 'So who else is coming tonight?' she asked.

'Some old friends are coming down from London. A few colleagues from New York. Local people.'

She hesitated. 'Do you ever see my half-brother, Rafe?'

His footsteps slowed and he shook his head. 'Not for ages. Not since he went out to Australia and cut himself off from his old life and nobody knew why.'

Remembering an offhand remark her father had once made, she glanced up at his rugged profile. 'I think it was something to do with a woman.'

'It's always to do with a woman, Amber. Especially when there's trouble.' He turned his head towards her and gave a hard smile. 'What do the French say? *Cherchez la femme.*'

'Is that cynicism I can hear in your voice? Did some girl break your heart, Conall?'

'Not mine, sweetheart. Mine's made of stone—didn't you know?' His eyes glittered. 'All I heard was that Rafe was heavily disillusioned by some woman and his life was never the same afterwards. It's a lesson for us all.'

He really *was* cynical, thought Amber as he introduced her to the party planner—a freckled redhead who clearly thought Conall was the greatest thing since sliced bread. Along with just about every other female present. Amber wondered if he was oblivious to the way the waitresses looked up and practically melted as they offered their trays of canapés and drinks. Whether he noticed that the female guests were fawning all over him. He *must* do—but, she had to admit, he handled it brilliantly. He was charming but he didn't flirt back—thus risking the wrath of their partners. She watched as he shook hands and made introductions as the room began to fill up, a smile creasing his rugged features.

She moved away, trying to remember that she was here as a member of his staff and not as his guest—wishing that she could retain a little immunity when she was close to him. She found herself a soft drink and stood in an alcove, watching as even more people arrived and the level of chatter increased. There was a discreet buzz of anticipation in the air, as if everyone was waiting for their royal guest, but Amber only became aware of the Prince's arrival when a complete silence suddenly descended on the ballroom.

People instantly parted to create a central path for him and the imposing man who walked in accompanied by two aides was instantly recognisable from the images Amber had downloaded from the Internet. With his immaculately cut dark suit and his golden skin gleaming, he had a charisma which was matched by only one other man in the room, who instantly stepped forward to greet him.

Amber watched as Conall gave a brief bow before shaking Luciano's hand and the string quartet broke into what was obviously the national anthem of Mardovia. And then a pair of midnight eyes were silently seeking her out and she found herself walking towards them, forcing herself to concentrate on the Prince and not on the rugged Irishman who had touched her so intimately.

'Your Royal Highness, this is Amber Carter—one of my assistants. Amber will be on hand tonight to provide anything you should require.'

That horrendous year at finishing school in Switzerland had taught Amber very little other than how to play truant and to ski, but it came up trumps now as she executed a deep and perfect curtsey. She rose slowly to her feet and the Prince smiled.

'Anything?' he drawled, his eyes roving down over her with an appreciative stare.

Amber wondered if she'd imagined Conall's faint frown and imperceptibly she nodded to the hovering waitress. 'Perhaps you would care for something to drink, Your Royal Highness?'

'Certo,' he answered softly in Italian, taking a glass of Kir Royale from the tray and then raising it to her in silent salute.

But Amber found herself enjoying the Prince's unexpected attention. For the first time in a long time she found herself encouraged by the sense that here was something she *could* do. She might not have any real qualifications but she'd watched enough of her father's wives and girlfriends fluttering around to know how *not* to behave if you were trying to play the perfect hostess. Even her mother had been able to pull it out of the bag when the need had arisen.

Unobtrusively she stood by to make sure the Prince wasn't approached by any stray star-struck guests as Conall introduced Luciano to several carefully vetted guests. It seemed he'd recently bought a penthouse apartment through Conall's company and she listened while the two men chatted with a local landowner about the escalating fortunes of the London property market. More waitresses appeared with tiny caviar-topped canapés but she noticed that the Prince refused them all. Eventually he turned to Conall.

'Do you think I have properly fulfilled my role as guest of honour,' he questioned drily, 'and given this occasion the royal stamp of approval?'

'You'd like to see the painting now?'

'I think you have tantalised me with it for long enough, don't you?'

Conall looked at her. 'Amber?'

She nodded, aware of two bodyguards who had suddenly appeared at the entrance to the ballroom and who now walked behind them towards the gallery. She thought what a disparate group they made as they made their way through the empty corridors.

The guard at the door stepped aside and Amber watched Luciano's reaction as he stepped forward to stand directly in front of the canvas. She thought that someone trying to negotiate a better price might have feigned a little indifference towards the painting, but the admiration on his face was impossible to conceal.

'What do you think?' asked Conall.

'It is breathtaking,' the Prince said slowly as he leaned forward to study it more closely. He murmured something in Italian to one of his aides and several minutes passed in silence before eventually he turned to Conall. 'We will discuss prices when you are back in London, not tonight. Business should never be distracted by pleasure.'

Conall inclined his head. 'I shall look forward to it.'

'Perhaps you could check that my car is ready? And in the meantime, I really think I must dance with your assistant who has looked after me so well all evening.' The Prince smiled. 'Unless she has any objections?'

The Prince's bright blue eyes were turned in her direction and Amber felt a stab of satisfaction. The Prince of Mardovia had told everyone that she'd done a good job—even though she'd done nothing more onerous than act as his gatekeeper—and now he wanted to dance with her. It was a long time since she could remember feeling this good about herself.

'I'd love to,' she said simply.

'Eccellente.'

She was aware of Conall's fleeting frown before he went to chase up the Prince's transport and aware of the envious glances of the other women in the ballroom as the Prince pulled her into his arms and the string quartet began to play a soft and easy waltz. Amber had been to some flashy parties in her time, but even she knew it wasn't every night of the week that you got to dance with a prince and Luciano ticked all the right boxes. He was supremely handsome and extremely attentive, but the weird thing was that it felt almost like dancing with her *brother*. Innocent and sweet, but almost dutiful. His arms around her waist felt nothing like Conall's had felt when he'd hauled her into his arms earlier. Despite the fact that he'd told her to forget it, she found herself remembering the way he had kissed her. Kissed her so hard that he'd left her feeling dazed.

'Devlin is your lover?' the Prince questioned suddenly, his voice breaking into her thoughts and amplifying them.

Slightly taken aback by his candour, Amber bit her lip. 'No!'

'But he would like to be.'

She shook her head. 'He hates me,' she said without thinking and then remembered that she was supposed to be there in the role of facilitator—not pouring out her heart to a royal stranger. 'I'm sorry—'

But Luciano didn't seem to notice for he lifted his hand to silence her apology. 'He may hate you, but he wants you. He watches you as the snake watches a chicken, just before it devours it whole.'

Amber shivered. 'That's not a very nice image to paint, Your Highness.'

'Maybe not, but it is an accurate one.' He gave her a cool smile. 'And you really should have mentioned that you speak Italian.'

Amber could feel a hot blush rising in her cheeks, so that any thought of denying it went straight out of the window. She looked up into Luciano's bright blue eyes. 'How—?'

'Not difficult.' He smiled. 'When I was speaking to my aide you were trying very hard not to react to what I was saying, but I am adept in observing reactions. I have had enough attempts made on my life to recognise subterfuge, even though I sometimes cannot help but admire it. Tell Conall I had always intended to give him a fair price for the painting.'

Amber tilted her chin. 'She's related to you, isn't she? The woman in the painting?'

He grew still. 'You recognised the family likeness, even though our colouring is quite different?'

Amber nodded. 'I'm...I'm quite good at doing that. I have a lot of half-brothers and sisters.'

'She is the daughter of my great-grandfather's brother who was born at the beginning of the last century. He fell in love with an Englishwoman and eloped with her to America. It caused a great scandal in Mardovia at the time.'

'I can imagine,' commented Amber.

Luciano glanced at his watch. 'At any other time

I would be fascinated to continue this discussion but look over there—the Irishman has returned and his expression tells me that he does not like to see you in my arms like this.'

'And you care what he thinks?'

'No, but I think you do.'

Amber stiffened. 'Maybe I do,' she admitted.

Luciano's eyes narrowed as he swung her round with a flourish, to the final few bars of the music. 'You are not aware of his reputation, I think?'

'With women?'

'With women, yes. And with business,' he commented drily. 'He is known for a detachment and a ruthlessness he has demonstrated tonight by placing a *spy* in my camp.'

Amber felt her cheeks grow pink. Hadn't she accused him of the very same thing? 'I'm sure that wasn't his intention at all,' she said doggedly.

The Prince smiled. 'Ah! Your loyalty to the man is touching—but do not look so alarmed, Amber. Conall and I know one another of old and I have great admiration for someone as ruthless as I am—but I would heed any sensible woman to exercise caution with such a man.'

Amber's cheeks were still burning as the Prince dropped his hands from her waist as Conall returned to escort him to his waiting car.

There was a loud buzz of chatter as the royal party left the room and Amber moved away from the dance floor and went to stand by the cool shelter of a marble pillar. With both men gone she felt like Cinderella—as if she no longer had any right to be here. As if any minute now her beautiful cream dress would turn into rags. She looked around. Maybe she should take the opportunity to slip out of the ballroom and go back to her room before Conall came back. Nobody would miss her. He might even be glad that she was out of his hair and he could party on without compunction.

But suddenly the decision was taken out of her hands because Conall had returned and was standing in the entrance to the ballroom, his dark suit hugging his muscular frame. He had undone a couple of buttons of his white silk shirt and Amber could see the faint smattering of dark hair there.

His eyes searched the room until he'd found her and as he began to walk towards her, her heart began to pound painfully in her chest. Would he be angry with her? She might have rather clumsily allowed the Prince to realise she was a linguist but he hadn't seemed to mind and she had done her best. Surely even Conall could understand that.

He was standing in front of her now, his midnight eyes shuttered. He didn't say a single word, just took her hand and led her onto the dance floor and Amber could feel her pulse rocketing skywards as he pulled her into his arms.

'Wh-what are you doing?' she questioned shakily, because she hadn't felt remotely like this when she'd been dancing with Luciano.

'Taking over where the Prince left off.' His eyes gleamed. 'Unless you have decided that dancing with mere mortals has no appeal compared to the heady delights of having a blue-blooded partner?'

'Don't be ridiculous,' she said. 'I'm quite happy to dance with you as long as you promise not to tread on my foot.'

His hands tightened around her waist. 'And that's your only stipulation, is it, Amber?'

Her eyes were fixed on the sprinkling of chest hair which was now exactly at eye level. 'I could think of plenty more.'

'Such as?'

'I wonder why you want to dance with me when you seem to have been glaring at me all evening.'

'Is that what I've been doing?'

'You know you have. Is it...' She hesitated. 'Is it because the Prince guessed that I spoke Italian?'

He laughed. 'He said you frowned when he used the word assassination. I guess most people would. And no, it's not because of that.'

'What, then?'

His hands tightened around her waist. 'Maybe because I have conflicting feelings about you.'

She lifted her face up and met the hard gleam of his eyes. He had *feelings* for her? She could do absolutely nothing about the sudden race of her heart—only pray he couldn't detect its erratic thumping. 'What do you mean?'

Idly, he began to rub his thumb up and down over her ribcage. 'Just that you arouse me. Deeply and constantly. And I can't seem to get you out of my mind.'

If anyone else had come out and said that Amber would have been shocked or scared, but somehow when Conall said it she was neither. 'And I'm supposed to be flattered by such a statement?'

'I don't know,' he said simply. 'My biggest concern is what I'm going to do about it.'

She could feel danger whispering in the air around them, but far more potent was the sense of excitement which made the danger easy to ignore. 'And the options are?'

'Don't be disingenuous, Amber, because it doesn't suit you.' Almost experimentally, he rolled his thumb over one of her ribs, slowly rubbing along the chiffon-covered bone. 'You know very well what the options are. I can take you upstairs so that we can finish off what we started earlier and maybe rid myself of this damned fever which has been raging in my blood since the moment I first saw you draped all over that white leather sofa.'

Somehow Amber stopped herself from reacting. Since *then*? 'Or?'

'Or I trawl this ballroom looking for someone who would make a more suitable bed partner on so many levels.' His voice dipped to a deep caress so that it sounded like velvet brushing over gravel. 'There's a third choice, of course—but not nearly so inviting. Because I could always go and take a long, cold shower and steer clear of all the complications of sex.'

Amber said nothing. He'd made her sound as disposable as a paper handkerchief. As forgettable as last night's tangled dreams. Yet he wasn't lying to her, was he? He wasn't dressing up his desire with fancy words and meaningless phrases—raising up her hopes before smashing them down again. He wasn't promising her the stars, but his underlying message was that he would deliver on satisfaction. And didn't she want that satisfaction for the first time in her life? Didn't she want to sample what other women just took for granted?

She thought about what the Prince had said to her. That a sensible woman would exercise caution. She guessed he'd been warning her off Conall Devlin, for whatever reason. But she wasn't known for being *sensible*, was she? She was known as a wild child—the party animal who was up for anything. And only she knew the truth—that all her wildness was nothing but a façade behind which she hid, a barrier which nobody had ever been able to break down.

But Conall Devlin had got closer than anyone else.

She closed her eyes as she felt his fingers pressing against her flesh and she was acutely conscious that they were inches away from her breast. Through the delicate fabric of her silk dress it felt as if he were touching her bare skin and she felt a shiver rippling down her spine. How did he *do* that? What power did he have which made her respond to him like this and make her so achingly aware of her own body? The hard jut of his hips and the potent cradle of his masculinity as he pressed himself closer should have intimidated a woman of her laughable experience, but it didn't. It just made her want more. Much more. Was she really prepared to turn her back on this opportunity to become a real woman at last?

Instinct made her lips part as she looked into his eyes and saw the sudden gleam of intensity in his darkened gaze.

'And don't I get a say in what happens?' she questioned, as lightly as if she had this kind of conversation every day of the week.

'Of course. You get to choose—because that is a woman's prerogative. Tell me what *you* want, Amber.'

The mood of the conversation had switched and beneath the teasing banter of his tone she could sense his sudden urgency. But still Amber held back, telling herself to confront the reality of what was happening here. For him this was just a liaison no different from countless others—apart from her name and her hair colour, she was probably as interchangeable as the last woman who had shared his bed.

And for her?

It was going to be no good if she started weakening. If she made the mistake of falling for him. She could only go ahead if she accepted it for what it was. Not stardust and roses, but a powerful sexual hunger. A physical awakening which was long overdue.

Rising up on tiptoe, she put her lips to his ear and only just refrained from sliding her tongue across the lobe.

'I want to have sex with you,' she whispered.

Conall stiffened, thinking he had misheard her. He must have done. She had been feisty and defiant every step of the way—surely she wasn't rolling over and capitulating *that* easily. And didn't he *want* her to go on resisting him for a little while longer, because it was so deliciously rare and because the conquest was never quite as good as the chase...

'You mean that?' he questioned softly, his fingertips continuing to slide over her silk-covered torso.

She nodded, her words uncharacteristically brief. 'Yes. Yes, I do.'

A smile curved the edges of his lips as he felt the heat begin to rise within him. 'Very well. This is what I want you to do. You will go upstairs to your room and wait for me while I say goodbye to my guests. But you will not undress before I arrive.' He paused. 'Because undressing a woman is one of the greatest pleasures known to man. Is that clear?'

She nodded—more obedient than he had ever seen her. 'Very clear.'

'I shall come to you before midnight.' He tilted her chin with his thumb and stared straight into her emerald eyes. 'But if before that you decide—for whatever reason—that you've changed your mind, then you must tell me and we will consider this conversation never to have happened. Do you understand?'

'Yes, Conall.'

He put his lips very close to her ear. 'I'm not quite sure how to cope with this unusually docile Amber.'

She turned her head to meet his gaze. 'Would you prefer defiance, then?'

'I'll let you know in graphic detail exactly what I'd prefer but I think it had better wait until we are alone. Because my words are having an unfortunate but predictable effect on my body, and having you this close to me is making me want to tear that dress off you and see the flesh beneath, and I don't think that would go down very well with my guests, do you?'

She shook her head but, to his surprise, her cheeks flushed a deep shade of pink and he felt a doubling of his desire for her. 'Go upstairs and wait for me,' he said roughly. 'Because the sooner this evening ends, the sooner we can begin.'

CHAPTER SEVEN

AMBER HEARD A CREAK behind her and turned to see the handle turning and the door slowly opening to reveal Conall standing rock still on the threshold of her bedroom. The light from the corridor spilled in from behind him, turning his muscular physique into a powerful silhouette, but not for long—because he closed the door and walked across the room, his eyes shuttered as he grew close and looked down at her. His voice sounded like velvet encasing steel.

'Changed your mind?'

She shook her head. Admittedly, she *had* been having second thoughts about their cold-blooded sexual liaison as she'd been sitting perched on the window seat waiting for him. Not undressing as per his curt instructions and feeling a bit like a sacrificial lamb in her evening dress as she stared out at the bright stars which spattered the night sky and the crescent moon which gleamed against the darkness. But her flutterings of apprehension were nothing compared to the stealthy creep of desire which was making her nerve endings feel so raw and her breasts so heavy and tingling. 'No,' she said unsteadily. 'I haven't changed my mind.'

Conall expelled the breath he hadn't realised he'd been holding because hadn't he almost wished she *had*? He'd been plagued by feelings of guilt the moment she had walked off the dance floor with her pale dress floating around her like a cloud. He had felt tortured by his conscience and even now something told him he should get out while he still could.

'I told your father that I would set you on the right path,' he growled.

She looked up into his face. 'And you have. You know you have. I felt so confident tonight—as if anything was possible and it was because of you and the chance you gave me. A few weeks ago I wouldn't have done that but you've made me see new possibilities. I'm a grown woman, Conall, not a child—so don't treat me like one. And my father is not my keeper.'

Transfixed by the unusually steadfast note in her voice and the rise and fall of her breasts, Conall felt the last of his resistance melting away as he took hold of her hands and lifted her to her feet. In the moonlight her face was almost as pale as her silky dress and, in vivid contrast, her dark hair spilled like ebony over her shoulders. She looked like a witch, he thought longingly. *Was* she a witch? Able to enchant him with things he suspected were the wrong things for a man like him? His mouth hardened. *So make sure she knows your boundaries. Make sure she doesn't read anything into what is going to happen.*

'I guess we'd better have the disclaimer conversation,' he said abruptly.

She blinked up at him. 'Disclaimer conversation?'

'Sure. I'm pretty certain a hard-partying woman like you isn't going to object to a one-night stand on moral grounds but just in case—I'd better make it clear that this is all this is going to be. One night. Great sex. But no more.' He raised his eyebrows. 'Any objections?'

'None from me,' she said, in that flippant way which was so much a part of her, though for a second he wondered if he had imagined the faint shadow which crossed over her face. 'So what are we waiting for?'

Heart pounding, he reached for the zip of her dress and slid it down. One small tug and it had pooled to her ankles and she was standing wearing nothing but her high-heeled silver shoes and her underwear.

Conall frowned because somehow her lingerie didn't match her sassy image. Her plain white bra looked like something a woman might wear to the gym and she had on a pair of those big knickers which had been the butt of a national joke for a while. It was not the lingerie of a woman who had boldly whispered to him on the dance floor that she wanted to have sex with him and that puzzled him.

Had she sensed his disquiet? Was that why she reached behind her and unclipped her bra—as careless as a woman getting changed on the beach? He stilled as her breasts spilled free and he felt a jerk of almost unbearable lust as he stared at them. Did she know that they were the stuff of his fevered fantasies—large yet pert, with their rosy-pink and perfect nipples? Of course she did. With a groan he pulled her into his arms and pushed back the spill of her hair as he kissed her. He kissed her until she was melting and her lips opened eagerly beneath his, until she began to move restlessly in his arms. And when he drew his face away, her eyes looked huge and dark in her face. As if she was completely dazed by that kiss. Conall shook his head a little. Come to think of it—wasn't he a little dazed himself?

'You are the most unfathomable woman I've ever met, Amber Carter,' he groaned, taking each nipple between a finger and a thumb and squeezing them until she squirmed with pleasure.

Her eyelids seemed to be having difficulty staying open. 'And is that a good thing, or a bad thing?'

'I haven't made my mind up yet. It's unusual, that's for sure.' He leaned forward and brushed his lips over hers. 'I keep thinking I've got you all worked out and then you go and confound all my expectations.'

'And what do you have me worked out as?'

He laughed and his voice grew serious as he traced the outline of her lips with his finger. 'One minute you're unbearably spoilt, with a sense of entitlement so strong it almost takes my breath away, while the next…'

But Amber halted his words by leaning forward to kiss him, mimicking the almost careless way he'd just brushed his lips over hers. She guessed what was coming and she didn't want to hear it. She didn't dare. She didn't want to hear about her flaws and she certainly didn't want him to work out why she was feeling out of her depth. He was a sexually experienced man—and a perceptive man—who was doubtless going to make some comment about her seeming gauche and innocent. Some bone-deep instinct told her he would run a mile if he knew the truth—and that was something she wasn't prepared to tolerate. Because she wanted Conall Devlin. She didn't care if it was a one-night stand. She couldn't think beyond the sudden urgent needs of her body and she wanted him more than she could remember wanting anything. More than the security she'd prayed for as a child, or the peace which had always eluded her. More than any of that.

So stop behaving like someone who is a stranger to intimacy. Start being the person he thinks you are.

Looping her arms around his neck, she slanted him a coquettish smile. 'Look, I know the Irish are famous for talking, but do you think we could save this conversation until later?'

And suddenly they seemed to be reading from the same page, because his eyes gleamed. 'Oh, I'm happy to skip the talking, sweetheart,' he promised, his voice laden with silken intent. 'What is it they say—action, not words?'

He picked her up and carried her over to the four-poster bed, laying her down on top of it and bending his head to a nipple. Her eyes closed as his tongue flicked over the puckered skin and his teeth gently grazed the engorged nub, making her wriggle her hips with helpless pleasure before he turned his attention to the other. Sweet sensation speared through her, flooding her body with a sudden rush of honeyed warmth as his dark head moved over her sensitive skin. Did he realise that her desire was rapidly building, or could he detect it from the subtle new perfume now scenting the air? Was that why he slipped his hand between her legs, burrowing beneath the plain white fabric of her briefs and brushing over the mound of curls before alighting on the heated flesh beneath?

She felt so wet. Maybe that was why he gave a low laugh which sent shivers down her spine. Amber's mouth dried as he began to move his finger against her so that her little gasp was scarcely more than a sigh. It felt as if he were building a wall of pleasure, brick by delicious brick, and she fell back against the pillows, her thighs parting of their own accord, when suddenly he stopped. Her eyes snapped open, terrified he had changed his mind. Her heart pounded. *He mustn't change his mind!*

But he was smiling as he shook his head. 'No,' he said. 'Not like that. Not the first time.'

He moved away from the bed and began to undress—removing his clothes and producing a small silver packet from his pocket with an efficiency which suggested he'd done this many times before. Of course he had. And although fear that she would somehow disappoint him began to bubble up inside her—it quickly disappeared the moment she saw him in all his naked glory.

Amber shivered. He was like a classical statue you might see in a museum—with broad shoulders tapering down to narrow hips and muscular legs. But statues didn't have tawny skin which glowed with life, nor midnight eyes which gleamed with hunger. Inevitably, her gaze was drawn down towards the cradle of his masculinity where, against a palette of jet-dark curls, his erection was thick and pale and prominent. Amber felt her pulse go shooting skywards. She'd never got this far before—she'd always fallen at much earlier hurdles—and perhaps she should have been daunted by what she saw. But she wasn't. It felt natural. As if it was supposed to happen. As if fate had intended it to happen—before she reminded herself that she wasn't going down that path. Stardust and roses weren't part of this equation, she reminded herself fiercely. This was sex. Nothing but sex. He'd told her that himself.

'I like it,' he murmured as he came over to the bed and pulled her into his arms.

'Wh-what?'

'The look on your face.' He smiled. 'As if this was the first time all over again. Have you spent years perfecting that look of wonder and innocence, Amber—knowing just how much it will turn a man on?'

If she'd written the script herself, there wouldn't have been a better time to tell him but Amber couldn't bring herself to say it. Because now he was kissing her and his hands were starfishing over her breasts and she could feel his hardness pressing against her belly.

'Conall,' she gasped as he pulled back for a moment to slide her panties down and she lifted up her bottom to help him.

'You were the one who didn't want to talk,' he murmured as he fumbled for the silver packet he'd put beside the bed. 'Though maybe you'd better say something to distract me because I've never had so much trouble putting on a damned condom.'

'Be…be careful.'

The smile on his lips died. 'Oh, don't worry, sweetheart. Having a baby with you was never part of my agenda.'

The stark statement was oddly painful and yet somehow it helped. It helped her focus on the way he was making her *feel* and not the conflicting thoughts which were swirling around inside her head.

So she kissed him back with a passion which came

from somewhere deep inside her, and with growing confidence began to explore the warm satin of his skin with her mouth and her fingers. And when he moved over her and parted her thighs, the fear she felt was only fleeting. She was twenty-four years old, for heaven's sake. It was time.

Conall gave a groan as he thrust into her, knowing he was going to have to be very careful because he was so aroused he wanted to come straight away. And she was so *tight*. His heart pounded like some caged animal locked inside his chest. Too tight. He gave a near-silent curse as realisation dawned on him and his body stilled. For a moment he almost achieved the impossible by starting to withdraw from her, but the moment was lost the second she cried out and he couldn't work out if the sound was pain or pleasure. Had he hurt her? He stared down into her face, into eyes which were wide—as if seeking some kind of approval—and instantly he shut his own with grim deliberation, not wanting her to see his anger or his disbelief as he began to move inside her. Part of him wanted to just spill his seed and have done with it, but the pride he took in his reputation as a lover made him take his time...

Duplicitous little *bitch*, he thought as he drove into her—each thrust making her gasp out her pleasure. With almost cold-hearted precision he did all the things to her which women liked best. He tilted up her hips to increase the level of penetration while he played with her clitoris. He rode her hard and he rode her slow, and only when he felt her body begin to tense did he let go—and then it was *his* time for bewilderment. Because it had never happened to him before. Not like this. Not at exactly the same time—as if they'd worked very hard at sexual choreography classes to ensure the ultimate in mutual fulfilment. So that as her back began to arch and her long legs began to splay, he couldn't even watch her—he was too busy focusing on his own orgasm, which was welling up inside him like an almighty wave, before taking him under.

Had he thought that the chase was always more tantalising than the conquest? He had been wrong.

Because all he was aware of was the convulsive jerk of his body and the molten rush of heat. Of the sweetest pleasure he had ever known flooding him… and his shuddered cry drowning out the distant hoot of the night owl.

CHAPTER EIGHT

'You acted...'

Conall's words trailed off and Amber didn't prompt him. She didn't want to talk and she didn't want to hear what he had to say. She didn't want to do anything except lie here and go over what had just happened, second by glorious second. To remember the way he'd kissed her. The way he'd pushed deep inside her—and then the growing awareness of her body's reaction, which had seemed too good to be true. Only it hadn't been. It had been very real and very true. Conall Devlin had made love to her and it had been perfect. She expelled a long, slow breath of satisfaction. Suddenly she could understand all the fuss and hype and everything which went with it. Sex was pretty potent stuff.

But then when it was over, he had withdrawn from her without even looking at her. He had just rolled over onto his back and lain there staring at the ceiling in complete silence. As if he was working out what he was going to say, and something told her she wasn't going to like it...

She was right.

'You acted like you'd been round the block a few times—and then some,' he accused.

She risked a glance at him then and almost wished she hadn't because it triggered off a craving to touch him again and that was the last thing he wanted, judging from the stony look on his face. *You haven't done anything wrong*, she told herself. *And he can only make you feel bad about yourself if you let him.*

'You're objecting to the fact I was a virgin?' she questioned, in a voice which was surprisingly calm. Maybe it was the endorphins rushing through her bloodstream which were responsible—making her feel as if she were floating in the sea, in bright sunshine. 'And you're objecting to the fact that I hadn't *been around the block*, is that what you're saying?'

He turned to look at her, his eyes gleaming in his tawny skin. 'What do you think? You knew what the deal was, Amber.'

'Deal?' she echoed. She raised her eyebrows. 'What deal was that?'

'I told you it was a one-night stand!' he exploded.

'And virgins aren't allowed to have one-night stands?'

'Yes. No! Stop wilfully misunderstanding me!'

'I'm confused, Conall. You still haven't told me why you're so angry.'

He glared at her. 'You know damned well why.'

'No, I don't.'

'There's an unspoken rule about sex—that if you're inexperienced, you tell the man.'

'Why? So that you could be "gentle" with me?'

'So that I could have turned around and walked right out again.'

'Because you didn't want me?'

Conall steeled himself against that uncertain note in her voice, reminding himself that she was a consummate actress. She'd played the vamp to an astonishingly successful degree and had fooled him completely. He'd fantasised about all the sexual tricks she might have learnt over the years. He'd been expecting accomplishment and slickness—not for her to cry out like that when he tore through her hymen. Or to clutch at him like a child with a new toy when he was deep inside her. That wonder on her face had not been feigned, he realised grimly.

'You know I wanted you. My body is programmed to want you. It's a reaction outside my control.'

'Gee. Thanks.'

He shook his head. 'The first time is supposed to be special. It's supposed to *mean* something and if I'd realised, I would have done the decent thing and walked away. But you weren't prepared to let that happen, were you, Amber? You saw something and you just went right ahead and took it because that's the kind of woman you are. Even though you must have known it would never have happened if I'd realised you were a virgin. But Amber always gets what Amber wants, doesn't she?'

'If that's what you want to think, then think it,' she said.

'I just don't understand why.' He frowned. 'How come someone who looks like you and acts like you has never actually had sex before now?'

Amber met the anger in his eyes and wondered how much to tell him. But what was the point in holding back—in trying to pretend that she was a normal woman who'd led a normal life?

'Because I don't really like men,' she said slowly. 'And I certainly don't trust them.'

'Which is why you put out for someone you only met a couple of weeks ago, who hasn't even taken you out on a date?'

Put like that, it made her sound plain stupid. As if she'd been caught scraping the very bottom of the barrel. Amber felt her cheeks growing hot, but she could hardly blame him for speaking the truth—even if it made her feel bad. And was she really going to let him take the moral high ground, just because she hadn't given some embarrassingly graphic explanation before he'd made love to her? Why *would* she ruin the mood and risk spoiling something which had felt so natural?

'I'm sure your colossal ego doesn't need me to tell you why I succumbed to you. You must realise that you're overwhelmingly attractive to women, Conall. I'm sure you've heard it many times before. It must be that blend of Irish charm coupled with a masterful certainty that you always know best.' She snuggled down a little further into the bedclothes, but her skin still felt like ice. 'It must be great to have that kind of unshakeable confidence.'

'We were talking about you, not me,' he growled. 'And you still haven't given me an explanation.'

'Do I have to?'

'Don't you think you owe me one?'

'I don't owe you anything.'

'Okay, then. How about as a favour to me for having given you so much pleasure in the last hour?'

Amber swallowed as she met the arrogant glitter in his eyes. In a way it was easier when he was being hateful because at least that stopped her from fostering any dreamy illusions about him. And she realised that this was the other side of intimacy—not the sex part but the bit where two people were naked in more ways than one. Because for once she couldn't run or hide from the truth. She felt exposed; vulnerable. Conall was demanding an explanation and in her heart she guessed she owed him one.

'Maybe it's because I didn't have the best role models in the world,' she said.

'You're talking about your father?' he questioned curiously.

'Not just my father. There were plenty of others. My mother's lovers, for starters.'

'There were a lot?'

'Oh, yes—you could say that.' She gave a hollow laugh. 'After my parents split, my father gave my mother loads of alimony—I think he was trying to ease his conscience about falling in love with a new woman. With hindsight it was probably a big mistake—because money buys you plenty of things, but not happiness. The biggest cliché in the world, I know, but true.' Amber was aware of the irony of her words. As if it had taken this to make her see things clearly. Because hadn't she experienced the closest thing she'd felt to joy in a long time when she'd been walking in that country lane that afternoon? And then just a few minutes ago, when Conall's naked skin had touched hers and he'd taken her to heaven and back? Only one of those things had cost her...and it couldn't be measured in monetary terms.

'So what happened?' he asked, his deep Irish voice penetrating her thoughts.

'My mother couldn't face staying in England with the humiliation of being replaced by wife number four, who was much younger—as well as being a lingerie model. So she decided to do an extensive tour of Europe—which translated into an extensive tour of European men. The trouble was that she was divorced and predatory, with a child in tow. Not the best combination to help her in her ardent pursuit of a new partner.' She shifted her legs beneath the duvet, taking care to keep them well away from his. 'Oh, there were plenty of men—but the men always seemed to come with baggage, usually in the shape of a wife. We were hounded out of Rome, and Athens, too. We were threatened in Naples and had to slip away in the dead of night. Only in Paris did she achieve any kind of acceptance because there the role of mistress is more or less accepted. Only she didn't like playing second fiddle to other men's wives, and...' Her words tailed off.

'And what?'

A wave of indignation swept over her as she met the hard glitter of his sapphire eyes. Why was he doing this? Interrogating her like some second-rate cop. Was he determined to ruin the amazing memory of what had just happened between them by making her retrace a past it was painful to revisit?

'I'm waiting, Amber,' he said softly.

Stubborn, hateful man. Amber stared straight up at the ceiling. 'I don't want to talk about it,' she said woodenly. 'She died, okay? I was brought back to England, kicking and screaming, and moved in with my father, who by that time was on wife number five. I didn't fit in anywhere—and I knew his latest wife didn't want me there. To him, I was a problem he didn't know how to cope with, so he just threw lots of money at it. I started doing loads of courses but only the ones he thought were suitable and, of course, I never saw them through. I didn't know how to deal with normal life—and I'd known so many creepy men when I was growing up that I simply wasn't interested in getting intimate with any of my own.'

'I see.'

Amber pulled the duvet right up to her neck—noticing he didn't object—before rolling on her side to face him. 'And what *do* you see, Conall?'

He gave a short laugh. 'I can see now why your father was so determined he help you escape from the rut you were in. I detected a sense of remorse in his attitude—a sense that he wanted to try to repair some of the mistakes he'd made in the past. He must have realised that giving you money was having precisely the wrong effect, and that's why he withdrew your funds.'

'Wow. You should be a detective!'

'But you didn't like being broke, did you, Amber?' he continued silkily. 'You didn't like having to knuckle down and do a hard day's work like the rest of the human race.'

'I thought I did a good job for you tonight with the Prince!' she defended, stung.

He nodded reluctantly. 'Oh, you did,' he said. 'He was very impressed with you and who wouldn't be, with your classy dress and your pearls? And, of course, the fact that you were gazing up at him on the dance floor and batting those witchy green eyes certainly didn't do you any harm. But I guess you quickly discovered that he wasn't interested in you and so that quicksilver mind of yours had to come up with an alternative plan.'

'Really? And what *plan* was this, Conall? Do enlighten me—this is absolutely fascinating.'

'I think I can understand why you were a virgin,' he said slowly. 'With a mother who was sexually voracious, you must have realised that virginity is the most prized gift a woman can offer a man. It's unique. A one-off.'

'You've lost me now,' she said faintly.

'Think about it. Because despite your lack of qualifications, you're a super-sharp woman, Amber. You know damned well what I'm talking about. You played the vamp with me. You realised there was real chemistry between us and that all I wanted was casual sex. It was a grown-up agreement between two consenting adults when suddenly you spring this surprise on me. You're a virgin! Though when I stop to think about it, maybe it isn't so surprising after all.' He gave a short laugh. 'Take a previously wealthy woman with nothing to offer but her innocence—and throw her into the arms of an old-fashioned man with a conscience and the result is predictable.'

'What *result*?'

Despite their cold hue, his eyes suddenly looked as if they were capable of scorching her skin.

'It doesn't matter—at least, not right now,' he said, his mouth twisting into a grim line. 'What an impetuous fool I was to have taken you to bed!'

'Then why don't you do us both a favour and get out of it right now?'

She wasn't expecting him to take her at her word, but he did—pushing back the bedclothes with an impatient hand and moving away from the bed as if it were contaminated. But the impact of seeing him unselfconsciously naked as he walked across the room was utterly compelling and Amber couldn't seem to drag her gaze away. He went to stand by the window and all she could see was his magnificent physique, silhouetted against the gleaming moon and scattered stars. And all she could think about was how pale his buttocks looked against the deep tawny colour of his back. How it had felt to have the rough power of his muscular legs entwined with her own, which had felt so light and smooth in comparison.

Only he had made her feel bad about what had happened—and bad about herself. As if she were using her virginity as some kind of bargaining tool. As if she were nothing but a cold-blooded manipulator.

So why did she still want him, despite his wounding words? Why did she want to feel his lips on her lips and his hands on her hips as he positioned himself over her, before thrusting deep inside her? Maybe she was one of those women who were only turned on by men who were cruel to them, just like her mother.

She licked her dry lips. 'Are you going now?' she croaked, because surely it would hurt less if he was gone.

He turned back to face her and at once she could see that he was aroused and, although she tried not to react, something in her face must have given away her thoughts because he gave a cold, hard smile.

'Oh, yes,' he said ruefully. 'I still want you, be in no doubt about that. Only this time I'm not going to be stupid enough to do anything about it.' Grabbing his clothes, he started pulling them on until he was standing in the now-creased suit he'd worn to the party.

'I'm going to bed,' he continued. 'I need to sleep on this and decide what needs to be done. I'll have breakfast sent up here tomorrow morning and then drive you back to London. Make sure you're ready to leave at eight.'

Amber shook her head. 'I don't want to drive back to London with you,' she said. 'I'll get the train, like I did before.'

'It's not a subject which is open for negotiation, Amber. You and I need to talk, but not now. Not like this.'

She lay there wide-eyed after he'd gone, hugging her arms around her chest. And although she went to the bathroom to shower his scent from her skin, it wasn't so easy to erase him from her memory and her night was spent fitfully tossing and turning.

She was up and dressed early next morning, telling herself she wasn't hungry but it seemed her body had other ideas. She devoured grapefruit, eggs and toast with an appetite which was uncharacteristically hearty, before going downstairs to find Conall waiting outside for her with his car engine running.

She tried not to look at him as she climbed beside him and she kept communication brief, but he didn't object to her silence and said very little on the journey back to London. She stared out of the window and thought about yesterday and how green the lush countryside had seemed—and how today it seemed like a once-bright balloon from which all the air had escaped.

He drove her straight to her apartment and as he turned off the engine she couldn't resist a swipe.

'Here we are—home at last,' she said with bright sarcasm. 'Though not for much longer, of course, because soon my big, bad landlord will be kicking me out onto the streets.'

'That's what I want to talk to you about,' he said, pushing open his door.

'You're not planning on coming in?'

'No, not planning,' he said grimly. 'I *am* coming in. And there's no need to look so horrified, Amber—I'm not going to jump on you the moment we get inside.'

Oddly enough, his assurance provided Amber with little comfort. Was it possible that one episode of sex had been enough to kill his desire for her for ever? Because the man who had been so hot and hungry for her last night was deliberately keeping his distance from her this morning.

She waited until they were inside and then she turned to him, noticing the dark shadows around his eyes. As if he had slept as badly as her. 'So. What's the verdict?'

His mouth was unsmiling and his voice was heavy. 'I think we should get married.'

Amber blinked in astonishment and, even though she knew it was *insane*, she couldn't quite suppress the flicker of hope which had started dancing at the edges of her heart. She pictured clouds of confetti and a lacy dress, and a rugged face bending down to kiss her. She swallowed. 'You do?'

'Yes.' Navy eyes narrowed. 'I know it's far from ideal but it seems the only sensible solution.'

'I think I need to sit down,' said Amber faintly, sinking onto one of the white leather sofas beneath the penetrating brilliance of his gaze. And now that her heart had stopped pounding with a hope she realised was stupid, she tried to claw back a little dignity. 'Whatever gave you that idea that I would want to marry you?'

His gaze burned into her. 'Didn't it enter your mind for a moment that giving me your virginity would trouble my conscience? I feel a responsibility towards you—'

'Then don't—'

'You don't understand,' he interrupted savagely. 'I have betrayed the trust of your father by taking advantage of you.' His voice hardened. 'And trust is a very big deal to me.'

'He won't know. Nobody will know.'

'*I* will know,' he said grimly. 'And the only way I can see of legitimising what has just happened is to make you my temporary wife.'

She stared at him defiantly. 'So you want to marry me just to make yourself feel better?'

'Not entirely. It would have certain advantages for you, too.'

She opened her mouth and knew she shouldn't say what she was about to say—but *why not*? He'd seen her naked, hadn't he? He'd been deep inside her body in a way that nobody else had ever been. He'd heard her cry out her pleasure with that broken kind of joy as she'd wrapped her legs around his back. What did she have to lose? 'What, like sex?'

But he shook his head, his hair glinting blue-black in the watery spring sunshine. 'No,' he said. 'Most emphatically not sex. I don't want the complications of that. This will purely be a marriage of convenience—a short-lived affair with a planned ending.'

She screwed up her eyes, trying not to react. One brief sexual encounter and already he'd had enough of her? 'I don't understand,' she said, desperately trying to hide the hurt she felt at his rejection.

He walked over to the window and stared out at the view for a moment before turning back to face her. 'Your father wanted you to stand on your own two feet—and as a wealthy divorcee you'll be able to do exactly that.'

'A wealthy divorcee?' she echoed hoarsely.

'Sure. What else did you think would happen—that twenty-five years down the line we'd be toasting each other with champagne and playing with the grandkids?' He gave a cynical smile. 'We'll get married straight away—because a whirlwind marriage always makes a gullible world think it's high romance.'

'But you don't, I suppose?'

His mouth hardened. 'I'm a realist, Amber—not a romantic.'

'Me, too,' she lied.

'Well, that makes it a whole lot easier, doesn't it? And you know what they say...marry in haste, repent at leisure. Only nowadays there's no need to do that. We'll split after three months and nobody will be a bit surprised. I'll settle this apartment on you and agree to some sort of maintenance. And if you want my advice, you should use the opportunity to go off and do something useful with your life—not go back to your former, worthless existence. Your father will see you blossom and flourish with your new-found independence. He's hardly in a position to berate you for a failed marriage—and my conscience will be clear.'

'You've got it all worked out, haven't you?' she said slowly.

'I deal in solutions.' His gaze drifted to her face. 'What do you say, Amber?'

She looked away, noticing a red wine stain on the white leather of the sofa as he waited for her answer. The trouble was that on some level she wasn't averse to marrying him and she wasn't quite sure why. Was it because she felt safe and protected whenever he was around? Or because she was hoping he'd change his mind about the no-sex part? Surely a virile man like Conall wouldn't be prepared to coexist platonically with a woman—no matter how fake or how short their relationship was intended to be.

And look what he was offering in return. At least as a divorcee she would have a certain respectability. A badge of honour that someone had once wanted her enough to marry her...

Except that he didn't. Not really. He didn't love her and he didn't want her.

That old familiar feeling of panic flooded through her. It felt just like that time when she'd been shipped off to her dad's after her mother had died. He hadn't wanted her, either, not really—and neither did Conall. It was a grim proposition to have to face until she considered the alternative. No money. No qualifications. No control. She swallowed. In an ideal world she would turn around and walk out, but where would she go?

Couldn't this marriage be a stepping stone to some kind of better future?

'Yeah, I'll marry you,' she said casually.

CHAPTER NINE

It wasn't a real wedding—so no way was it going to feel like one.

It was a line Amber kept repeating—telling herself if she said it often enough, then sooner or later she'd start believing it. Her marriage was nothing but a farce. A solution to ease Conall's conscience and set her up financially for the future. This way, nobody would have to lose face. Not her and not Conall.

But weddings had a sneaky knack of pressing all the wrong buttons, no matter how much you tried not to let them. Despite the example set by both her parents, Amber found herself having to dampen down instincts which came out of nowhere. Who knew she would secretly yearn for a floaty dress with a garland of flowers in her hair? Because floaty dresses and flowers were romantic, and this had nothing to do with romance—Conall had told her that and she had agreed with him. This was a transaction, pure and simple. As emotionless as any deal her Irish fiancé might cut in the boardroom.

So she opted for a dress she thought would be *suitable* for the civil ceremony—a sleek knee-length outfit by a well-known designer, with her hair worn in a heavy chignon and a minimalist bouquet of stark, arum lilies.

The ceremony was small. Her father, still in his ashram, had not been able to attend—and Conall had insisted on keeping the celebrations short and muted.

'I don't want this to turn into some kind of rent-a-crowd,' he'd growled. 'Inviting a bunch of my friends to meet a woman who isn't going to be part of my life for longer than a few weeks is a waste of everyone's time. As long as we give the press the pictures they want, nobody will care.'

But on some level *Amber* had cared. She tried to convince herself that it was a relief not to have to invite anyone and have to maintain the farce of being a blissfully happy bride. She told herself that she was perfectly cool with the miniskirted Serena and another of Conall's glamorous assistants being their only two witnesses on the day.

But hadn't some stupid part of her *wanted* Conall to take her into his arms when he'd slipped the thin gold band on her finger—and to kiss her with all the passion he'd displayed on that moonlit night in his country house? He hadn't, of course. He had waited until they got outside, where a bank of tipped-off photographers was assembled, and it was only then that he had kissed her. From the outside it must have looked quite something, for he held her close and bent over her in a masterful way which made her heart punch out such a frantic beat that for a minute she felt quite dizzy. But his lips had remained as cold and as unmoving as if they'd been made from marble—and it didn't seem to matter what she said or did, she couldn't remember seeing him smile.

They had taken the honeymoon suite at the Granchester Hotel, even though Conall had an enormous house in Notting Hill, which Amber had visited just twice before. But both occasions had felt dry and rather formal and she'd felt completely overwhelmed by the decidedly masculine elements of his elegant town house.

'I think it's best if we stay on neutral territory for the first few days.' His words had been careful. 'It lets the world know we're man and wife, but it will also allow us to work out some workable form of compromise as to how this...*marriage* is going to work.' He'd paused and his midnight-blue eyes had glinted. 'Plus the hotel is used to dealing with the press.'

The hotel seemed used to dealing with pretty much everything. Their suite was huge, with a dining room laid up to serve them a post-wedding meal, a vast sitting room, and a hot tub on the private and very sheltered rooftop garden. Rather distractingly, the king-sized bed had been liberally scattered with scarlet rose petals—something which had made Conall's mouth harden as he'd walked into the bedroom, while pulling loose his tie.

'Why the hell do they *do* that?' he asked.

Amber paused in the act of removing the pins from her hair, relieved to be able to shake it free after the tensions of the long day, even though a feeling of apprehension about the night ahead was building up inside her. 'Presumably they like to think they're adding to the general air of romance.'

'It's so damned corny.'

Kicking off her cream shoes, Amber sank down

on one of the chairs and looked at him, a trace of defiance creasing her brow. 'So now what?'

It was a question Conall had been dreading and one he still hadn't quite worked out how to answer, despite it looming large in his thoughts during the days since she'd agreed to marry him, while they'd waited for the necessary paperwork to go through. Hadn't he thought she might phone him up and tell him she'd changed her mind? That she'd tell him it was insane in this day and age for two people to go through with a marriage neither wanted, just because they'd had casual sex and she had been a virgin?

There had been a big part of him which had *wanted* her to do that. Because whichever way you looked at it, he was now trapped with her for the next three months. Their relationship had to look real, which meant he'd have to be with her—as a new husband would be expected to be with his wife. And he didn't *do* sustained proximity. He liked his freedom and the ability to come and go. He always demanded an escape route and a get-out clause whenever he was in a relationship. And this *wasn't* a relationship, he reminded himself grimly.

He walked over to the ice bucket, which was sitting next to two crystal flutes and yet more scarlet roses, and pulled out a bottle of vintage champagne.

'I think we deserve a drink, don't you?' he said, glancing over at her as he popped the cork.

'Please.'

Trying hard to avert his gaze from the splayed coltishness of her long legs, he handed her a glass. 'Here.'

Amber took the glass and studied the fizzing

golden bubbles for a moment before looking up into his eyes. 'So what shall we drink to, Conall?'

He sat down opposite, deliberately settling himself as far away from her as possible. What he would *like* to drink to wasn't a request for long life or happiness. No. What he needed right then was to be granted some sort of immunity. A sure-fire way to stop thinking about her sensuality—a sensuality which seemed even more potent now that he'd sampled her delicious body for himself. He wondered how it was possible for a woman to be so damned sexy when she'd only ever had sex once before.

He felt his throat thicken, but he had vowed that he was going to forget that night and put it out of his mind. To push away the ever-creeping temptation to do it to her all over again...and again. He swallowed as he felt the hard throb of desire at his groin and the sudden distracting thunder of his pulse. 'To an argument-free three months?'

She raised her eyebrows. 'You think that's possible?'

'I think anything is possible, if we put our minds to it.'

'Okay. Then—purely on the subject of logistics—I'd like to know how this arrangement is supposed to work when there's only one bed?'

Sipping his champagne, he fixed her with a steady look. 'In case you hadn't noticed, it's a very big bed.'

'And you won't be...'

'Won't be what?'

'I don't know.' She shrugged. 'Tempted?'

'To leap on you?' He gave a short laugh. 'Oh, I'm one hundred per cent certain I'll be tempted because you are an extremely beautiful woman and you blew my mind the other night. But I can resist anything when I put my mind to it, Amber. Even you.'

She put the glass down on the table and tucked her legs up neatly beneath her. It was a demure enough pose—but that didn't stop his body jerking in response, nor prevent the sudden urgent desire to slide his fingers all the way up her silken thighs and to feel if she was wet for him. Was that why a sudden brief look burned between them and why she suddenly started shifting awkwardly on the chair, as if a colony of ants had crawled into her panties?

'Well, we're going to have to do *something* to pass the time.' She glanced around. 'And I haven't noticed any board games.'

'I don't think you'll find board games are the activity of choice in a world-famous honeymoon suite,' he said drily.

'So we might as well find out more about each other. A sort of getting-to-know-you session.' She fixed him with a bright smile. 'It'll come in useful if ever we're forced to compete on one of those terrible *Mr and Mrs* TV shows, before we get our divorce finalised. I've told you plenty of stuff about me but you're still one great big mystery, aren't you, Conall?'

And that was the way he liked it. Conall drank some more champagne. Being enigmatic was a lifestyle choice. Keep people away and they couldn't get close enough to cause you pain. Because pain meant you couldn't think straight. It made you lash out and lose control. He'd lost control once—big time—and it had scared the hell out of him. It had almost ruined his life and he had vowed it would never happen again.

But you lost control with Amber the other night, didn't you? You had sex with her even though you'd told yourself it wasn't going to happen. You plunged deep into her body even though your head was screaming at you to withdraw. And you couldn't. You were like a fly caught in her sticky web.

Briefly, he closed his eyes. The way she'd made him feel had been like nothing else he'd ever experienced—as if he'd been teetering on the brink of some dark abyss, about to dive straight in. If he'd had his way, he would have walked away and never seen her again.

But Amber was his wife now and that changed all the rules. He was with her for the duration and there wasn't a damned thing he could do about it. And they were holed up in this hotel with a self-imposed sex ban. What else were they going to do but talk? Surely he needed something to occupy his thoughts other than how much he'd like to rip that damned white dress from her body. He could always have her sign a confidentiality agreement when the time came to settle the divorce. And in the meantime, wasn't there something *liberating* about for once not having to hide behind the barriers he had erected to stop women from getting too close?

'So what do you want to know about me?' he drawled. 'Let me guess. Why I've never married before? That's usually the number-one question of choice for women.'

'Why are you so cynical, Conall?'

'Maybe life has made me that way,' he said mockingly. 'Is it cynical to state the truth?'

Their gazes clashed. He thought her narrowed eyes looked like bright slithers of green glass in her pale face.

'How come you and my father are so close?'

'I told you. I used to work for him a long time ago.'

'But that doesn't explain the connection between you.' She ran her fingertip around the rim of her champagne glass before shooting him another glance. 'A connection which was intimate enough for him to ask you to take charge of my life. Why does he trust you so much, when there are very few people he does trust?'

Conall's mouth hardened. 'Because once he did me a big favour and I owe him.'

'What kind of favour?'

Putting his glass down, he leaned back in the chair and cushioned his head on his clasped hands. 'It's a long story.'

'I like long stories.'

Conall let his gaze drift over her. Maybe it was better to revisit the uncomfortable landscape of the past, than to sit here uncomfortably thinking about what a beautiful bride she made. 'It started when I won a scholarship to your brother's school,' he said. 'Did you know that?'

She shook her head.

'A full scholarship which enabled the illegitimate son of an Irish housekeeper to attend one of the finest schools in the country. It's where I learnt to ride and to shoot.' He gave a short laugh. 'To behave like a true English gentleman.'

'Except you aren't, are you?' she said slowly. 'Not really.'

He met her faintly mocking gaze. 'No, you're right. I'm not. But you have two choices when you go to a place like that—either you try to blend in and mimic all the other boys around you, or you attempt to stay the person you already are. It was because my mother had been so strict about making me study that I was there in the first place and so I vowed to stay true to my roots. I was determined she would never think I was rejecting her values.' There was silence for a moment. Up here in the totally soundproof hotel suite, he thought that the rest of the world seemed a long way away. 'And I think Ambrose admired that quality. I'd actually met him before I won the scholarship, and became friends with his son. I'd polished the windscreen of his car a couple of times, because my mother worked as housekeeper for some of his friends. The Cadogans.'

She nodded. 'I know the Cadogans.'

'Of course you do. Everyone does. They're one of the most well-connected families in England.' He heard his voice become rough, as if someone had just attacked it with coarse sandpaper. And suddenly it stopped being just a memory. It came back to him and hit him, like an unexpected wave sneaking up behind you and knocking you off your feet. He could feel his heart pounding heavily. His skin felt heated and he wanted suddenly to escape. He wanted to get out of that damned suite and start walking. Or walk right over to the chair where she sat and haul her into his arms.

'You were saying?'

Her cool prompt made the mists clear and he was tempted to tell her that he'd changed his mind and it was none of her business. But he had bottled this up for more years than he cared to remember and mightn't it be therapeutic to let it out and for Amber to see her father in a good light for once? He cleared his throat. 'My mother had worked for the family ever since she'd got off the ferry from Rosslare. They worked her long and hard but she never complained—she was grateful that they'd allowed her to bring her baby into the house.' He raised his eyebrows. 'I guess it's unusual for you to hear it this way round. To hear what life is like *below stairs*?'

'Being rich is no guarantee of happiness,' she said flatly. 'I thought that was one thing you and I agreed on. And please don't stop your story just when it was getting interesting.'

'Interesting? That wouldn't have been my word of choice.' His mouth twisted. He thought that there were some memories which never lost their power to wound...was it any wonder he'd buried it so deeply? 'One day a diamond ring went missing—which just happened to be a priceless family heirloom—and my mother was accused of stealing it by one of the Cadogan daughters.' His heart twisted as he remembered his mother's voice when she'd phoned him and the way she'd tried to disguise her shuddering sobs. Because in all the years of heartbreak—those times when she'd waited vainly for a letter or a card from her family in Ireland—he had never once heard her cry. 'My mother was as honest as the day was long. She couldn't believe she was being labelled a thief by a family whose house she had worked in for all those years. A family she thought trusted her.' There it was again. Trust. That word which didn't mean a damned thing.

A clock chimed in one of the suite's adjoining rooms.

'What happened?' Amber asked as the chimes died away.

He gave a heavy sigh. 'In view of her long service record they decided not to press charges but they sacked her and eventually she found a job as a cleaner in a big girls' school. But she never got over it.' He felt the lump which rose in his throat. The sense of helplessness. Even now. 'She died months later—years before her time.'

'Oh, Conall.'

But he held up his hand in an imperious gesture because he didn't need Amber Carter's pity, or for her to soften her voice like that. He didn't want token *kindness*. 'That might have been the end of it if I hadn't gone back to the house and got one of the daughters to talk to me, to find out what had really happened.'

There was a pause and he noticed she didn't prompt him to continue—maybe if she had he would have stopped—but when he started speaking again he could hear the shakiness in his own voice.

'She told me that the ring had been stolen by her sister's boyfriend—a boy high on drugs and keen to purchase more. It was all hushed up, of course. My mother had simply been the scapegoat.' He gave a bitter laugh. 'So I took it on myself to exact some sort of revenge.'

'Oh, Conall,' she whispered. 'What did you do?'

'Don't look so fearful, Amber. I didn't hurt anyone,

if that's what you're thinking—but I hurt them where I knew it would matter. One night, under the cover of darkness, I took a spray can and let rip—covering their beautiful stately house with graffiti which was designed to let the world know just how corrupt they were. I caused a lot of damage to the place and they called the police. It was my word against theirs. They were one of the oldest and most respectable families in the country while I was just...' he shrugged '...a thug with a motive.'

She was silent for a moment. 'And where did my father come in?' she asked eventually.

Conall stared straight ahead, remembering the stench of unwashed bodies and the sound of voices shouting in the adjoining cells. His own cell had been small and windowless and he'd seen a glimpse of a different path which had lain before him—a path he hadn't wanted to take.

'When I was sitting in the detention centre,' he said slowly, 'with my offer of a place at university having been withdrawn and looking at the possibility of a jail term—Ambrose arrived, and vouched for me. Rafe must have called him. He said I'd been a friend of his son's for many years and that this was a one-off deviation. I don't know if he spoke to the Cadogans but all the charges against me were dropped and he offered me a job in his construction company—at the very bottom rung of the ladder. He told me I needed to prove myself and he never wanted to hear of me wasting my time and my education again. So I worked my way up—determined not to abuse his faith in me. I learnt the building trade from the inside out. I worked every hour that God sent and saved every penny I had, until I could buy my first property. And the rest, as they say, is history.'

Amber understood a lot more about Conall Devlin now—and much of it she admired. But not all. He was hard-working and loyal, but he was also heartless. But at least now she could understand some of his prejudice towards her. *Of course* he would despise someone who represented everything he most deplored. To him she was just another of those spoilt and privileged people who stamped their way through life, not caring who they trod on—just as the Cadogans had done to his mother.

She could see the pain on his face even though he was doing his best to hide it—but hiding pain was something she recognised very well. And despite everything—despite this whole crazy, mixed-up situation—all she wanted was to go up to him and put her arms around him. Sitting there in his wedding suit with his tie pulled loose and his dark hair all ruffled, he looked more approachable than she'd ever seen him and she felt a great wave of emotion welling up inside her. In that moment she hated the Cadogans and what they had done to his mother and she found herself silently applauding the graffiti. The most natural thing in the world would be to go over there and kiss him. To comfort him with her body, which was crying out to be touched by him. But sex was off the menu. He'd told her that.

She glanced at the ornate archway which led through to the bedroom and the vast, petal-strewn bed and wondered how she was going to be able to get through the night—any night—when she was forbidden to touch him. And she wanted to touch him.

She wanted to feel those expert fingers caressing her and to rediscover the pleasures of sex. Should she *accidentally* roll up against him during the night, or pretend she was having a nightmare?

She drank another mouthful of champagne. No. She sensed that she would get nothing from Conall if she was anything other than truthful. He was already furious because she'd kept her virginity a secret—if she started to play games with him now he would have zero respect for her. She could spend the next three months tiptoeing round him while the tension between them grew, or she could do the liberated thing of reaching out for what she most wanted. And what did she have to lose?

'Conall?'

'No more questions, Amber,' he warned impatiently. 'I'm done with talking about it.'

'I wasn't going to ask you any more questions about the past. I was wondering more how we're going to spend this short-lived marriage of ours.' She lifted her shoulders in a shrug, suddenly aware of the softness of her body beneath the heavy material of her wedding dress. And that Conall's dark blue gaze seemed fascinated by the movement. Any movement she made, come to think of it. Should that give her the courage to carry on? 'Because despite what I said earlier, we can't talk all the time, can we? We've already done the past and we both know there isn't going to be any future.'

'You sound like someone asking a question who has already decided what the answer is going to be.'

'Maybe I have.' She hesitated. 'All you have to do is agree with me.'

Their eyes met.

'Agree with *what*, Amber?'

'I'd like…' She licked her lips. 'What I'd really like—is for you to teach me everything you know about sex.'

CHAPTER TEN

FOR A MOMENT Conall thought he must have misheard her because it sounded like one of those fantasies men sometimes had about women. Teach her everything he knew about sex? His mouth hardened. So that she could claw her manicured nails deeper into his flesh and learn more about him than she already did?

'Why, Amber?' he questioned, trying to ignore the sudden flare of heat in his blood.

'Isn't it obvious? Because I know so little and you know so much.' She seemed to be struggling to find the right words, which he guessed wasn't surprising in the circumstances. 'And I…'

'Oh, please, don't stop now,' he said silkily. 'This is just starting to get interesting.'

She wriggled her shoulders again and Conall got a sudden disturbing flashback of how she'd looked when she'd been naked in bed, those green eyes all wide and hungry just before he'd entered her. Another fierce hit of blood made an erection jerk beneath his suit trousers.

'I know this arrangement between us isn't meant to last, but—'

'Let me guess?' he interrupted. 'One day your

knight in shining armour is going to come galloping over the horizon and carry you away, and in the meantime you'd like to learn how best to turn him on?'

A little angrily, she pushed a fallen lock of hair away from her face.

'That wasn't what I was going to say. I told you. I'm not crazy about men but I've realised that I like sex. At least, I don't have very much experience to base it on, but I certainly like the sex I had with you. And it seems a pity not to capitalise on that, don't you think?'

Her cheeks suddenly went pink and, in the silence which followed, Conall could hear the shallow sound of his own breathing.

'You want to treat me like some kind of stud?'

'That's a little defensive, Conall. Couldn't we describe it as making the most of your expertise?'

'And this would be sex without strings?'

'Naturally.'

'With no boundaries?'

'That would depend on the boundaries.'

Conall laughed. This was getting more and more like a fantasy by the minute. Gorgeous, defiant Amber asking him to teach her everything he knew about sex—with no strings?

'So what would you say if I asked you to strip for me right now?'

'I'd say that I have no experience of stripping and would be prepared to give it a try, but...'

He raised his eyebrows as he saw a trace of insecurity cross her features. 'But?'

'I want sex,' she whispered, 'but I don't want you to make me feel like an object.'

And that whispered little appeal somehow pierced

his conscience and made him realise he was behaving like a boor.

'Is that what I was doing?' he said softly.

'Yes.'

He stood up and walked over to her. 'Then I guess I'd better wipe the slate clean and start all over again. Come here and let me see what I can do.'

Amber felt herself melting as he pulled her to her feet and took her face between his hands, before bending to place his lips on hers. She told herself she must be true to her words and not read anything into it, but it wasn't easy. Not when he kept brushing his lips over hers like that, as if he had all the time in the world—teasing her and tormenting her so that she felt like a cat having a cotton reel dangled before its eyes. As he skimmed his palms down over her dress she could feel the instant response of her body.

'Want to take a shower?' he murmured.

'I guess,' she said unsteadily.

He took her by the hand and led her to the giant bathroom which had an enormous wet room attached. Amber was trying to stop herself from trembling because, after having been so upfront about expressing her needs, she could hardly turn round and tell him she was having second thoughts, could she?

Because she was. Suddenly she was scared. She realised that she was going to get exactly what she had asked for—and no more. No matter how good this felt, or how much it mimicked tenderness—she needed to remember that it meant nothing. *So just enjoy it for what it is*, she told herself fiercely. *Don't demand more than he will ever give you.*

The tiled floor felt cool beneath her bare feet and

he was tilting up her chin, so that their eyes were on a collision course, and it gave her a thrill of pleasure to read the raw blaze of hunger in his gaze.

'I don't know the protocol for removing a wedding dress,' he said. 'Are there all kinds of hidden panels?'

'Nope.' She gave the familiar Amber smile as she slid down the zip and stepped out of the gown. The easy, confident smile which had always hidden a multiplicity of insecurities. 'It's all me.'

It was gratifying to see his boggle-eyed look in response to what lay beneath, and maybe on some subliminal level Amber had been hoping for this outcome all along. Last time she'd undressed in front of him she had been wearing her plain bra and those hideous big knickers—which she had now replaced with some of the most provocative lingerie she'd been able to find.

Something blue was what brides traditionally wore and she had chosen a shade of blue for her underwear—the same sapphire hue as his shuttered eyes. Wisps of silk and gossamer-fine lace pushed her breasts together so that they appeared to be spilling out of the bra like ice cream piled high on twin cones. The tiny high-cut panties barely covered her bottom and he gave a small groan of appreciation as he splayed his fingers possessively over the silky triangle at the front.

'Wow. X-rated stuff,' he said softly before peeling them off and unclipping her bra. 'And the kind of lingerie I always imagined you wearing.'

'You did a lot of that, did you?' She tipped her head to one side as he stared at her breasts. 'Thinking about me in my underwear?'

'I refuse to answer that question, on the grounds it might incriminate me. And I think you'd better learn to undress me, Amber. I think my hands are shaking too much to do it with any degree of style.'

Hers were still shaking, too, and she didn't know if he noticed but she didn't care. Because suddenly she was hungry for him. Hungry to feel his hands on her skin again and that slow burst of pleasure as he pushed deep inside her.

She eased the jacket from his shoulders and laid it on a nearby stool. Next came his shirt and she freed each stubborn button until at last she could let it flutter free. She turned her attention to his belt and then slid the zip of his trousers slowly down. She gave an instinctive murmur of delight as he sprang free, hard and proud against the palm of her hand, and, even though this was a totally new experience for her, she told herself not to be shy. *Every woman has to learn some time*, she thought—and suddenly she was grateful to be learning from someone as magnificent as Conall. Experimentally, she trickled a finger down over the stiff shaft but the steely clamp of his fingers around her wrist and the stern look on his face halted her.

'No,' he said. 'To touch a man when he is as aroused as this will make me come all over your fingers and will delay the gratification you are seeking.'

Amber wanted to disagree with him. She wanted to tell him that it would delight her to see him at the mercy of her touch. And she wanted to tell him not to be so anatomical about it all—to protest that surely sex was about more than just physical *gratification*. But she didn't say a word and not just because she didn't have the experience to back up her claim or because his words were so *graphic*. Because he was sliding on a condom and turning on the shower and hot water was gushing freely down into the wet room as he pushed her beneath the jets.

Sweet sensation flooded over her as his arms wrapped around her and he stepped in beside her. She was aware of the hot water gushing over her and the slippery feel of Conall's hair-roughened skin as he drew her closer. His dark head was bent and he closed his lips down over one nipple to suck greedily on the hardened tip. She gasped as his fingers slid between her legs and she couldn't tell whether the warmth which flooded through her came from the shower or from inside her own body. Her head fell back as he thrummed her there insistently, the urgent rhythm building relentlessly inside her.

He had made her come once before when he had been deep inside her—but the sensation of this second orgasm took her by surprise because it happened so quickly. One minute she was revelling in him touching her and the next she was gasping out her pleasure as violent spasms racked through her body. She was still gasping when he wrapped her legs around his hips and eased himself inside her, and she clamped her hands on his shoulders as he levered her back against the tiled wall and drove into her.

He was so big. A slow moan escaped from her lips. So very big. As if he had been made to fit inside her like that. As if her own body had been designed to accommodate him and only him. She could feel the heat building again and she sensed his own sudden restraint, as if he had felt it, too—so that when the spasms exploded deep inside her again, she heard him expel a deep and ragged breath. She felt his own jerking movements and heard him groan and she was completely overcome by the sensation of what was happening to her. She must have been. Why else, when her head flopped helplessly onto his shoulder, should she have the salty taste of tears on her lips?

Her eyes were closed as he turned the shower off and wrapped her in a towel, patting her completely dry before carrying her into the bedroom. He set her down on the floor while, with an impatient hand, he yanked off the bedcover so that all the red rose petals scattered down onto the beautiful Persian rug. Like giant spills of blood, she thought, with a sudden clench of her heart, as he put her into bed and climbed in next to her.

'My hair is going to go crazy if I don't brush it,' she murmured.

'Do you want to brush it?' His lips skated over her neck and his words were muffled as he murmured against her skin. 'Or could you think of something else you'd rather do?'

Her head tipped back to accommodate his lips and her eyes closed. There was really no contest. 'Something else.'

It took longer this time. As if it were happening in slow motion. His fingertips seemed determined to acquaint themselves with every centimetre of skin. His kisses were lazy and his thrusts were deep, and her orgasm seemed to go on and on for ever. Afterwards he held her trembling body very tightly and lay there, just stroking her still-damp hair, while her cheek rested against his chest and she listened to the muffled thunder of his heartbeat.

Her eyes felt heavy and her limbs seemed to be weighed with lead. Just keeping her eyes open felt like the biggest effort in the world but there was something she needed to know, and through fluttering lashes she tipped her head back to look at him.

'Conall?' she said.

'Mmm?'

She hesitated. 'You thought I'd want to know why you'd never married before and seemed surprised when I didn't pursue it.'

'And?'

'I'm pursuing it now.' Her gaze was steady. 'Why not?'

Conall took his hand away from her head, wondering why she had reacted in such a dull and predictable way and so comprehensively ruined the soft mood which had settled over him. Give a woman a little intimacy and she tried to take everything. But maybe this would be the ideal time to drive home his fundamental principles, despite the fact that he'd just enjoyed the most mind-blowing sex. He shook his head in slight disbelief. For someone who was so inexperienced, she was so *hot*. When he touched her he felt a fierce and elemental hunger he had trouble reining in. But Amber needn't know that. He felt the beat of a pulse at his temple. Amber *mustn't* know that.

'I'm surprised that someone with your history should ask that,' he drawled. 'For me, it always seemed like backing a horse with an injured leg.'

'So that's the only reason? Because the odds are stacked against it?'

She was very persistent, he thought. 'You ask too many questions, Amber,' he said softly. 'And a man doesn't like to be interrogated straight after sex.'

She met his gaze and maybe she read something in his eyes which made her realise that his patience was wearing thin.

'Okay. Shall we have some more sex, then?' she questioned guilelessly.

Silently he applauded her lack of inhibition as he thought about some of the things he'd like to do to her. To put his head between her thighs and to taste her, just for starters. He'd like to see what she looked like on all fours, with that magnificent bottom pressed into him as he took her from behind. But he was still feeling *exposed*, from all the things he'd told her, and it was time to regain control. The sex, he decided, could wait.

'Not right now, I'm afraid.'

She sounded disappointed. 'Really?'

He pushed back the sheet and got out of bed, walking over to the wardrobe and rifling through for some of the clothes he'd unpacked before the ceremony. Pulling out a pair of jeans and a sweater, he shot her a regretful glance.

'I have some work I need to do,' he said. 'And you should sleep for a while. It's been a long day. I'll wake you up for dinner later. Would you like to go out somewhere? Or I can have the hotel reserve us a table in one of the restaurants downstairs if you prefer?'

Her body tensing beneath the duvet, Amber stared at him in confusion. Dinner was the last thing on her mind. What she wanted was for him to get in beside her and to cradle her in his arms. She wanted to drift off to sleep with him *beside* her and wake up with his black head on the pillow next to hers, so that she could lean over and kiss him and have him make love to her again. But judging by his body language as he carried his clothes towards the adjoining dressing room—that was the last thing Conall wanted.

'Can't work wait?' she questioned.

'Sorry.' He flicked her a cool look. 'It may have slipped your memory but it's my job which is paying for our stay here.'

It was a statement obviously designed to remind her that she was nothing but one of life's freeloaders, and it didn't miss its mark. Amber flinched as he turned his back on her.

She didn't know how a naked man could walk across a room looking so unbelievably in command, but somehow Conall managed it. The pale jut of his buttocks and the powerful thrust of his thighs were like poetry in motion, she thought, silently willing him to turn around and look at her. Just once.

But he closed the door behind him without a second glance.

CHAPTER ELEVEN

IT WAS LIKE playing a game of cat and mouse. A game which had no rules. But despite Amber's joking remark about boundaries, there were plenty of those.

Don't ask.

Don't expect.

And don't feel. Especially that. Don't feel anything for your enigmatic and gorgeous husband, other than desire, because he certainly won't tolerate any outward show of emotion.

But Amber was fast discovering she wasn't a switch which could be flicked on and off. She couldn't blow hot one minute and cold the next. Unlike Conall.

He had woken her up on that first evening with his hand lazily caressing her breast and, after a blissful hour between the sheets, they had gone downstairs to dine in the Granchester's midnight room. Glowing lights on an indigo ceiling mimicked the night skies and the exotic flowers on every table were all fiery oranges and red. And although the hotel took their guests' privacy seriously, someone in the restaurant managed to capture a photo on their cell phone, which found its way into one of the newspapers. It was funny to look at it. Or not, depending on your viewpoint. Conall was leaning in to listen to something Amber was saying and, for that frozen slice of time, it actually managed to look as if he *cared*. Which was a lie. A falsehood. All he cared about was projecting the right *image*. Of making what they had look real to the outside world. But how could it, when it wasn't real?

After five days of relative confinement and wall-to-wall sex, the newlyweds moved into Conall's Notting Hill house, and Amber found herself living in a brand-new neighbourhood. It was a tall, four-storeyed house, overlooking a central square with a beautiful, gated garden and in any other circumstances, she might have been overjoyed to spend time in such a glorious environment. But she felt displaced, surrounded by Conall's things—with nothing of her own in situ except for her clothes. It was *his* territory and he had neither the need nor the desire to modify it in any way to accommodate her. And what was the point, when she would be moving out again in three months, when their short-lived marriage was over?

'I don't know if you've thought about how you're going to spend your time while I'm at work?' he'd said, eyebrows raised in mild question—after he'd finished showing her how the extremely complicated coffee machine worked.

Amber hadn't really thought about it. The recreational shopping which used to consume her now held no appeal and she seemed to have outgrown the people she'd hung out with before. She guessed the truth was that there was only one person she wanted to spend time with and that was the man she'd married—but that was clearly a one-way street. Because Conall was an expert at compartmentalising his life—a skill which seemed beyond her. Or maybe it was because he simply didn't *have* any feelings for her, beyond those of desire and responsibility.

After wake-up sex, he left the house for work and Amber found herself resenting the fact that Serena got to see him all day, while she had to be content with the few measly hours left by the time he finally made it home. At least the May weather was warm enough for her to sit outside and she bought herself a sketch pad and took a book to read in the garden square beneath one of the lilac bushes which scented the air with its heady fragrance.

She'd been there for a couple of weeks when she received a letter from her father, forwarded by Mary-Ellen, telling her how delighted he was to hear of her marriage to Conall.

He's a man I've always admired. Probably the only man on the planet capable of handling you.

And Amber could have wept, because deep down didn't she agree with her father's words? Didn't she revel in the way her new husband made her feel—like a contented, purring pussycat? Weren't the times she was able to snatch with the powerful Irishman the closest thing to heaven she'd ever known?

But Conall doesn't feel that way, she reminded herself. For him this marriage was nothing but a burden—driven by a longstanding debt to her father and an overdeveloped sense of responsibility.

She found herself thinking about the future, even though she tried not to—about what she would miss when it was all over. The sex, of course—but it was all the other things which were proving so curiously addictive. It was breakfast in bed at the weekends and waking up in the middle of the night to find yourself being kissed. It was walking around London and discovering that it seemed like an entirely different city when you were seeing it through someone else's eyes, even if you were aware that your companion would rather be somewhere else.

She made herself a cup of coffee and walked across the kitchen to stare out of the window at the quiet Notting Hill street. Last night she'd woken up as dawn was breaking and the truth had hit her like an intruder trying to break in through the basement window. The realisation had shocked and scared the life out of her—once she'd finally had the guts to admit it. That she was falling for Conall and wanted to give their relationship a real chance. To work on what they'd got and see if it had the potential to last. She wanted more of him, not less, and wouldn't she spend the rest of her life regretting it if she didn't even *try* to explore its potential?

In a frantic attempt to rewind the tape—and show him she wasn't just some vacuous airhead—she started cooking elaborate meals in the evening. Fragments of a half-finished *cordon bleu* cookery course came back to her, so that she was able to present her bemused husband with a perfect cheese soufflé or the soft meringues floating in custard which the French called *îles flottantes*.

She started reading the international section in the newspaper so she could discuss world affairs with him, over dinner. And if at times she realised she was in danger of becoming a caricature of an old-fashioned housewife, she *didn't care*. She wanted to show him that there was more to flaky Amber than the mixed-up socialite who used to fall out of nightclubs.

But if she was hoping for some dramatic kind of conversion, she hoped in vain. Her cool but sexy husband remained as emotionally distant as he had ever been. And even though she adored the powerful sexual chemistry which fizzed between them, she found herself thinking it would make a nice change to have dinner together without at least one course growing cold, while Conall carried her off to the bedroom.

She wasn't sure if she had communicated some of her restlessness, but one morning Conall paused by the doorway as he was leaving for work.

'You've been cooking a lot lately,' he said. 'I think you're due a break, don't you?'

'Is that a polite way of telling me you're fed up with my food?'

He raised his eyebrows. 'Or a roundabout way of wondering if you'd like to go out for dinner tonight?'

'Even though it's a weeknight?' She tried to clamp down the stupid Cinderella feeling which was bubbling up inside her. 'I'd love to.'

'Good.' He glanced out of the window as his driver pulled up. 'Book somewhere for eight and call the office to let them know where. I'll meet you there.'

Amber booked the table and dressed carefully for dinner, aware that she felt as bubbly and as excited as if this were a bona fide first date. She'd read a lot in the newspapers about the Clos Maggiore restaurant, known as 'London's Most Romantic'. The irony of its reputation wasn't lost on her but she'd also read that the food was superb. And she wasn't asking for *romance*—she knew he didn't do *that*. She was just asking for more of the same.

She picked out a discreetly sexy dress—a silk jersey wrap in scarlet—and she was bubbling over with excitement as she hailed a cab and directed it to Covent Garden.

But her happy and expectant mood quickly began to dissolve because he didn't turn up at eight. Nor at eight-twenty. With tight lips, Amber shook her head as the waiter offered her another glass of champagne. She'd already had one on an empty stomach and now her head was swimming. She felt a bit ridiculous sitting alone when all the other tables were occupied by people talking and laughing with each other. The rustic mirrored room was supposed to resemble a garden and somehow it managed to do just that. Just a few steps away from the world-famous market and you could find yourself sitting beneath a ceiling from which hung sprigs of thick white blossom, which looked so realistic that you almost felt you could reach up and pick one. It looked almost magical, but the feeling of dread which had started to build up inside her made Amber feel anything but magical.

Did she really think that one dinner out meant that everything was suddenly going to be perfect? As if he were suddenly going to stop keeping her locked away in her own tiny little box, which was so separate from the major part of his life. That was, if he could even be bothered to show.

Surreptitiously, she glanced at her watch, not wanting anyone to think she'd been stood up—but what if she *had*?

And then, exactly thirty-five minutes after the appointed time, there was a faint commotion at the door and Conall appeared in the flowered archway. The other diners turned to look at him as he walked over to the table and sat down, ignoring the glass of champagne which the waiter placed before him.

'You're late,' she said.

'I know I am and I'm sorry.'

'What happened?' she demanded. 'Did *Serena* keep you busy?'

He frowned. 'I'm not sure what you're trying to imply, Amber—but I'm not going to rise to it. I was on a call to Prince Luciano and I could hardly cut the negotiations short to tell him I was due at dinner.'

'But it didn't occur to you that *I* might like to be involved, seeing that I was there when you first showed him the painting?'

Conall stared at her. He could see she was angry and he knew it was partly justified, but what the hell did she expect? He hadn't planned to be late, but then—he hadn't planned for the Mardovian royal to ring him to talk about the painting. And no, he hadn't thought to involve Amber in the deal because *this was not her life and it never would be.* Soon she would be gone and their marriage nothing but a memory. Didn't she realise that the boundaries he'd imposed were in place to protect them both? *That* was why he kept an emotional distance from her, why he had never repeated those earlier confidences he had shared with her, when he'd opened up to her more than he'd ever opened up to anyone and had been left feeling raw and vulnerable. What was the point of getting close to someone when the end was already in sight? When he never got close to anyone.

Yet it was harder than he'd imagined to keep his distance from the woman he'd married, or to keep thoughts of her at bay during his working day. Hard not to remember how it felt when she was in his arms at night. The growing sense that he was in danger of losing control. His mouth twisted. Because he would never lose control. Never again.

'No, of course it didn't occur to you,' she continued, her voice shaking. 'Because I'm of no consequence to you, am I? None at all!'

Conall leaned back in his chair, his narrowed eyes wary. This marriage of theirs wasn't real, so why the hell was she making out as if it were? 'You sound a little hysterical, Amber.'

Amber went very still, feeling like a small child who had been reprimanded by a very severe teacher. And suddenly all her words were coming out in a haphazard rush. Words she'd thought often enough but never planned to say, in her determination to be the cool and casual Amber she knew she was supposed to be. 'I'm fed up with being allocated a few hours in the morning before you go to work and then just sandwiched in at night, when you can be bothered to tear yourself away from the office and your beloved Serena. Weekends are better—but you still manage to spend a great deal of time working.'

'Will you please lower your voice?' he demanded.

'No. I will not lower my voice.' She sucked in a breath, aware that two worried-looking waiters were now hovering at the edge of the room and some of the lovey-dovey couples had gone completely quiet and were staring at them with mounting looks of horror on their faces as if registering that a full-blown row was escalating. *This is what it's like for me*, thought Amber miserably, trying not to envy all those couples their closeness and unity, but failing to do so. *This is what it's like for me. This is the reality of my marriage.*

And suddenly she realised how stupid she'd been. What was it they said? That you couldn't make a silk purse out of a sow's ear. Just as you couldn't make a real marriage out of something which had only ever been a coldly executed contract. Why even try?

Had she really thought she could endure three months of this? Of trying to *just* enjoy sex when all the time her heart was becoming more and more involved with this stubborn man and would continue to do so with every second which passed? She was a woman, for heaven's sake—not a machine! She might try but she couldn't keep her emotions locked away, even if her husband had managed to do so with such flair. *Because he doesn't have any emotions!*

She leapt to her feet and some of Conall's champagne slopped over the side of the glass as the cutlery on the table clattered. She saw the dark look of warning in his eyes but she ignored it with a sudden carelessness which felt almost *heady*.

'I'm sick of being married to a man who treats me as if I'm part of the furniture!' she flared. 'Who always puts his damned work first. Who doesn't ever want to talk about stuff. *Real* stuff. The stuff which matters. So maybe I ought to admit what's been staring me in the face right from the start. It's over, Conall. Got that? *Over for good!*'

She tried to tug the gold band from her finger but, stubbornly, it refused to budge. Picking up her handbag, she rushed straight out of the restaurant, aware of Conall saying something to the waiters as he followed, hot on her heels. She'd planned to hail a cab but she didn't have time because Conall had reached her with a few long strides and was propelling her towards his waiting car—holding her by the elbow, the way she'd sometimes seen police do in films when they were arresting someone.

'Get in the car,' he said grimly and as soon as the door was closed behind him he turned on her, his face a mask of dark fury. 'And start explaining if you would—what the *hell* was that all about?'

'What's the point in repeating it? It's the truth. You don't make enough time for me.'

'Of course I don't. Because this isn't real, Amber.' The bewilderment in his tight voice sounded genuine. 'Remember?'

'Well, if it isn't real, then we need to show the watching world that there's discord between us. We can't just break up after our supposedly *romantic* whirlwind marriage without some kind of warning. We need to show that cracks have already begun to appear in our relationship and tonight should have helped.'

There were a few seconds of disbelieving silence.

'You mean,' he said, clearly holding onto his temper only by a shred. 'You mean that the undignified little scene you created back there was all just part of some charade? That you disturbed those people's dinner in order to manufacture a spat between us?'

Wasn't it better to let him think that, rather than reveal the humiliating truth that she'd wanted to search for something deeper? That her stupid aching heart was craving the love he could never give her.

'But it's true, isn't it?' she questioned, biting her lip to stop tears spilling from her eyes. 'There are cracks. It's been cracked right from the get-go. All that stuff you said about me realising some of my talents was completely meaningless. You could have done the courtesy of having me sit in on the conference call with Prince Luciano about the Wheeler painting, but you didn't. You didn't even bother to mention the negotiations. To you I'm nothing but an invisible socialite who happens very inconveniently to turn you on.'

'Well, at least you're right about something, Amber, because you certainly turn me on,' he said grimly. 'And yes, I often find myself wishing that you didn't.'

Something dark and heavy had entered the atmosphere—like the claustrophobic feeling you got just before a thunderstorm. But he didn't say another word until the front door had slammed behind them and Amber thought he might slam his way into his study or take a drink out into the garden, or even shut himself in the spare room, but she was wrong. His gaze raked over her and she saw a flicker of something dark and unknown in the depths of his sapphire eyes.

He moved like a predator, striking without warning—reaching out for her dress and hooking both hands into the bodice. He ripped it open, the delicate material tearing as easily as if it had been made of cotton wool. Amber shivered because cold air was suddenly washing over her skin and because the expression in his eyes was making her feel...*excited* and he nodded as he looked into her face, as if he had seen in it something he recognised, something he didn't like.

'And your desire for me is just as inconvenient, isn't it, Amber?' he taunted. 'You wish you didn't want me, but you just can't help it. You want me now. You're aching for me. Wet for me.'

Her lips were parched as they made a little sound, though she didn't know what she was trying to say. She could scarcely breathe, let alone think. Excitement fizzed over her skin even though she told herself she should have been appalled when her panties suffered the same fate as her dress and fluttered redundantly to the hall floor. Appalled when he started to unfasten his trousers, struggling to ease the zip down over his straining hardness.

But she wasn't appalled.

She was relieved—for surely that was a moan of relief she gave as he eased his moist tip up against her and then thrust deep inside her. She gasped. Was it anger which made this feel so raw and so incredible as she ripped open his shirt to bare his magnificent torso? Or simply the frustration that this was the only way she could express her growing feelings for him? She could bury her teeth into the hair-roughened skin of his chest and nip at him like a small animal. And although he was giving a soft laugh of pleasure in response, she knew he wouldn't be laughing when it was over.

He didn't even kiss her and she knew better than to reach her mouth blindly towards his in silent plea. And anyway, there wasn't really time for kissing. There wasn't time for anything but a few hard and frantic thrusts. It was so wild and explosive that she gave a broken cry as her orgasm took her right under and his own cry sounded like some kind of feral moan—as if something dark had been dragged up from the depths of his soul. It was only when he withdrew from her, seconds later—quickly turning his back so she couldn't see his face—that she realised he had forgotten to use a condom.

He was breathing very heavily and it was several seconds before he had composed himself enough to turn around and stare at her and his eyes looked dark and tortured. He was shaking his head from side to side.

'That should never have happened.' His bitter words sounded as if they had been dipped in acid.

'It doesn't matter.'

'Oh, but it does, Amber. It really does.' His lips twisted. 'I can't believe I just did that. That *we* just did that. It was…it was *out of control*. I don't want to live my life like that, and I won't. This marriage was a mistake and I don't know why I fooled myself into thinking it could be anything else.'

Amber stared into his eyes and saw the contempt written there, along with a whole lot of other things she would rather not have seen. Once before he had looked at her as if she were something which had been dragged in from the dark, and it was the same kind of look he was giving her now. But back then he hadn't known her and now he did. It was rejection in its purest form and it hurt more than anything had ever hurt.

Biting back the sob which was spiralling up inside

her throat, she bent down to grab her tattered panties, before rushing upstairs towards the bedroom and slamming the door behind her.

CHAPTER TWELVE

THE END OF the marriage was played out in the papers, just as the beginning had been, and Amber found herself reading the headlines with a sense of being outside herself. As if she were some random little dot high up on the wall, looking down at the mess she'd made of her life.

And it was a mess, all right. She stared down at the photo taken of them at the Granchester on their wedding night—that false and misrepresentative photo snatched by a fellow diner—while she read the accompanying text.

Whirlwind marriage over. Golden couple split.

But it turned out to be surprisingly easy to dismantle their short-lived union. Or maybe not so surprising. Because a marriage undertaken to settle a long-term debt could never be anything other than doomed, no matter how strong the sexual chemistry between them was.

During their last conversation together, Conall had told Amber he intended being 'generous' in his settlement—but she had shaken her head.

'I don't want your charity,' she'd said, trying desperately to hold on to her equilibrium when all she'd wanted was for him to put his arms around her, and to love her.

'An admirable attitude, if a little misguided,' he'd responded coolly. 'And a waste of everyone's time if you don't accept your side of the deal.'

A waste of everyone's time? She had glared at him then, because glaring helped keep the ever-threatening tears at bay.

'I'm offering you the apartment and a monthly maintenance payment,' he'd said. 'You won't have to move.'

She told herself it was pointless to deliberately make herself homeless and so, even though she rejected his offer of monthly maintenance, she accepted the deeds of the apartment and immediately put it up for sale. She couldn't bear the thought of living in a block owned by Conall and the nightmare prospect of running into him. She would buy somewhere smaller, in a less dazzling and expensive area, and use the profit she made to support herself. She would start living within her means and take no maintenance from him. And she intended to get a job.

She sold her diamond watch—slightly taken aback by how much it was worth—and with the money raised she booked onto a short degree course in translation and interpretation at the University of Bath. It was a beautiful city and far enough away from London to know that there would be no risk of running into Conall. By a fortuitous chance there was a course starting almost immediately and Amber leapt at it eagerly. It gave her something to do. Something to replace the miserable thoughts which were whirling round in her head. She didn't want to do some boring job involving grain quotas, but surely there would be other opportunities open to her? Some which might even involve travel. But first she needed a bona fide qualification and so she moved into a rented room in a house on the outskirts of the city and began to work harder than she'd ever worked in her life.

She'd never shared a flat or lived on a reduced budget before and she soon became used to running out of milk, or eating cornflakes for lunch. She discovered that a cheap meal of pasta could taste fantastic when you shared it with three other people and a bottle of cheap wine. And if at night she found sleep eluding her and tears edging out from between her tightly closed eyes, she would hug her arms around her chest and tell herself that soon Conall Devlin would be nothing but a distant memory.

Would he?

Would she ever forget that rare smile which sometimes dazzled her? That lazy way he had of stroking her hair just after they'd made love?

Had sex, she corrected herself as she tossed and turned in the narrow bed. He'd only married her because of the debt he'd felt he owed her father. Other than that, it had really only ever been about the sex. It must have been—because when she'd told him not to bother contacting her again just before she'd left London, Conall had taken her at her word. To Amber's initial fury and then through the dull pain of acceptance, she realised he was doing exactly as she had asked him to do. He hadn't called. Not once. Not a single text or a solitary email had popped into her inbox to check how she was doing in her new life. All negotiations had been dealt with through his lawyers. And she was just going to have to learn to live with that.

June bled into July and a monumental heatwave brought the country almost to a standstill. Sales of ice cream and electric fans soared. Riverbeds dried and the grass turned a dark sepia colour. There was even talk of water rationing. One evening Amber was sitting in the dusty garden after college, when she heard the doorbell ringing loudly through the silent house. It was so hot she didn't want to move and as a rivulet of sweat trickled down her back she hoped someone else would answer it.

She could hear the distant sound of voices. A deep voice which she didn't really register because she was holding her face up, trying to find the whisper of breeze she thought she had detected on the air. And then she heard footsteps behind her and a deep voice that sent shivers racing down her spine—shivers which should have been welcome in the extreme heat, if they hadn't been underpinned by emotions far too complex to analyse.

She lifted her head slowly, telling herself not to react—but how could she possibly *not* react when she'd spent weeks thinking of him and dreaming of him? Hadn't it been an integral part of some of her wildest fantasies that he should suddenly appear in this house, like this? Greedily, her gaze ran over him. His eyes were as shuttered as they had ever been and his jaw was still shadowed blue-black. His concession to the warmer weather meant he was wearing a T-shirt with his jeans, which immediately made her start wishing it were the dead of winter, because then she wouldn't have to stare at that hard, broad torso. She wouldn't have to remember when those rippling biceps had wrapped themselves so tightly around her before carrying her off to bed.

'Conall!' Her throat felt dry and constricted. Her head felt light. 'What are you doing here?'

'No ideas?'

She shook her head. 'No.'

'Even though there's a question we both know needs answering?'

She licked her lips. 'What question is that?' she said hoarsely.

There was a pause. 'Are you carrying my baby?'

The pause which followed was even longer. 'No.'

Conall was taken aback by the shaft of regret which speared through his body and embedded itself deep in his heart. He was briefly aware of the fact that somewhere inside him a dim light had been snuffed out. He wondered how it was possible to want something more than you'd ever wanted anything, and only discover that once the possibility was gone.

He stared into Amber's pale face. At the tremble of her lips. He thought how different she looked from the woman he'd found fast asleep on that white leather sofa. Calmer. With an air of serenity about her which gave him a brief punch of pleasure. But he could see anger flickering in her grass-green eyes as she drew her shoulders back and brushed a lock of ebony hair away from her face with an impatient hand.

'Okay, you've had the answer you presumably wanted, so now you can go.'

'I'm not going anywhere.'

She narrowed her eyes. 'What I don't understand, Conall, is why you've come all this way in order to ask a question which didn't need to have been asked in person. You could have texted or emailed me. Even phoned. But you didn't.'

'It isn't about the question.'

'No? Then what is it about?'

Conall met her gaze and let her fury wash over him like a fierce tide. He had tried to stay away from her—telling himself that it was for her own good, as well as his. But something just kept drawing him back to her—and now that he was here, he felt curiously exposed. He knew she deserved nothing less than the truth, but that still didn't guarantee him the outcome he longed for. It was fork-in-the-road time, he realised. It was time to stop hiding behind the past. To reject the emotional rules he'd lived by for so long. 'I don't know if you can ever forgive me for the way I behaved on our last evening together,' he said, in a low voice.

She frowned. 'You mean...what happened in the hall?'

'Yes,' he said roughly. 'That's exactly what I mean.'

She shrugged with the expression of someone who planned to say exactly what was on their mind—and to hell with the consequences. 'We had some pretty raw and basic sex, which I thought you'd enjoyed—I certainly did, even if you completely ruined my dress and some perfectly good underwear.'

His mouth gave a flicker of a smile. 'You're missing the point, Amber.'

'Am I?' Her voice went very quiet. So quiet it was almost a whisper. 'Yet you were the one who taught me that no sex was bad sex, unless one person happened to object to it.'

'Yes, I know I did. But I lost control.' He felt a lump in his throat. 'For a moment I saw red. I felt consumed by something which seemed to consume *me*. It was as if I was powerless to stop what was happening and I didn't like that.'

'So what? Everyone loses control some time in their lives—especially after a blistering row. What's the matter, Conall—did you think you were going to run off to find a handy canister of paint and start spraying graffiti all over the walls?' She gave an impatient shake of her head. 'I don't have a degree in psychology, but I've seen enough therapists in my teenage years to realise that what you call *staying in control* means never letting any emotion out—so that when you do, it just explodes. So why not do what everyone else does and just let yourself *feel* stuff?'

Her words made sense and deep down he knew it, but did he have the courage to admit that? The courage to reach inside himself for something he'd buried for as long as he could remember? Because yes, that something was emotion. His mother had been uptight, he recognised that now—she'd allowed herself to be defined by a youthful indiscretion, so keen never to repeat it that she had locked away all her feelings and desires. And hadn't he done the same?

There had been other factors, he recognised that, too. He'd grown up in a house where he'd never fitted in. A house where his intellect and natural athleticism had made him physically and mentally superior to the men who ruled the Cadogan household—but their wealth and power had allowed them to patronise him. Amber had accused him of having a chip on his shoulder right at the beginning of their relationship—and she had been right.

But he'd learnt his lesson. Or tried to. He had come here today with only one thing on his mind, and that thing was her.

He looked at her. 'What if I told you that I agree with every word you say?'

She narrowed her eyes suspiciously. 'And what's the catch?'

'No catch. If you can accept that I've been a fool. That I've been arrogant and stubborn and short-sighted in nearly letting the most wonderful thing which has ever happened to me slip through my fingers. And that is you. You I want. And you I miss.' His voice deepened, but there was a break in it. 'Because I love you, Amber, and I want you back.'

She shook her head, struggling a little as she got out of the deckchair. 'But you don't *do* love,' she said. 'Remember?'

'I didn't do a lot of things. If you want the truth, I didn't really live properly until I met you.' He gave a short laugh. 'Oh, don't get me wrong—to the outside world I had everything. I made more money than I knew what to do with. I ate in fine restaurants and owned amazing houses, with great works of art adorning my walls. I could travel to any place in the world and stay in the best hotels, and date pretty much any woman I wanted.' He stopped speaking and for a few seconds he seemed to be struggling to find the right words.

'But I don't want any other woman but you because everyone pales in comparison to you, Amber,' he said, and his voice was raw. 'I thought you represented everything I didn't want—but it turns out you're everything I do. You're sharp. Irreverent. Adaptable. You make me laugh and, yes, you frustrate the hell out of me, too. But you always challenge me—and I'm the kind of man who needs a challenge. And so...'

'So?' she echoed a little breathlessly as he walked across the scorched brown grass and took her in his arms.

'We did a lot of stuff in public—*for* the public. But this is private. This is just for us. I have something I want to give you, but only if you can tell me something—and I want complete honesty from you.' He swallowed. 'And that is whether you love me back.'

Amber savoured the moment and made him wait for a few seconds—she felt almost as if it was her *duty* to do so. Because Conall had made her feel very insecure in his time and he needed to know that they shouldn't put each other through this kind of thing, ever again. But she couldn't hide the smile which had begun to bloom on her face. It spread and spread, filling her with a delight and a sunny kind of joy.

'Yes, I love you,' she said simply. 'I love you more than I can ever say, my tough and masterful Irishman.'

'Then I guess I'd better do this properly.' He glanced around, but, although the garden was deserted except for a dejected-looking starling pecking at the bare ground, they were still visible to the bedroom windows of the adjoining houses.

'Is there anywhere more private we could go?'

Breathlessly she nodded and laced her fingers in his, leading him up the rickety old stairs until they reached the tiny box room which was her bedroom. She watched his face as he looked around, seeing disbelief become admiration and then avid curiosity. He walked across the bare floorboards to the painting she was halfway through, and stared very hard at the vibrant splashes of yellow and green, edged with black.

Turning round, he looked at her. 'You've been painting,' he said.

'Yes.' Her voice was a little unsteady. 'And I have you to thank for that. I realised that you were right. That you didn't say things you didn't mean—and your praise has somehow managed to resurrect my crushed self-belief.' She smiled. 'I may never be able to sell any of these—I may not even want to. But you made me believe in myself, Conall—and that's worth more to me than anything.'

'I'm hoping this might be worth something to you, too—in purely romantic terms, rather than monetary ones,' he said gruffly as he produced a small box from the back pocket of his jeans.

And to Amber's shock he went down onto one knee as he held up a ring with an emerald at its centre—big as a green ice cube—surrounded by lots of diamonds. 'Will you marry me again, Amber? Only in a church this time. Properly. Surrounded by family and friends?'

Amber felt like a princess as she stared at the glittering ring, even though Conall had once reprimanded her for behaving like one. But this was different and she suddenly realised why. She was *his* princess and she always would be. He'd changed her in many ways, but she'd helped change him, too. He'd tamed her—a bit—and somehow she'd managed to tame him right back.

She drew in a deep breath. 'Yes, Conall, I'll marry you again today, tomorrow, next year or next week. I'll marry you any way you want, because you have given me back something I didn't realise I'd lost—and that something was myself,' she said, and now she didn't bother to hide the tears which were welling up in her eyes, because how could she berate him for not showing emotion and then do exactly the same herself? Even so, it was a couple of minutes until she had stopped crying enough to be able to speak. 'You made me realise that there was something inside the empty shell of a person I'd become,' she whispered. 'And I thank you for that from the bottom of my heart. It's one of the many reasons why I love you with every cell of my body, my darling. And why I always will.'

EPILOGUE

Outside, the night was dark and the snow tumbled down like swirling pieces of cotton wool. Conall looked at the layer of white on the ground which was steadily growing thicker. In a few short hours it had transformed the Notting Hill garden into a winter wonderland.

'I really think...' he turned away from the window and walked over to where his wife was just finishing brushing her hair '...that we ought to think about leaving.'

Amber put the brush down and looked at him, a lazy smile on her face. 'In a minute. There's plenty of time—even with the snow. The table isn't booked until eight. Kiss me first.'

'You, Mrs Devlin, are a terror for wanting kisses.'

Her eyes danced in response. 'And you're not, I suppose?'

'I confess to being rather partial to them,' he admitted, pushing her hair away from her face and bending his head towards her, kissing her in a way which never failed to satisfy and frustrate him in equal measure. He never kissed her without wanting her and he couldn't ever imagine not wanting her.

They couldn't get enough of each other in every way that mattered, and he thanked God for the day he'd walked into her life and seen her lying fast asleep amid the debris of a long-forgotten party.

His vow to marry her *properly* had remained true and deeply important to him and their wedding had taken place in a beautiful church not far from their country house. He remembered slowly turning his head to look at Amber as she walked down the aisle, his heart clenching with love and pride. She'd looked like a dream in her simple white dress, fresh flowers holding in place a long veil which floated to the ground behind her. As Conall had remarked to her quietly at the reception afterwards, if there was any woman on the planet who was qualified to wear virginal white, it was her. And when challenged on the subject by his feisty wife, he agreed that it gave him a feeling of utter contentment to know he was the only man she had ever been intimate with. And although she might have teased him about his old-fashioned attitude, deep down he knew she felt the same.

Ambrose had returned from his ashram in time for the ceremony, bronzed a deep colour, with clear eyes and looking noticeably thinner. He'd announced that he'd fallen in love with his yoga teacher and she was planning on joining him in England, just as soon as she got her visa sorted. Amber had briefly raised her eyebrows, but told Conall afterwards that she had learnt you had to live and let live, and that nobody was ever really in a position to judge anyone else. And Conall had opened up her mind to the realisation that her father wasn't all bad—he just had flaws and weaknesses like everyone else. They all did.

And families could be complicated. She knew that, but she also knew it felt better when they were together, rather than apart. She'd encouraged Conall to trace some of his mother's relatives, discovering that the world had moved on and nobody was remotely bothered by the fact that a grown man had been born not knowing who his father was. Several of his aunts were still alive and he had lots of cousins who were eager to meet him, which was one of the reasons why they'd chosen Ireland as their honeymoon destination.

Her half-brother Rafe even made it back from Australia in time for the wedding—causing something of a stir among the women present. Almost as much as the guest of honour—Prince Luc—who could be overheard telling Serena that he had played matchmaker to the happy couple.

The Prince had bought the Wheeler portrait and it now hung next to its sister painting in his Mediterranean palace and next month Conall and Amber were visiting the island of Mardovia, to see them together—at the Prince's invitation. Amber was very excited about the prospect of speaking Italian in front of her husband, very aware that it turned him on to listen to her saying stuff he simply didn't understand! Just as she was excited by the part-time art course she'd started to attend in London, where her tutor encouraged her distinctive style of painting just as much as her husband did.

But tonight they were going to Clos Maggiore—their favourite restaurant—where they'd had the furious row which had been such a flashpoint in their relationship, but where tonight they would sit happily beneath the boughs of white blossom, as contented as any of the other couples who ate there. And Amber would refuse her customary glass of pink champagne and tell Conall what she suspected he would be delighted to hear, even though it had come as something of a shock to her when she'd found out. She thought they'd been so careful...

She looked up into his shuttered eyes. Would he be a good father? A lump rose up in her throat. The very best. Just as he was the very best husband, lover and friend a woman could ever want.

'I love you, Conall Devlin,' she whispered.

His eyes crinkled into a smile—a faint question in their midnight depths. 'I love you, too, Amber Devlin.'

And suddenly she didn't want to wait until they were in the restaurant, gorgeous though it was. This was private, just for them, just like the time when he'd knelt on the bare floorboards of her tiny room in Bath and produced an emerald ring as big as a green ice cube. Feeling stupidly emotional, she tightened her arms around his neck and brushed her lips over his as the excitement grew and grew inside her. 'And this might be a good time to tell you my news...'

* * * * *

THE ARGENTINIAN'S
BABY OF SCANDAL

This story is for Megan Crane, with whom I shared an unforgettable trip to the west of Ireland...and for Abby Green – the diva of Dublin!

CHAPTER ONE

Lucas Conway surveyed the blonde who was standing in front of him and felt nothing, even though her eyes were red-rimmed and her cheeks wet with tears.

He felt a pulse beat at his temple.

Nothing at all.

'Who let you in?' he questioned coldly.

'Y-your housekeeper,' she said, her mouth working frantically as she tried to contain yet another sob. 'The one with the messy hair.'

'She had no right to let anyone in,' Lucas returned, briefly wondering how the actress could be so spiteful about someone who'd supposedly done her a good turn. But that was women for you—they never lived up to the promise of how they appeared on the outside. They were all teeth and smiles and then, when you looked beneath the surface, they were as shallow as a spill of water. 'I told her I didn't want to be disturbed.' His voice was cool. 'Not by anyone. I'm sorry, Charlotte, but you'll have to leave. You should never have come here.'

He rose to his feet, because now he felt something, and it felt like the fury which had been simmering inside him for days. Although maybe fury was the wrong word to use. It didn't accurately describe the hot clench to his heart when he'd received the letter last week, did it? Nor the unaccustomed feeling of dread which had washed over him as he'd stared down at it. Memories of the past had swum into his mind. He remembered violence and discord. Things he didn't want to remember. Things he'd schooled himself to forget. But sometimes you were powerless when the past came looking for you...

His mouth was tight as he moved out from behind his desk, easily dwarfing the fair-haired beauty who was staring up at him with beseeching eyes. 'Come with me. I'll see you out.'

'Lucas—'

'Please, Charlotte,' he said, trying to inject his voice with the requisite amount of compassion he suspected was called for but failing—for he had no idea how to replicate this kind of emotion. Hadn't he often been accused of being unable to show *any* kind of feeling for another person—unless you counted desire, which was only ever temporary? He held back his sigh. 'Don't make this any more difficult than it already is.'

Briefly, she closed her swollen eyelids and nodded and he could smell her expensive perfume as he ushered her out of his huge office, which overlooked the choppy waters of Dublin Bay. And when she'd followed him— sniffling—to the front door, she tried one last time.

'Lucas.' Her voice trembled. 'I have to tell you this because it's important and you need to know it. I know there isn't anyone else on the scene and I've missed you. Missed being with you. What we had was good and I... I love you—'

'No,' he answered fiercely, cutting her short before she could humiliate herself any further. 'You don't. You can't. You don't really know me and if you did, you certainly wouldn't love me. I'm sorry. I'm not the man for you. So do yourself a favour, Charlotte, and go and find someone who is. Someone who has the capacity to care for you in the way you deserve to be cared for.'

She opened her mouth as if to make one last appeal but maybe she read the futility of such a gesture in his eyes, because she nodded and began to stumble towards her sports car in her spindly and impractical heels. He stood at the door and watched her leave, a gesture which might have been interpreted as one of courtesy but in reality it was to ensure that she really did exit the premises in her zippy little silver car, which shattered the peace as it sped off in a cloud of gravel.

He glanced up at the heavy sky. The weather had been oppressive for days now and the dark and straining clouds were hinting at the storm to come. He wished it would. Maybe it would lighten the oppressive atmosphere, which was making his forehead slick with sweat and his clothes feel as if they were clinging to his body. He closed the door. And then he turned his attention to his growing vexation as he thought about his interfering housekeeper.

His temper mounting, Lucas went downstairs into the basement, to the kitchen—which several high-profile magazines were itching to feature in their lifestyle section—to find Tara Fitzpatrick whipping something furiously in a copper bowl. She looked up as he walked in and a lock of thick red hair fell into her eye, which she instantly blew away with a big upward gust of breath, without pausing in her whipping motion. Why the hell didn't she get it cut so that it didn't resemble a birds' nest? he wondered testily. And why did she insist on wearing that horrible housecoat while she worked? A baggy garment made from some cheap, man-made fibre, which he'd once told her looked like a relic from the nineteen fifties and completely swamped her slender frame.

'She's gone, then?' she questioned, her gaze fixed on his as he walked in.

'Yes, she's gone.' He could feel the flicker of irritation growing inside him again and, suddenly, Tara seemed the ideal candidate to take it out on. 'Why the hell did you let her in?'

She hesitated, the movement of her whisk stilling. 'Because she was crying.'

'Of course she was crying. She's a spoiled woman who is used to getting her own way and that's what women like her do when it doesn't happen.'

She opened her mouth as if she was about to say something and then appeared to change her mind, so that her next comment came out as a mild observation. 'You were the one who dated her, Lucas.'

'And it was over,' he said dangerously. 'Months ago.'

Again, that hesitation—as if she was trying her hardest to be diplomatic—and Lucas thought, not for the first time, what a fey creature she was with her amber eyes and pale skin and that mass of fiery hair. And her slender body, which always looked as if it could do with a decent meal.

'Perhaps you didn't make it plain enough that it was over,' she suggested cautiously, resting her whisk on the side of the bowl and shaking her wrist, as if it was aching.

'I couldn't have been more plain,' he said. 'I told her in person, in as kind a way as possible, and said that perhaps one day we could be friends.'

Tara made a clicking noise with her lips and shook her head. 'That was your big mistake.'

'My big mistake?' he echoed dangerously.

'Sure. Give a woman hope and she'll cling to it like a chimp swinging from tree to tree. Maybe if you weren't so devastatingly attractive,' she added cheerfully, resuming her beating with a ferocity which sent the egg whites slapping against the sides of the bowl, 'then your exes wouldn't keep popping up around the place like lost puppy dogs.'

He heard the implicit criticism in his housekeeper's voice and the tension which had been mounting inside him all week now snapped. 'And maybe if you knew your place, instead of acting like the mistress of my damned house, then you wouldn't have let her in in the first place,' he flared as he stormed across the kitchen to make himself a cup of coffee.

Know her place?

Tara stopped beating as her boss's icy note of censure was replaced by the sound of grinding coffee beans and a lump rose in her throat, because he'd never spoken to her that way before—not in all the time she'd worked for him. Not with that air of impatient condemnation as if she were some troublesome minion who was more trouble than she was worth. As she returned his gaze she swallowed with confusion and, yes, with hurt—and how stupid was that? Had she thought she was safe from his legendary coldness and a tongue which could slice out sharp words like a knife cutting through a courgette? Well, yes. She had. She'd naively imagined that, because she served him meals and ironed his shirts and made sure that his garden was carefully weeded and bright with flowers, he would never treat her with the disdain he seemed to direct at most women. That she had a special kind of place in his heart—when it was clear that Lucas Conway had no heart at all. And wasn't the fact of the matter that he'd been in a foul mood for this past week and growing snappier by the day? Ever since that official-looking letter had arrived from the United States and he'd disappeared into his office for a long time, before emerging with a haunted look darkening the spectacular verdant gleam of his eyes?

She ran a wooden spoon around the side of the bowl and then gave the mixture another half-hearted beat. She told herself she shouldn't let his arrogance or bad mood bother her. Maybe that was how you should expect a man to behave when he was as rich as Lucas Conway—as well as being the hottest lover in all of Ireland, if you were to believe the things people whispered about him.

Yet nobody really knew very much about the Dublin-based billionaire, no matter how hard they tried to find out. Even the Internet provided little joy—and Tara knew this for a fact because she'd looked him up herself on her ancient laptop, soon after she'd started working for him. His accent was difficult to figure out, that was for sure. He definitely wasn't Irish, and there was a faint hint of transatlantic drawl underpinning his sexy voice. He spoke many languages—French, Italian and Spanish as well as English—though, unlike Tara, he knew no Gaelic. He was rumoured to have been a bellhop, working in some fancy Swiss hotel, in the days before he'd arrived in Ireland to make his fortune but Tara had never quite been able to believe this particular rumour. As if someone like Lucas Conway would ever work as a bellhop! He was also reputed to have South American parentage—and with his tousled dark hair and the unusual green eyes which contrasted so vividly with his glowing olive skin, that was one rumour which would seem to be founded in truth.

She studied him as the machine dispensed a cup of his favoured industrial-strength brew of coffee. He'd had more girlfriends than most men had socks lined up in a top drawer of their bedroom, and was known for his exceptionally low boredom threshold. Which might explain why he'd dumped the seemingly perfect Charlotte when she—like so many others before her—had refused to get the message that he had no desire to be married. Yet that hadn't stopped her sending him a Valentine's card, had it—or arranging for a case of vintage champagne to be delivered on his birthday? 'I don't even particularly *like* champagne,' had been his moody aside to Tara as he'd peered into the wooden case, and she remembered thinking how ungrateful he could be.

Yet it wasn't just women of the sexy and supermodel variety who couldn't seem to get enough of him. Men liked him, too—and old ladies practically swooned whenever he came into their vicinity. Yet through all the attention he received, Lucas Conway always remained slightly aloof to the adulation which swirled around him. As if he was observing the world with the objectivity of a scientist, and, although nobody would ever have described him as untouchable, he was certainly what you might call unknowable.

But up until now he'd always treated her with respect. As if she mattered. Not as if she were just some skivvy working in his kitchen, with no more than two brain cells to rub together. The lump in her throat got bigger. Someone who didn't *know her place*.

Was that how he really saw her?

How others saw her?

She licked lips which had suddenly grown dry. Was that how she saw herself? The misfit from the country. The child who had grown up with the dark cloud of shame hanging over her. Who'd been terrified people were going to find her out, which was why she had fled to the city just as soon as she was able.

She told herself to leave it. To just nod politely and Lucas would vacate the kitchen and it would all be forgotten by the time she produced the feather-light cheese soufflé she was planning to serve for his dinner, because he wasn't going out tonight. But for some reason she couldn't leave it. Something was nagging away at her and she didn't know what it was. Was it the strange atmosphere which had descended on the house ever since that letter had arrived for him, and she'd heard the sound of muffled swearing coming from his office? Or was it something to do with this weird weather they'd been having, which was making the air seem as heavy as lead? Her heart missed a beat, because maybe it was a lot more basic than that. Maybe it all stemmed from having seen someone from home walking down Grafton Street yesterday, when she'd been window-shopping on her afternoon off.

Tara had nearly jumped out of her skin when she'd spotted her—and she was easy to spot. At school, Mona O'Sullivan had always been destined for great things and her high-heeled shoes and leather trench coat had borne out her teacher's gushing prophesy as she'd sashayed down Dublin's main street looking as if she didn't have a care in the world. A diamond ring had glittered like a giant trophy on her engagement finger and her hair had been perfectly coiffed.

Tara had ducked into a shop doorway, terrified Mona would see her and stop, before asking those probing questions which always used to make her blush to the roots of her hair and wish the ground would open up and swallow her. Questions which reminded Tara why she was so ashamed of the past she'd tried so desperately to forget. But you could never forget the past, not really. It haunted you like a spectre—always ready to jump out at you when you were least expecting it. It waited for you in the sometimes sleepless hours of the night and it lurked behind the supposedly innocent questions people put to you, which were anything but innocent. Was that why she had settled for this safe, well-paid job tucked away on the affluent edge of the city, where nobody knew her?

She wondered if her gratitude for having found such a cushy job had blinded her to the fact that she was now working for a man who seemed to think he had the right to talk to her as if she were nothing, just because he was in a filthy mood.

She stilled her spoon and crashed the copper bowl

down on the table, aware that already the air would be leaving those carefully beaten egg whites—but suddenly she didn't care. Perhaps she'd been in danger of caring a bit too much what Lucas Conway had for his supper, instead of looking after herself. 'Then maybe you should find yourself someone who does know their place,' she declared.

Lucas turned round from the coffee machine with a slightly bemused look on his face. 'I'm sorry?'

She shook her head. 'It's too late for an apology, Lucas.'

'I wasn't apologising,' he ground out. 'I was trying to work out what the hell you're talking about.'

Now he was making her sound as if she were incapable of stringing a coherent sentence together! 'I'm talking about *knowing my place*,' Tara repeated, with an indignation which felt new and peculiar but oddly... *liberating*. 'I was trying to be kind to Charlotte because she was crying, and because I've actually spent several months of my life trying to wash her lipstick out of your pillowcases—so it wasn't like she was a complete stranger to me. And I once found one of her diamond studs when it was wedged into the floorboards of the dining room and she bought me a nice big bunch of flowers as a thank-you present. So what was I expected to do when she turned up today with mascara running all down her cheeks?' She glared at him. 'Turn her away?'

'Tara—'

'Do you think she was in any fit state to drive in that condition—with her eyes full of tears and her shoulders heaving?'

'Tara. I seem to have missed something along the way.' Lucas put his untouched coffee cup down on the table with as close an expression to incomprehension as she'd ever seen on those ruggedly handsome features. 'What's got into you all of a sudden?'

Tara still didn't know. Was it something to do with the dismissive way her boss's gaze had flicked over her admittedly disobedient hair when he'd walked into the kitchen? As if she were not a woman at all, but some odd-looking robot designed to cook and clean for him. She wondered if he would have looked like that if Mona O'Sullivan had been standing there whipping him up a cheese soufflé, with her high heels and her luscious curves accentuated by a tight belt.

But you dress like a frump deliberately, a small voice in her head reminded her. *You always have done. You were taught that the safest way to be around men was to make yourself look invisible and you heeded that lesson well. So what do you expect?*

And suddenly she saw exactly what she might expect. More of the same for the countless days which lay ahead of her. More of working her fingers to the bone for a man who didn't really appreciate her—and that maybe it was time to break out and reach for something new. To find herself a job in a big, noisy house with lots of children running around—wouldn't that be something which might fulfil her?

'I've decided I need a change of direction,' she said firmly.

'What are you talking about?'

Tara hesitated. Lucas Conway might be the biggest pain in the world at times, but surely he would give her a glowing reference as she'd worked for him since she'd been eighteen years old—when she'd arrived in the big city, slightly daunted by all the traffic, and the noise. 'A new job,' she elaborated.

He narrowed his stunning eyes—eyes as green as the valleys of Connemara. 'A new job?'

'That's right,' she agreed, thinking how satisfying it was to see the normally unflappable billionaire looking so perplexed. 'I've worked for you for almost six years, Lucas,' she informed him coolly. 'Surely you don't expect me to still be cooking and cleaning for you when you reach retirement age?'

From the deepening of his frown, he was clearly having difficulty getting his head around the idea of retirement and, indeed, Tara herself couldn't really imagine this very vital man ever stopping work for long enough to wind down.

'I shouldn't have spoken to you so rudely,' he said slowly. 'And that *is* an apology.'

'No, you shouldn't,' she agreed. 'But maybe you've done me a favour. It's about time I started looking for a new job.'

He shook his head and gave a bland but determined smile. 'You can't do that.'

Tara stilled. It was a long time since anyone had said those words to her, but it was the refrain which had defined her childhood.

You can't do that, Tara.
You mustn't do that, Tara.

She had been the scapegoat—carrying the can for the sins of her mother and of her grandmother before her. She had been expected to nod and keep her head down, never to make waves. To be obedient and hardworking and do as she was told. To stay away from boys because they only brought trouble with them.

And she'd learned her lessons well. She'd never been in a relationship. There hadn't been anyone to speak of since she'd arrived in Dublin and had gone on a few disastrous dates, encouraged by her friend Stella. She tried her best to forget the couple of encounters she'd shared with one of the farm hands back home, just before she'd left for the big city and landed the first job she'd been interviewed for. The agency had warned her that Lucas Conway was notoriously difficult to work for and she probably wouldn't last longer than the month but somehow she had proved them wrong. She earned more money than she'd ever imagined just by keeping his house clean, his shirts ironed and by putting a hot meal in front of him, when he wasn't gallivanting around the globe. It wasn't exactly brain surgery, was it?

On that first morning she had slipped on her polyester housecoat and, apart from a foreign holiday every year, that was where she'd been ever since, in his beautiful home in Dalkey. She frowned. Why did Lucas even *own* a place this big when he lived in it all on his own, save for her, carefully hidden away at the top of the vast house like someone in a Gothic novel? It wasn't as if he were showing any signs of settling down, was it? Why, she'd even seen him recoil in horror when his friend Finn Delaney had turned up one day with his wife Catherine and their brand-new baby.

'You can't stop me from leaving, Lucas,' she said, with a touch of defiance. 'I'll work my month's notice and you can find someone else. That won't be a problem—people will be queuing up around the block for a job like this. You know they will.'

Lucas looked at her and told himself to just let her go, because she was right. There had been dozens of applicants for the job last time he'd advertised and nothing much had changed in the years since Tara had been working for him, except that his bank balance had become even more inflated and he could easily afford to hire a whole battalion of staff, should the need arise.

But the young redhead from the country did more than just act as his housekeeper—sometimes it felt as if she kept his whole life ticking over. She didn't mind hard work and once he had asked her why she sometimes got down on her hands and knees to scrub the kitchen floor, when there was a perfectly serviceable mop to be had.

'Because a mop won't reach in the nooks and crannies,' she'd answered, looking at him as if he should have known something as basic as that.

He frowned. She wasn't just good at her job, she was also reliable, and no laundry could ever press a shirt as well as Tara Fitzpatrick did. It was true that sometimes she chattered too much—but on the plus side, she didn't go out as often as other young women her age so she was always available when he needed her. If he asked her to cook when he had people over for dinner she happily obliged—and her culinary repertoire had greatly improved since he'd arranged for her to go on an upmarket cookery course, after pointing out there were other things you could eat, rather than meat pie. As far as he knew, she never gossiped about him and that was like gold to him.

He didn't want her to leave.

Especially not now.

He felt the pound of his heart.

Not when he needed to go to the States to deal with the past, having been contacted by a lawyer hinting at something unusual, which had inexplicably filled him with dread. A trip he knew couldn't be avoided, no matter how much he would have preferred to. But the attorney's letter had been insistent. He swallowed. He hadn't been back to New York for years and that had been a deliberate choice. It was too full of memories. Bitter memories. And why confront stuff which made you feel uncomfortable, when avoidance was relatively simple?

Lucas allowed his gaze to skim down over the old-fashioned denim jeans Tara wore beneath her housecoat. Baggy and slightly too short, they looked as if they'd be more appropriate for working on a farm. No wonder she'd never brought a man back in all the time she worked for him when injecting a little glamour into her appearance seemed to be an unknown concept to her. And wasn't that another reason why he regarded her as the personification of rock-like reliability? She wasn't surreptitiously texting when she should have been working, was she? Nor gazing into space vacantly, mooning over some heartbreaker who'd recently let her down. Despite her slender build, she was strong and fit and he couldn't contemplate the thought of trying to find a replacement for her, not when he was focussed on that damned letter.

He wondered how much money it would take to get her to change her mind, and then frowned. Because in that way Tara seemed different from every other woman he'd ever had dealings with. She didn't openly lust after expensive clothes or belongings—not if her appearance was anything to go by. She wore no jewellery at all and, as far as he knew, she must be saving most of the salary he paid her, since he'd seen no signs of conspicuous spending—unless you counted the second-hand bicycle she'd purchased within a fortnight of coming to live here. The one with the very loud and irritating bell.

Lucas wasn't particularly interested in human nature but that didn't mean he couldn't recognise certain aspects of it, and it seemed to him that a woman who wasn't particularly interested in money would be unlikely to allow a salary increase to change her mind.

And then he had an idea. An idea so audacious and yet so brilliant that he couldn't believe it hadn't occurred to him before. Sensing triumph, he felt the flicker of a smile curving the edges of his mouth.

'Before you decide definitely to leave, Tara,' he said, 'why don't we discuss a couple of alternative plans for your future?'

'What are you talking about?' she questioned suspiciously. 'What sort of plans?'

His smile was slow and, deliberately, he made it reach his eyes. It was the smile he used when he was determined to get something and it was rare enough to stop people in their tracks. Women sometimes called it his killer smile. 'Not here and not now—not when you're working,' he said—a wave of his hand indicating the rows of copper pans which she kept so carefully gleaming. 'Why don't we have dinner together tonight so we can talk about it in comfort?'

'Dinner?' she echoed, with the same kind of horrified uncertainty she might have used if he'd suggested they both dance naked in Phoenix Park. 'You're saying you want to have dinner with me?'

It wasn't exactly the way he would have expressed it—but want and need were pretty interchangeable, weren't they? Especially to a man like him. 'Why not?' he questioned softly. 'You have to eat and so do I.'

Her gaze fell to the collapsing mixture in her bowl. 'But I'm supposed to be making a cheese soufflé.'

'Forget the soufflé,' he gritted out. 'We'll go to a restaurant. Your choice,' he added magnanimously, for he doubted she would ever have set foot inside one of Dublin's finer establishments. 'Why don't you book somewhere for, say, seven-thirty?'

She was still blinking at him with disbelief, her pale lashes shuttering those strange amber eyes, until at last she nodded with a reluctance which somehow managed to be mildly insulting. Since when did someone take so long to deliberate about having dinner with him?

'Okay,' she said cautiously, with the air of someone feeling her way around in the dark. 'I don't see why not.'

CHAPTER TWO

THE AIR DOWN by the River Liffey offered no cooling respite against the muggy oppression of the evening and Lucas scowled as they walked along the quayside, unable to quite believe where he was. When he'd told Tara to choose a restaurant, he'd imagined she would immediately plump for one of Dublin's many fine eating establishments. He'd envisaged drawing up outside a discreetly lit building in one of the city's fancier streets with doormen springing to attention, instead of heading towards a distinctly edgy building which stood beside the dark gleam of the water.

'What is this place?' he demanded as at last they stopped beneath a red and white sign and she lifted her hand to open the door.

'It's a restaurant. A Polish restaurant,' she supplied, adding defensively, 'You told me to choose somewhere and so I did.'

He wanted to ask why but by then she had pushed the door open and a tinny bell was announcing their arrival. The place was surprisingly full of mainly young diners and an apple-cheeked woman in a white apron squealed her excitement before approaching and flinging her arms around Tara as if she were her long-lost daughter. A couple of interminable minutes followed, during which Lucas heard Tara hiss, *'My boss...'* which was when the man behind the bar stopped pouring some frothy golden beer to pierce him with a suspicious look which was almost challenging.

Lucas felt like going straight back out the way he had come in but he was hungry and they were being shown to a table which was like a throwback to the last century—with its red and white checked tablecloth and a dripping candle jammed into the neck of an empty wine bottle. He waited until they were seated before he leaned across the table, his voice low.

'Would you mind telling me why you chose to come and eat here out of all places in Dublin?' he bit out.

'Because Maria and her husband were very kind to me when I first came to the city and didn't know many people. And I happen to like it here—there's life and bustle and colour on the banks of the river. Plus it's cheap.'

'But I'm paying, Tara,' he objected softly. 'And budget isn't an option. You know that.'

Tara pursed her lips and didn't pass comment even though she wanted to suggest that maybe budget *should* be an option. That it might do the crazily rich Lucas Conway good to have to eat in restaurants which didn't involve remortgaging your house in order to pay the bill—that was if you were lucky enough to actually *have* a mortgage, which, naturally, she didn't. She felt like telling him she'd been terrified of choosing the kind of place she knew he usually frequented because she simply didn't have the kind of wardrobe—or the confidence—

which would have fitted into such an upmarket venue. But instead she just pursed her lips together and smiled as she hung her handbag over the back of her chair, still pinching herself to think she was here.

With him.

Her boss.

Her boss who had turned the head of everyone in the restaurant the moment he'd walked in, with his striking good looks and a powerful aura which spoke of wealth and privilege.

She shook her hair, which she'd left loose, and realised that for once he was staring at her as if she were a real person, rather than just part of the fixtures and fittings. And how ironic it should be that this state of affairs had only come about because she'd told him she was leaving, which had led to him bizarrely inviting her to dinner. Did he find it as strange as she did for them to be together in a restaurant like this? she wondered. Just as she wondered if he would be as shocked as she was to discover that, for once. she was far from immune to his physical appeal.

So why was that? Why—after nearly six years of working for him when her most common reaction towards him had been one of exasperation—should she suddenly start displaying all the signs of being attracted to him? Because she prided herself on not being like all those other women who stared at him lustfully whenever he swam into view. It might have had something to do with the fact that he had very few secrets from her. She did his laundry. She even ironed his underpants and she'd always done it with an unfeigned impartiality. At home it had been easy to stick him in the categories marked 'boss' and 'off-limits', because arrogant billionaires were way above her pay grade, but tonight he seemed like neither of these things. He seemed deliciously and dangerously accessible. Was it because they were sitting facing each other across a small table, which meant she was noticing things about him which didn't normally register on her radar?

Like his body, for example. Had she ever properly registered just how broad his shoulders were? She didn't think so. Just as the sight of two buttons undone on his denim shirt didn't normally have the power to bring her out in a rash of goosebumps. She swallowed. In the candlelight, his olive skin was glowing like dark gold and casting entrancing shadows over his high cheekbones and ruggedly handsome face. She could feel her throat growing dry and her breasts tightening and wondered what had possessed her to agree to have dinner with him tonight, almost as if the two of them were on a date.

Because he had been determined to have a meal with her and he was a difficult man to shift once he'd set his mind on something.

She guessed his agenda would be to offer her a big salary increase in an attempt to get her to stay. He probably thought she'd spoken rashly when she'd told him she was leaving, which to some extent was true. But while she'd been getting ready—in a recently purchased and discounted dress, which was a lovely pale blue colour, even if it was a bit big on the bust—she'd decided she wasn't going to let him change her mind. And that his patronising attitude towards her had been the jolt she needed to shake her out of her comfort zone. She needed to leave Lucas Conway's employment and do something different with her life. To get out of the rut in which she found herself, even though it was a very comfortable rut. She couldn't keep letting the past define her—making her too scared to do anything else. Because otherwise wouldn't she run the risk of getting to the end of her days, only to realise she hadn't lived at all? That she'd just followed a predictable path of service and duty?

'What would you like to drink?' she questioned. 'They do a very good vodka here.'

'Vodka?' he echoed.

'Why not? It's a tradition. I only ever have one glass before dinner and then I switch to water. And it's not as if you're driving, is it?' Not with his driver sitting in a nearby parking lot in that vast and shiny limousine, waiting for the signal that the billionaire was ready to leave.

'Okay, Tara, you've sold it to me,' he answered tonelessly. 'Vodka it is.'

Two doll-sized glasses filled with clear liquor were placed on the tablecloth in front of them and Tara raised hers to his—watching the tiny vessel gleam in the candlelight before lifting it to her lips. *'Na zdrowie!'* she declared before tossing it back in one and Lucas gave a faint smile before drinking his own.

'What do you think?' she questioned, her eyes bright.

'I think one is quite enough,' he said. 'And since you seem to know so much about Polish customs, why don't you choose some food for us both?'

'Really?' she questioned.

'Really,' he agreed drily.

Lucas watched as she scrolled through the menu. She

seemed to be enjoying showing off her knowledge and he recognised it was in his best interests to keep her mood elevated. He wanted her as compliant as possible and so he ate a livid-coloured beetroot soup, which was surprisingly good, and it wasn't until they were halfway through the main course that he put his fork down.

'Do you like it?' she questioned anxiously.

He gave a shrug. 'It's interesting. I've never eaten stuffed cabbage leaves before.'

'No, I suppose you wouldn't have done.' In the flickering light from the candle, her freckle-brushed face grew thoughtful. 'It's peasant food, really. And I suppose you've only ever had the best.'

The best? Lucas only just managed to bite back a bitter laugh as he stared into her amber eyes. It was funny the assumptions people made. He'd certainly tried most of the fanciest foods the world had to offer—white pearl caviar from the Caspian Sea and matsutake mushrooms from Japan. He'd eaten highly prized duck in one of Paris's most famous restaurants and been offered rare and costly moose cheese on one of his business trips to Sweden. Even at his expensive boarding school, the food had been good—he guessed when people were paying those kinds of fees, it didn't dare be anything but good. But the best meals he'd ever eaten had been home-made and cooked by Tara, he realised suddenly.

Which was why he was here, he reminded himself. *The only reason he was here.*

So why were his thoughts full of other stuff? Dangerous stuff, which made him glad he'd only had a single vodka?

He stared at her. Unusually, she'd left her hair loose

so that it flowed down over her narrow shoulders and the candlelight had transformed the wild curls into bright spirals of orange flame. Tonight she seemed to have a particularly fragile air of femininity about her, which he'd never noticed before. Was that something to do with the fact that for once she was wearing a dress, instead of her habitual jeans or leggings? Not a particularly flattering dress, it was true—but a dress all the same. Pale blue and very simple, it suited her naturally slim figure, though it could have done with being a little more fitted. But the scooped neck showed a faint golden dusting of freckles on her skin and drew his attention to the neatness of her small breasts and, inexplicably, he found himself wondering what kind of nipples she had. Tiny beads of sweat prickled on his brow and, not for the first time, he wished that the impending storm would break. Or that this damned restaurant would run to a little air conditioning. With an effort he dragged his attention back to the matter in hand, gulping down some water to ease the sudden dryness in his throat.

'The thing is,' he said slowly, putting his glass down and leaning back in his seat, 'that I don't want you to leave.'

'I appreciate that and it's very nice of you to say so, but—'

'No, wait.' He cut through her words with customary impatience. 'Before you start objecting, why don't you at least listen to what I'm offering you first?'

She trailed her fork through a small mound of rice on her plate so it created a narrow valley, before looking up at him, a frown creasing her brow. 'You can't just throw more money at the problem and hope that it'll go away.'

'So we have a problem, do we, Tara?'

'I shouldn't have said that. It's nothing to do with you, not really. It's me.' She hesitated. 'I need a change, that's all.'

'And a change is exactly what I'm offering you.'

Her amber eyes became shuttered with suspicion. 'What do you mean?'

He took another sip of water. 'What if I told you that I'm going to be leaving Dublin for a while, because I have to go to the States?'

'You mean on business?'

'Partly,' he answered obliquely. 'I'm thinking of investing in some property there. I need to spread my money around—at least, that's what my financial advisors are telling me.'

'This wouldn't have anything to do with that letter, would it?' she questioned curiously.

He grew still. 'What letter?'

'The one…' The words came out in a rush, as if she'd been waiting for a chance to say them. 'The one which arrived from America last week.'

Lucas wondered if she'd noticed his reaction at the time. If she'd seen the shock which had blindsided him. It suddenly occurred to him how much of his life she must have witnessed over the years—a silent observer of all the things which had happened to him. And wasn't that another reason for keeping her onside? Bringing another stranger into his home would involve getting to know a new person and having to learn to trust them and that was something to be avoided, because he didn't give his trust easily. His mouth hardened and his jaw firmed. And it wasn't going to happen. No way. Not when there was a much simpler solution.

'I'm planning a minimum six-month stay and I'm thinking of renting an apartment because the idea of spending that long living in a hotel isn't what you'd call appealing.' He slanted her his rare, slow smile. 'And that's where you come in, Tara.'

'Where?' she questioned blankly.

'I want you to come to New York with me.' He paused. 'Be my housekeeper there and I'll increase your salary—'

'You pay me very generously at the moment.'

He shook his head with a trace of impatience. Who in their right mind ever pointed out that kind of thing to their employer? 'The cost of living is higher there,' he said. 'And this will give you the opportunity to try living in a brand-new city. This could be a win-win situation for both of us, Tara.'

He thought she might show excitement and more than a little gratitude, not a look of sudden suspicion, which hooded her eyes. Inexplicably, he found his gaze drawn to the delicate bowed outline of her lips, which he'd never really noticed before. Well, of course he hadn't. He'd never been this close to her before, had he? Close enough to detect her faint scent, which was like no other perfume he'd ever encountered. Nor realised that her clear skin was porcelain-pale apart from those few freckles which dusted the upturn of her nose. He shook his head, perplexed by the observation and by the inexplicable rise of heat in his blood.

'New York,' she said slowly.

'You said you wanted a change. Well, what greater change from Dublin town than living in the buzzing metropolis of Manhattan? Didn't you go on a trip there last Christmas?'

She nodded.

'And didn't you have a good time?'

Once again, Tara nodded. She'd saved up and gone with her friend Stella, who was a nanny in nearby Dun Laoghaire, and they'd done the whole New York holiday thing together. A fun-packed snow and shopping trip, marred only by the fact that Tara had fallen over on the ice rink outside the Rockefeller building and grazed both her knees. 'We had a very good time.'

'So what's stopping you from saying yes?' he probed.

Tara nibbled on the inside of her lip, reminding herself that her plan had been to get *away* from Lucas—not to sign up for more of the same. She needed to remove herself from the influence of a powerful man who was selfishly pursuing his own interests. He certainly wasn't thinking about what was best for *her* at the moment, was he? Only what was best for him.

And yet.

She ran her fingertip over the frosted surface of her water glass. If she looked at it objectively couldn't this be the best of all possible outcomes? A trip to a glamorous city she was already familiar with, without all the uncertainty of having to fix herself up with a job? Wouldn't a spell in America provide the inspiration she needed to turn her life around and decide what she wanted to do next?

But still she held back from saying yes because something seemed to have changed between her and

Lucas tonight. Something she couldn't quite put her finger on because she had no experience of this sort of thing. Was she imagining the tension which was stoking up between the two of them, like when you threw a handful of kindling on the fire? She certainly wasn't imagining the heart-racing feeling she was getting whenever she stared into his gorgeous green eyes—not to mention the fact that her body was behaving in a way which wasn't normal. At least, not normal for her. Her nipples were aching and there was a delicious syrupy feeling deep in the very core of her. She could feel a weird kind of restlessness she'd never experienced before, which was making her want to squirm uncomfortably on the wooden seat, and she was having to concentrate very hard not to keep wondering what it would be like to be kissed by him.

Was it because they were in the falsely intimate setting of a candlelit restaurant, making her wish she'd chosen somewhere brighter? Or because she'd stupidly decided to wear a dress and wash her hair—as if this were a real date or something? And now she was left feeling almost *vulnerable*—as if she'd lost the protective barrier which surrounded her when she was working at his house and cleaning up after him.

He was still studying her with an impatient question in his eyes, as if he wasn't used to being kept waiting. Come to think of it—he wasn't.

'Well?' he demanded.

'Can I have some time to think about it?' she said.

He looked surprised and Tara guessed that most women wouldn't have thought twice about accompanying their billionaire boss to a glamorous foreign city with the offer of a pay-rise.

'How long do you want?' he demanded.

Tara chewed on her lip. Should she ask her friend Stella's advice? She certainly didn't have anyone else to ask. She'd been so young when her mother died that she hardly remembered her and her grandmother had passed away just before she'd come to work for Lucas. 'A few days?' she suggested and gave a little shrug. 'Maybe you'll change *your* mind in the meantime?'

'If you continue to prevaricate like this, then maybe I will,' he retorted, not bothering to hide his displeasure. 'Let's just get the bill and go, shall we?'

'Okay.' She rose to her feet. 'But I need to use the washroom first.'

Still unable to believe she wasn't grabbing at his job offer with eager hands, Lucas watched as she walked through the restaurant, his gaze mesmerised by the curve of her calves, which led down to the slenderest ankles he'd ever seen. Suddenly he could understand why men living in the Victorian age had found them highly arousing.

He told himself to look away but somehow he couldn't. Somehow Tara Fitzpatrick's back view seemed to be the most beautiful thing he'd looked at in a long time, with those red curls spilling wildly over her shoulders. Her dress was slightly creased from where she'd been sitting but it was brushing against a bottom firmed by hard work and regular cycling—a realisation which was rewarded by an unwanted hardening at his groin. What the hell was happening to him? he wondered irritably. Was it simple physical frustration? Had

Charlotte's unexpected appearance at his house this afternoon reminded him just how long it had been since he'd had sex? He remembered their split, when he'd grown bored with her and bored with bedding her. Because despite the actress's undeniable beauty and sexual experience, hadn't making love to her sometimes felt as if he were making love to a mannequin? *And there hadn't been anyone since, had there?* Not even a flicker of interest had stirred in his blood, despite the many come-ons which regularly came his way.

With an impatient shake of his head, he glanced at his cell-phone to see what the markets were doing, but for once his attention was stubbornly refusing to focus and when he looked up, Tara was back. She must have attempted to brush the fiery curls into some kind of submission, because they looked half-tamed. Her eyes were bright and her air of youthful vitality made his heart clench with something he didn't recognise. Was it cynicism? He shook his head, confused now and slightly resentful because he'd come out tonight thinking this was going to be a straightforward exercise and it was turning into anything but.

'The bill, Tara,' he said impatiently. 'Have you asked for it?'

'I've done more than that.' She gave a wide smile. 'I've paid it.'

'You've paid it?' he repeated slowly.

'It's very reasonably priced in here,' she said. 'And it's the least I can do, since we came here in your car.'

As he followed her out of the restaurant—after a farewell even more ecstatic than their greeting—Lucas found himself trying to remember the last time a woman had offered to pay for a meal. Not recently, that was for sure. Not since those days when he'd had nothing and heiresses had sniffed around him like dogs surrounding a piece of fresh meat. When he'd been forced to leave his fancy school because there had been no money—or so he'd been told. But pride had made him refuse to accept the charity of women who had been hungry for his virile body. He'd fed himself. Sometimes he'd eaten the food left lying around after a meal in the directors' dining room. And sometimes he just used to go without. Tara had been wrong when she'd suggested he'd never eaten peasant food, he thought, the harsh reminder of those days making his jaw clench as his car purred smoothly down the quayside towards them.

But when he joined her on the back seat the bitter memories were dissolved by a rush of something far more potent. Lucas felt a beat of promise and of heady desire. Flaring his nostrils, he inhaled her subtle scent, which was more like soap than perfume. Half turning his head, he saw the brightness of her hair and suddenly he wanted to tangle his fingers in it. One slender thigh was placed tantalisingly close to his—a gesture he suspected was completely lacking in provocation—yet right now it seemed the sexiest thing he'd ever encountered. He swallowed as desire beat through him like an insistent flame and if it had been anyone else he might have reached out and caressed her. Touched her leg until she was squirming with pleasure and widening her thighs and whispering for him to touch her some more.

But this was Tara and he couldn't do that because she worked for him. *She worked for him.* She made his bed and cooked his meals. Ironed his shirts and kept his garden bright. She was an employee he wanted to accompany him to America. She wasn't a prospective lover—not by any stretch of the imagination. He stared straight ahead, attempting to compose himself as the traffic lights turned red.

Her heart pounding and her shoulders tense, Tara told herself to stop feeling so nervous as the powerful car purred through the city streets because *none of this was a big deal*. She'd just had dinner with her boss—that was all—and he'd just offered her a job in America, which was a massive compliment, wasn't it? She'd never been in his chauffeur-driven car before either, and travelling home in such luxury should have been a real treat. Yet she was finding it difficult to appreciate the soft leather or incredibly smooth suspension as they travelled through Dublin. All she could think about was how *different* Lucas seemed tonight and how her reaction towards him seemed to have undergone a dangerous and fundamental shift. From being a demanding employer, he seemed to have morphed into a man she was having difficulty tearing her eyes away from. For the first time ever, she could understand why he inspired such a devoted following among women. Suddenly, she *got* why someone as beautiful as Charlotte would be prepared to humiliate herself in order to wheedle herself a way back into his life.

And I don't want to feel this way, she thought. *I want to go back to the way it was before, when I tolerated him more than idolised him and was often infuriated by him.*

The car pulled into the driveway of his Dalkey house but instead of being relieved that the journey was over, all Tara could feel was a peculiar sense of disappointment. Blindly, she reached for the door handle, her usually dextrous fingers flailing miserably as she failed to locate it in the semi-darkness.

'Here,' said Lucas, sounding suddenly amused as he leaned across her to click a button. 'Let me.'

Of course. The door slid noiselessly open because it was an electronic door and didn't actually have a handle! What a stupid country girl she must seem. But Tara's embarrassment at her lack of savvy was exacerbated by a heart-stopping awareness as Lucas's arm brushed against hers. She swallowed. He'd touched her. *He'd actually touched her.* He might not have meant to but his fingers had made contact and where they had it felt like fire flickering against her skin.

Scrambling out of the car into an atmosphere even stickier than earlier, she cast a longing look towards the heavy sky, wishing it would rain and shatter this strange tension which seemed to be building inside her, as well as in the atmosphere. She scrabbled around in her handbag to fish out her key but her fingers were trembling as she heard a footfall behind her and Lucas's shadow loomed over her as she inserted it tremblingly into the lock.

'You're shaking, Tara,' he observed as she opened the door and stepped into the house.

'It's a cold night,' she said automatically, even though that wasn't true. But he didn't correct her with a caustic comment as he might normally have done.

And the strange thing was that neither of them moved to put on the main light once the heavy front door had swung shut behind them, and the gloom of the vast hallway seemed to increase the sense of unreality which had been building between them all evening.

There was something in the air. Something indefinable. Tara felt acutely aware of just how close Lucas was. His eyes were dark and gleaming as he stared down at her and she held her breath as, for one heart-stopping moment, she thought he was going to kiss her. She felt as if he was going to pull her into his arms and crush his lips down on hers.

But he didn't.

Of course he didn't.

Had she taken complete leave of her senses? He simply clicked the switch so that they were flooded with a golden light, which felt like a torch being shone straight into her eyes, and the atmosphere shattered as dramatically as a bubble being burst. A hard smile was playing at the edges of his lips and he nodded, as if her reaction was very familiar to him.

'Goodnight, Tara,' he said in an odd kind of voice. And as he turned away from her, she could hear the distant rumble of thunder.

CHAPTER THREE

THE NEXT FEW days were an agony of indecision as Tara tried to make up her mind whether or not to accept Lucas's job offer. She tried drawing up a list of pros and cons—which came up firmly weighted in favour of an unexpected trip to America with her boss. Next she canvassed her friend Stella, who told her she'd be mad not to jump at the chance of joining Lucas in New York.

'Why wouldn't you go?' Stella demanded as she folded up one of the tiny smocked dresses belonging to the twin baby girls she nannied for. 'You *loved* New York when we went last Christmas. Apart from the ice-rink incident, of course,' she added hastily. 'And that man really should have been looking where he was going. It's a no-brainer as far as I can see, so why the hesitation?'

Tara didn't answer. She thought how lame it would sound if she confessed that something felt different between her and Lucas and that something unspoken and sexual seemed to have flowered between them that night. Or would it simply seem deluded and possibly arrogant to imply that Dublin's sexiest billionaire might be interested in someone like her?

But something *had* changed. She wasn't imagining it. The new awkwardness between them. The shadowed look around his eyes when she'd brought in his breakfast the morning after that crazy dinner, which had made her wonder if his night had been as sleepless as hers. The flickering glance he'd given her when she'd put the coffee pot down with trembling fingers before he'd announced that he was flying to Berlin later that morning and would be back in a couple of days—and could she possibly give him her answer about accompanying him to America by then?

'Yes, of course,' she'd answered stiffly, wondering why she was dragging her feet so much when she knew what she *ought* to say. She practised saying it over and over in her head.

It's a very kind offer, Lucas—but I'm going to have to say no.

Why?

Because... Because I've fallen in lust with you.

How ridiculous would that sound, even if it weren't coming from someone who could measure her sexual experience on the little finger of one hand?

But it was easier to shelve the decision and even easier when he wasn't around So Tara just carried on working and when she wasn't working, she did the kind of things she always did when Lucas was away. She swam in his basement pool and began to tidy up the garden for winter. She made cupcakes for a local charity coffee morning and went to Phoenix Park with Stella and her young charges. She listened to Lucas's voicemail telling her he'd be late back on Thursday night and not to bother making dinner for him.

And still the wretched weather wouldn't break. It was so heavy and sticky that you felt you couldn't breathe properly. As if it was pressing against your throat like an invisible pair of hands. Sweat kept trickling down the back of her neck and despite piling her rampant curls on top of her head, nothing she did seemed to make her cool.

On Thursday evening she washed her hair and went to bed, listening out for the sound of Lucas's chauffeur, who had gone to collect him from the airport. It wasn't even that late, but several days of accumulated sleeplessness demanded respite and Tara immediately fell into a deep sleep, from which she was woken by a sudden loud crack, followed by a booming bang. Sitting bolt upright in bed, she tried to orientate herself, before the monochrome firework display taking place outside her bedroom window began to make sense. Of course. It was the storm. The long-awaited storm which had been building for days. Thank heavens. At least now the atmosphere might get a bit lighter.

Another flash of lightning illuminated her bedroom so that it looked like an old-fashioned horror film and almost immediately a clap of thunder echoed through the big house. The storm must be right overhead, she thought, just as heavy rain began to teem down outside the window. It sounded loud and rhythmical and oddly soothing and Tara sank back down onto the pillows and lay there with her eyes wide open, when she heard another crash. But this time it didn't sound like thunder. Her body tensed. This time it sounded distinctly like the sound of breaking glass.

Quickly, she got out of bed, her heart pounding and

her bare toes gripping the floorboards. What if it was a burglar? This was a big house in a wealthy area and didn't they say thieves always chose opportunistic moments to break in? What better time than amid the dramatic chaos of a wild thunderstorm?

Pulling on her dressing gown, she knotted the belt tightly around her waist and wondered if she should go and wake Lucas. Of course she should—if he was back. Yet she was dreading knocking on his bedroom door in a way she would never have done before she'd agreed to have dinner with him. Back then—in that unenlightened and innocent time before she'd started to fantasise about him—she wouldn't have been in an angsty state of excitement, wondering what she'd find. She knew he didn't wear pyjamas because she did his laundry for him. And that was the trouble. She knew so much about him and yet not nearly enough.

Quietly, she pushed open her bedroom door and crept along the corridor, her head buzzing. At least she'd made up her mind about how to deal with his job offer—because no way could she join Lucas in America now, not if she was harbouring stupid ideas about what it would be like to…to…

She cocked her head and listened. Was that the creak of a footstep on the stairwell she could hear, or just the normal sounds of the big house settling down for the night? It was difficult to tell above the sound of the drumming rain. Peering over the bannister, she could see light streaming from Lucas's room on the floor below and she crept downstairs towards it.

She had just reached his door when a figure appeared at the top of the stairs and Tara nearly jumped out of her skin when she realised that Lucas was standing there wearing nothing but a pair of faded denims, which he had clearly just slung on, because the top button was undone. And his chest was bare. Gloriously and deliciously bare—his washboard abs as beautifully defined as the powerful curves of his forearms. Tara felt the sudden flip of her heart and was furious with herself—because wasn't it shocking to be noticing something like that at a time like this? She was supposed to be investigating a night-time disturbance, not eying up her half-naked boss like some kind of man-hungry desperado.

'Lucas!' she breathed. 'It's you.'

'Of course it's me—who else did you think it would be? Father Christmas?' he snapped. 'And what the hell are you doing, creeping around the place like a damned wraith?'

She was still flustered by the sight of him wearing so few clothes, and her reply came blurting out, the words tumbling over themselves in their eagerness to be said. 'I... I heard a crash from downstairs and I thought it might be...' she shrugged '...a burglar!'

'And you thought the best way to deal with some potentially violent nutter was to confront him with nothing more effective than an indignant look in your eyes?' His gaze bored into her. 'Are you out of your mind, Tara?'

Tara licked her bone-dry lips. Yes, that was a pretty accurate description of the way she was feeling right now. But she could hardly tell him the reason why, could she? She could hardly explain that her fixation about him had been so great that it hadn't left room in her head for anything else, and certainly not common sense. 'So what was the crash?' she questioned. 'Did you find out?'

Lucas scowled, aware that his body was hardening in a way which was *not* what he wanted to happen. And the reason for his suddenly urgent desire was the most perplexing thing of all. Tara was standing there in some passion-killer of a dressing gown, which looked as if it had been made from an old bedspread, and yet a powerful sexual hunger was pumping through his veins. It defied all logic, he thought—just as his behaviour had done in the few days since they'd been apart. He'd been busy in Berlin, buying fleets of electric cars and planning to lease them out to businesses at a highly profitable rate. He'd had several high-powered meetings with the German transport minister and had been taken to an entrancing *Schloss*, situated outside the capital, where busty blondes had served them foaming tankards of beer. Yet all the time there had been a constant soundtrack playing in his mind as if it was on some infernal loop and giving him no peace. It had begun with Tara and ended with Tara and had involved plenty of X-rated images of how her pale and freckled body might look if it were naked in his bed.

Why the hell was he thinking so graphically about a woman he'd never even given a second glance to before?

Somehow he managed to drag his thoughts back to the present, realising that she was regarding him with a question in her eyes, and somehow he managed to dredge up a memory of what she'd asked him. 'It was something breaking in the kitchen,' he informed her tightly. 'You'd left a window in the pantry open and the wind made some figurine fall.'

'Oh, dear.' She bit her lip. 'I'd better go and tidy it up.'

'No. Leave it until morning,' he said firmly. 'You shouldn't be clearing up broken china at this time of night—though the ornament is beyond repair, I'm afraid.'

Tara nodded, her mouth working with an unexpected flare of emotion, despite all her mixed feelings about where that little statue had come from. She'd only put it there because she'd been planning to clean it tomorrow. 'Can't be helped.'

'Was it something special?'

It wasn't the kind of thing he usually asked and for a moment she almost told him about the figurine of St Christopher—the patron saint of travellers—which her mother had taken with her when she'd left for England, setting out on a life which was supposed to be so different from what she'd left behind. But why would you start explaining a woman's broken dreams to a man who probably wasn't really interested—and a man who was only half dressed? Wouldn't that lead to questions and then yet more questions, which might end up with her revealing telltale details about her background? And nobody wanted to hear those, least of all herself. She might as well write on a placard: *This is why I am such a freak*. She shook her head and turned away but not before the salty prickle of tears had stung her eyes.

Had Lucas seen it? Was that why his voice suddenly gentled in a way she'd never heard before?

'Tara?' he said.

Impatiently fisting away the tears, Tara didn't know what she'd been expecting but it wasn't for Lucas to turn her around to look at him. It was just a hand placed on her upper arm, through the thick barrier of her dressing gown. The type of reassuring gesture anyone might make to someone who was on the verge of crying, but it didn't feel remotely like that. It felt...*electric*. Tara had grown up in a house where physical contact was frowned upon, where nobody actually *touched* each other—and nobody had touched her in years. Was it that which made her response to Lucas so instant? Her blood was heating, like syrup on an open flame, and her body felt as if it were dissolving from the inside out. She sucked in a shuddered breath and somehow it seemed inevitable he should pull her into his arms. It was comfort, she told herself. That was all.

But it didn't feel like comfort. It felt like heaven. Like a taste of something she'd never quite believed in. He was so big and powerful—so warm and strong—that it seemed only natural to let her head fall to his shoulder and for her breath to fan the silken skin of his neck. Tara had no idea how long that wordless embrace lasted. It might have been a few seconds but, there again, it could have been longer. Suddenly he pushed her head away so he could look at her, his eyes searching her face long and hard, and she'd never seen him look so disorientated. As if he were in some weird kind of dream and was expecting to wake up at any minute.

But he didn't wake up—and neither did she. They remained standing in the same spot, staring into each other's eyes as if it were the first time they'd ever seen each other.

'You'd better go back to your own room,' he said unsteadily.

Afterwards, Tara would ask herself what had possessed her to behave in such an uncharacteristic way.

Was it the certainty of knowing she wasn't going to be working for him much longer which made her throw caution to the wind? Or just the fact that she'd never felt like this before—as if her body were on fire with a burning need too powerful to be ignored? For once she wanted to cast aside the roles she'd been given in life. To forget the person she'd been taught to become. Obedient Tara. Wary Tara. The woman who had never stepped out of line because that way lay danger and she had been fearful of what might happen if she refused to comply.

But now there was no fear, only an audacity which felt newly minted and exhilarating.

'Why?' she questioned.

Her question hung in the air.

'You know why,' he ground out.

And somehow she did. Even though she had no experience of such matters, Tara could tell that Lucas Conway wanted her in exactly the same way as she wanted him. It was explicit in the tension which radiated from his powerful body and the hectic gleam which was glittering from his eyes. Her mouth was dry as she gazed at his lips and the temptation to kiss them was just too strong to resist. Because those lips held the tantalising promise of something else—something she was keen to explore. Suddenly she reached up to wind her arms around his neck, her thumbs stroking the dark waves of hair which covered the base of his neck, and she heard him suck in a breath.

'Go to bed, Tara,' he growled.

Again, that boldness. That strange, uncharacteristic boldness as she repeated her own guileless question. 'Why?'

'I don't want to take advantage of you.'

'We're not playing a game of tennis, Lucas.'

'You know what I mean,' he growled. 'I'm your employer.'

'Not right now you're not,' she declared fiercely. 'Unless you're planning on demanding I go and fix you a midnight snack or iron a shirt for you.'

An unexpected smile curved at his lips as Lucas realised how his humble housekeeper seemed determined to confound all his expectations tonight—in fact, to blow them clean away. She'd fearlessly come downstairs to tackle a potential thief like some kind of modern-day warrior queen. With her pale skin and red curls streaming down her back like a pre-Raphaelite painting, she looked fragile and ethereal and yet she was turning him on. Very, very much. And suddenly he couldn't stem his desire any longer, not with her slim body so near and her mouth so tantalisingly close. He angled his head to kiss her, wondering if he was breaking some kind of fundamental rule. Some unspoken moral code. And then he cursed himself for even posing such a stupid question. Of course he was. Big time. He knew that. But knowing didn't change anything—how could it when she was kissing him back with a hunger which felt as fierce as anything he'd ever encountered?

Her lips were as soft as petals and he could sense all the sweet promise in her slim young body. Already he felt as if he wanted to explode. As if he could tear that ugly dressing gown from her body and do it to her right there, up against the wall outside his bedroom. Yet something held him back and not just because this was the first time and instinct told him to savour it, in case there wasn't a repeat. There was also part of him—a growingly distant part of him, admittedly—which wondered if one of them was going to suddenly come to their senses. As if something would suddenly shatter this strange spell and leave them facing each other with an air of disbelief and embarrassment.

But that wasn't happening. The only thing on the agenda right now was that the kiss was growing deeper—and the first tentative thrust of her tongue was making his groin grow deliciously hard. Hell. What kind of sorcery was she wielding when she was doing so little? And why was her body still hidden from his hungry gaze, beneath the folds of that unspeakable dressing gown?

Pulling his mouth away from hers, he saw nothing but dazed compliance in her eyes and was unprepared for the ecstatic thundering of his heart in response. When was the last time he'd felt this...*excited* about having sex with a woman? Was it because this was the last thing he'd ever imagined happening, or because she was so different from anyone he'd ever been intimate with?

He thought about leading her to his bedroom in a way he'd done with other women countless times over the years, when instead he did something which had never happened before. Picking her up, he planted his foot in the centre of the door and kicked it wide open.

'Lucas!' breathed Tara, her voice sounding almost shocked as he carried her towards his bed, which was softly illuminated by the glow of a nearby lamp.

'What's the matter, Tara?' he growled. 'Don't you like the masterful approach?'

She shook her head so that her curls shimmered down her back like a halo of fire and he could see her licking her lips before her next words came out with a rush of bravado. 'I don't like you kicking the paintwork when I'm the one who has to clean it!'

He laughed—which was extraordinary because he didn't usually associate humour with sex—but his mirth was quickly forgotten as he lowered her to her feet. Pulling open the sash of her dressing gown, he narrowed his eyes on discovering she wasn't naked underneath. Far from it. A baggy T-shirt of indeterminate colour hung to the middle of her lithe thighs. 'You certainly aren't dressed for seduction,' he observed wryly as he peeled it over her head.

'I'm right...right out of silk negligees,' she breathed as he smoothed his hands down over her ruffled curls.

Once again, he could hear a trace of vulnerability behind her flippant response and so he kissed her some more while he dealt with his zip, which was straining almost painfully over his hardness. He waited for her to offer to help him, but she didn't—and maybe that was a good thing. He wasn't sure he trusted anyone to touch him when he was this close to coming.

Kicking off his jeans, he urgently peeled back the duvet, sinking her down onto the mattress and wrapping his arms tightly around her so that they were skin-on-skin. He could hear her gasp as his erection sprang against her belly and for one last time he heard a whisper of warning in the recesses of his mind. *Are you sure you're doing the right thing?* But her long legs were tangling with his with unashamed excitement and when he slid his hand between her thighs, she was so wet and warm and slippery. He wasn't sure at all, he realised, but the only power on earth which could stop him now was Tara herself and, judging by the way she was writhing beneath him, that wasn't going to happen any time soon.

'Oh,' he said, his voice dipping with approval as he whispered his fingertip over the engorged little bud which was slick with desire.

'Oh,' echoed Tara as a shimmer of incredible sensation swept over her. Was this what had been spoken about with such venom when she'd been growing up? The most wicked thing in the world which could bring with it terrible consequences?

He lowered his lips to hers again and the sweetness of his kiss made her heart want to burst from her chest. How was it possible to *feel* this good? She closed her eyes in ecstasy as he began to kiss her breasts, his tongue flicking against one nipple so that it peaked into his mouth as if it had been made for just that purpose. She quivered as his fingertips skated over her skin, leaving a trail of goosebumps in their wake as he explored her breasts and belly and the jutting bones of her hips. Suddenly she wanted to touch him back in the same intimate way but she was shy and scared—wondering if her inexperience would put him off and bring this all to an abrupt end.

She thought: *Am I going to be passive about this, or am I going to be a participant?* For the first time in her life, couldn't she just go with what she wanted to do rather than thinking about what was the *right* thing to do? Fired by a fierce tide of hunger, she whispered her hand down his spine and then drifted her fingertips to the flat planes of his stomach. Did he sense she was going to move her hand further down to explore his hardness for the first time? Was that why he gave a low laugh of expectation?

In the soft light she could see the pale pole of his hardness contrasted vividly against the burnished hue of his olive skin and Tara wondered why she wasn't feeling the fear she had expected on seeing an aroused man for the first time in her life. Because this felt perfectly natural, that was why. This was what was *supposed* to happen between a man and a woman.

Tentatively, and with the lightness of touch which made her such a good pastry-maker, she started to stroke him—but he endured the exploratory skate of her fingers for no more than a minute before shaking his head.

'If you carry on doing that, this will not end well,' he growled softly, reaching out for a foil packet on the locker and tearing it open with impatient fingers. Then he lifted her up to position her over him, so she was intimately straddling him, his tip nudging against her new-found wetness.

Tara gasped as he splayed his hands over her breasts, his thumbs playing with her thrusting nipples, which instantly made her want to squirm with pleasure—although she wasn't exactly in the ideal position to do any squirming.

'Ride me, Tara,' he urged huskily. 'Ride me.'

She didn't get a chance to tell him she didn't really know what he was talking about because, suddenly, he was pulling her down onto him so that his erection was pushing deep inside her, as if he was done with talking and couldn't wait a second longer. Pushing up right into her so that he filled her completely, and the warm rush of unexpected pleasure was slightly offset by the unexpected shock of what was happening to her body. She could feel her muscles tense and the briefest split of pain. She closed her eyes and when she opened them again, she found Lucas staring up at her with an expression of disbelief on his rugged features and something else.

Was it regret?

Or was it anger?

'You're a virgin?' he bit out.

Breathlessly, she nodded.

He said something she didn't understand—she thought it might be in Italian, though what did she know?—and it sounded incredulous. He put his hands on either side of her hips and for a moment she thought he was going to remove her from his body and tell her to get out. But he didn't. With a look of intense concentration on his face, he flipped her over onto her back while he was still inside her, displaying a skill which spoke volumes about his experience. And once she was on her back he smoothed away the wild disarray of curls from her face and stared down at her.

'I think I'd better be the one in charge from now on, don't you?' he said thickly.

She nodded, terrified of saying the wrong thing. Terrified he was going to stop. Because she couldn't bear that—not when those amazing feelings were building up inside her again and he was bending his head to kiss her more deeply than before. And she was floating now. Floating off into a sweet and strange new world where nothing existed except the sensation of Lucas Conway thrusting deep inside her, his mouth capturing hers in kiss after kiss. He moved slowly at first and then faster—as if her body was sending out an unspoken command which he correctly interpreted and acted upon.

She didn't think it would happen. Not the first time. She might have been innocent but she'd read all the magazine articles, like everyone else. And when it did, her orgasm was nothing like she'd expected. Because how could she ever have anticipated that something could feel this good? As if the sweet spasms which were racking her body had transformed her, so that for a moment she felt as if she'd redefined what it meant to be human.

Her fingers dug into the damp skin at his back and she kissed his neck over and over again as his own movements changed. His thrusts became more urgent and she heard his shuddered groan just before he collapsed on top of her. She wrapped her arms around him and in that moment she felt as if she'd tumbled into paradise and never wanted to leave. But nearly six years of a boss-employee relationship couldn't be dissolved in a couple of minutes and the unmistakable balance of power between them hadn't changed. So she lay there perfectly still and waited to hear what Lucas had to say.

CHAPTER FOUR

TARA STARED OUT at the sodden morning to where the previous night's storm had left the garden completely battered—as if some giant malevolent fist had pummelled the shrubs and flowers and left them leafless and sad. Gloomily surveying the damage to her previously well-tended shrubs, she found herself wondering if Lucas was in the air by now. If he was already beginning the process of forgetting her. Probably. No doubt it would be a speedy process in his case—less so in her own, she suspected—as she remembered the awkward words which had followed their passionate bout of sex.

It had been the worst conversation of her life—though of course she'd been too young to remember her grandmother telling her that her mammy was dead, which she supposed she must have done. Worse even than the time she'd discovered the truth about her tarnished legacy—not from the person who *should* have told her, but from a sniggering trio of bullies on a freezing cold school playground in the rural wilds of Ballykenna.

Nope. She sighed as she turned away from the window. It had been an all-time low to hear Lucas's chilly statement as he'd coolly detached himself from her satiated and naked body and rolled to the other side of the bed, his voice as distant as the great space which had suddenly appeared between them. And, just as she must have done twenty times over—she found herself reliving that post-sex scenario, word by excruciating word.

It had started with Lucas. A flat, hard assessment which allowed no room for manoeuvre.

'That should never have happened.'

The trouble was that on one level she had agreed with him. It shouldn't. While on another level...

The flip side of the coin was that she'd been lying there, basking in emotion and reaction and a million other things besides. She'd felt fulfilled and relieved—yes, relieved—grateful that she was capable of feeling all the stuff other women felt and that her body was functioning just fine. For a few crazy, misplaced minutes before her boss had spoken, she'd actually been thinking that maybe she *could* go to New York with him, after all. That perhaps they could carry on doing... well, doing *this*. All right, it hadn't been the most conventional beginning in the world—but the world wasn't a conventional place these days and who was to say they couldn't have some kind of relationship, even if it didn't last? But Lucas hadn't wanted to hear that. He hadn't wanted to hear anything which smacked of eagerness. Presumably what he'd wanted was an unflappable response which echoed his own sentiments—one which reassured him that she wasn't about to start reading something into a foolish act of passion which meant nothing in the grand scheme of things.

'No,' she'd said slowly. 'I suppose it shouldn't.'

'I can't believe what we just did. I just can't believe

it.' He had shaken his tousled dark head. 'I should have—'

'Honestly, Lucas, you don't have to explain,' she had butted in quickly, her voice sounding much sharper than usual and he'd turned his head to look at her in surprise, as if thinking she didn't usually talk that way to him, which of course she didn't. But then, they weren't usually lying buck-naked in bed, were they? And because she couldn't bear the thought of him voicing any more regrets and leaving her with nothing but uncomfortable memories of her first ever sexual experience—which happened to have completely blown her away—she had somehow forced a smile to her lips. She'd even managed a half-shrug, glad that her expression was mostly hidden by the thick fall of her curls. 'Things got out of hand, that's all. It's not a big deal. Really.'

'But you were a *virgin*, Tara.'

'So what? Everybody is a virgin at some point in their life. I had to lose it some day.'

'But not with…'

His words had tailed off but she'd wondered what he had been about to say. Not with someone like me, probably. Someone who was completely out of her league. A commitment-phobe billionaire who normally dated the kind of women most men lusted after, not a skinny redheaded employee who'd hardly even been kissed before.

'I can't offer you anything, Tara,' he had continued fiercely. 'If that's what you're thinking.'

How *dared* he presume to know what she was thinking? Hiding her hurt behind righteous indignation, Tara had decided to fight against the negative opinion he seemed to be forming of her.

'You thought I was holding out for the man I'd one day marry?' His look of surprise had told her she'd judged it correctly. 'That I wanted to trade my innocence for a big white dress and a triumphant march down the aisle? You think the only reason we country girls come to the city is because we're looking for a husband? Well, don't worry, Lucas. I'm not—and if I was, I wouldn't choose someone who clearly has no intention of ever settling down. Just like I'm not expecting anything to come of this. You're right—it shouldn't have happened and it certainly won't happen again. For one thing, you're off to New York, aren't you? And I'm staying here in Dublin to find myself another job, which was always the plan.'

Unlike that night over dinner, this time he hadn't attempted to persuade her to stay and Tara felt angry at herself for having supposed he might. And hurt, too. That was the stupid thing. Her heart gave a funny little twist. He obviously couldn't wait to put as many air miles between them as possible. She'd thought she couldn't possibly feel any worse than she did, and then he had proceeded to rub salt into the wound by being unusually considerate.

'Look, I don't want you to feel you have to rush into anything.' His words had been careful but he had seemed oblivious to the irony in them as he'd reached out to glance at his watch. 'You must use the house here in Dalkey for as long as it takes you to find a job you really like. I'll be away for at least six months and I don't want you feeling as if you've got to grab the first thing which comes to hand just to get away from here.'

He'd made her feel like a charity case but somehow

Tara had hidden her humiliation behind a tight smile as she'd scrambled off the bed. 'Thanks, I appreciate it.'

'Tara?'

'What?' Her voice had been toneless as she'd turned around to answer his deep command. And wasn't it crazy how the human spirit continued to hope no matter how much the odds were stacked against it? Hadn't she secretly been praying he was going to tell her to get right back into bed when one look at the shuttered indifference on his face had told her that any such hope was pointless? 'What is it?' she'd said.

He had shrugged, even though she'd been able to see his body shift uncomfortably on the bed and the rigid outline of his erection beneath the sheet had been abundantly clear. She had felt herself blush and had been grateful that the dim light of the room had hidden her embarrassment.

'Nothing,' he'd growled. 'It doesn't matter.'

So she had picked up her abandoned dressing gown and T-shirt and returned to her room without another glance at the naked man on the rumpled bed, and if she'd thought he might come running after her—well, he hadn't done that either.

In the morning she'd overslept—which she *never* did—and when she'd gone downstairs, she'd found a note lying on the table. A simple note. A note which was damning despite its air of considered politeness. Or maybe because of it.

Tara,
In view of what happened last night, I've brought my trip to New York forward by a few days. I'm sure you'll understand the reasons why.

Good luck with all that you do—you've been the best housekeeper I've ever had and any references I provide will reflect that opinion.

I've paid you in advance for six months, so take your time choosing your next position.
Lucas

What position was he talking about? she'd wondered with a mild tinge of hysteria as she'd crumpled the note in her palm before hurling it into the fire where it had combusted into a bouquet of bright flames. The one which involved her straddling him before taking him deep inside her body?

But recriminations and casting blame were going to get her nowhere. She needed to think clearly and objectively and, most of all, she needed a new job. She went to a couple of employment agencies and scrolled through the newspapers for domestic vacancies, but nothing compared to working for Lucas. She even went on a couple of interviews but her heart wasn't in it and despite her glowing references she was turned down for both jobs, which didn't exactly do wonders for her self-esteem.

She was longing to confide in Stella but something held her back. Was it because she thought her friend might be shocked by what she'd done—essentially enjoyed a night of casual sex with her employer? Stella couldn't be more shocked than she was herself, Tara thought grimly as she polished the fine furniture in Lucas's sitting room, trying to keep herself busy. And she discovered very quickly that it was easy to procrastinate. To act as if nothing had really changed, except that it had.

Something had *really* changed.

Her periods had always been as regular as clockwork and so she was concerned from the very first day of being late. But there again, it was weird how your mind did its best to protect you by concealing the truth and cloaking it in all kinds of possibilities. She told herself that there'd been so much upheaval lately it was no wonder she was a little out of sorts. She blamed the sudden dip in the temperature as autumn suddenly swept through the city. She managed to keep these various myths alive for a whole fortnight. It was only when she'd been unable to keep her breakfast down, or her lunch for that matter—and Stella had popped round unexpectedly to find her sitting white-faced in the kitchen—that the whole horrible truth came tumbling out, though it still needed a little prompting.

'So. Are you going to tell me what's going on, Tara?' her friend demanded. 'About why you're looking so awful and acting so distracted?'

Licking her tongue over bone-dry lips, Tara prepared to say something she was glad her grandmother wasn't alive to hear. Or her mother for that matter. 'I'm...pregnant.'

There were a few astounded seconds while Stella appeared to be having some difficulty digesting what she'd just been told. 'I wasn't aware you were seeing anyone,' she said at last, carefully. 'Have I missed something?'

And here it was. The horrible reality. Did she try to dress it up into acceptable bite-sized chunks so that her friend might understand? Tara wondered desperately. No, there wasn't a single chunk of this which could in any way be described as acceptable. In the end she managed to condense it down into a couple of bald sentences which she still found difficult to believe.

'I had sex with Lucas,' she said. 'And I'm expecting his baby.'

'You had sex with Lucas Conway?'

'I did.'

'You're kidding me?'

'I'm afraid I'm not.'

Stella shook her head from side to side, her thick black hair gleaming in the autumn afternoon sunshine. 'I wasn't even aware you fancied him!' she exclaimed, blinking at her in astonishment. 'Or that you were his type!'

'I didn't. And I'm not.'

'So what happened?'

Tara shrugged and the bitter taste in the back of her throat only intensified. 'I still can't quite work it out.'

'Well, *try*, Tara.'

Tara worried her teeth into her bottom lip before meeting her friend's incredulous gaze. 'He said something pretty mean to me, which focussed me into thinking I should get a new job.'

'Which I've been saying to you for ages,' said Stella darkly.

'He told me he didn't want me to leave—'

'Please don't tell me he *seduced* you so you'd change your mind?'

Tara shook her head. 'Of course he didn't. It wasn't like that.'

'Then just how was it, Tara?'

How could you put into words something which had flared between the two of them over dinner that evening? Something which had changed the way they were with each other, so they'd suddenly gone from being boss and employee to a man and a woman who were achingly aware of the other? Even if you could, it wasn't something you'd dare admit to a friend, for fear of coming over as slightly deranged—or even stupid. Both of which were probably true in her case. 'It just happened,' she said simply. 'I can't explain it.'

There was a pause and Stella's eyes bored into her. 'So now what happens?'

This was the question which really needed answering and Tara knew that there was no alternative than to face the thing she was dreading more than anything else.

'I'm going to have to go to New York and tell him.'

CHAPTER FIVE

THE WORLD AS he knew it had just come to an end but Lucas kept his expression blank as he finished reading the letter the attorney had given him. It had shocked and sickened him—the final sentence dancing before his eyes—but somehow he kept it together. He could feel the punch of his heart and the faint clamminess at his brow, but his hands were steady as he folded the piece of paper carefully and slipped it back inside the envelope.

'Do you have any queries, Mr Conway?' the lawyer was asking him. 'Anything you'd like to discuss with us, regarding the contents?'

A million things, thought Lucas grimly—and then some. But they were the kind of questions which couldn't be answered by some anonymous attorney he could see was burning up with curiosity. Not when he could manage to work out the most important bits for himself.

And suddenly it was as if a heavy mist had lifted and everything which made up the sometimes confusing landscape of his past suddenly become clear. It explained so many important things. Why his 'father' had always been so cruel to him and why his mother…

His mother.

He felt a twist of something which felt more like anger than pain as finally he understood why he'd never felt as if he belonged anywhere. *Because he didn't. His parents were not his parents and he was not the man he'd thought himself to be. Everything had changed in the time it took to read that letter.*

And yet nothing had changed, he reminded himself grimly. Not really. He was still Lucas Conway, not Lucas Gonzalez. A pulse flickered at his temple. And no way was he ever going to call himself Lucas Sabato, his birth name. He shook his head. He was the man he had set out to be. A truly self-made man.

'We had some difficulty tracking you down after your father's death,' the lawyer was saying smoothly. 'Given that you'd changed your name and settled in Europe. And given, of course, that you were estranged from your family.'

Behind his desk the man was looking at him with a hopeful expression, as if waiting for Lucas to put him out of his misery and reveal why he had been so keen to conceal his true identity for all these years. Lucas felt his mouth flatten.

Because he had no intention of enlightening the lawyer.

No intention of enlightening anyone.

Why should he? His inner life had always been his and his alone—his thoughts too dark to share. And they had just got a whole shade darker, he realised bitterly, before pushing them away with an ease born of habit. Much simpler to adopt the slick and sophisticated image he presented to the world—the one which discouraged people to dig beneath the surface. Because who in their right mind wanted to explore certain and unremitting pain?

Hadn't that been one of the unexpected advantages to becoming a billionaire at such an early age—that people were so dazzled by his wealth, they didn't stop to explore his past too deeply? Or rather, people became so obsequious when you were loaded, that *you* were able to control how you wanted conversations to play out. He was good at evasion and obfuscation. He didn't even tell people where he'd been born—sidestepping curious questions with the same deft touch which had enabled him to become one of the youngest billionaires in all Ireland. His accent had helped to obscure his background, too. It had been difficult to place—his cultured New York drawl practically ironed out by years of multilingual schooling in Switzerland. And Ireland had provided the final confusing note—with the soft, lilting notes he had inevitably picked up along the way.

'Thanks for all your help,' he said smoothly as he rose to his feet, tucking the envelope into the inside pocket of his jacket.

He was barely aware of the lawyer shaking his hand or the secretary outside who stood up and smoothed her pencil skirt over her shapely bottom as he passed by, her hopeful smile fading as he failed to stop by her desk. Outside he was aware of the faint chill in the air. The reminder that fall was upon them. After a busy couple of weeks of business meetings, things had looked very different this morning when he'd lined up another apartment viewing, intending to stay in the city for a minimum of six months. Yet there was no reason to change that plan, he reminded himself. No reason at all. He hadn't been back here in years because he hadn't wanted to run into his father, but the man who had erroneously claimed that title was now dead and he wasn't going to let that bastard reach out from beyond the grave and influence him any more. Why *not* reclaim the city of his youth and enjoy it as he had never been able to do before?

With a quick glance at his watch, he set off by foot to meet the real-estate agent. He walked along Fifth Avenue, his body tensing as he stared up at the Flatiron building he hadn't seen since he'd been, what…fourteen? Fifteen? That had been the last time he'd spent his school vacation here. That particular homecoming had ended in the usual violence when his father had raised his fist to him but Lucas had turned his back and simply walked away, trying to block out the sound of the other's man's taunts which had been ringing in his ears.

'Not man enough to fight?'

It had been a flawed assessment because for the first time ever, Lucas had felt too *much* of a man to fight back. He'd filled out that summer and his muscles had been hard and strong. The almost constant sport he'd done at his fancy Swiss boarding school had made him into a fine athlete and deep down he knew he could have taken out his adoptive father, Diego Gonzalez, with a single swipe.

And the reason he hadn't was that because he was afraid once he started, he wouldn't know when to stop. That he would keep punching and punching the cruel bully who had made his life such a misery.

So he had carried on walking and not looked back.

The only other time he had returned had been for his mother's funeral, when the two men had sat on opposite sides of the church without speaking. With the cloying scent of white lilies making him want to retch, Lucas remembered staring at the ornate scrolling on the lavish coffin, realising he'd never really known the woman he'd thought at the time had given birth to him. And he had been right, hadn't he? He hadn't known her at all.

But he wasn't going to dwell on that. He had spent his life rejecting the past and he wasn't going to change that now.

Deliberately focussing his attention on the here and now, he saw a woman standing up at the lights in front of him and the tawny colour of her hair made him think about Tara, even though that was something else he had decided was off-limits. He'd told himself that it had been a mistake. That maybe it had happened because he'd been thrown off-balance by what had lain ahead of him in New York. But at least he had let her down gently and no real harm had been done. And as she'd said herself—she'd had to lose her virginity some time.

Yet his eagerness to put her out of his mind hadn't been the plain sailing he'd expected. His night-time dreams had been haunted by memories of her slim, pale body and the delicious tightness he'd encountered as he had entered her. He would wake up frustrated and angry—with a huge erection throbbing uncomfortably between his thighs.

He still couldn't quite believe he'd had sex with her—his innocent housekeeper. Someone who, despite her fiery curls, had always seemed to blend into the background of his life, so that he hadn't regarded her as a woman at all—just someone to cook and clean and scrub for him. But she'd been a woman that night in his bed, hadn't she? All milky limbs and hair which had glowed like fire as the storm had flashed through the sky with an elemental force which had seemed to mimic what had been taking place in his bed. He found himself recalling the passion with which she'd kissed him and the eagerness with which she'd fallen into his arms. And then the unbelievable realisation—of discovering he was her first and only lover.

How could he have been so reckless?

His uncomfortable preoccupation was interrupted by the vibration of the cell-phone in his pocket and when he pulled it out his fingers froze around the plastic rectangle as he saw the name which had flashed up onto the screen. He shook his head in slight disbelief, as if his thoughts had somehow managed to conjure up her presence.

Tara.

Quickly, he calculated the time in Dublin and frowned. Getting on for ten in the evening, when normally she would have been laying the table for his breakfast, before retiring to her room at the top of the house. Of course, he wasn't there to make breakfast for, so she was free to do whatever she wanted, but that wasn't the point. The point was that she was ringing him.

Why was she ringing him?

He couldn't think of a conversation they could possibly have which wouldn't be excruciatingly uncomfortable, but, despite wanting to let the call go to voicemail, he knew he couldn't ignore her. He might wish he could take back that night and give it a different outcome but that wasn't possible. And she'd been a faithful employee for many years, hadn't she? Didn't he owe her a couple of minutes of conversation, even if it was going to be something of an ordeal? What if there'd been a burglary—a bone fide one this time, not just some holy statue crashing to the floor in the middle of a storm?

He felt an unmistakable wave of guilt as his thumb hit the answer button. 'Tara!' he said, his voice unnaturally bright, and he thought how usually he would have greeted such a call with a faint growl—the underlying message that he hoped she had a good reason for ringing. 'This is a surprise!'

'Is it a bad time to ring?'

She sounded nervous. Maybe she was remembering that other time when she'd called him and he'd been abroad, with a model called Catkin. Despite the warning look he'd given her, Catkin had picked up his phone and answered it, her voice laughing and smoky with sex. He remembered Tara's stuttering embarrassment when she'd finally come on the line and the way the model had sniggered beside him, loud enough to be heard. And with that loathsome demonstration of feminine cruelty, she had unwittingly put an end to their relationship.

'I'm dodging pedestrians on Fifth Avenue, Tara,' he said lightly. 'So you may have trouble hearing me above all the traffic noise.'

'Oh.'

She sounded flat now and he thought how their easy familiarity seemed to have been replaced by an odd new formality as he asked a question which sounded more dutiful than caring. 'Nothing's wrong, I hope?'

Her response was cautious. As if she was picking out her words—like someone sorting through the loose change in their pocket while searching for a two-euro coin. 'Not exactly.'

Not exactly? What the hell was that supposed to mean? *Please don't start telling me that you miss me or that—God forbid—you've decided you're in love with me.* 'No burst pipes in the basement?' he enquired, his forced joviality not quite hitting the mark.

'No, nothing like that. Lucas, I have... I have to talk to you.'

He could feel his heart sink because this sounded exactly as he'd feared. He'd had too many of these conversations in the past with women unable to recognise that their needs were very different. That the sex they'd shared meant nothing—it was just sex. She probably wanted to see him again, and soon—while he most definitely wanted to close the page on it. 'I thought that's exactly what we *were* doing,' he said smoothly.

'No. I don't mean a phone call. I mean face to face!' she burst out, her voice tinged with a desperation he'd never heard there before.

'But I'm in New York, Tara,' he told her, almost gently, because if he was going to have to let her down—which he suspected he was—then he needed to be kind about it. Because wasn't it his own damned fault that his housekeeper was now clearly pining for him? 'And you're in Dublin.'

'No, I'm not,' she corrected, sounding a little more confident now. 'I've just flown into LaGuardia.'

'LaGuardia?' he echoed incredulously. 'You mean you're in New York?'

'Obviously.' Her voice became terse.

Afterwards Lucas would wonder how he could have been so stupid, but that was only afterwards, when the hard, cold facts had finally percolated into his disbelieving brain. Maybe it was the double whammy of finding out the truth about his parentage which had sucked all the sense and perception out of him. Which meant he was able to shelve the glaringly obvious reason why Tara Fitzpatrick had taken it into her head to follow him to America, and to give a nod of acknowledgement to the curvy real-estate agent who had appeared outside the main entrance of the apartment block.

'Look, I haven't got time for this now, Tara. I'm meeting someone. Hi, Brandy,' he said, forcing a smile before putting his mouth close to the phone and hissing into it. 'Can you take a cab from the airport?'

'Of course I can!' She sounded angry now. 'I'm not a complete fool.'

'Meet me in the bar of the Meadow Hotel at seven. We can talk then.'

He cut the call and walked up the stairs towards the elegant town house, where the agent was slanting him a great big smile.

CHAPTER SIX

Despite all her bravado, Tara wondered if Lucas had deliberately chosen to meet her in the most inaccessible bar in New York. It was situated deep in the bowels of the fanciest hotel she could ever have imagined—a place which instantly made her feel overheated, overdressed and scruffy. She'd worn a thick sweater with her jeans because it was autumn and the city was supposed to be colder than Dublin—but the temperature inside the hotel made it feel more like summer and consequently there were little beads of sweat already appearing on her brow and stubborn curls were sticking to the back of her neck, like glue. And she couldn't take the sweater off because she had only a very old vest top on underneath.

After convincing the granite-faced doorman that her appointment was genuine, she was instructed to put her anorak and old suitcase in the cloakroom, where she was given a look of frank disbelief by the attendant. Her long scarf she kept draped round her neck out of habit, like an overaged child still clutching a security blanket. Tucking her ticket into her purse, she walked through the huge foyer—past impossibly thin women on impossibly high heels who were smiling adoringly into the faces of much older men—and never had she felt quite so awkward. Several times she had to ask for directions and was made to feel even more self-conscious for not knowing where she was going. As if showing any kind of ignorance meant you'd failed a test you hadn't even realised you were taking.

Eventually she found the bar, which was situated down a dimly lit passageway—dimly lit and daunting with its understated display of quiet opulence and a lavish oriental feel. Standing in front of a display of coloured glasses and bottles, a barman was vigorously shaking a cocktail mixture as if it were a pair of maracas, playing to the group of businessmen sitting on tall stools at the bar in front of him. It was definitely a man's room but Tara was met with nothing but disparaging glances, indicating that without the clothes, the sophistication or the glamour, she was the wrong kind of woman to drink in a place like this. And didn't that simple fact acknowledge more clearly than words ever could just how awful the predicament in which she now found herself?

Where *was* Lucas? she thought, with a tinge of desperation as she sat down at a vacant table in the corner of the room and snuck a glance at her watch. And who was this woman called Brandy he'd been meeting when she'd telephoned him from the airport? She felt her self-esteem take another dramatic nose-dive as a familiar voice broke into her reverie.

'Tara?'

Thank heavens. Her heart pounded with relief. It was Lucas and he must have entered the room without her noticing because he was standing right beside her. She could detect his subtle scent as his shadow enveloped her, making her acutely aware of his powerful body. As befitted the sophisticated environment, he was wearing a suit, a crisp shirt and a tie—but, despite the elegant exterior, Tara knew all too well what lay beneath the sophisticated city clothes.

And suddenly he was no longer her soon-to-be ex-boss who had migrated to the opposite side of the globe, but the man with whom she'd shared all kinds of intimacies. The man with whom she had lain naked—skin next to warm and quivering skin. Who had stroked her eager body with infinite precision and licked his tongue over her puckering nipples. Had she really lost her virginity to the man she'd worked for and never looked twice at for all those years? Had he really thrust deep inside her as he'd taken her innocence and introduced her to that terrible and exquisite joy? How did something like that even *happen*?

Her heart began to race even faster. It was one thing being in Dublin and deciding that telling him to his face was the only way to impart her unwanted news—but now she wondered if she had been too hasty. Should she have sent him an email, or a text, even though it would have been an extremely impersonal method of communicating that she was carrying his baby? Suddenly what she was about to tell him seemed unbelievable—especially here, in this setting. Because this was his world, not hers. It was quietly moneyed and privileged—and it was pretty obvious that she stuck out like some country hick with her home-knitted scarf and cheap jeans.

'H-hello, Lucas,' she said.

'Tara.'

His voice was non-committal as he gave a brief nod of recognition, but as he turned to look at her properly Tara almost reeled back in shock because his face looked *ravaged*—there was no other word for it. The faint lines which edged his mouth seemed deeper—as if someone had coloured them in with a charcoal pencil. And despite the dim golden glow cast out by the tall light nearby, she could detect a bleak emptiness in his green eyes. As if the Lucas she knew had been replaced by someone else—a cool and indifferent stranger, but one who was radiating a quiet and impenetrable fury. Lucas was no even-tempered, angelic boss, but she'd never seen him looking like this before. What was responsible for such a radical change? Was he angry that she'd turned up without warning and was this to be her punishment—being given the ultimate cold shoulder for daring to confront him like this?

Well, his reaction was just too bad and she wasn't going to let it get to her. She couldn't afford to. She wasn't some desperate ex-lover chasing him to the far ends of the earth because she couldn't accept their relationship was over, but the woman who was carrying his baby. She needed to do this and she would do it with dignity.

'I know this is unexpected.'

'You can say that again.' He sat down opposite her, loosening his tie as he did so, but his powerful body remained tense as he looked at her. 'Have you ordered yourself a drink?'

Now was not the time to explain that she'd been too intimidated by the ambidextrous barman to dare to open her mouth, aligned with the very real fear that buying something here would eat dangerously into her limited budget. 'Not yet.'

'Would you like to try one of their signature cocktails?' He fixed her with an inquiring look and she knew him well enough to recognise that his smile was forced. 'They come with their own edible umbrella and are something of an institution.'

She tried not to look ungrateful, even though she found his tone distinctly patronising. But he was summoning a waitress who was travelling at the speed of light in her eagerness to serve him and Tara told herself not to be unreasonable. She had to look at it from his point of view. They'd had some bizarre unplanned sex and now it must look as if she were trying to gatecrash his new life. Because he still didn't know why she was here and what she was about to tell him—and it was going to come as a huge shock when he did.

So the sooner she did it, the better.

Nervously, she cleared her throat. 'Just a glass of water would be fine for me.'

The darkness on his face intensified, as if he had suddenly picked up on some of the tension which was making her push nervously at the cuticles of her fingernails, like someone giving themselves a makeshift manicure. He glanced up at the eager server who was hovering around his chair. 'Bring us a bottle of sparkling water, will you?'

'Coming right up, sir.'

And once they were on their own, all pretence was gone. The courteous civility he'd employed when asking her what she wanted to drink had all but disappeared.

All that was left in its place was a flintiness which was intimidating and somehow *scary*, because it suddenly felt as if the man sitting opposite was a complete stranger, and Tara shifted uncomfortably on the velvet seat, dreading what she had to tell him.

'So. I'm all ears. Are you going to tell me why you're here, Tara?' Those curiously empty green eyes fixed her with a quizzical look. 'Why you've made such a dramatic unannounced trip?'

Tara sucked in a deep breath, wishing that the water had arrived so that she could have refreshed her parched mouth before she spoke. Wishing there were some other way to say it. She sucked a hot breath into her lungs and expelled it on a shudder. 'I'm… I'm having a baby,' she croaked.

There was a silence. A long silence which even eclipsed Stella's reaction when she'd told her the news. Tara watched Lucas's face go through a series of changes. First anger and then a shake of the head, which was undoubtedly denial. She wondered if he would try bargaining with her before passing through stages of depression and acceptance—all of which she knew were the five stages of grief.

'You can't be,' he said harshly.

Tara nodded. This was grief, all right. 'I'm afraid I am.'

'You can't be,' he repeated, leaning forward so that his lowered voice was nothing more than a deep hiss of accusation. 'I used protection.'

Tara licked her lips, pleased when the server arrived with their bottle to interrupt their combat, although the silence grew interminably long as she poured the water and it fizzed and foamed over two ice-filled crystal glasses. It was only when the woman had gone and Tara had forced herself to gather her composure long enough to take a deep and refreshing mouthful that she nodded. 'I realise that. And I also understand that the barrier method isn't a hundred per cent reliable.'

Incredulously, he looked at her. 'The *barrier* method?' he echoed. 'Who the hell calls it that any more?'

'I read it in a book about pregnancy.'

'When was it published? Some time early in the eighteenth century?'

Tara urged herself to ignore his habitual sarcasm, which right now seemed more wounding than it had ever done before. This was way too important to allow hurt feelings and emotions to get in the way of what really mattered, which was the tiny life growing inside her. But neither was she prepared to just sit there and allow Lucas to hurl insults at her, not when he was as much to blame as she was. *And I don't want to feel blame,* she thought brokenly. *I don't want my baby to have all the judgmental stuff hurled at it which I once had to suffer.*

She put her glass down on the table with a shaky hand and the ice cubes rattled like wind chimes. 'Being flippant isn't going to help matters.'

'Really? So do you have a magic formula for something which *is* going to help matters, because if so I'm longing to hear it?'

'There's no need to be so...*rude!*'

He leaned forward so that the tiny pulse working frantically at his temple was easily visible. 'I'm not being rude, I'm being honest. I never wanted children, Tara,' he gritted out. 'Never. Do you understand? Not from when I was a teenage boy—and that certainty hasn't diminished one iota over the years.'

She told herself to stay calm. 'It wasn't exactly on my agenda either,' she said. 'But we're not talking hypothetical. This is real and I'm pregnant and I thought you had a right to know. That's all.'

Lucas stared at her, half wondering if she was going to suddenly burst out laughing and giggle, *'April Fool,'* and he would be angry at first, but ultimately relieved. He might even consider taking her up to his hotel room and exacting a very satisfying form of retribution—something which would give him a brief respite from the dark reality which had been visited upon him in that damned lawyer's office. But this was October, not April, and Tara wouldn't be insane enough to fly out here without warning unless what she said was true. And she wasn't smiling.

He thought about the ways in which he could react to her unwanted statement.

He could demand she take a DNA test and quiz her extensively about subsequent lovers she might have dallied with after he'd taken her innocence. But even as he thought it he knew only a fool would react in that way, because deep down he knew there had been no lover in Tara Fitzpatrick's life but him.

He could have a strong drink.

Maybe he would—because the time it took to slowly sip at a glass of spirit would give him time to consider his response to her. But not here. Not with half of New York City's movers and shakers in attendance and a couple of people he recognised staring at him curiously from the other side of the room. He wasn't surprised at their expressions, because never had anyone looked more as if they shouldn't be there than Tara Fitzpatrick, with her thick green sweater the colour of Irish hills and her striking hair piled on top of her head, with strands tumbling untidily down the sides of her pale face.

He saw that her ridiculously over-long scarf was wound around her neck—the multicoloured one she'd started knitting when she first came to work for him and which had once made him sarcastically enquire whether she ever planned to finish it. 'I don't know how to cast off,' had been her plaintive reply, and he had smiled before suggesting she ask someone. But he wasn't smiling now.

Was he ashamed of her? No. He'd broken enough rules in his own life to ever be described as a conformist and he didn't care that his skinny housekeeper was sporting a pair of unflattering jeans rather than a sleek cocktail dress like the few other women in the bar. And besides, hadn't he just discovered something about himself which would shock those onlookers in the bar and fill them with horror and maybe even a little pleasure at hearing about someone else's misfortune, if they knew the truth about him? The Germans even had a phrase for that, didn't they? Schadenfreude. That was it.

He needed to get away from these blood-red walls, which felt as if they were closing in on him, so he could try to make sense of what she'd told him. As if giving himself some time and space would lessen the anger and growing dread which were making his heart feel as heavy as lead.

'We can't talk here,' he ground out, rising to his feet. 'Come with me.'

She nodded obediently. Well, *of course* she would be obedient. Hadn't that been her role ever since she'd entered his life? To carry out his wishes and be financially recompensed for doing that—not to end up in his bed while he gave into an unstoppable passion which had seemed to come out of nowhere.

'Where are we going?' she questioned, once they'd exited the bar and were heading back down a dimly lit corridor towards the foyer.

'I have a room here in the hotel.'

'Lucas—'

'You can wipe that outraged look from your face,' he said roughly as he slowed down in front of the elevator. 'My mind is on far more practical things than sex, if that's what you're thinking.'

'Would you mind keeping your voice down?' she hissed.

'Isn't it a little late in the day for prudery, Tara?'

'I'm not being a prude,' she said, in a low voice. 'I just don't want every guest in this hotel knowing my business.'

He didn't trust himself to answer as he ushered her into the private elevator and hit the button for his suite. In tense and claustrophobic silence they rode to the top, his thoughts still spinning as he tried to come to grips with what she'd told him. But how could he possibly do that, when he'd meant what he said? He'd never wanted to be a father. Never. His experience of that particular relationship had veered from non-existent to violent—and he'd never had a loving mother to bail him out. At least now he knew the reason why, but that didn't make things any better, did it? In many ways it actually made them worse.

'In here,' he said tersely as the doors slid noiselessly open and they stepped into the penthouse suite of the Meadow Hotel, which was reputed to command one of the finest views of the Manhattan skyline. It was growing dark outside and already lights were twinkling like diamonds in the pale indigo sky. Most people would have automatically breathed their admiration on seeing such an unparalleled view of the city. But not Tara. She barely seemed to notice anything as she stood in the centre of the room and fixed those strange amber eyes on him.

'I came because I felt you had a right to know,' she began, as if she had prepared the words earlier.

'So you said in the bar.'

'And because I felt it better to tell you face to face,' she rushed on.

'But you didn't think to give me any warning?'

'How could I have done that without telling you what it was about?' She was quiet for a moment. 'I wanted to see your face when I told you.'

'And did my reaction disappoint you?'

'I'm a realist, Lucas. It was pretty much what I thought it would be.' She sucked in a deep breath. 'But I want you to know that this has nothing to do with any expectations on my part. I'm just giving you the facts, that's all. It's up to you what you do with them.'

Lucas flinched, suddenly aware of his heart's powerful reaction as he acknowledged he was to be a father. But it clenched in pain, not in joy. 'Brandy,' he said harshly. 'I'll order strong tea for you, but I think I need brandy.'

Her reaction was not what he'd been expecting. He'd thought she might be slightly pacified by him remembering the way she liked her tea—but instead she turned on him with unfamiliar fury distorting her face. 'Can't you leave your girlfriend out of it for a minute?' she flared. 'Can't we at least have this discussion in private without you talking to her?'

'Excuse me?' He narrowed his eyes. 'I'm afraid you've lost me, Tara. I haven't a clue what you're talking about.'

'You were meeting someone called Brandy when I called you from the airport!' she accused.

It might have been funny if it hadn't been so serious but Lucas was in no mood for laughing. 'That's the name of the house agent, not my girlfriend,' he gritted out, but her chance remark put him even more on his guard. Was she already showing signs of sexual jealousy? Already planning some kind of mutual future which would be a disaster for them both, despite her fiery words to the contrary? Well, the sooner he disabused her of that idea, the better. 'The drinks can wait. Why don't you take a seat over there, Tara?'

Tara didn't want to take a seat. She wanted to be back at home in her iron-framed bed in Dublin, where she could see the sweep of the Irish sea in its ever-changing guises. Except that it *wasn't* her home, she reminded herself painfully—it was Lucas's. She bit her lip. But it was the closest she'd ever come to finding a place where she felt safe and settled—far away from all the demons of the past. 'I'd prefer to stand, if it's all right by you,' she said stiffly. 'I've been sitting on a long flight for hours and I need to stretch my legs.'

He nodded but she couldn't miss the faint trace of frustration which briefly hardened his eyes. Was he finding it difficult to cope with the fact that, since she was no longer technically his employee, he could no longer order her around as he wanted?

'As you wish,' he said. His drink seemingly forgotten, he stared at her. 'So where do we go from here?'

She wished he would show more of the emotion she'd seen in the bar a little while ago. It might have been mostly anger and negativity but at least it was *some* kind of feeling—not this icy and remote person who seemed nothing like the Lucas Conway she knew.

But she didn't know him, did she? Not really. And not just because he kept so much of himself hidden that people called him a closed book. You couldn't really know someone you worked for—not properly—because their interactions had only ever been superficial. Yes, she'd witnessed different sides of his character over the years—but ultimately she'd just been a person on his payroll and that meant he'd treated her like an employee, not an equal.

Had he ever treated his girlfriends as equals? she wondered. Judging by the things she'd witnessed over the years she would say that, no, he had not. If you were heavily into equality, you didn't pacify dumped exes by giving them expensive diamond necklaces rather than an explanation of what had gone wrong. *And you are not his girlfriend,* Tara reminded herself bitterly. *You are just a woman he had sex with and now you're carrying his baby.*

His baby.

Her fingers crept to touch her still-concave belly and she saw him follow the movement with the watchful attention of a cheetah she'd once seen on a TV wildlife programme, just before it pounced on some poor and unsuspecting prey.

'How...pregnant are you?' he questioned, lifting that empty gaze to her face.

He said the word *pregnant* like someone trying out a new piece of vocabulary, which was rather ironic given that he was such a remarkable linguist. And Tara found herself wanting to tell him that it felt just as strange for her. That she was as mixed up and scared and uncertain about the future as he must be. But she couldn't admit to that because she needed to be strong. Strong for her baby as well as for herself. She wasn't going to show weakness because she didn't want him to think she was throwing herself in front of him and asking for anything he wasn't prepared to give.

'It's still very early. Seven weeks.'

'And you're certain?'

'I did a test.'

'A reliable test?'

Silently, she counted to ten. 'I didn't buy some dodgy kit at the cut-price store, if that's what you're hinting at, Lucas. I'm definitely pregnant.'

'Have you seen a doctor?'

She hesitated. 'No. Not yet.' Would it sound ridiculous to tell him that she'd baulked at going to see the friendly family doctor in Dalkey—himself a grandfather—terrified of how she was going to answer when he asked her about the father of her baby? Terrified he would judge her, as people seemed to have been doing all her life.

She watched as Lucas walked over to the cocktail cabinet—a gleaming affair of beaten gold and shiny chrome—but he seemed to think better of it and turned back to face her, that remote expression still making his face look stony and inaccessible.

'So what do we do next?' He raised his dark brows. 'Any ideas? You must have had something in mind when you flew all this way to tell me. You want to have this baby, I take it?'

Tara screwed her face up as a blade of anger spiked into her and for a moment she actually thought she might burst into tears. 'Of course I want this baby!' she retaliated. 'What kind of a woman wouldn't want her baby?'

She wondered what had caused that look of real pain to cross his face and thought it ironic that if they had some of the closeness of real lovers, she might have asked him. But they weren't *real* lovers. They were just two people who had let passion get the better of them and were having to deal with the consequences.

'So is it a wedding ring you're after?' he enquired caustically. 'Is that it?'

'I've no desire to marry someone who finds it impossible to conceal his disgust at such a prospect!'

'I can't help the way I feel, Tara. I'm not going to lie. I told you I never wanted children,' he gritted out. 'And the logical follow-on from that is that I never wanted marriage either.'

'I didn't come here for either of those things,' she defended. 'But at least now I know exactly where I stand.'

Her fingers tightened around the strap of her bag, which was still tied diagonally across her chest like a school satchel—in case anyone had tried to mug her. 'And since I've done what I set out to do, I'll be on my way.'

'Oh, really?' Dark eyebrows shot up and were hidden by his tousled dark hair. 'And where do you think you're going?'

She drew her shoulders back proudly. 'Back to Dublin, of course.'

He shook his head. 'You can't go back to Dublin.'

'Oh, I think you'll find I can do anything I please, Lucas Conway,' she answered, and for the first time in many hours she actually found comfort in a sense of her own empowerment. 'And you can't stop me.'

But it was funny how sometimes your own body could rebel and that you had no idea what was going on inside you. Maybe it was the economy flight which had been extremely cramped, or perhaps it had something to do with the dreadful food she'd been served during that journey, which she personally wouldn't have given to a dog. Add to that her see-sawing hormones and troubled emotions and no wonder that a sudden powerful wave of nausea washed over her.

Did her face blanch? Was that why Lucas stepped forward, an unfamiliar look of concern creasing his face as he reached out towards her? 'Tara? Are you okay?'

There was no delicate way to say it, even though it was an intimacy she had no desire to share with a man who'd shown her not one iota of compassion or respect since she'd got here.

She swayed like a blade of grass in the wind. 'I think I'm going to be sick!' she gasped.

He muttered something in French—or was it Italian?—and Tara moaned in dismay as he caught hold of her before she fell, lifting her up into his arms. Last time he'd carried her it had been a shortcut to his bed—and hadn't that been the beginning of all this trouble?—but this time he merely carried her to the nearest bathroom so she could give into the intense nausea which was gripping her. And as she bent over the bowl and started to retch he was still there, brushing away the curls which were dangling around her face, even though she tried to push him away with her elbow.

'G-go away,' she gasped, mortified.

'I'm not going anywhere.'

'I don't want you seeing me like this.'

'Don't worry about it, Tara,' he drawled. 'I've been on enough school football trips to have witnessed plenty of boys being sick.'

'It's not the same,' she moaned.

'Stop talking.'

She did but it took a while before she felt better-which was presumably why she allowed Lucas to dab at her face with a deliciously cool cloth. Then, after a moment of cold, hard scrutiny, he handed her some paste and a spare toothbrush.

'Wash up and take as long as you like. Call me if you need me. I'll be right outside.'

Tara waited until he had closed the bathroom door behind him, and as she staggered to her feet to the mirror she looked in horror at the white-faced reflection staring back at her. Her eyes were huge and haunted and her hair couldn't have been more of a mess, which was saying something. She tugged at the elastic band so that her curls tumbled free and shook her head impatiently.

What had she *done*?

Thrown up in front of a man who didn't want her here. Given him news he didn't want, a fact which he'd made no attempt to hide. Even worse, she was thousands of miles from home.

Past caring about her old vest top, she peeled off her too-hot sweater, splashed her face with water and then vigorously washed her hands until the suds stopped being grey. Then she brushed her teeth until they were minty-fresh and removed a hotel comb from its little packet of cellophane. It was slightly too small to properly attack her awry curls but she managed to marginally tame them before going over to the door. Whatever happened, she would cope, she thought grimly. Look what her mother and her granny had done during times when having a baby out of wedlock was the worst thing which could happen to a woman. She dug her teeth into her lip. It was true that their lives had been pretty much wrecked by circumstances but they had *managed*. And she would manage too.

Pushing open the door, she found Lucas waiting outside, his body tense and his features still dark with something which may have been concern but was underpinned with something much darker.

His question was dutiful rather than concerned. 'How are you feeling?'

'Better now,' she informed him stiffly.

'I'll ring for the doctor.'

'Please don't bother. I don't need a doctor, Lucas. Women often get sick when they're pregnant. I'd just like you to call me a cab and I'll stay in the hostel I've booked for tonight—and tomorrow I'll see about getting the first flight back to Ireland.'

He shook his head and now there was a look of grim resolution in his eyes. 'I'm afraid that's not going to happen, Tara.'

She tilted her chin in disbelieving challenge. 'You mean you're going to physically stop me?'

'If I need to, I will—because I would be failing in my duty if I allowed you to travel around New York on your own tonight, especially in your condition,' he agreed grimly. 'There's only one place you're going right now and that's to bed.'

'I'm not—'

'Oh, yes,' he said, in as firm a voice as she'd ever heard him use. 'You most certainly are. There's a guest suite right along the corridor. I've put your things in there. And it's pointless arguing, Tara. We both know that.'

Tara opened her mouth to object but he was right because she recognised that resolute light in Lucas's eyes of old. She'd seen it time and time again when he'd been in the middle of some big negotiation or trying to pull off a deal which nobody had believed could ever happen. Except that he made things happen. He had the wherewithal and the clout to mould people and events to his wishes. And didn't part of her *want* to lie down on a soft bed and close her eyes and shut out reality? To have sleep claim her so that maybe when she opened her eyes again she would feel better.

But how was that going to work and what could possibly make this situation better? She had let history repeat itself and she knew all too well the rocky road which lay ahead. But none of that bitter knowledge was a match against the fatigue which was seeping through her body and so she nodded her head in reluctant agreement. 'Oh, very well,' she mumbled ungratefully. 'You'd better show me the way.'

Lucas nodded, indicating the corridor which led to the guest accommodation, though he noticed she kept as far away from him as possible. Yet somehow her reluctance ignited a flicker of interest he wasn't prepared for and certainly didn't want. He frowned. Maybe it was because women didn't usually protest about staying in his hotel suite or try to keep him at arm's length like this. He was used to sustained adoration from ex-lovers, even though he was aware he didn't deserve such adoration. But women would do pretty much anything for a man with a big bank account who gave them plenty of orgasms, he thought cynically.

He'd tried to convince himself during the preceding weeks that the uncharacteristic lust he'd felt for Tara Fitzpatrick had gone. It *should* have gone by now. But to his surprise he realised it hadn't and he was discovering there was something about her which was still crying out to some atavistic need, deep inside him. Even when she was in those ill-fitting jeans and a vest top, he couldn't help thinking about her agile body. The pale breasts and narrow hips. The golden brush of freckles which dusted her skin. He remembered the way he had lowered her down onto his rocky hardness and that split-second when he had met the subtle resistance of her hymen. And yes, he had felt indignation that she hadn't told him—but hadn't that been quickly followed by a primitive wash of pleasure at the thought that he was her first and only lover?

His throat grew dry as he continued to watch her. The red curtain of curls was swaying down her back, reminding him of the way he'd run his fingers through their wild abundance, and the hot punch of desire which had hardened his groin now became almost unendurable.

Yet she was pregnant. His skin grew cold with a nameless kind of dread—a different kind of dread from the one he had experienced in the lawyer's office. She was carrying his child.

And in view of what he had learned today—wouldn't any child which had sprung from his loins have an unknown legacy?

He opened the bedroom door and saw the unmistakable opening of her lips as her roving gaze drank in the unashamed luxury of her surroundings and it was a timely reminder that, despite her innocence, she was still a woman. And who was to say she wouldn't be as conniving as all other women, once she got into her stride? 'I hope it meets with your satisfaction,' he drawled. 'I think you'll find everything in here you need, Tara.'

Did she recognise the cynical note in his voice? Was that why she turned a defiant face up to his?

'I'm only staying the one night, mind.'

He wanted to tell her that she was mistaken, but for once Lucas kept his counsel. Let her sleep, he thought grimly—and by morning he would have decided what their fate was to be.

CHAPTER SEVEN

TARA OPENED HER eyes and for a moment she thought she'd died and gone to heaven. She was lying in a bed—the most comfortable bed she'd ever slept in—in a room which seemed composed mostly of huge windows. Windows to the front of her and windows to the side, all looking out onto the fairy-tale skyline of New York. She blinked as she levered herself up onto her elbows. Like giant pieces of Lego, the tall buildings soared up into the cloudless October sky and looked almost close enough to touch. Sitting up properly, she leaned back against the feathery bank of pillows and looked around some more—because last night she'd been too dazed and tired to take in anything much.

It was…amazing, she conceded. The ceiling was made of lacquered gold, the floors of polished parquet, so that everything around her seemed to gleam with a soft and precious life. On an exquisite writing desk stood a vase of pure white orchids so perfect that they almost didn't look real. And there, in one corner of the room, was her battered old suitcase, looking like a scruffy intruder in the midst of all this opulence.

She flinched.

Just like her, really.

Lucas must have put a glass of water on the bedside table and she reached out and gulped most of it down thirstily. On slightly wobbly legs she got out of bed and found the en-suite bathroom—a monument to marble and shiny chrome—and, after freshening up and brushing her hair, thought about going to find Lucas. She needed to talk about returning to Ireland and he needed to realise that she meant it and he couldn't keep her here by force. But her legs were still wobbly and the bed was just too tempting and so she climbed back in beneath the crisp sheets and before she knew it was dozing off.

She was woken by the sensation of someone else being in the room and her eyelids fluttered open to find Lucas standing beside the bed, staring down at her. His jaw was unshaven and the faint shadows shading the skin beneath his vivid green eyes made it look as if he hadn't had a lot of sleep. Black jeans hugged his narrow hips and long legs and his soft grey shirt was unbuttoned at the neck, offering a tantalising glimpse of the butterscotch-coloured skin beneath. Tara swallowed. It should have felt weird to have her one-time boss standing beside her bed while she lay beneath the duvet wearing nothing more than a baggy T-shirt, but somehow it didn't feel weird at all.

This is my new normal, she thought weakly. The same normal which was making her breasts sting with awareness as her gaze roved unwillingly over his powerful body. *Because this man has known you intimately,* she realised. *Known you in a way nobody else has ever done.* She felt a clench of exquisitely remembered desire, low in her belly, and before she could stop them vivid images began to flood her mind as she remembered how it felt to encase him—big and hard and erect. Despite everything she'd been brought up to believe, it hadn't felt shameful at all. It had felt *right*. As if she hadn't known what it really meant to be alive and to be a woman—until Lucas Conway had entered her and she'd given that little gasp as brief pain had morphed into earth-shattering pleasure.

Her heart was thumping so hard she was afraid he might notice its fluttering movement beneath her T-shirt and so she sat up, her fingers digging into the duvet, which she dragged up to a deliberately demure level, just below her chin. Only then was she ready to give him a cautious nod. 'Good morning.'

He returned the nod but didn't return the sentiment. 'Did you sleep well?'

'Very well, thank you.'

'Good.'

They stared at each other cautiously, like two strangers forced into close proximity. Tara cleared her throat, wishing she could get rid of the sense of there being an unexploded time bomb ticking away unseen in one corner of the room. But maybe that was what babies really were. She forced her attention to the pale sunlight which splashed over the wooden floor. 'Is it late?'

'Just after eleven.'

'Right.' Her fingers didn't relax their hold on the duvet. 'I need to start thinking about leaving—and it's no good shaking your head like that, because I don't work for you any more, Lucas. You can't just tell me no and expect me to fall in with your wishes, just because that's what I've always done before.'

His eyes narrowed and she saw the hard light of the practised negotiator enter them, turning them into flinty jade colour. 'I wouldn't dream of laying down the law—'

'You've had a sudden personality change, have you?'

He completely ignored her interjection, and didn't respond to the humour which was intended. 'We need to talk about where we go from here,' he continued. 'Just hear me out, will you, Tara?'

Once again she shifted awkwardly but the movement didn't manage to shift the syrupy ache between her thighs, which was making her wish that he would tumble down on top of her.

And where did that come from?

Since when had she become so preoccupied with sex?

She swallowed.

Since the night Lucas Conway had introduced her to it.

With an effort she dragged her thoughts back to the present, wondering why he was talking so politely. He must want something very badly, she thought, instantly on her guard. 'Okay,' she said.

He traced his thumb over the dark shadow at his jaw, drawing her unwilling attention to its chiselled contours. 'Would you like coffee first?'

'I'm not drinking coffee at the moment, thank you. I've already had some water and I think you're playing for time. So why don't you just cut to the chase and tell me what's on your mind, Lucas?'

Lucas's jaw tightened with frustration. It was easy to forget that she'd been working for him and sharing his house for years. Longer than he'd lived with anyone at a single stretch—and that included his parents. But despite the relative longevity of their relationship, Tara didn't really *know* him—not deep down. Nobody did. He made sure of that because he'd been unwilling to reveal the dark emptiness inside him, or the lack of human connection which had always made him feel disconnected from the world. Now he understood what had made him the man he was. He'd been given a kind of justification for his coldness and his lack of empathy—but that was irrelevant. He wasn't here to focus on his perceived failings. He was here to try to find a solution to an unwanted problem.

'You don't have any family, do you, Tara?'

She flinched. 'No. I told you at my interview that my grandmother brought me up after my mother died, and my grandmother has also since passed.'

Lucas nodded. Had she? He hadn't bothered probing much beyond that first interview, because if you asked someone personal questions, there was always the danger they might just ask them back. And Tara had impressed him with her work ethic and the fact that, physically, he hadn't found her in the least bit distracting. *What a short-sighted fool he had been.*

Because the truth was that she was looking pretty distracting right now—with those wild waves of hair bright against the whiteness of the pillow and her amber eyes strangely mesmeric as they surveyed him from beneath hooded eyelids.

'Why don't you put some clothes on?' he said, shooting the words out like bullets. 'And we'll have this discussion over breakfast.'

'Okay.' Tara nodded, not wanting to say that she didn't feel like breakfast—just relieved he had turned his back and was marching out of the room, wanting to be free of the terrible *awareness* which had crept over her skin as his green gaze had skated over her in that brooding and sultry way.

After showering and shrugging on an enormous bathrobe, she found him drinking coffee in the wood-panelled dining room—another room which was dominated by the Manhattan skyline and she was glad of the distraction.

'I can't believe the size of this place,' she said, walking over to the window and looking down at a green corner of what must have been Central Park. 'Why, even the bathroom is bigger than the hostel Stella and I stayed in last Christmas!'

'I'm not really interested in hearing how you saw New York on a budget,' he drawled. 'Just sit down and eat some breakfast, will you?'

As she turned around Tara was about to suggest it might do him good to stay in the kind of cramped accommodation which *most* people had to contend with, but then she saw a big trolley covered with silver domes which she hadn't noticed before. On it was a crystal jug of juice, a basket covered by a thick linen napkin, and on a gilded plate were little pats of butter—as yellow as the buttercups which used to grow in the fields around Ballykenna. She'd thought she wasn't hungry but her growling stomach told her otherwise and she realised how long it had been since she'd had a square meal. And she'd been sick last night, she reminded herself.

She walked towards the trolley to help herself but Lucas stayed her with an imperious wave of his hand.

'No. I don't want you collapsing on me again,' he instructed tersely. 'Sit down and I'll serve you.'

Tara opened her mouth to tell him she was perfectly capable of serving herself, but then a perverse sense of enjoyment crept over her as he offered cereal and eggs, fruit and yoghurt, and she sat there helping herself with solid silver spoons. Because if she allowed herself to forget her awful dilemma for a moment, this really *was* role reversal at its most satisfying! The food was delicious but she ate modestly, a fact which didn't escape Lucas's notice.

'No wonder you always look as if a puff of wind could blow you away,' he observed caustically. 'You don't eat enough.'

She buttered a slice of toast. 'My book on pregnancy says little and often if you want to try to avoid nausea.'

'Just how many books on pregnancy are you reading just now?'

'As many as I need. I know nothing about motherhood and I want to be as well prepared as possible.'

Wincing deeply, he sucked in a lungful of air. 'You say you want this baby—'

'I don't just *say* it. Lucas—I mean it,' she declared fiercely. 'And if for one moment you're daring to suggest—'

'I wasn't suggesting anything,' he cut across her, his expression darkening. 'And before you fly off the handle, let me make my views plain, just so there can be no misunderstanding. Which is that I'm glad you've chosen to carry this child and not...'

'Not what?' Tara questioned in bewilderment as his mouth twisted.

'It doesn't matter,' he snarled.

'Oh, I think it does.' She drew in a deep breath, putting her napkin down and realising almost impartially that her fingers were trembling. 'Look, we're not the same as we used to be, are we? We're no longer boss and employee.' She looked at him earnestly. 'I'm not sure how you'd define our relationship now—the only thing I'm sure about is that we're going to be parents and that means we need to be honest with each other. I'm not expecting you to say things you don't mean, Lucas, but I am expecting you to tell me the truth.'

The truth. The words sounded curiously threatening as they washed over him and Lucas stared at her. For a man who had spent his life denying and concealing his feelings, her heartfelt appeal seemed like a step too far and his instinct was to stonewall her. Yet he recognised that this was like no other situation he'd ever found himself in. He couldn't just buy himself out of this, not unless he was prepared to throw a whole lot of money her way and tell her that he wanted to cut all ties with her and his unborn child for ever.

He would have been a liar if he'd said he wasn't tempted...

But how could he do that, given the bitter reality of his own history which had been revealed to him by that damned lawyer? Wouldn't that mean, in effect, that he was as culpable as his own mother had been?

And look how that had turned out.

'Have you given any thought to how you see your future?' he demanded.

Tara shook her head. 'Not really. Have you?'

'Finish your breakfast first.'

But Tara's mouth felt dry with nerves and it was difficult to force anything else down, especially under that seeking green gaze—and she noticed he hadn't touched anything himself except two cups of inky coffee. 'I've finished,' she said, dabbing at her lips with a heavy-duty linen napkin.

He placed the palms of his hands on the table in front of him, looking like a man who meant business. 'So,' he said, his emotionless gaze still fixed on her. 'It seems there are several options available to us. We just have to work out which is the most acceptable, to both of us.'

Tara nodded. 'Go ahead,' she said cautiously. 'I'm all ears.'

He nodded. 'Obviously I will provide for you and the baby, financially.'

'Do you want me to do a dance of joy around the room just because you're accepting responsibility?'

His frown deepened. 'It's not like you to be quite so…irascible, Tara.'

Tara didn't know what irascible meant but she could guess. Should she tell him her crankiness stemmed from fear about the future, despite his offer of financial support? Surely even Lucas could work that out for himself. She studied the obdurate set of his jaw. Maybe that was hoping for too much. He was probably thinking about his own needs, not hers. And suddenly she realised that she couldn't afford to be vulnerable and neither could she keep second-guessing him. She was responsible for the life she carried and she needed to be strong.

'Why don't we just stick to the matter in hand?' she questioned coolly. 'Tell me what you have in mind.'

Was he surprised by her sudden air of composure? Was that why he subjected her to a look of rapid assessment? It was a look Tara recognised all too well. It was his negotiating look.

'You have no family and...neither do I,' he said slowly. 'And since I'd already made plans to stay in New York for the next few months, I see no reason to change those plans, despite the fact that you're pregnant.'

She thought how cleverly he had defined the situation, making it sound as if the baby had nothing to do with him. But perhaps that was exactly how he saw it, and Tara certainly wasn't going to push him for answers. She was never going to beg him, not for anything. Nor push him into a corner. 'Go on,' she said calmly.

'You could stay here and return to Ireland in time for the birth,' he continued. 'That would free you from unwanted scrutiny—or the questions which would undoubtedly spring up if you went back home.'

And now the surreal sense of calm she'd been experiencing suddenly deserted her. Tara could feel colour flooding into her cheeks as she pushed back her chair and sprang to her feet, her hair falling untidily around her face. 'I see!' she said, her voice shaking with emotion as she pushed a thick wave over her shoulder. 'You're trying to hide me away in a country where nobody knows me! You're ashamed of me—is that it?'

'If there's any shame to be doled out, then it's me who should bear it,' he retorted, though he seemed mesmerised by her impatient attentions as she brushed away her unruly hair with a fisted hand. 'I was the one who took your virginity!'

Was it her pregnancy which made Tara feel so volatile? Which made her determined to redefine his view of what had happened that fateful night, because didn't his jaundiced summary of events *downgrade* it? Or was it simply that she had carried the burden of shame around for a whole lifetime and suddenly the weight was just too much to bear? 'I wasn't some *innocent victim* who just fell into the arms of an experienced philanderer,' she declared.

'Thanks for the uplifting character reference,' he said drily.

'That wasn't how it happened,' she continued doggedly. 'That night we were just...'

'Just what, Tara?' he prompted silkily.

She stared down at her bare feet for a moment before lifting her heavy-lidded gaze to his. 'We were just a man and woman who wanted each other and status didn't come into it—not yours, nor mine,' she whispered. 'Surely you're not going to deny that, Lucas?'

Lucas was taken aback by her candour and surprised by his response to it, because an emotional statement like that would usually have made him run for the hills. Maybe it was the naïve way she expressed herself which touched something deep inside him—something which unfurled the edges of the cold emptiness which had always seemed such an integral part of him. For a moment he felt almost...*exposed*—as if she were threatening to peel back a layer of his skin to see what lay beneath. And no way did he wish her to see the blackness of his soul.

So that when his groin grew rocky it felt almost like

a reprieve, because wasn't it simpler to allow desire to flood him? To let lust quieten all those nebulous feelings he hadn't addressed since leaving the lawyer's office and which had been compounded by the bombshell Tara had dropped in his lap soon afterwards? He looked at the wild spill of her hair and her sleepy amber eyes. The towelling bathrobe she had pulled on was swamping her slender body in a way which should have been unflattering, but it only seemed to emphasise her fragility and suddenly he knew he wanted her again and he didn't care if it was wrong. Because the worst had already happened, hadn't it—what else could possibly eclipse the prospect of unwanted fatherhood?

Slowly yet purposefully, he walked across the dining room towards her and now her cat-like eyes weren't quite so sleepy. Their pupils had dilated so they looked night-dark against her pale skin.

'Lucas?' she questioned faintly. 'What do you think you're doing?'

'Oh, come on, Tara.' His voice dipped. 'You're a clever woman. Surely you've got *some* idea.'

He saw her touch her tongue to her mouth. Heard the sigh which escaped from her lips and a heavy beat of satisfaction squeezed his heart as he met her hungry gaze. He reached out and pulled her into his arms and instantly she melted against him, the quick tilt of her face silently urging him to kiss her.

So he did.

He kissed her for a long time—long enough for her to start wriggling distractedly, in a way which only stoked his growing desire. He covered her lips in kisses, then turned his mouth to her throat, loving the way her head fell back to give him access to her neck and revelling in the way her thick hair brushed so sensually against his hand. He undid the robe and bent his head to kiss her tiny breasts, flicking his tongue hungrily over her thrusting nipples. And when her hips circled in wordless plea against his aching groin, he inched his fingers up her thigh. Up over the silken surface of her skin he stroked her until at last he found her tight little nub and began to play with her and she was begging him not to stop. Until she was letting him back her up against the dining-room table and he was seriously thinking about sweeping all the crystal and silver and breakfast remains to the floor—and to hell with the mess—when he drew back and looked down into her dazed face.

'Let's go to bed,' he growled, his hands on her shoulders now.

Tara's throat constricted. Her breasts were aching and the syrupy heat between her thighs was making her wish he'd start touching her there again. She wished he hadn't stopped. That he'd just carried on with what he'd been doing and ravished her right there, in the dining room. She might have only had sex once before, but she badly wanted to do it again. She wanted to be carried along on an unstoppable tide of passion like the first time—she didn't want to have to make a *decision* about her actions.

But that was naïve—and short-sighted. She couldn't regard sex like candy—something she could just take when she felt like it. Not when there were so many issues they still hadn't addressed. Wouldn't that be totally irresponsible? There were a baby and a future to think of.

And without that baby she wouldn't be here in his arms like this, would she? She would be back home in Ireland while Lucas carried on with the rest of his life without her.

'No,' she said, shrugging his hands from her shoulders and taking a step backwards, even though her quivering skin still seemed to bear the delicious imprint of his fingers. With firm fingers she pulled the front of her robe together and knotted the belt tightly. 'This is not going to happen.'

His expression told her he didn't believe her. To be honest, she couldn't quite believe it herself.

'Are you serious?' he demanded.

'That's the whole point, Lucas,' she said, and suddenly her voice acquired a note of urgency as she stared into his beautiful face. 'I am. Very serious. I mean, what precisely are you offering mc here?'

The flattening of his mouth told its own story. A cynical indication that he now found himself on familiar territory—that these were female demands being thrown at him, something which had been happening all his life. 'I should have thought it was perfectly obvious what I'm offering you, Tara,' he said. 'Sex, pure and simple. Because the bottom line is that we still want each another—surely you're not going to deny that?'

No. She couldn't deny what was obviously the truth—not when her nipples were pushing insistently against her robe, and his frustrated gaze indicated that their silent plea hadn't gone unnoticed.

'So why not capitalise on that?' he continued, with silky assurance. 'Stay with me here in New York and be my lover?'

The passing seconds seemed to drag into minutes as his words sank in. 'Your lover?' she verified slowly, thinking it was an inaccurate description when there was no actual *love* involved.

'Sure. It makes perfect sense. I can make sure you look after yourself and we can enjoy some pretty incredible downtime.' He gave a slow smile as his gaze travelled to the tiny pulse which was hammering at her neck. 'What's not to like?'

The fact he had to ask was telling, but Tara reminded herself that Lucas had never been known for his sensitivity to other people's feelings. She told herself he wasn't trying to insult her, or hurt her—he was just doing what he always did and taking what he wanted. And right now he wanted sex.

Perhaps if she'd been a different kind of woman she might have agreed. If she'd been worldly-wise she might have smiled contentedly and sealed the deal in the master bedroom of this luxury hotel suite. But not only was she inexperienced, she was also afraid. Afraid she would read more into physical intimacy than Lucas ever intended. Afraid of falling under his spell as she'd seen so many other women do and then being heartbroken when he tired of her, as inevitably he would. After all, this passion had happened so suddenly—it was likely to end just as abruptly, even if he hadn't already had a track record for short-lived affairs.

She still knew so little about him. He was the father of her child yet she didn't have a clue what his own childhood had been like, because he'd never told her. Just as he hadn't told her what—if any—role he wanted to play in their baby's life. Wasn't the sensible thing to do to stay here and address all these issues in a calm and collected way? Not let desire warp her judgement and threaten to turn her into an emotional wreck.

'Yes, I will stay here,' she said slowly and then, before he could touch her again and make her resolve waver, she started backing towards the door. 'But not as your lover, although I will continue to be your housekeeper.'

'My...housekeeper?' he repeated blankly.

'Why not? That was the role you originally offered me, before—'

'Before you spent the night in my bed?' he growled.

'It wasn't the whole night, Lucas. I left shortly after two a.m., if you remember.' She cleared her throat and forged on. 'If you're moving into an apartment you'll need someone in post here and nobody knows the job better than me. It'll allow us to get to know one another better and to think about what's best for the future.'

'Wow,' he said sarcastically. 'That sounds like fun.'

She told herself afterwards that he could have tried to persuade her otherwise, but he didn't. Of course he didn't. Maybe he was already having second thoughts. As he stood silhouetted against the Manhattan skyline, he seemed to symbolise cool, dark composure—while she felt churned-up, misplaced and frustrated.

'I'd just like us to be honest with each other. You know. Open and transparent. Surely that's not too much to ask?' But her voice was a dying croak and her cheeks burning hot, as she turned away from his mocking gaze and fled from the dining room.

CHAPTER EIGHT

'TARA.' LUCAS SUCKED in an impatient breath. 'What the *hell* do you think you're doing?'

A bright clump of hair was falling untidily into her eyes as the apartment door swung open and Tara stepped inside, dumping two bulging bags of groceries on the floor right by his feet.

'I'm bringing home the shopping,' she answered. 'What does it look like I'm doing?'

With a snort of something which felt like rage, Lucas picked up the bags and carried them into the kitchen, aware that she was following him and that his temper was building in a way which was becoming annoying familiar. He waited until he had planted the hessian sacks in the centre of the large table before turning round to confront her. She could be so stubborn! So infuriatingly hard-working! Maybe it had been a mistake to move out of the luxury hotel and into a place of his own, so that Tara could resume her housekeeper duties—especially if she was going to keep up this kind of pace. But she had insisted, hadn't she? Had set her lips in a firm and determined line, and Lucas had found himself going along with her wishes.

'You shouldn't be carrying heavy weights,' he objected.

'Two bags of shopping is hardly what I'd call heavy. Women in rural Ireland have been shifting far more than that for centuries.'

'But we aren't *in* rural Ireland!' he exploded. 'We're in the centre of Manhattan and there are plenty of services which will have stuff delivered right to your door. So why don't you use one of them?'

'What, and never go outside to see the day?' she retorted. 'Cooped up on the seventy-seventh floor of some high-rise apartment block so that I might as well be living on Mars?'

'This happens to be one of the best addresses in all of New York City!' he defended, through gritted teeth.

'I'm not disputing that, Lucas, and I'm not denying that it's very nice—but if I'm not careful I'll never get to see anyone and that's not how I like to live. I've discovered an old-fashioned Italian supermarket which isn't too many blocks away. And I like going there—I've become very friendly with the owner's wife and she's offered to teach me how to make real pasta.'

Remembering the Polish restaurant she'd taken him to in Dublin what now seemed like light years ago, Lucas silently counted to ten as Tara began putting away the groceries.

'At least you seem to be settling in okay,' he observed, watching her sweater ride up to show a narrow white strip of skin as she reached up to put some coffee beans in the cupboard.

'Indeed I am, though it's certainly very different from life in Ballykenna. Or Dublin, for that matter.

But it's not so bad.' She pushed tubs of olives and fresh juice into the refrigerator and bent to pick up a speck of something from the granite floor. 'And the people are the same as people everywhere.'

There was a pause as he watched her tuck an errant wave of hair behind her ear, which somehow seemed only to emphasise its habitual untidiness.

'You know, you're really going to have to do something about your appearance,' he said.

Her shoulders stiffened and, when she turned round, her amber eyes were hooded. 'Why?' she demanded suspiciously. 'What's wrong with it?'

He made a dismissive movement towards her outfit—a gesture provoked by frustration as well as disbelief that his life had been so comprehensively turned upside down by one annoyingly stubborn woman. He still couldn't get his head round the fact that she was pregnant, and not just because it was such an alien concept to a man who had never wanted a child of his own. It was compounded by the fact that she didn't look pregnant yet—and her body was as slim as it had ever been. Not that he'd seen any of it, he thought moodily. Not since that first morning, when they'd very nearly had sex on the dining-room table, before she'd had second thoughts and pushed him away.

What woman had ever refused him?

None, he thought grimly. Tara Fitzpatrick was the first.

The painful jerk at his groin punished him for the erotic nature of his thoughts, yet for once he seemed powerless to halt them. They'd been living in close proximity for almost three weeks yet not once had she wavered in her determination to keep their relationship platonic. He shook his head.

Not once.

At first, he'd thought her stand-off might be motivated by pride, or a resolve to get some kind of commitment from him before agreeing to have sex again, despite her defiant words about not wanting marriage. He'd thought the undoubted sizzle of chemistry which erupted whenever they were together would be powerful enough to wear down her defences. To make her think: what the hell? And then give into what they both wanted.

But she hadn't. And hadn't he felt a grudging kind of respect for her resilience, even if it was making him ache so badly every night?

Perhaps it was that frustration which had made him go out and find this apartment. Tara had been complaining that with fleets of chambermaids and receptionists and waiters, there was nothing much for her to do at the hotel—so he had ordered Brandy to come up with some more rental places for him to look at. Eventually she had found a penthouse condominium on West Fifty-Third Street, a place which had caused even his jaded palate to flicker with interest as Brandy had shown him and Tara through each large and echoing room. Eight hundred feet above the ground, the vast condo had oversized windows which commanded amazing views over park, river, city and skyline. There was a library, a wine room, a well-equipped gym in the basement and a huge pool surrounded by a vertical garden. Most women would have been blown away by the undeniable opulence and upmarket address.

But Tara wasn't like most women, he was rapidly coming to realise. She had been uncharacteristically quiet when he'd given her an initial tour of the building. He'd watched her suspiciously eying Brandy and she had then proceeded to exclaim that he couldn't possibly be planning to live in a place that size. He remembered the shock on Brandy's face—probably worried she was about to lose her commission. But that was exactly what he was planning to do, he had explained. In New York you needed to display the trappings of success in order to be taken seriously, and luxury was the best way in which to go about it.

'Wealth inspires confidence,' he'd told her sternly afterwards, but she had shrugged as if she didn't care and he thought she probably didn't.

'You still haven't told me what's wrong with my appearance!' Her soft Irish brogue voice broke into his thoughts as she closed the door of the refrigerator and, plucking her navy-blue overall from a hook on the back of the door, began to shrug it on.

He stared at her. Where did he begin? Aware of the volatility of her mood—something he guessed had to do with fluctuating hormones—Lucas strove to find the right words. 'In Ireland you used to cook dinner whenever I had people over, and I'd like to be able to entertain here, too. In fact, I've arranged to hold a small dinner next week.' He jerked his head towards the impressive vista of skyscrapers. 'Show off the view.'

'It sounds as if there's a "but" coming,' she observed as she did up the last button of her uniform.

Lucas sighed. Maybe there was no easy way to say this. 'That...that thing you insist on wearing,' he said, his gaze sweeping over the offending item and noticing for the first time that her breasts seemed a little bigger than before and that the material was straining very slightly across the bust. A pulse hammered at his temple. 'It's not really very suitable for serving guests.'

'But you never complained when I wore it in Dublin!'

'In Dublin, you came over as someone mildly eccentric—while here you're in danger of being classified as some kind of screwball.'

'Some kind of screwball,' she repeated, in a hollow voice. 'Is that what you think?'

He wasn't surprised to see her face whiten but he was surprised how uncomfortable it made him feel. 'No, it's not what *I* think and it wasn't meant to be an insult, Tara,' he amended hastily. 'Anyway, there's a simple solution.'

'Oh, really?' she said moodily.

'Sure. You can go shopping. Get yourself some new clothes. It's fixable. I'm happy to pay for whatever it takes.'

He thought that a man might reasonably expect to see a woman's eyes light up at the prospect of a lavish buying expedition when someone else was paying. But Tara failed to oblige. He could see her biting her lip and for one awful moment he thought she was going to cry and that made him feel oddly uncomfortable. Her face screwed itself up into a fierce expression but when she spoke, her voice was quite steady.

'Whatever it takes,' she repeated. 'You're saying you want me to buy new clothes to make sure that I look the part—whatever the part is?'

'That's one way of looking at it.' He flicked her unruly curls a glance. 'And maybe you could do something about your hair while you're at it.'

She drew herself up very straight. 'So what you're really saying is that you want to make me look nothing like myself?'

'That's a rather dramatic summary of what I just said, Tara. Think of it as making the best of yourself for once.'

'You certainly seem to have been giving it some thought.' Suddenly that fierce look was back. 'Yet you didn't even bother asking me what the doctor said when I went to see him yesterday, did you, Lucas?'

Lucas met the accusation in her eyes, his body growing tense. He knew he was still in denial about impending fatherhood. That he was doing what he always did when confronted with something he didn't want to deal with, or which caused him pain. He blocked it. Locked it away. Stored it in a dark place never to be examined again. But you couldn't keep doing that when there was a baby involved. No matter how much he tried to pretend it wasn't happening. He kept thinking that one morning he was going to open his eyes and discover that he was the same Lucas as before, one with no ties or commitments.

And that was never going to happen.

And lately he'd been experiencing the occasional flicker of curiosity—uneasy little splinters of thought which spiked away at him at the dead of night when he lay in bed, aching for Tara. He kept remembering the final line of the letter written by the woman who had subjected him to a life of misery. His mother. Except that she was *not* his real mother, despite the fact that she had spent her life pretending to be. Surely no real mother would have treated their child with such disregard and cruelty. And surely no real mother would have tried to justify their behaviour with the flimsiest of excuses. His mouth hardened with contempt. She had done it because she was desperate for the love of a man who didn't really want her. Because she had put her desire for Diego Gonzalez above everything else, hopelessly pursuing it with single-minded determination which had pushed her adopted son into the shadows. And that was what people did for *love*, he summarised bitterly as he processed the accusation Tara had just thrown at him. They manipulated and they lied.

'Okay. Tell me. What *did* the doctor say?' he said.

But his dutiful question seemed to irritate her more than please her and she answered it like someone recounting the words by rote. She and the baby had been pronounced perfectly healthy, she told him tartly, and she had been booked in for a scan the following week. Her eyes had narrowed like a watchful cat. 'Perhaps you'd like to accompany me, Lucas?'

'We'll see,' he said, non-committally, pulling back the cuff of his shirt to glance at his watch. 'I have a meeting scheduled, so I'd better run. And in the meantime, do you want to organise yourself a shopping trip?'

Tara met the faintly impatient question in his eyes and tried to tell herself he wasn't being unreasonable, though in her heart she wasn't sure she believed it. But then, she was mixed up and confused and out of her depth in so many ways. Frightened about the future and unsure about the present. Every morning she awoke to a slew of different emotions but she'd refused to let them show, knowing that bravado was the only way of surviving this bizarre situation.

Her feelings about Lucas didn't help and she thought how much easier it would be if she didn't want him so badly. If only she could blind herself to the certainty that he could break her heart. She sighed, because in many ways she couldn't fault him. He had accepted her demand for no intimacy with composure and then hadn't she driven herself half mad wishing he hadn't accepted it *quite* so calmly? Perhaps she'd imagined he would come banging on her door at night, demanding she let him in. Or just walk in without asking, slide in between her sheets and take her into his arms. And wasn't there a big part of her that wished he *would* adopt such a masterful role and take the decision right out of her hands?

But no. He'd found this apartment within walking distance of Central Park—with the assistance of the intimidating Brandy—and had booked her in to see a wonderful obstetrician in Lexington, who had immediately made her feel at ease. In some ways their familiar working pattern had simply been transferred to a brand-new setting, except that here she had no bicycle because even she had to concede that in New York it was too dangerous.

Yet despite their superficial compatibility, she recognised that he was still a stranger to her. Despite that one-off night of intimacy, she knew no more about Lucas Conway than when they'd been living in Dublin. Back then it hadn't been relevant—but now she was carrying his baby and it was. Didn't she have the *right* to know something about him?

'If I agree to smarten up my appearance to fit in with your billionaire image…' she hesitated, lifting her gaze to his '…will you agree to do something for me?'

His green gaze was shot with cynicism. 'Ah. This sounds like bargaining territory to me.'

'Maybe it is—but that's irrelevant. Because I know nothing about you. Do you realise that, Lucas? You're the father of my baby and yet you're practically a stranger to me…' As her words tailed off she heard a trace of vulnerability in her own voice. Did he hear it too? Was that why his face darkened? But he relented, didn't he? Even if he did clip out the words like bullets.

'What do you want to know?'

Everything. But Tara sensed that if she asked for too much, she would get nothing at all.

'What was in that letter?' she questioned suddenly.

'The letter?' he said, and she knew he was playing for time.

'You know very well which letter. The one you received just before you came out here.'

The one which made you act so strangely and look so haunted.

She hesitated and said it exactly as it was. 'Which made you look so angry. Who was it from, Lucas?'

It was then that Lucas realised just how much Tara Fitzpatrick *did* know about him. Probably more than any other living person. His mouth hardened. But that was the thing about having a housekeeper. You thought they just existed in the shadows of your life. You thought they were there simply to enable things to run smoothly—but in reality they were watching you and listening to you. Absorbing all the comings and goings like a detached observer. And although her pregnancy meant Tara could no longer be described as detached—didn't that make her entitled to know the truth?

A truth he had firmly locked away. A truth he had never talked about with anyone before.

His throat dried as he looked into the soft question in her eyes and suddenly he found himself wanting to confide in her—to share the ugly facts with someone. 'It was from my father's...' His mouth twisted as he said the word. 'His attorney.

'Your *father*?' She blinked at him in surprise.

He nodded. 'He died a few months back.'

'You never said—'

'Well, I'm saying now. There was no reason to tell you before,' he said. 'And before you look at me with that reproachful gaze—I didn't go to his funeral because I hated him and he hated me.' He paused for a moment, long enough to get his breathing under control but he could do nothing about the painful clench of his heart. 'They found a letter from my mother among his belongings. A letter addressed to me, which I never received, even though it was written a long time ago, just before she died. But it seemed she didn't have the sense or the wherewithal to give it to her own lawyer. She entrusted it to her husband, which was a dumb thing to do because he kept it all this time and I only got to hear about it after his death.'

Her face creased with concentration as if she was trying to piece together a puzzle of facts. 'So is New York where you were born?'

He shook his head, his laugh bitter as, unwittingly, she asked the most pertinent question of all. 'It's where I grew up. I don't know where I was born because last week I discovered that my mother and father weren't my real parents.'

'You mean...' she frowned again '...that they kept that fact hidden from you?'

'Yes, they did. Though there's a more accurate way of putting it. They lied to me, Tara. All through my life they lied.' He saw her wince. 'Because they couldn't bear to tell me the truth.'

'And was the truth so very awful?' she whispered.

'Judge for yourself.' There was silence for a moment before he shrugged, but his shoulders still felt as if they were carrying a heavy weight. 'The woman I called my mother was in her forties when she married a man who was decades younger. She was a hugely wealthy heiress and he was a poor, good-looking boy from Argentina—who happened to have a pretty big gambling habit. Her Alabama family cut her off when she married Diego and the two of them moved to Manhattan. In her letter she explained that he wanted a child but her age meant she was unable to give him one.' He gave a bitter laugh. 'So she did what she'd spent her whole life doing. She tried to solve a problem by buying her way out of it. That's when she bought me.' He gave a bitter laugh. 'My mother bought me, Tara. But when the deal was done she discovered that having me around wasn't the quick solution to her troubles she thought I would be. She'd bought me, but she didn't want me and neither did Diego. Suddenly I was in the way and a child isn't as easy to dispose of as one of the fancy sports cars my father loved to drive.'

And Tara stared at him dumbly, in horror and in shock.

CHAPTER NINE

'YOUR MOTHER *BOUGHT* YOU?' Tara demanded, eventually getting her voice back. 'She actually paid money for you?'

'She did.' His jaw tightened. 'I guess the illegal trade in selling babies has always gone on and back then it was pretty unregulated. She found someone who was willing to part with their infant child—for the right price, of course.'

'I can't believe it,' she breathed.

But Lucas seemed to barely hear her. It was as if having bottled it up—that he could do nothing to now stop the words spilling bitterly from his mouth.

'A child's memory only kicks in fragmentally,' he continued harshly. 'But I gradually became aware of the fact that he seemed to resent me from the get-go and then to hate me—only I could never understand why. It couldn't have helped that he obviously felt trapped in a marriage to a woman he clearly didn't love—only he loved her fortune too much to ever walk away.' But that hadn't lessened the tension, had it? His mother sobbing and kneeling on the floor in front of her younger husband, begging him not to leave her. And Diego gloating like a boastful schoolboy about the lipstick she'd found on his collar. Lucas snapped out of his painful reverie to find Tara staring at him, her eyes like two amber jewels in her pale face.

'What…happened?' she whispered.

He shrugged. 'They sent me away to boarding school in Europe to get me out of the way. And when I came home for the holidays…' he paused and maybe admitting this was the hardest part of all, harder even than the sharp blows to his kidneys '…he used to beat me up,' he finished, on a rush.

'But, surely he couldn't get away with something like that?'

'Oh, he was very careful. And clever, too. He only used to mark me where it wouldn't show.' He heard her sharp intake of breath and she opened her lips as if to say something, but he carried on—wanting to excise the dark poison which had lived inside him for so long. 'The summer I realised I could hurt him back was the last summer I ever came here and that's when I broke all ties with them.'

'But what about your mother?' she breathed. 'Do you think she was aware that Diego was cruel to you?'

He gave a cynical laugh as he gazed at her with weary eyes. 'Do you really think it's possible for a woman not to know when a child is being beaten within the home, even in a house as big and cold and dysfunctional as ours?'

'Oh, Lucas.' Her bottom lip had grown pinker from where she'd been worrying it with her teeth and he saw the genuine consternation on her face. 'That's terrible. I can't—'

'I didn't tell you because I wanted your sympathy, Tara.' Ruthlessly, he cut across her faltered words. 'I told you because you asked and because you of all people now have a right to know. Maybe now you can understand why I started a new life for myself and left the old one far behind. When my mother died my father was such a gambler it wasn't long before there was no money left to pay for my schooling in Switzerland, so at sixteen I got myself a job as a bellhop in a fancy Swiss hotel—'

'So that bit was true,' she interrupted wonderingly before offering an explanation to the frowning question in his eyes. 'There were rumours swirling around Dublin that you'd been a bellhop but I couldn't ever imagine you doing a job like that.'

For the first time, he smiled—and the rare flash of humour on his troubled face made Tara's heart turn over with an emotion she didn't dare analyse.

'You'd be surprised at what a comprehensive education it was,' he said. 'I watched and learned from all the customers who'd made money and a couple of them gave me advice on how to make it big. When I got to Ireland I changed my name and that changed everything. I worked hard and saved even harder and I had a little luck sprinkled over me on the way.' He gave a short laugh. 'Though maybe I deserved a little luck by then.'

But Tara didn't seem interested in the details about how he'd made his fortune. Instead she was frowning with intensity, as she did when she was trying to work something out, often a new recipe.

'I guess you did.' She hesitated. 'But going back to the letter.'

'I thought we'd moved on from the letter.'

Seemingly undaunted, she continued. 'Was there any information about your birth mother in it?'

'I know her name.'

'And have you…have you followed it up?'

'What do you think?' he snapped.

'Don't you think you might? I mean, you might have…' She shrugged. 'Well, you might have other relatives who—'

'I'm not interested in relatives,' he said coldly. 'I've had it with family. Surely you can understand why? And I don't want to talk about it any more.'

He stared at her almost resentfully, wanting to blame her for having unburdened himself like this, but the hard stir of his groin was making him think about something other than the past. The flood of desire was a welcome antidote to the pain which had resulted from his confession and had left him feeling as if someone had blasted him with an emotional blowtorch. And now he was empty and hurting inside. Did she sense that? Could she detect the hunger in his body which was demanding release? Was that why she walked over to where he was standing and wordlessly hooked her arms around his neck, pressing her face against his cheek and planting there a kiss so soft that it made his heart turn over with something nameless and unfamiliar? Something underpinned with danger, despite all its dark deliciousness.

He wanted to push her away and compose himself but his need for her was stronger than his need for equilibrium and he pulled her into his arms and held her close. His heart pounded. So close. The faint scent of her sex was already redolent in the air and something inside him melted as instantly as ice hitting hot water. Their gazes clashed for the nanosecond it took before their lips fused and they shared the most passionate kiss he could ever remember. And when there was no breath left in his lungs, he reluctantly drew his head away, his eyes silently asking her a question and she answered it with a silent nod. This time she didn't call a halt to what was happening as he laced his fingers in hers. Instead, she let him lead her to the master bedroom, where he pulled the navy-blue ribbon from her hair and all those unruly waves tumbled around her shoulders with fiery profusion.

'Lucas?' she said, and he heard the uncertainty in her voice—as if wanting him to define what was happening. But he couldn't. Or rather, he wouldn't. He would never lie about his feelings for her. This didn't go deep. It was one level only. Simple physical need. 'I want you,' he said, very deliberately. 'That's all.'

Tara sucked in a ragged breath, wondering if it could be enough. But it had to be enough, because nothing else was on offer. And surely she could be grown up enough to admit that she wanted him—unconditionally. Surely she wasn't demanding words of love or commitment in order to enjoy sex with the father of her baby. Her mouth dried. Some people might say they'd already made progress in their relationship because he'd confided in her—something which had never happened before. He'd told her the awful truth about his upbringing—which made even her own seem less bad. Should she have filled him in on some of her own, awful personal history? She thought not. Not then and certainly not now when he seemed to need her very badly, and all she wanted was to bring a little comfort and joy into his life. Hers, too. Was that so wrong?

'I want you, too,' she said shakily.

'But before we go any further, there's one thing we need to get straight, which is that I'm not offering undying love, or certain commitment. I can't put my hand on my heart and promise to be with you for the rest of my life, Tara,' he emphasised harshly. 'Because that's not what I do. You know that.'

She shook her head. 'I don't care.'

She could see his throat constrict as he undid the buttons of her uniform before quickly dispensing with the T-shirt and jeans beneath. And when he began to tug impatiently at his silk shirt, she found herself fantasising about what their baby might look like when it was born. Would it be a boy? she wondered yearningly as he lifted her up and laid her down on the bed. A boy who would grow up to be like his father—charismatic and powerful but with a dark side which was hiding so much pain? Or would it be a redheaded little girl, destined to be swamped by her own insecurities?

But her questions were forgotten as his naked body was revealed to her—all honed muscle and soft shadow and the subtle gleam of olive skin. His limbs were hair-roughened and his desire was achingly obvious and she should have been daunted but she wasn't. She stared at him with longing as the bed dipped beneath his weight and when he took her in his arms again, his skin felt deliciously warm against hers. Was it the conversation they'd just had which suddenly made Tara feel less of a conquest and more of an equal? Which gave her the courage to explore his body in a way she would never have dared do before? Tentatively at first but with growing assurance, she stroked his skin, her fingertips running over washboard abs, down over the flat hardness of his stomach, to whisper shyly at the dark brush of hair beyond.

'Tara?' he said softly.

'What?'

'Don't keep doing that.'

'You don't like it?'

'I like it too much,' he growled.

'What...what shall I do instead?'

He gave a soft laugh. 'Part your thighs for me.'

She lifted her head as she did exactly that, their gazes clashing as, very deliberately, he slipped his hand between her legs and began to finger the creamy-moist folds with a light touch which sent a wild shudder through her body.

'L-Lucas,' she breathed.

'Shh... Don't say a word. Just feel it. Feel what I'm doing to you. It's good, isn't it?'

'Y-yes. It's very good.'

With delicate precision he strummed her where she was wet and aching, until she was writhing helplessly on the mattress and making unintelligible little gasps. Sensation speared at her with each feather-light touch as he propelled her towards some starry summit, so that she felt like an unexploded firework which was hurtling though the sky. And when the eruption came, he entered her at the same moment—so she could feel herself still clenching around his hardness as their bodies were intimately joined. It felt exquisitely erotic and unexpectedly emotional and as she looked up into the dark mask of his beautiful face, she touched her fingertips to his cheek.

'Lucas,' she said shakily, trying to bite back the soft words of affection which were hovering on her lips.

He stilled as he searched her face. 'It doesn't hurt?'

'No. It's…it's gorgeous.'

'I've never done it without protection before,' he husked. 'Never.'

She couldn't respond to his appreciative murmur because her eager body was short-circuiting her addled brain, making rational thought impossible as a second orgasm swept her up on a breathless wave. In fact there was no time to address his question until afterwards, when he had choked out his own pleasure and she could feel the sticky trickle of his seed running down her thigh in a way which felt deliciously intimate. Her heart was pounding and her skin was suffused with satisfied heat, but she forced herself to turn over to face the Manhattan skyline outside the window as she tried to get her muddled thoughts into some kind of order.

Because she could sense she was on the brink of something risky. Something which needed to be reined in and controlled. Yes, they'd just had the most amazing sex but in the middle of it hadn't Lucas gloated about never having had unprotected sex before while she'd been getting all emotional about him? And that was the fundamental difference between them. He required sex and nothing more and so she needed to be vigilant about her emotions. To make sure she didn't get sucked into a bubble of love and longing which would burst at the slightest provocation.

'Tara,' he said softly.

His finger was tracing a delicate path between her buttocks and she felt herself quiver in response. 'What?' she questioned, as casually as possible.

'I suspect what we've just done has made you change your mind about us being lovers.'

His assurance was as unshakable as his arrogance and she wanted to tell him that, no, she hadn't changed her mind at all. She wanted to declare that this had been another impetuous mistake which mustn't be repeated. But she couldn't keep running away from the consequences of her actions, could she? She couldn't keep letting sex 'happen' and then act like a scared little girl afterwards.

What she wanted was impossible. Like most people she wanted what she'd never had—in her case a secure home and a child raised within a loving family—despite all her proud protestations to the contrary. Lucas had offered none of these things and, having heard about his own childhood, she could understand why. It didn't matter that his parents hadn't been his birth parents—what mattered was that they had lied and been cruel to him. His whole upbringing had been built on a web of deceit and had destroyed his trust in other people. No wonder he was such a commitment-phobe who had never wanted marriage. No wonder he sometimes seemed to view women as the enemy, because to him they were. His birth mother had sold him and his adopted mother had lied to him and condoned her husband's violence towards him.

But he'd offered to support her and the baby, hadn't he? He hadn't said he wanted to be hands-on, but surely that was a start—a single block on which to build. She didn't know what the future held—nobody did—but there was no reason why they couldn't have a grown-up relationship within certain boundaries. Just so long as she didn't start weaving unattainable fantasises—and maybe for that reason alone, she needed to maintain an element of independence.

So she turned over and touched her fingertip to his face, tracing it slowly along the outline of his sensual lips. 'Yes, I'll be your lover,' she said. 'But I'm not going to give up my role as housekeeper.'

His eyes narrowed. 'Are you out of your mind?'

'Not at all. I need to work and that's my job. Otherwise, what am I going to do all day while you wheel and deal—go out to lunch and have my nails painted?' Her smile was serene as she met his disbelieving expression and she wouldn't have been human if she hadn't enjoyed that small moment of triumph. 'I've never had any desire to be a kept woman, Lucas, and I don't intend to start now.'

CHAPTER TEN

SUNLIGHT CAME STREAMING in through the huge windows, bathing Tara's body with a delicious glow, though the only thing she was really aware of was Lucas's hand, which was splayed proprietorially over one breast, while the other was tucked possessively around her waist. But possessive was a misnomer and any sense she *belonged* to him was simply an illusion, she reminded herself fiercely. The touchy-feely-couldn't-seem-to-keep-his-hands-off-her side of his character was just another feature of the fantastic sex they'd recently enjoyed. A physical reaction, that was all.

He was lazily stroking her nipple so that it was proud and aching, even though she had just gasped out one of the shuddering orgasms which had become so much a part of her daily life. Yet the crazy thing was that the man beside her felt as much of a stranger as he'd ever done—despite having told her about his childhood and despite having just been deep inside her body. Had she hoped that physical intimacy would automatically morph into mental intimacy? That the bond between them would grow stronger—maybe even unbreakable—the longer they spent together wrapped in each other's arms like this?

Yes, she had. Guilty on all counts. But what did she know about such matters when he was her first and only lover? Her mentor, too. In the most delicious way possible, he had tutored her in every aspect of sex. He'd taught her how to uninhibitedly enjoy her body and not to be shy about expressing her needs, but none of that seemed to have impacted on their relationship. Despite the physical closeness of sharing their bed each night and the often teasing banter they enjoyed much as before, nothing fundamental had changed within their relationship. Emotionally, at least, he was as detached as he had ever been.

Was that because, in spite of his obvious disapproval, she'd insisted in maintaining her role as his housekeeper—thus reinforcing the boss/employee dynamic which had always existed between them? She didn't think so. What else was she going to do all day if she wasn't cooking and cleaning—lie around in some cliché of a negligee waiting for Lucas to return from one of his business meetings? She would go out of her mind with boredom if she did that. Anyway, she didn't have a negligee—cliched or otherwise—because somehow she still hadn't got around to the shopping trip Lucas had suggested she take to avoid looking like 'a screwball'.

'Are you awake?' His murmured voice was soft against her hair.

Her thoughts still full of fundamental insecurities, Tara nodded. 'Mmm...'

The bedclothes rustled as he shifted, turning her round to face him so that their eyes were level and Tara prayed her face didn't give away her feelings. Feelings she was trying desperately hard to hide, because she knew Lucas was no stranger to the emotion she and countless women before her had experienced...

She was falling for him. Falling deep and falling hard.

She was scared to use the word *love* but it was the only one which seemed appropriate to describe the see-sawing of her feelings and the great rush of joy which powered her heart whenever he walked into the room. When he kissed her she sometimes felt she could faint with pleasure and when he made love to her, her happiness threatened to spill over. It didn't seem to matter how much she tried to deny what she was feeling, it made no difference. She wasn't sure how it had happened. If it was because he'd taken her innocence and made her pregnant.

Or because, beneath his glossy patina of success, he was wounded and hurting inside and that made her want to reach out to protect him?

He lifted a strand of hair and wound it slowly around his finger and Tara was reminded of one of those fishermen back home—the way they used to slowly reel in their catch, before leaving the floundering fish gasping for air on the quayside.

'You still haven't been shopping,' he observed.

'I know.' She shrugged her bare shoulders. 'But I haven't seemed to be able to find the time.'

'Then *make* the time, Tara. Better still. Why don't I schedule an appointment with a personal shopper and drop you off at Bloomingdale's? That way you won't be able to wriggle out of it the way you seem to have been doing.'

She blinked. 'What's Bloomingdale's?'

He frowned. 'You're kidding?'

'Lucas, this is a big city and I'm exploring it the best I can! I can't be expected to know every single name which trips off your tongue.'

'It just happens to be one of the best department stores in the city, possibly the world,' he commented drily. 'And I'll drop you off there tomorrow morning, on my way to work.'

'But we might not be able to get an appointment so soon,' she objected.

His brief smile managed to be both dismissive and entitled. 'Don't worry about that,' he drawled as he parted her thighs with insistent fingers. 'We'll get one. You haven't forgotten that you're cooking dinner for six on Friday, have you?'

'No, Lucas. I haven't forgotten. I've been racking my brains to come up with a menu for days.' She swallowed. 'And you doing that to me isn't exactly helping me work out what to give them for dessert.'

'Damn the dessert,' he growled.

But by the following morning Tara felt sick with nerves at the thought of presenting herself to a professional stylist, horribly aware of the plainness and age of her bra and pants and wishing she could skip the whole ordeal. Because it turned out that Lucas had been right and there were any number of slots available for a man like him at short notice.

Reluctantly, she joined him in the back of his car, which then proceeded to get snarled up in the early-morning traffic. It was stop-start all the way and Tara started to feel even more queasy. 'It's very stuffy in here.'

'I'll turn up the A/C.'

'I don't want any more air-conditioning. I want to get out and walk,' she croaked.

He shot her a quick glance. 'Are you okay?'

'I will be when I'm outside in the fresh air.'

'Fine. Come on, I'll walk you there.'

'Honestly, there's no need. I can find the store perfectly well on my own and I don't want you to be late for your meeting.'

'Tara,' he said patiently, his voice underpinned with a hint of impatience. 'It's pointless objecting. I'm taking you there. End of discussion.'

He tapped the glass and spoke to his driver, then helped Tara out of the car. She saw a glamorous woman blinking at her in bemusement as she stepped onto the sidewalk in her sweatpants and trainers, swamped by a big old anorak she'd brought with her from Dublin. But it was great to be outside, despite the stationary traffic and ever-hooting cars. As Lucas fell into a steady walk beside her, she thought how well he seemed to know the streets and when she remarked on this, he shrugged.

'I grew up near here.'

'Whereabouts?'

'It doesn't matter.'

'I think it does.' She came to a sudden halt and a speed-walking man who was holding a cup of coffee above his head had to swerve to avoid her. 'I'd like to see where you lived, please.'

Lucas bit back an exasperated retort, but he altered his steps accordingly, making no attempt to hide his displeasure. If it had been any other woman than Tara he would have refused point-blank. He would have delivered a rebuke which suggested that unless she started behaving as he wanted her to behave, their relationship would be over. But it wasn't any other woman. It was Tara and she was pregnant and therefore he could never completely finish a relationship with her because, one way or another, they would be tied through their child for the rest of their lives. He wondered if she had any idea how much that terrified him or if she'd begun to guess at the self-doubts which flooded through him. Was that why there had been a subtle shift in her mood lately? Why she'd become unpredictable and emotional. Had it just dawned on her that he could never be the man she probably wanted him to be? Why, only yesterday when he'd arrived home, her eyes had been red-rimmed from crying and she'd been unwilling to provide an explanation of what had upset her. It was only later that she'd blurted out about hearing a radio request show playing 'Danny Boy', after which she'd been overcome by a wave of temporary homesickness.

Deep down, he knew their situation was untenable in its current form. That in just over six months' time she would give birth to his child and everything would change. He realised that she wanted reassurance he would be there for her, and in the important ways he would. Providing for her financially was always going to be simple—but giving her the emotional support he suspected she needed was not. Why promise to be the man he could never be? Why bolster her hopes, only to smash them and let her down? Surely it would be kinder to let her know where she stood right from the start.

His footsteps slowed as he reached Upper East Side, his heart clenching as he came to a halt outside an opulent mansion which was edged by elegant railings and neatly trimmed greenery. Outwardly, it seemed that very little had changed. There were still those two old-fashioned-looking streetlights he'd used to stare down on from within the echoing loneliness of his childhood bedroom.

'This is it,' he said reluctantly, his gaze lifting upwards to the four-storeyed building.

'Gosh,' breathed Tara, loosening her long scarf as she craned her neck to look up at it. 'It's massive. You must have rattled around in it like peas inside a tin can.'

He gave a bitter smile. 'Oh, I don't know. Furniture and objects can occupy an astonishing amount of space and it's amazing what you can do with nineteen rooms and an unlimited budget. Especially when someone else is paying for it.'

'Nineteen rooms?' she verified incredulously. 'In New York?'

He nodded. 'The dining room was modelled on the one at the Palace of Versailles and there's a hand-painted ballroom with a pure gold ceiling—not to mention a corridor wide enough to ride a bicycle down.'

'Is that what you used to do?'

'Only once,' he said flatly. That had been the first time his 'father' had hit him. His nanny—one in a long line of indifferent women in whose care he'd spent most of his time—had spotted the bruise when he was getting ready for bed, readily accepting his explanation that he'd acquired it after falling over. Later he'd discovered that the nanny in question had been sleeping with Diego. He'd overheard an indiscreet maid exclaiming that the woman had been discovered naked with him on the floor of the library, a litter of used condoms beside them. All he could remember about that particular incident had been his mother screaming. And then sobbing as she had dramatically stabbed at her wrists with a blunt blade which had refused to cut.

Tara stared at him. 'You must have felt very isolated there. My own...' she ventured hesitantly, before plucking up the courage to say it. To reassure him that her own life hadn't been all roses around the cottage door. Well, it had—but there had been very sharp thorns on those roses. 'My own childhood was pretty isolated. In fact, my grandmother—'

'Look, I really don't have time for this,' he said, with an impatient narrowing of his eyes as he glanced at his watch. 'And I have an imminent meeting. The city tour is over and so is the glimpse into my past. Come on, let's get you to Bloomingdale's—it's only ten minutes' walk away.'

His dismissive attitude hurt. It hurt far more than it should have done, but that was a result of her own stubbornness—not something *he* had done. Because Lucas was just behaving in the way he'd always behaved. How many times did he need to say it for her to finally get the message that he wasn't interested in deepening their relationship? He didn't *want* to know about her past. What had made her the person she was. What had made her happy and what had given her pain. She was someone he was forced to spend time with because of the baby and someone he liked having sex with, but that was as far as it went.

So put up or shut up, she told herself fiercely as Bloomingdale's came into view—with all the different flags fluttering in the autumn breeze and a quirkily dressed brunette called Jessica waiting for them. After initial introductions, she gave Tara a thorough once-over before fixing her with a warm smile and turning to Lucas.

'Don't worry, Mr Conway. She's in good hands.'

Lucas gave a brief nod. 'Thanks. Just do what it takes. I'll be back tomorrow night in time for dinner, Tara. Okay?'

Tara nodded and thought how crazy the whole situation was. Right up until they'd left the apartment that morning they'd been hungrily exploring each other's bodies—yet now, in the cold and clear light of day, she was expected to give him a cool farewell, as if she meant nothing to him.

Because she didn't.

'Right,' said Jessica, turning towards Tara as Lucas's car pulled away from the kerb. 'Let's get this fairy dust working.'

It was an experience Tara had never thought could happen to someone like her. Pushing all her troubled thoughts resolutely from her mind, she felt positively Cinderella-like as Jessica led her through all the plush and beautifully lit departments, which were perfumed with all manner of delicious scents. She'd been planning to purchase only a modest wardrobe but it seemed Lucas had forewarned the personal shopper this might be the case because she was overruled in pretty much everything.

'I've never owned a shirt like this before,' she observed wonderingly, running her fingertips over the delicate fabric. 'I'll save it for best.'

'Ah, but you'll need more than one,' responded Jessica, with a smile. 'Which means you won't have to.'

In the space of a couple of hours, Tara went from being someone who'd never owned a single silk shirt, to someone who now had several. For the snowy New York winter she snuggled into an oversized metallic anorak, its hood lined with shaggy faux fur, which Jessica told her was fresh off the runway, while for more formal occasions came a mid-length coat in midnight blue, the warmest coat Tara had ever worn. An accompanying cobalt scarf was plucked from a rainbow selection and Jessica's gaze travelled ruefully to the overly long home-knit, which lay abandoned on a nearby chair like a large and neglected woollen snake. 'You might want to find that another home,' she suggested gently.

Tara felt a momentary pang before being persuaded into the first of many dresses—slinky shirtwaisters and soft knits which Jessica said emphasised her slim frame. Next came boots—long boots and ankle boots—plus a pair of trendy shoes with lace inserts to go with a swingy chiffon shirt and boxy denim jacket. There were exquisite embroidered bras and matching thongs, as well as T-shirt bras with more practical pants. And Tara felt momentarily overwhelmed as she acknowledged that it had been Lucas's murmured appreciation which had made her revel in her own body instead of being ashamed of it. He'd never moaned about the state of her underwear, had he? Not really. He'd always been more concerned in taking it off than complaining about how faded it was.

She blinked away the sudden tears which had sprung to her eyes as she tried on the jeans which were an entirely different breed from the baggy ones which had always been her mainstay. Fashioned from soft and stretchy denim, they hugged her bottom but allowed for future expansion, though there was still no visible sign of a pregnancy bump. She wanted to tell the shopper that in a few months' time none of these gorgeous outfits would fit—but she could hardly start telling her personal business to a complete stranger, could she?

'It's been a pleasure doing business with you, Mrs Conway,' said Jessica as the session drew to a close.

Tara shook her head—despairing at her instinctive pang of yearning at the thought of being Lucas's wife. *It's because your own mother was never married,* she told herself. *Nor her mother before that. You're just secretly craving the respectability you never had, which made your own childhood such a misery. But things are different these days and nobody cares if a child is born out of wedlock.* 'I'm not Lucas's wife,' she said calmly. 'I'm actually his housekeeper—and I was wondering if you happen to sell aprons here?'

To Jessica's credit, she didn't look a bit fazed by what have been an unusual request. 'Of course,' she said. 'Come with me.'

The morning ended with a rock-star experience at the hair salon, where Tara sipped cinnamon-flavoured latte as large chunks were hacked from her curls. The result was...well, unbelievable, really—and several of the stylists had clustered around the mirror to say so. Her hair looked just as thick as before but it was more... manageable somehow. Little fronds framed her face and, where layers had been chopped into it, the colour seemed more intense and the texture more lustrous.

She was aware of heads turning as she left the salon in her brand-new jeans, pale jumper and the boxy denim jacket. And she'd never had that experience before. Of men's eyes following her as she slid into the back of the chauffeur-driven car which Lucas had ordered for her.

She remembered her grandmother's disapproval of fancy clothes—understandable given her own monastic upbringing, but a bit tough on a growing teenager who had been forced to wear second-hand outfits, which had only increased the amount of bullying she'd received.

The apartment was quiet and, since Lucas wouldn't be back until tomorrow, she had a whole day and a night without him. The only time she'd been on her own since she'd arrived here—which meant no distractions as she prepared for her very first dinner party in America. She looked down at the list of people he'd invited—an official from the Irish embassy and his wife, an Italian businessman named Salvatore di Luca and his girlfriend Alicia, and an 'unnamed guest' who seemed to have been added since last time she'd looked at it.

She wasn't going to deny that it was going to be weird serving Lucas and his guests and playing the role of servant, all the while knowing she would be sharing his bed once everyone had gone home. But surely it was better that way.

It had to be. Because if they stopped being lovers... She bit her lip and silently corrected herself. *When* they stopped being lovers, if the baby drove a wedge between them, or when he tired of her as history dictated he would—then surely it would be less traumatic not to have become used to being his partner in public, and then have that role wrenched away from her. Such a brutal change of circumstance would surely leave her feeling neglected, unloved and unwanted.

And hadn't she already experienced enough of those feelings to last a lifetime?

Smoothing down her pale cashmere sweater, she went into the kitchen, realising that she needed to get a move on with her planning. Without her stack of cookery books, she was forced to fire up her computer to look up some recipes online, but she scrolled through them uninterestedly.

Until suddenly she had a brilliant idea.

CHAPTER ELEVEN

THE FIRST THING Lucas heard when he walked through the door was the sound of music. His steps stilled and he paused to listen, even though he was running late. Irish music. Some softly lilting air which managed to be both mournful and uplifting at the same time—in the way of all Irish music. He frowned as he heard a peel of laughter which sounded familiar and then the chink of crystal, followed by more laughter.

With a quick glance at his watch he moved swiftly towards the library, quietly pushing open the door to see his guests standing with their backs to him, listening to something Tara was saying as she tilted a bottle of champagne into someone's glass.

He almost did a double-take as for a moment he felt as if the light were playing tricks on him, because the woman in question looked like Tara and sounded like Tara, and yet...

He screwed up his eyes.

And *yet*...

Surely that wasn't *Tara*?

Her hair was scooped on top of her head but for once there wasn't a riot of frizzy curls tumbling around her face. The sleek red waves were coiled like sleeping serpents—emphasising the slim, pale column of her neck. He swallowed, because her hair wasn't the only thing which was different. She was wearing a dress. And stockings. And... Again, he frowned. She had on some flirty little apron which made her look... She looked as if she was about to leave for a party where the specified dress code was Sexy French Maid. His groin grew rocky and he realised he didn't want to focus on her appearance, or the evening was going to become one long endurance test before he could take her to bed.

He realised his guests must have heard him for they were turning to greet him and as he apologised for his lateness he saw a wry look on Brett Henderson's face—because, as a world-acclaimed movie star and key member of British acting royalty, he wasn't used to being kept waiting.

But Lucas's somewhat garbled explanations about late planes and fog on the San Franciscan runway were cut short by a dismissive wave from the Irish Embassy official.

'Oh, don't you worry about that, Lucas—we've been fine here.' Seamus Hennessy beamed, and so did his wife, Erin. 'We're hardly missed you at all and Tara's been looking after us grandly, so she has!'

For the first time since he'd walked in, Tara turned to look at him and gave a shy smile, which contrasted with the sensual allure of her outfit, and Lucas was taken aback by the resultant shiver which rippled its way down his spine as he met her heavy-hooded amber gaze. He found himself wishing he could just dismiss the guests, skip supper and take her straight to bed—yet his need for her unsettled him.

'Do you all have drinks?' he questioned pleasantly. 'Good. Tara? I wonder if I could have a quick word in the kitchen.'

He didn't say anything as they left the library and neither did he comment as they passed the dining room, even though he could see she must have gone to a lot of trouble to lay the table for dinner. Unlit candles protruded from centrepiece swathes of fragrant greenery mixed with cherry-coloured roses, and all the crystal and silver was gleaming beneath the diamond shards of the overhead chandelier. He waited until they were in the kitchen and completely out of earshot before he turned on her and the feelings which had been growing inside him now erupted.

'What happened?' he demanded. 'You don't look like you!'

Faint colour stained her cheeks as she glanced down at her outfit before looking up again to meet his accusing gaze. 'You mean you don't like it?'

'I told you to buy yourself some new clothes,' he ground out. 'Not to look like the personification of every man's fantasy maid.'

She screwed up her face. 'It's an apron, Lucas!' she said crossly. 'And perhaps you ought to make your mind up about where you really stand! You were always criticising my old uniform for being too frumpy and now you're complaining that this one is too sexy!'

Confused, he shook his head. 'It's the way you wear it,' he said slowly.

'Or rather, the way you perceive it—which is your

problem, not mine. Make up your mind what it is you want because I haven't got the time or the appetite for this. And now, if you'll excuse me—' she lifted her chin in as haughty a gesture as he'd ever seen her use '—I really do need to get on with serving dinner.'

He wanted to reach out and stay her with a hungry kiss but something stopped him and it wasn't just pride. It was anger. And jealousy—and he didn't *do* jealousy or possession.

But the true and very bitter fact seemed to be that he *did*.

He forced himself to snap out of his foul mood and, since he often hosted dinners without a woman by his side, it shouldn't have been a problem. Seamus and Erin were easy company and Salvatore di Luca's latest squeeze worked for the United Nations and had some very illuminating things to say about the current political situation in Europe, which usually would have interested him. But for once he found his attention wandering and the biggest fly in the ointment was Brett Henderson flirting like crazy with Tara. And she wasn't exactly discouraging him, was she? Did she really have to simper like that as she told him how much she'd enjoyed the film in which he'd played a shape-shifting wizard?

Lucas was forced to watch as the mellifluous Englishman returned the love-fest by purring all kinds of compliments about his housekeeper's home-made lasagne.

'A really lovely woman in a nearby Italian store taught me how to make fresh pasta!' she was telling him proudly.

'What, here? In cynical old New York City?' joked Seamus.

'Tara has a particular naïve charm all of her own,' said Lucas coolly, and he couldn't miss the look of fury she directed at him as she brought out the tiramisu.

Eventually they all went home and Lucas tried to ignore the sound of Brett asking Tara for her email address. And it wasn't until Seamus and Erin had extracted a promise that the housekeeper would attend a ceilidh at the embassy that they finally took their leave.

The apartment seemed very big and very quiet as Lucas walked back into the library and found Tara clearing away glasses. 'Did you give Brett your email address?' he demanded.

'And if I did? Is that such a crime?' She straightened up to look at him and he had never seen such a look of quiet fury in her eyes. 'Unless you think...' She shook her head as if in disbelief. 'Unless you really think that I would encourage one man in a romantic fashion, when I'm in a physical relationship with another?'

Physical relationship. He didn't like the sound of that, but he supposed he couldn't doubt its accuracy. 'You were sending out all kinds of mixed messages tonight.'

'That's all in your head,' she retorted, bending towards the table once more. 'I was being friendly, that's all.'

'Leave that,' he said as she resumed putting crystal glasses onto a tray with such force he was surprised they didn't shatter.

'I'd rather do it now than in the morning.'

'I don't care—'

'No,' she interrupted suddenly and this time when she straightened up, the quiet fury in her eyes had been replaced with something stronger—something which blazed like fire. 'You couldn't have made that more plain if you'd tried! But maybe I'm fed up with the Lucas Conway approach to staff management! You taught me to cook something other than pie so I would be worthy of catering for your fancy guests and I ticked that off the list, didn't I? Then you decided to dress me up like one of those paper dolls you find in a child's magazine—and I went along with that, too. Heaven forbid that I should look like some screwball! But you're still not satisfied, are you, Lucas? And nothing ever *will* satisfy you, because basically you don't know yourself and you have no desire to learn about yourself, because you're a coward.'

The room went very silent. 'Excuse me?' he questioned, his words like ice. 'Did you just call me a coward?'

'You heard exactly what I said.'

Tara met his stony gaze and couldn't quite believe she'd done it but she couldn't back out now, no matter what the repercussions might be. Because she loved him and she wanted him to stop running away from his past—even if that meant the end of what the two of them shared. And even if it was, would that really be such a great loss? You couldn't really share anything with a man with no emotions, could you? A man who resolutely refused to allow himself to *feel* stuff.

'You can't live properly until you reconcile yourself with your past—and I don't think I can carry on like this until you do,' she breathed. 'Maybe you don't have any living blood relatives, but isn't that something which warrants a little investigation? Don't you want to know why your mother sold you? To find out who your real father is and whether either of them are alive? To discover whether she had any more children and if you have any brothers or sisters?' Her face suddenly crumpled. 'I know that when I—'

'No!' Furiously, he cut across her—the slicing wave of his hand a gesture of finality. 'I'm done with confessionals and I certainly don't want to waste any more of my evening listening to you, while you start unburdening your soul. To be honest, I'm tired, and I'm bored. I don't know how many times I've told you that I never wanted that kind of relationship and unless you can accept that, then I agree—we have no kind of future. So perhaps you might like to think about that. And now, if you'll excuse me—I'm going to bed. I'll see you in the morning.'

Tara's heart was pounding with shock as he turned and walked out of the library without another word. She could hear his footsteps going upstairs, along the corridor towards the master bedroom, and just for a moment she actually considered following him, until she drew herself up short.

Was she completely *insane*? He might as well have taken out a full-page ad in *The Washington Post*, saying, *Leave me alone*. He'd told her he'd see her in the morning, and he'd done it with that cold and condemning look in his eyes. That wasn't the action of a man who wanted to cuddle and make up—that was a man who had been pushed to his limits. He was angry with her— but not nearly as angry as she was with herself. How long was she planning to hang around and get treated like someone who didn't really matter? Because she *did* matter. Not just for her baby's sake, but for her own.

She crept along to the second bedroom, uncomfortably aware that this was only the second night they'd spent apart since they'd resumed their sexual relationship—and she thought how big and lonely the bed seemed without him. Predictably, sleep was a long time in coming and when it did, dawn was just beginning to edge into the sky because she hadn't bothered to close the drapes.

When she awoke, the apartment was completely silent and, quickly, she got out of bed, wandering from room to room looking for Lucas, knowing with a sinking sense of certainty that she wasn't going to see him. The lingering aroma of coffee and some juiced halves of orange were the only signs of his presence. He must have had breakfast and then left. She looked around to see if there was a note, but of course there wasn't. And a huge pang of stupid longing swept over her as she tried to imagine what it would be like if he *was* the kind of man who left little messages dotted around the place. Affectionate words or cartoons, scribbled onto Post-it notes and stuck to the front of the refrigerator or left lying on a pillow. But those things only happened in films. or between real-life couples who genuinely loved one another. He'd only ever left her a note once before—when he'd brought forward his New York trip after they'd slept together and he'd told her he'd give her a good reference!

Back then he couldn't wait to get away from her and she wouldn't be here now if that night hadn't produced a child. Lucas would have moved on. And so would she. She'd have found herself a job as housekeeper to someone else and would now be throwing herself enthusiastically into her new role. Perhaps the discovery that she could enjoy sex might have provided some hope for the future—making her wonder if one day she'd be able to enjoy dating men who were more suitable than Lucas Conway.

Her stomach turned over at the thought of being held in any other arms than his. It made her feel violently sick to think of any lover other than Lucas and the longer she allowed this situation to continue, the harder it was going to be to ever give him up. Because that time would come, most definitely—as surely as the sun rose over Manhattan each morning. They'd already had their first serious row and they'd both said some pretty wounding things. Maybe she should be grateful for his honesty. At least he wasn't encouraging her to build fanciful daydreams and maybe it was time she stopped trying to pretend that this relationship of theirs was going anywhere. Surely it would be better—for both of them—if they re-established the boundaries and negotiated a different kind of future. She swallowed, knowing that the only way to do that was to put distance between them.

For her to go home to Ireland. Back to where she belonged.

She cleared up the debris from the dinner party, then went into the en-suite wet room and stood beneath the cascading shower, trying to enjoy the moment, but the luxury products were wasted on her. She took extra time washing and drying her hair and even more time selecting what to wear. Which clothes to take and which to leave behind. She stared a little wistfully at the chiffon skirt and lace insert shoes; the silky dresses and impossibly fine cashmere sweaters. She loved those clothes—loved the way they made her feel—but they had no place in the life she was about to resume. So she took the shiny anorak, the jeans, the darker of the sweaters, the warmest dresses-as well as all of the underwear. Then she called a cab and checked she had money and her passport. It was only as she was leaving that she realised she couldn't just *go*—not without saying something. So she went slowly into the library where she picked up a pen and, with a heavy heart, began to write.

Lucas stared down at the note and a flare of something which felt close to pain clenched at his heart. But it wasn't pain, he told himself furiously. It was disappointment. Yes, that was it. Disappointment that Tara Fitzpatrick had just done a runner like some thief in the night. And after everything he'd done for her...

He tugged his cell-phone from his pocket and jabbed his finger against her number. It rang for so long that he thought it was going to voicemail, but then she picked it up and he heard that sweetly soft Irish brogue.

'Hello?'

'You're at the airport, I assume?' he clipped out.

'I am. I've managed to get the last seat on a flight which is leaving for Dublin in...' there was a rustle as, presumably, she lifted her arm to look at her watch '... twenty minutes' time.'

'So you're running out on me,' he said coldly. 'Without even bothering to tell me you were going. Now who's the coward, Tara?'

'No, Lucas,' she corrected. 'The cowardly thing to have done would be not to have picked up this call.'

He could feel control slipping away from him and he didn't like it, because hadn't his legendary control allowed him to make his world manageable? Hadn't taking command enabled him to rise, phoenix-like, from the ashes of his upbringing and forge himself a successful life? 'Why didn't you at least wait around until I was back from my meeting when we could have discussed this calmly, like grown-ups?' he demanded.

He heard a fractured sound, as if she was having difficulty slowing down her suddenly rapid breathing. But when she spoke she sounded calm and distant. Very distant. He frowned. And not like Tara at all.

'You once left me a note when you couldn't face having an important conversation with me. Do you remember that, Lucas? Well, it's my turn now—and I'm doing it for exactly the same reasons. I didn't want a protracted goodbye, nor to have to offer explanations, or listen to any more accusations. I don't want bitter words to rattle around in my brain and imprint themselves on my memory, when we need to keep this civilised. So I'll be in touch when I'm settled and you can see as much or as little of our baby as you want. That's all.' She drew in a deep breath before letting it out in a husky sigh. 'Don't you understand? I'm setting you free, Lucas.'

Something swelled up inside him like a growing wave—something dark and unwanted. How *dared* she offer him his freedom, when it was not hers to give? Did she consider him as some kind of puppet whose strings she could tug whenever the mood took her—just because she carried a part of him deep inside her? The dark feeling grew but deliberately he quashed it, because he needed to think clearly—his mind unobstructed by neither anger nor regret. Because maybe she was right. Maybe it *was* better this way. Better she left when things were tolerably amicable between them. Time and space would do the rest and once the dust had settled on their impetuous affair, they would be able to work out some kind of long-term plan. He would be good to her. That was a given. He would provide her with the finest home money could buy and all the childcare she needed. And he would...

He swallowed, wondering why his throat felt as if it had been lined with barbed wire which had been left out in the rain. Even if fatherhood was an unknown and an unwanted concept—that didn't mean he wasn't going to step up to the plate and be dutiful, did it? To be there for his child as his own father had never been there for him.

And if he found that impossible?

Why *wouldn't* he find it impossible, when he had no real template for family life? And wouldn't it then follow that he was probably going to let her and the baby down, somewhere along the line?

He swallowed as Tara's accusations came back to ring with silent reproach in his ears.

'Don't you want to know why your mother sold you? To find out who your real father is and whether either of them are alive? To discover whether she had any more children?'

His mouth hardened. No, he didn't want to know

any of those things. Why should he? In an ideal world he would have gone back to the life he'd had before. The one with no surprises. No analysis. No whip-slim woman challenging him with those sleepy amber eyes. But it wasn't that simple. Nothing ever was.

He cleared his throat. 'Just let me know when you get back to Dalkey,' he said coolly. 'And please keep me up to speed with your plans. I will return to Ireland in time for the birth.'

CHAPTER TWELVE

RAIN LASHED LOUDLY against the window and a gale howled like some malevolent monster in the dark night. In the distance Tara could hear trees creaking and the yelp of a frightened dog. She rolled over and shivered beneath the duvet, trying to breathe deeply, and, when that didn't work, to count backwards from one hundred. Anything, really, which would bring the oblivion and ease she craved in the form of sleep, if only for a few hours.

Because it was hard. She wasn't going to lie. If this was what being in love was like, then she wanted it out of her system as quickly as possible. The pain was unbearable. Pain like she'd never known. As if someone were inserting a burning poker into each ventricle of her heart. And the torture wasn't just causing physical pain—it was mental too, because the memory of Lucas was never far from her mind. It hovered in the background of her thoughts throughout every second of the day. The knowledge that he was no longer part of her life was like a heavy weight pressing down on her shoulders, so that most of the time she felt weary, even when she shouldn't have done.

She missed his face, his body, his banter. She missed being in his arms at night, wrapped in all that warm and powerful strength as he made love to her, over and over again. Angrily, she clenched her hands into two white-knuckled fists. Because that was a ridiculously romantic interpretation of what had taken place. They'd had amazing and exquisite sex, that was all, and presumably that was what he did with all the other women who had shared his bed—which perhaps made their dogged pursuit of him more understandable. She was the one who had elevated it to a level which was never intended, with her fanciful words of *love*. And in doing that, hadn't she followed the path of so many foolish women before her—her mother and her grandmother included? For the first time in her life, she acknowledged that Granny might have had a point in her often expressed and jaundiced view about men, as she'd waved her stick angrily in the air.

'I tell you, they're not worth it, Tara! Not a single one of them!'

But, outwardly at least, Tara was determined to present a positive face to the world. She made sure she looked after herself—exercising sensibly, eating regularly and faithfully keeping all her appointments at the hospital, who pronounced themselves delighted with her progress. She even continued to dress in the new style which had been shown to her so comprehensively in New York. She liked the way the new clothes made her feel. She liked the soft whisper of silk and cashmere against her skin and she liked wearing trousers which actually fitted her, rather than flapping around her legs. If she'd learnt one thing it was that her body was nothing to be ashamed of and that there was nothing wrong with wanting to take care of her appearance.

It was only at night, under the forgiving cloak of darkness, that she cried big salty tears which rolled down her cheeks and fell silently into her sodden pillow. That she ached to feel Lucas beside her again, even though in her heart she knew that was never going to happen. And each morning she awoke to sombre grey Dublin skies, which seemed to echo the bleakness of her mood.

But she was strong and she was resilient, and, once she'd adjusted to her new life, things began to improve. Or rather, once she'd accepted that Lucas wasn't going to suddenly turn up and sweep her off her feet—that was the turning point. She knew then she had to embrace the future, not keep wishing for something which was never going to happen. There was to be no fairytale ending. Lucas wasn't going to suddenly appear on the doorstep, his face obscured by a bouquet of flowers with a diamond ring hidden in his pocket. He'd told her he would be back for the birth—which was still four whole months away—which gave her plenty of time to erase him from her aching heart.

Aware that his Dalkey house held too many poignant memories, she began to bombard local employment agencies with her CV and quickly found a job—though not, as originally planned, in a big, noisy family. With a baby of her own on the way, she decided it was better to keep focussed on that. Her new position was as housekeeper to a couple of academics, in their big house overlooking Caragh Lake, in beautiful County Kerry. Dana and Jim Doyle had both sat in on her interview, where Tara had been completely upfront about her situation.

'I'm pregnant and no longer with the father of my child. I don't know if that's going to be a problem for you,' she'd blurted out, 'but he is providing generous financial support for us both.'

'So do you really *need* to work?' Dana had asked gently.

'No, but I've always worked.' Tara's reply had been simple. She was unable to imagine the long days stretching ahead without some kind of structure to them, terrified of all those hours which could be devoted to pining for a man who didn't want her.

How long before she stopped feeling this way? Before her body stopped craving his touch and her lips his kiss?

She emailed Lucas her new address and he sent an instant response, asking if she had everything she needed. The answer to that was obviously no and yet, for some reason, the question infuriated her. Why did people keep asking her what she *needed* when she had a warm bed, a roof over her head, and a secure job, which was a lot more than many people had? Her needs weren't the problem but her wants were.

She stared into the mirror.

She still wanted Lucas—wasn't that the most agonising thing of all?

Her hand moving down to her growing bump, she told herself that these feelings would fade. They *had* to fade—because everything did eventually. The bullying at school—once unendurable—had leached from her consciousness once she'd left Ballykenna. Even the reason for that bullying—all the shame surrounding her ancestry—had receded, so that she hardly thought about it any more. And that had come about because she'd made a determined effort to erase it from her mind.

So do that now, with Lucas, or you'll spend the rest of your life as a ghost of a person, longing for something which can never be yours.

Tara bit her lip.

He was the father of her child. Nothing else.

Her mouth firmed.

Nothing.

As he was driven through the sweeping Argentinian landscape, Lucas felt the pounding of his heart. It was pounding like an out-of-control speed train. As he got out of the car he became aware that his mouth was dry and recognised that this was the closest he'd ever come to fear. Or maybe it was just apprehension. Glancing up at the big sign which read Sabato School of Polo, he took a moment to realise that someone must have heard the sound of his car and a man was walking towards him.

The man's build was much like his own—long-legged, strong and muscular—though the thick tumble of dark hair was distinctly longer. He wore casual riding clothes and leather boots which were dull with dust—an outfit which was in marked contrast to Lucas's own bespoke linen suit. But as he grew closer, Lucas found himself staring into a pair of dark-lashed and slanting green eyes, so unnervingly like his, as were the chiselled jaw and high slash of cheekbones.

And now the pounding of his heart became deafening as he acknowledged who it was who stood before him. His older brother. He swallowed. His only brother. For a moment neither man said anything, just stared long and hard, their faces set and serious. Two powerful tycoons confronted by the bitter reality of their past, which had somehow merged into the present.

'Alejandro,' said Lucas eventually.

The man nodded. 'I've spent a long time trying to find you, Lucas,' he breathed slowly.

And that was the main difference between them, Lucas acknowledged. That his brother's deep voice was accented, its lilting cadence emphasising the Spanish of his mother tongue. Lucas felt his heart clench, realising that his brother had known their real mother, while he had not, and he felt a bitter pang he hadn't expected before replying to his brother's statement. 'I changed my name,' he said, at last.

Alej nodded and then smiled, expelling a long sigh of something which sounded like relief. 'Want to tell me about it? Over a beer maybe, or even a ride? I don't even know if you ride—how crazy is that?'

For the first time Lucas smiled as he chose the latter option, even though he hadn't been on a horse in a while and even though his brother was an ex-world-champion polo player who could outride most people. But for once, he wasn't feeling competitive and he didn't care if Alej outshone him in the saddle. He wanted clarity in which to confront the past—not alcohol clouding or distorting the things which needed to be said. He wanted to hear the facts as they were, no matter how much they might hurt.

And they did hurt. No two ways about it. He had thought he was prepared for the pain which might be awaiting him when he heard the full story of how he came to be adopted, but afterwards wondered if perhaps he'd been naïve. Because was anyone ever really *prepared* for pain? Intellectually you might think you knew what to expect, but on a visceral level it always hit you with a force which could leave you breathless.

Hacking out over the lush green pastures, they rode for a long time, sometimes talking, sometimes lapsing into thoughtful silences, until the sinking sun had begun to splash the landscape with coral and Alej turned to him.

'You must be thirsty by now. Think it's time for that beer?'

Lucas nodded. 'Sure do.'

As if by unspoken consent, they urged their mounts into a fierce gallop as they headed back towards the stables and Lucas was glad for the sudden rush of adrenalin which surged through his veins. Glad too that the rush of air dried the tears he could feel on his cheeks.

His brother's car was waiting to take them to Alej's *estancia*, where his wife Emily was waiting with their baby Luis, and Lucas stepped into the warm family home and felt a rush of something he'd never experienced before. Was it envy or regret? he wondered. Because as Alej lifted the squealing Luis high in the air and the beautiful Emily stirred something in a pot which smelt delicious, Lucas realised that he too could have had this. A home and a family. With Tara. The woman who had encouraged him to come here. Who had made him dare raise the curtain on his past and look directly into the face of his brother and his troubled ancestry.

He swallowed as Emily handed him a frosted bottle of beer.

He could have had all this.

And he had blown it.

He didn't sleep well that night, even though the bed was supremely comfortable and the steak which Alej cooked for dinner the best he'd ever eaten, especially as it had been served with Emily's delicious spicy vegetables. But in the days which followed, he was given a tantalising taste of the country of his birth. He grew to understand it a little and to like it enormously so that by the time it came to leave, he experienced a distinct pang as he dropped a kiss on the baby's downy head and hugged Emily goodbye. He didn't say much as Alej drove him to the airport. He didn't need to. He knew that something powerful had been forged between the two of them during the past week, a bond which had been severed so many years ago but which had somehow, miraculously, endured.

At the airport the two men embraced. Then Lucas took one last look at the sweeping mountains he could see in the distance and, somewhere in his heart, knew he'd be back. 'You know, you and the family must visit me in Ireland.'

'Por supuesto.'

Once again their gazes clashed with the sense of something unspoken. And then he was in the aircraft and clipping his seat belt before the private jet barrelled along the runway and soared up into the cloudless sky. For a while Lucas stared down at the retreating rooftops of Buenos Aires, before settling back in his seat.

It was a long flight but for once he couldn't concentrate on work matters—even though he was able to communicate with his assistant on the ground. And somewhat predictably, when the plane touched down in Dublin, it was to a grey and blustery day. He thought how tiny Ireland seemed in comparison to the sweeping landscape of the country he'd just left. A pulse was beating at his temple as he stared down at the email his assistant had sent him earlier and, slowly, he gave his driver the address. All during the car journey to Caragh Lake, Lucas was aware of the racing of his heart and sudden clamminess of his palms—as if his body were trying to keep him focussed on what his mind was trying so hard to resist. But the dark thoughts kept flapping back, like insistent crows.

What if he couldn't do this?

What if she didn't want him? Could he blame her if she didn't? His mouth hardened. And mightn't that be best? Wouldn't that guarantee her some kind of peace, even if peace was a concept he couldn't ever imagine finding for himself? Not now, anyway.

Despite its size, the big house wasn't easy to find, tucked away in a leafy lane and overlooking a beautiful lake. As Lucas lifted the heavy door knocker he could hear it echoing through the large house and it seemed to take for ever before he heard the approach of oddly familiar footsteps, and when the door opened he saw Tara standing there. His heart leapt. The new Tara. The one with the feathery soft hair which made her look so sleek.

She was blinking at him in disbelief. 'Lucas?'

He heard the strangled note in her voice but of far more concern was the sudden blanching of her skin and the way her eyes had widened. Because there was no welcome in their amber depths and no smile on her soft lips. And her next words compounded his thumping fears.

'What are you doing here?' she demanded.

'Isn't it obvious? I've come here to see you.'

'And now you have. See? And I'm fine.'

She went to push the door shut again but he held up the palm of his hand.

'Tara.' His voice softened. 'That's not what I meant and you know it.'

Her face had lost none of its suspicion. 'You didn't warn me you were coming.'

'I thought unannounced was better.'

'Better? Better for who? Yourself, of course—because that's the only person you ever think about, isn't it?' Her voice rose. 'Are you crazy, Lucas? Didn't you think it mightn't be suitable for you to just come *barging* in like this? I might have been cooking lunch for Mr and Mrs Doyle.'

He didn't feel it prudent to point out that he'd had one of his assistants find out when her bosses were attending a conference on marine science in Sweden, and had timed his flight to Ireland accordingly. 'And are you allowed no life of your own?' he questioned archly.

The corners of her unsmiling mouth lifted but not with a smile—more like a rueful acknowledgement of some grim fact. 'You're probably better qualified than anyone to answer that question, Lucas. But that's beside the point. Why are you here?' She sucked in a deep breath, her hand leaning on the door jamb. 'Why are you here when you told me that you'd be back in time for the birth and that's still sixteen weeks away, by Dr Foley's reckoning.'

For the first time Lucas allowed his gaze to move from her face to her body and he was unprepared for the savage jolting of his heart. She looked...

His throat grew dry. He'd never really understood the description 'blooming' when applied to a pregnant woman, mainly because such a field was outside his area of interest. But he understood it now. She was wearing an apron covering a woollen dress of apple-green, and he could see that her slender frame had filled out. There was more flesh on her bones and her cheeks were fuller and, if he ignored the faint hostility in her gaze—which wasn't easy—he could see a radiance about her which seemed to make her glow from within. But it was the curve of her belly which made his heart begin to race.

Hesitation was something unfamiliar to him but he could sense he needed to be careful about what he said next—more careful than he'd ever been in his life—because she was still prickling with hostility. 'I'm here because I need to speak to you. To tell you things that perhaps you need to hear.'

Tara flinched, trying to put a lid on the rush of emotion which was flowing through her body. Because this wasn't fair. He'd told her he would see her for the birth, which was months away—precious months when she was supposed to be practising immunity when it came to looking into his beautiful face, that shadowed jaw and those emerald-bright eyes.

But she couldn't tell him that, could she? If she

hinted that she couldn't cope with an unexpected visit from him, then wouldn't that make her appear weak?

She had no idea what he was about to say since she hadn't heard very much from him since she'd left America. For all she knew he might be about to announce that he'd finally met the love of his life, despite having vowed that he didn't *do* love. But stranger things had happened and some gorgeous New Yorker might have possessed just the right combination of beauty and dynamism to capture the billionaire's elusive heart.

And if that were the case, then wasn't it better to get it over with?

'You'd better come in,' she said grudgingly.

She was achingly aware of his presence as he followed her into the hallway, wishing her thoughts didn't keep going back to that first night, when it had all started. If only you could rewrite the past. If, say, she hadn't let Charlotte in that day, then none of this might ever have happened. But you couldn't rewrite the past and, anyway, would she really want to go back to the Tara she'd been back then? The unfulfilled misfit of a woman who'd never known real pleasure? And yes, the flip side to pleasure was emotional pain—unbearable pain for quite a while now—but you learnt through such experiences, didn't you? You learnt to cope and you became stronger—strong enough to handle an unscheduled visit from the man whose child you carried.

'Would you like coffee?' she questioned, expecting him to say no.

But Lucas never did what you expected him to do.

'Actually, I would. I've missed your coffee, Tara.'

'I don't want any of your old flannel.'

His gaze was cool and unabashed. 'It isn't flannel. I'm merely stating a fact. Though they brew some pretty amazing stuff in Argentina.'

She blinked. 'Argentina?'

'Why don't you make the coffee first?' he said gently. 'And then we'll talk.'

Her instinctive fury at his reversion to the dominant role was supplanted by a natural curiosity but, grateful for the chance to get away from the distraction of that piercing green gaze, Tara hurried from the room. She returned minutes later, hating herself for having first checked her appearance in the kitchen mirror, because it wasn't as if she wanted to impress him, was it?

He was standing with his back to her, looking down over the sweeping emerald lawn and, beyond that, the darker green of the trees, through which you could see the silver glimmer of the lake and, fringing those, the gentle hills of Ireland. Something poignant shafted at Tara's heart but she forced herself to suppress it, because she needed to keep calm.

He turned to face her and she could feel an annoying shiver of awareness but she quashed it. With a hostess-like air, she indicated that he should sit down and watched as he lowered his powerful frame into one of the worn velvet seats which the non-materialistic Dana Doyle had told her they'd had for years. And when she'd given him his coffee, just the way he liked it, Tara perched on a more upright chair opposite, not quite trusting her trembling fingers to hold the water she'd poured for herself.

'So,' she said, with a tight smile. 'What is it that you want to speak to me about, Lucas?'

She was unprepared for the sudden darkness which crossed his rugged features, like a black cloud suddenly obscuring the face of the moon. And for a look of something she'd never seen in his eyes before, something which on anyone else she might have described as desolation. But Lucas didn't do desolation and she wasn't here to analyse his moods or to try to get inside his head. This was a matter-of-fact meeting and he probably wanted to discuss financial support for her and the baby.

He stared down at the inky brew in his cup and put it down untasted, before lifting his gaze to hers.

'I took your advice,' he said simply. 'And went to Argentina.'

CHAPTER THIRTEEN

'You went to Argentina,' Tara repeated slowly.

He nodded. 'I did.'

There was a momentary pause. 'And what did you find there, Lucas?'

She was staring deep into his eyes, her expression as distant as ever he'd seen it, and Lucas wondered if coming here unannounced had been a crazy idea. But he owed her this. He owed her the knowledge which had first shocked and then saddened him. And he owed it to himself to discover whether he had messed everything up.

'I found my brother there,' he said simply.

'You have a brother?'

'I do. His name is Alej—Alejandro Sabato— and he has a family of his own. His wife is English and she's called Emily and they have a young baby, Luis.'

'That's nice,' she said stiffly.

He wanted to tell her about the terrible pain in his heart because he'd missed her so much, but old habits died hard and for the time being he sought refuge in facts. 'He'd actually been trying to find me, but because I'd changed my name his investigators kept coming up with blanks. Anyway, he was able to fill me in on everything I needed to know.'

Her gaze was still steady. 'Which is?'

He shrugged his shoulders, for there was no easy way to say this, no acceptable way of defining the harsh facts surrounding his conception. 'My mother was a prostitute and my father was one of her clients,' he bit out. 'A drunken thief who used to spend long periods in prison, and when he was released he would come out, beat her up and make her pregnant.'

She licked her lips and he could see a swallowing movement in her throat. 'So how did you come—?'

'To be brought up in one of the most expensive parts of one of the most expensive cities in the world?' he supplied, and she nodded. 'My mother had given birth to Alej just a year earlier and she was having enough trouble feeding one child, let alone another. So she decided to sell me. I suppose it made perfect economic sense. She went to see someone in Buenos Aires—someone who put her in touch with a rich American heiress—'

'Your mother?' she interrupted breathlessly.

'No!' he negated viciously. 'Wanda Gonzalez never earned the right to call herself that during her lifetime, so I'm damned sure I'm not going to honour her with that title now she's dead.' He gave a bitter laugh. 'She had specified that she wanted a birth mother from Argentina, so that I would resemble my "father" as much as possible.'

'And did you?' she questioned curiously. 'Resemble him, I mean?'

He shook his head. 'Not really. We had the same hair colour, but that was about it—I was bigger, stronger, more powerful.' He gave a short laugh. 'And that's how I came to be brought up amid such great wealth in Manhattan, while Alejandro lived a very different life in Argentina—that is, until he escaped from abject poverty to become one of the world's greatest polo players.'

'Alejandro Sabato,' she ventured slowly, with a nod of her flame-bright hair. 'Yes, I've heard of him.'

'I'm sure you have. He was a bit of a poster-boy for the sport in his time. But I haven't come here to talk about my brother, Tara.'

She became instantly alert. 'No?' she challenged.

He wanted her to make this easy for him. To soften her lips into a smile. To send him a soft, unspoken message with her eyes so he could get up and walk right over there. Pull her hungrily into his arms and kiss her as he'd dreamt of doing ever since she'd walked out of his New York apartment. Because if he started kissing her and they began to make love, surely it would blot away some of the pain.

But something stopped him and it was the sense that this was the biggest deal he'd ever tried to pull off and he couldn't afford to get it wrong. Yet getting it wrong was a distinct possibility, even though he knew how to wheel and deal in a boardroom. When to talk and when to let silence work for you. He knew about joint venture capital, about leasing out cars or lorries which people couldn't afford to buy themselves, but he knew nothing about telling a woman that he loved her. And wasn't that the crux of what he really wanted to say to her? The most important thing.

No. First up he needed to acknowledge what she had done for him. To tell her some of the things he had felt.

Still felt. 'I wanted to be angry with my mother and to blame her for the life into which I was born,' he whispered. 'And for a while I was. But then I realised that she'd taken a bad situation and tried to make it better. It can't have been easy to give me away, but she did. And she did it for me, so I wouldn't starve—and so that Alej wouldn't starve either. She probably thought she was giving me the best chance she could—she wasn't to know that Wanda was weak and Diego was cruel.'

'Lucas,' she said, and for the first time he could hear a softening of her voice and saw concern pleating her brow, as if she had detected his pain and wanted to soothe it away.

But he shook his head to silence her because he needed to say it, to let it all out so it could no longer gnaw away at him.

'I would never have found this out if you hadn't encouraged me to find my brother,' he said. 'You are responsible for that, Tara. For the bond I now have with my brother. For the discovery that I have a nephew and a sister-in-law. But when I saw that family of theirs it was like a dagger to my heart.'

'Lucas!' she said, as if she could hardly believe he was saying stuff like this, and wasn't there a part of him who could hardly believe it himself?

'I realised then that I had been given the opportunity to have a loving family—with you,' he said huskily. 'And because of my pride and arrogance and my cold and unfeeling heart, I had probably blown it. But I'm hoping against hope that I haven't blown it and I'm asking you to give me another chance because... I love you, Tara.'

She was shaking her head as if she didn't believe it, but the brief clouding of her eyes told him she didn't *dare* believe it and he knew he wasn't in the clear yet.

'I love your spirit and the way you answer me back,' he continued softly, and his eyes crinkled. 'Even although sometimes that trait makes me as mad as hell. I like the way you're loyal and true and that beneath your often prickly exterior there beats a heart of pure gold.' He swallowed. 'The first time I made love to you, it was like nothing I'd ever experienced. The way you made me feel was completely alien to me—'

She pursed her lips together. 'That's why you couldn't wait to dash away the next morning and fly to New York early?'

'Because it scared the hell out of me,' he admitted. 'It made me feel vulnerable, in a way I hadn't allowed myself to feel for years. And then, when I told you stuff I'd kept bottled up for so long and you comforted me with your arms and with your body...' He swallowed. 'You just rocked my world. You're still rocking it. Even now when I told you about my real mother and father, you just accepted it calmly. I was watching your face and you didn't seem appalled, or shocked. You didn't start expressing fears about what bad blood I may have being passed onto our baby.' He saw her flinch. 'Listen to me, Tara, I know I handled it badly but I didn't know at the time *how* to handle it. But now I do. I'm asking you to forgive me and telling you that since you've been gone my life seems empty. To tell you that I want to marry you and spend the rest of my life with you. To give our child love and security, as well as to each other. To create a family. A real family. The kind of family which neither of us has ever had before. That is…that is if you feel you could ever love me too. So what do you say, Tara Fitzpatrick?'

Right then Tara was finding it impossible to say *anything*, she was feeling so choked up. Because Lucas might not be carrying a big bunch of flowers and a diamond ring, but he *was* telling her he loved her and he was asking her to marry him.

But he still didn't know, did he?

He didn't know everything about her because she'd kept her own guilty little secrets. And although she'd tried several times to tell him about her past—hadn't she been quietly glad when he'd cut her short? Hadn't that given her the justification she'd needed to bury it even deeper—to act as if she were Tara Goody-Two-Shoes—in which case, perhaps *she* was the coward, after all.

'I'm not the woman you think I am,' she said slowly.

'You're everything—'

'No. I'm not. Hear me out, Lucas. Please. Because this is important.' She stood up, because it was difficult sitting there in the piercing green spotlight of his gaze. So she walked around the Doyles' lovely old sitting room, with its faded furniture and leaf-framed view over the silvery lake, and gave a small sigh as she began her story. 'My mother was a nurse in England when she got pregnant by someone whose name I was never told.' Her voice grew reflective. 'She never saw him again, so she came back to Ireland with me and I was brought up by my grandmother, while Mammy went out to work. We lived pretty much hand to mouth, in a little cottage on the outskirts of Ballykenna, and when I was two, my mother got breast cancer—'

'Tara.'

'No, Lucas,' she said fiercely. 'Let me finish. She got breast cancer and it was very aggressive. It was obviously very sad but I can't remember much about it, or maybe I just blocked it out. She died very quickly and I was left in the sole care of my grandmother.' She swallowed as she made an admission she'd never dared make before, even to herself. To realise that just because someone went through the mechanics of caring for you, didn't mean that they liked you or loved you. Especially if you reminded them of their own failings.

'She was a cold and bitter woman,' she continued, with a wince. 'Though it took me a long time to find out why. To discover why she hated men so much and why she used to dress me like a frump.' She swallowed. 'And why the other children used to laugh at me behind my back.'

'Why?'

She drew in a deep breath. Here it was. The truth—in all its unvarnished clarity. 'My grandmother had been a nun and my grandfather a priest and their liaison was a huge scandal at the time, because my mother was the result of that liaison. Oh, they tried to hush it up but everyone knew. And I think that some of the burden of the guilt my grandmother carried around with her must have transferred itself onto me. It's why I was terrified of men and of intimacy until I met you, Lucas.'

She didn't know what she expected him to do, but she'd imagined *some* moment of reflection while he processed what she'd just told him. As if he'd need time to come to terms with her revelation and maybe to get his head around what a massive scandal it had been at the time. But instead he was getting up out of the faded velvet chair and crossing the room with a purposefulness which was achingly familiar to her. And when he put his arms around her and pulled her close, she started to cry and once she had started she couldn't seem to stop. The tears came hard and fast and Tara realised she was crying for all kinds of reasons. She was crying for the women of earlier generations who'd had to deal with judgement and being shunned. And she was crying for her poor dead mother who would never know her grandchild. Those tears were of sorrow, but hot on their heels came tears of gratitude, and joy—for being fit and healthy and carrying a child beneath her fast-beating heart. A child who...

She turned her wet face up to Lucas and saw compassion and love blazing from his green eyes and that gave her the courage to tell him. 'I love you, Lucas,' she whispered. 'So much. And yes, I want to spend the rest of my life with you.'

He nodded, but didn't speak, just drew his arms around her even tighter and for now that was enough.

It was more than enough.

EPILOGUE

'LUCAS...' TARA GAVE a luxurious stretch as she felt the warm lips of her husband tracking over her bare stomach, making her flesh shiver into little goosebumps. *Again.*

She swallowed down her growing desire, because they'd only just made love, hadn't they? Was it always going to be this good? she wondered dreamily.

'We'll...we'll be late for dinner.'

'Dinner isn't until nine-thirty,' he whispered. 'You know they eat late in Argentina.'

'Yes, but even so.' She fluttered her fingertips to his bare shoulders. 'We really ought to be getting dressed.'

'Say that with meaning, Tara.' There was a note of laughter in his voice as he moved to lie on top of her. 'And perhaps we will.'

Within minutes she was gasping out his name as he drove into her and he was kissing away the sounds of her helpless little cries as she came. But even though a deep lethargy crept over her afterwards, Tara forced herself to wriggle out from beneath Lucas's hard, honed flesh and head for the en-suite bathroom, because they had a whole delicious evening ahead of them. Quickly, she showered and, when Lucas took her place to stand beneath the powering jets, she returned to the bedroom to slither into a silky black jersey dress and matching pumps, before creeping along the corridor to where Declan was fast asleep, in a cot beside his bigger cousin, Luis.

For a moment she just stood there, gazing down at the dark heads of the two sleeping babes, and a great wave of love and contentment swelled up inside her. They were so lucky, she thought, with a sudden twist of her heart. So very lucky. All of them.

She and Lucas had been married in Dublin just before the birth of their beloved son, Declan. Her friend Stella had been bridesmaid and the celebrations had been memorable for many reasons, not least because Stella had rebuffed the advances of the Italian billionaire Salvatore di Luca, which was pretty much unheard of. And the guest of honour had been Brett Henderson—the actor who had caused Lucas to be so jealous in New York—who had offered to sing a song at their wedding, about love changing everything.

'He's clearly still smitten,' Lucas had grumbled, when she'd excitedly shown him the email.

'Rubbish,' Tara had disagreed. 'I think he just likes a woman with an Irish accent—in which case he'll have plenty to choose from at the reception! Our friends will never forgive us if we say no, Lucas. And besides, nobody could disagree with the sentiments of the song he's planning to sing, could they?'

And Lucas had no answer to that.

Their honeymoon had been postponed until Declan was six months old, when they went on an extended stay with Alej, Emily and Luis at their beautiful Argentinian *estancia*. The two women had hit it off immediately and it had warmed Tara's heart to see Lucas bonding with the brother he was quickly getting to know. Her husband was learning about the land of his birth, too, and had changed his name back to his birth name—not the one he'd seen written above a pub on the very first night he'd arrived in Dublin, completely alone. As Lucas Sabato he was building a mother-and-baby unit outside Buenos Aires, to support women and children who had fallen on hard times. Tara swallowed. To help prevent another helpless baby being given up because his mother couldn't afford to feed him...

And tonight they would eat outside beneath the stars with Emily and Alej and count every single one of their blessings.

She heard soft footsteps behind her and felt the whisper of Lucas's lips against her neck. His arm snaked around her waist and for a moment the two of them were silent as they stood looking down at their son.

'It's crazy,' said Lucas softly.

'What is?'

He shrugged. 'How I've gone from being a man with nothing to a man who has everything.'

She turned to look at him, an expression of bemusement on her face. 'Some people wouldn't describe a relatively young billionaire as a man with nothing.'

He shook his head. 'All the money in the world doesn't come close to the way I feel when I look at you, and Declan. Because you have given me all that is properly precious. You gave me courage to seek out my family and doing that has enriched my life. You have given me a beautiful son. But most of all, you've given me your love and that is priceless.' He tilted her chin, his voice a little unsteady. 'You are my everything, Tara Sabato, do you realise that?'

He had taken her breath away with his soft words and Tara had to dab furiously at her eyes to stop her mascara running. 'And you are my everything,' she answered fiercely. 'For the first time in my life I feel as if I have a real home and that you and Declan are the beating heart of that home. And I love you. I love you so much. You do know that, don't you, Lucas?'

Tenderly, Lucas stared down into the amber gleam of her eyes. The woman he admired more than any other. Who was strong and smart and brave and beautiful. His equal. His wife. His love. 'Do I know that?' He smiled as he wiped a mascara-coloured teardrop away from her freckled cheek. 'You betcha.'

* * * * *

DI SIONE'S VIRGIN MISTRESS

For Sarah-Jane Volkers who will know exactly why this book is dedicated to her when she reads it! And to the brilliant Rafael Vinoly, whose words painted such a perfect vignette of Long Island life...

CHAPTER ONE

Dante Di Sione felt the adrenaline pumping through his body as he walked into the tiny airport terminal. His heart was pounding and his forehead was beaded with sweat. He felt like he'd been running. Or just rolled away from a woman after a bout of particularly energetic sex. Even though it was a long time since he could even remember *having* sex. He frowned. How long?

His mind raced back over the past few weeks spent chasing across continents and flitting in and out of different time zones. He'd visited a dizzying array of countries, been presented with a whole shoal of red herrings and wandered up against several dead ends before arriving here, in the Caribbean. All in pursuit of a priceless piece of jewellery which his grandfather wanted for reasons he'd declined to share. Dante felt the tight clench of his heart. A dying man's wish.

Yet wasn't the truth that he had been tantalised by the task he'd been given and which he had taken on as a favour to someone who had given him so much? That his usually jaded appetite had been sharpened by a taste of the unusual. Truth was, he was dreading going back to his high-octane world of big business and the slightly decadent glamour of his adopted Parisian home. He had enjoyed the unpredictability of the chase and the sense that he was stepping outside his highly privileged comfort zone.

His hand tightened around the handle of his bag which contained the precious tiara. All he needed to do now was to hang on to this and never let it go—at least, not until he had placed it at his grandfather's sickbed so that the old man could do what he wanted with it.

His mouth felt dry. He could use a drink, and… something else. Something to distract him from the fact that the adrenaline was beginning to trickle from his system, leaving him with that flat, empty feeling which he'd spent his whole life trying to avoid.

He looked around. The small terminal was filled with the usual suspects which this kind of upmarket Caribbean destination inevitably attracted. As well as the overtanned and ostentatiously wealthy, there seemed to have been some photo shoot taking place, because the place was full of models. He saw several giraffe-tall young women turn in his direction, their endless legs displayed in tiny denim shorts and their battered straw hats tilted at an angle so all you could see were their cute noses and full lips as they pouted at him. But he wasn't in the mood for anyone as predictable as a model. Maybe he'd just do a little work instead. Get on to René at his office in Paris and discover what had been going on in his busy and thriving company while he'd been away.

And then his gaze was drawn to a woman sitting on her own. The only pale person in a sea of tanned bodies. Her hair was blond and she looked as fragile as spun sugar—with one of those pashmina things wrapped around her narrow shoulders which seemed to swamp her. She looked *clean*. He narrowed his eyes. Like she'd spent most of her life underwater and had just been brought up to the surface. She was sitting at the bar with an untouched glass of pink champagne in front of her, and as their eyes met, she picked up her glass, flustered, and began to stare at it as if it contained the secret to the universe—though he noticed she didn't drink any.

Was it that which made him start walking towards her, bewitched by a sudden demonstration of shyness which was so rare in the world he inhabited? With a few sure strides he reached her and put his bag down on the floor, right next to a remarkably similar brown leather carry-on. But then she lifted her head and all he could think about was the fragile beauty of her features.

'Hi,' he said.

'Hi,' she said in a very English accent as she blinked up at him through thick lashes.

'Have we met before?' he questioned.

She looked startled. Like someone who had been caught in an unexpected spotlight. She dug her teeth into her lower lip and worried them across the smooth rosy surface.

'I don't think so,' she said, then shook her head so that the strands of fair hair shimmered over her narrow shoulders like a silky cascade of water. 'No, we haven't. I would have remembered.'

He leaned on the bar, and smiled. 'But you were staring at me as if you knew me.'

Willow didn't answer—not straight away—her

head was too full of confusion and embarrassment combined with a powerful tug of attraction which she wasn't quite sure how to handle. Yes, *of course* she had been staring at him because—quite honestly—who wouldn't?

Beneath the pashmina, she felt the shiver of goose bumps as she met his mocking gaze, acknowledging that he was probably the most perfect man she'd ever seen—and she worked in an industry which dealt almost exclusively with perfect men. Dressed with the carelessness only the truly wealthy could carry off, he looked as if he'd only just fallen out of bed—though probably not his own. Faded jeans clung to unbelievably muscular thighs, and although his silk shirt was slightly creased, he still managed to convey a sense of power and privilege. His eyes were bright blue, his black hair was tousled and the gleam of his golden olive skin hinted at a Mediterranean lineage. Yet behind the brooding good looks she could detect a definite touch of steel—a dangerous edge which only added to his allure.

And Willow was usually left cold by good-looking men, something she put down to a certain shyness around them. Years of being ill, followed by a spell in an all-girls school, had meant that she'd grown up in an exclusively female environment and the only men she'd ever really met had been doctors. She'd been cocooned in her own little world where she'd felt safe—and safety had been a big deal to her.

So what was it about this man with the intense blue eyes which had made her heart start slamming against her ribcage, as if it was fighting to get out of her chest?

He was still looking at her questioningly and she tried to imagine what her sisters would say in similar circumstances. They certainly wouldn't be struck dumb like this. They'd probably shrug their gym-honed shoulders and make some smart comment, and hold out their half-empty glasses for a refill.

Willow twisted the stem of the champagne glass in between her finger and thumb. *So act like they do. Pretend that gorgeous-looking men talk to you every day of the week.*

'I imagine you must be used to people staring at you,' she said truthfully, taking her first sip of champagne and then another, and feeling it rush straight to her head.

'True.' He gave a flicker of a smile as he slid onto the bar stool beside her. 'What are you drinking?'

'No, honestly.' She shook her head, because surely the champagne must be responsible for the sudden warmth which was making her cheeks grow hot. 'I mustn't have too much. I haven't eaten anything since breakfast.'

He raised his eyebrows. 'I was going to ask if it was any good.'

'Oh. Yes. Of course. Right. Silly of me. It's…' Feeling even more flustered, Willow stared at the fizzing bubbles and drank a little more, even though suddenly it tasted like medicine on her tongue. 'It's the best champagne I've ever had.'

'And you often drink champagne on your own at airports, do you?' he drawled.

She shook her head. 'No. Actually, I'm celebrating the end of a job.'

Dante nodded, knowing this was his cue to ask

her about her job, but the last thing he wanted was to have to listen to a résumé of her career. Instead, he asked the bartender for a beer, then leaned against the bar and began to study her.

He started with her hair—the kind of hair he'd like to see spread over his groin—because although he wouldn't kick a brunette or a redhead out of bed in a hurry, he was drawn to blondes like an ant to the honeypot. But up close he could see anomalies in her appearance which made her looks more interesting than beautiful. He noted the almost-translucent pallor of her skin which was stretched over the highest cheekbones he'd ever seen. Her eyes were grey—the soft, misty grey of an English winter sky. Grey like woodsmoke. And although her lips were plump, that was the only bit of her which was—because she was thin. Too thin. Her slim thighs were covered in jeans onto which tiny peacocks had been embroidered, but that was as much as he could see because the damned pashmina was wrapped around her like an oversize tablecloth.

He wondered what had drawn him towards her when there were other more beautiful women in the terminal who would have welcomed his company, rather than looking as if a tiger had suddenly taken the seat beside her. Was it the sense that she didn't really fit in here? That she appeared to be something of an outsider? And hadn't he always been one of those himself? *The man on the outside who was always looking in.*

Maybe he just wanted something to distract him from the thought of returning to the States with the tiara, and the realisation that there was still so much which had been left undone or unsaid in his troubled family. Dante felt as if his grandfather's illness had brought him to a sudden crossroads in his life and suddenly he couldn't imagine the world without the man who had always loved him, no matter what.

And in the meantime, this jumpy-looking blonde was making him have all kinds of carnal thoughts, even though she still had that wary look on her face. He smiled, because usually he let women do all the running, which meant that he could walk away with a relatively clear conscience when he ended the affair. Women who chased men had an inbuilt confidence which usually appealed to him and yet suddenly the novelty of someone who was all tongue-tied and flustered was really too delicious to resist.

'So what are you doing here?' he questioned, taking a sip of his beer. 'Apart from the obvious answer of waiting for a flight.'

Willow stared down at her fingernails and wondered how her sisters would have answered *this*. Her three clever, beautiful sisters who had never known a moment of doubt in their charmed lives. Who would each have doubtless murmured something clever or suggestive and had this gorgeous stranger tipping back his dark head and laughing in appreciation at their wit. They certainly wouldn't have been sitting there, tying themselves up in knots, wondering why he had come over here in the first place. Why was it only within the defining boundaries of the work situation that she was able to engage with a member of the opposite sex without wishing that the floor would open up and swallow her?

This close, he was even more spectacular, with

a raw and restless energy which fizzed off him like electricity. But it was his eyes which were truly remarkable. She'd never seen eyes like them. Bluer than the Caribbean sky outside. Bluer even than the wings of those tiny butterflies which used to flutter past on those long-ago summer evenings when she'd been allowed to lie outside. A bright blue, but a hard blue—sharp and clear and focused. They were sweeping over her now, their cerulean glint visible through their forest of dark lashes as he waited for her answer.

She supposed she should tell him about her first solo shoot as a stylist for one of the UK's biggest fashion magazines, and that the job had been a runaway success. But although she was trying very hard to feel happy about that, she couldn't seem to shake off the dread of what was waiting for her back in England. Another wedding. Another celebration of love and romance which she would be attending on her own. Going back to the house which had been both refuge and prison during her growing-up years. Back to her well-meaning sisters and overprotective parents. Back to the stark truth that her real life was nowhere near as glamorous as her working life.

So make it glamorous.

She'd never seen this man before and she was unlikely to see him again. But couldn't she—for once in her life—play the part which had always been denied to her? Couldn't she pretend to be passionate and powerful and *desirable*? She'd worked in the fashion industry for three years now and had watched professional models morph into someone else once the camera was turned on them. She'd seen them become coquettish or slutty or flirtatious with an ease which was breathtaking. Couldn't she pretend that this man was the camera? Couldn't she become the person she'd always secretly dreamed of being, instead of dull Willow Hamilton, who had never been allowed to do *anything* and as a consequence had never really learned how to live like other women her age?

She circled the rim of the champagne glass with her forefinger, the unfamiliar gesture implying—she *hoped*—that she was a sensual and tactile person.

'I've been working on a fashion shoot,' she said.

'Oh.' There was a pause. 'Are you a model?'

Willow wondered if she was imagining the brief sense of *disappointment* which had deepened his transatlantic accent. Didn't he like models? Because if that was the case, he really *was* an unusual man. She curved her lips into a smile and discovered that it was easier than she'd thought.

'Do I look like a model?'

He raised his dark eyebrows. 'I'm not sure you really want me to answer that question.'

Willow stopped stroking the glass. 'Oh?'

His blue eyes glinted. 'Well, if I say no, you'll pout and say, *Why not?* And if I say yes, you'll still pout, and then you'll sigh and say in a weary but very affected voice, *Is it that obvious?*'

Willow laughed—and wasn't it a damning indictment of her social life that she should find herself shocked by the sound? As if she wasn't the kind of person who should be giggling with a handsome stranger at some far-flung spot of the globe. And suddenly she felt a heady rush of freedom. And excitement. She looked into the mocking spark of his eyes and decided that she could play this game after all.

'Thank you for answering me so honestly,' she said gravely. 'Because now I know I don't need to say anything at all.'

His gaze became speculative. 'And why's that?'

She shrugged. 'If women are so unoriginal that you can predict every word they're going say, then you can have this conversation all by yourself, can't you? You certainly don't need me to join in!'

He leaned forward and slanted her a smile in response and Willow felt a sense of giddy triumph.

'And that would be my loss, I think,' he said softly, his hard blue eyes capturing hers. 'What's your name?'

'It's Willow. Willow Hamilton.'

'And is that your real name?'

She gave him an innocent look. 'You mean Hamilton?'

He smiled. 'I mean Willow.'

She nodded. 'It is—though I know it sounds like something which has been made up. But it's a bit of a tradition in our family. My sisters and I are all named after something in nature.'

'You mean like a mountain?'

She laughed—*again*—and shook her head. 'A bit more conventional than that. They're called Flora, Clover and Poppy. And they're all very beautiful,' she added, aware of the sudden defensiveness in her tone.

His gaze grew even more speculative. 'Now you expect me to say, *But you're very beautiful, too.*' His voice dipped. 'And you respond by...'

'And I told you,' interrupted Willow boldly, her heart now pounding so hard against her ribcage that she was having difficulty breathing, 'that if you're so astute, you really ought to be having this conversation with yourself.'

'Indeed I could.' His eyes glittered. 'But we both know there are plenty of things you can do on your own which are far more fun to do with someone else. Wouldn't you agree, Willow?'

Willow might not have been the most experienced person on the block where men were concerned and had never had what you'd call a *real* boyfriend. But although she'd been cosseted and protected, she hadn't spent her life in *total* seclusion. She now worked in an industry where people were almost embarrassingly frank about sex and she knew exactly what he meant. To her horror she felt a blush beginning. It started at the base of her neck and rose to slowly flood her cheeks with hot colour. And all she could think about was that when she was little and blushed like this, her sisters used to call her the Scarlet Pimpernel.

She reached for her glass, but the clamp of his hand over hers stopped her. Actually, it did more than stop her—it made her skin suddenly feel as if it had developed a million new nerve endings she hadn't realised existed. It made her glance down at his olive fingers which contrasted against the paleness of her own hand and to think how perfect their entwined flesh appeared. Dizzily, she lifted her gaze to his.

'Don't,' he said softly. 'A woman blushing is a rare and delightful sight and men like it. So don't hide it and don't be ashamed. And—just for the record—if you drink more alcohol to try to hide your embarrassment, you're only going to make it worse.'

'So you're an expert on blushing as well as being an authority on female conversation?' she said, aware that his hand was still lying on top of hers and that it was making her long for the kind of things she knew she was never going to get. But she made no attempt to move her own from underneath and wondered if he'd noticed.

'I'm an expert on a lot of things.'

'But not modesty, I suspect?'

'No,' he conceded. 'Modesty isn't my strong point.'

The silence which fell between them was broken by the sound of screaming on the other side of the terminal and Willow glanced across to see a child bashing his little fists against his mother's thighs. But the mother was completely ignoring him as she chatted on her cell phone and the little boy's hysteria grew and grew. *Just talk to him*, thought Willow fiercely, wondering why some people even bothered *having* children. Why they treated the gift of birth so lightly.

But then she noticed that Blue Eyes was glancing at his watch and suddenly she realised she was missing her opportunity to prolong this conversation for as long as possible. Because wouldn't it be great to go home with the feeling of having broken out of her perpetual shyness for once? To be able to answer the inevitable question, *So, any men in your life these days, Willow?* with something other than a bright, false smile while she tried to make light of her essentially lonely life, before changing the subject.

So ask him his name. Stop being so tongue-tied and awkward.

'What's your name?' asked Willow, almost as if it was an afterthought—but she forced herself to pull her hand away from his. To break that delicious contact before he did.

'Dante.'

'Just Dante?' she questioned when he didn't elaborate further.

'Di Sione,' he added, and Willow wondered if she'd imagined the faint note of reluctance as he told her.

Dante took a sip of his beer and waited. The world was small, yes—but it was also fractured. There were whole groups of people who lived parallel existences to him and it was possible that this well-spoken young Englishwoman who blushed like a maiden aunt wouldn't have heard of his notorious family. She'd probably never slept with his twin brother or bumped into any of his other screwed-up siblings along the way. His heart grew cold as he thought about his twin, but he pushed the feeling away with a ruthlessness which came easily to him. And still he waited, in case the soft grey eyes of his companion suddenly widened in recognition. But they didn't. She was just looking at him in a way which made him want to lean over and kiss her.

'I'm trying to imagine what you're expecting my response to be,' she said, a smile nudging the edges of her lips. 'So I'm not going to do the obvious thing of asking if your name is Italian when clearly it is. I'm just going to remark on what a lovely name it is. And it is. Di Sione. It makes me think of blue seas and terracotta roofs and those dark cypress trees which don't seem to grow anywhere else in the world except in Italy,' she said, her grey eyes filling with mischief. 'There. Is that a satisfactory response—or was it predictable?'

There was a heartbeat of a pause before Dante

answered. She was so *unexpected*, he thought. Like finding a shaded space in the middle of a sizzling courtyard. Like running cool water over your hot and dirty hands and seeing all the grime trickle away. 'No, not especially predictable,' he said. 'But not satisfactory either.'

He leaned forward and as he did he could smell the tang of salt on her skin and wondered if she'd been swimming earlier that morning. He wondered what her body looked like beneath that all-enveloping shawl. What that blond hair would look like if it fell down over her bare skin. 'The only satisfactory response I can think of right now is that I think you should lean forward and part your lips so that I can kiss you.'

Willow stared at him—shocked—as she felt the whisper of something unfamiliar sliding over her skin. Something which beckoned her with a tantalising finger. And before she had time to consider the wisdom of her action, she did exactly as he suggested. She extended her neck by a fraction and slowly parted her lips so that he could lean in to kiss her. She felt the brush of his mouth against hers as the tip of his tongue edged its way over her lips.

Was it the champagne she'd drunk, or just some bone-deep *yearning* which made her open her mouth a little wider? Or just the feeling of someone who'd been locked away from normal stuff for so long that she wanted to break free. She wanted to toss aside convention and not be treated like some delicate flower, as she had been all her life. She didn't want to be Willow Hamilton right then. She wanted the famous fairy godmother to blast into the Caribbean airport in a cloud of glitter and to wave her wand and transform her, just as Willow had been transforming models for the past week.

She wanted her hair to stream like buttery silk down her back and for her skin to be instantly tanned, shown to advantage by some feminine yet sexy little dress whose apparent simplicity would be confounded by its astronomical price tag. She wanted her feet to be crammed into sky-high stilettos which still wouldn't be enough to allow her to see eye to eye with this spectacular man, if they were both standing. But she didn't want to be standing—and she didn't want to be sitting on a bar stool either. She wanted to be lying on a big bed wearing very sexy underwear and for those olive fingers to be touching her flesh again—only this time in far more intimate spots as he slowly unclothed her.

All those thoughts rushed through her mind in just the time it took for her own tongue to flicker against his and Willow's eyes suddenly snapped open—less in horror at the public spectacle she was making of herself with a man she'd only just met than with the realisation of what was echoing over the loudspeaker. It took a full five seconds before her befuddled brain could take in what the robotic voice was actually saying, and when it did, her heart sank.

'That's me. They're calling my flight,' she said breathlessly, reluctantly drawing her mouth away from his, still hypnotised by the blazing blue of his eyes. With an effort she got off the stool, registering the momentary weakness of her knees as she automatically patted her shoulder bag to check her passport and purse. She screwed up her face, trying to act like what had happened was no big deal. Trying to pretend that her breasts weren't tingling beneath her pashmina and that she kissed total strangers in airports every day of the week. Trying not to hope that he'd spring to his feet and tell her he didn't want her to go. But he didn't.

'Oh, heck,' she croaked. 'It's the last call. I can't believe I didn't hear it.'

'I think we both know very well why you didn't hear it,' he drawled.

But although his eyes glinted, Willow sensed that already he was mentally taking his leave of her and she told herself it was better this way. He was just a gorgeous man she'd flirted with at the airport—and there was no reason why she couldn't do this kind of thing in the future, if she wanted to. It could be the springboard to a new and exciting life if she let it. That is, if she walked away now with her dignity and dreams intact. Better that than the inevitable alternative. The fumbled exchange of business cards and the insincere promises to call. Her waiting anxiously by the phone when she got back to England. Making excuses for why he hadn't rung but unable—for several weeks at least—to acknowledge the reason he hadn't. The reason she'd known all along—that he was way out of her league and had just been playing games with her.

Still flustered, she bent down to grab her carry-on and straightened up to drink in his stunning features and hard blue eyes one last time. She tried her best to keep her voice steady. To not give him any sense of the regret which was already sitting on the horizon, waiting to greet her. 'Goodbye, Dante. It was lovely meeting you. Not a very original thing to say, I know—but it's true. Safe journey—wherever you're going. I'd better dash.'

She nearly extended her hand to shake his before realising how stupid that would look and she turned away before she could make even more of a fool of herself. She ended up running for the plane but told herself that was a good thing, because it distracted her from her teeming thoughts. Her heart was pounding as she strapped herself into her seat, but she was determined not to allow her mind to start meandering down all those pointless *what if* paths. She knew that in life you had to concentrate on what you had, and not what you really wanted.

So every time she thought about those sensual features and amazing eyes, she forced herself to concentrate on the family wedding which was getting closer and the horrible bridesmaid dress she was being made to wear.

She read the in-flight magazines and slept soundly for most of the journey back to England, and it wasn't until she touched down at Heathrow and reached into the overhead locker that she realised the carry-on bag she'd placed in the overhead locker wasn't actually *her* bag at all. Yes, it was brown, and yes, it was made of leather—but there all similarities ended. Her hands began to tremble. Because this was of the softest leather imaginable and there were three glowing gold initials discreetly embossed against the expensive skin. She stared at it with a growing sense of disbelief as she matched the initials in her head to the only name they could stand for, and her heart began to pound with a mixture of excitement and fear.

D.D.S.

Dante Di Sione.

CHAPTER TWO

DANTE'S PLANE WAS halfway over northern Spain when he made the grim discovery which sent his already bad mood shooting into the stratosphere. He'd spent much of the journey with an erection he couldn't get rid of—snapping at the stewardesses who were fussing and flirting around him in such an outrageous way that he wondered whether they'd picked up on the fact that he was sexually excited, and some hormonal instinct was making them hit on him even more than usual.

But he wasn't interested in those women in too-tight uniforms with dollar signs flashing in their eyes when they looked at him. He kept thinking about the understated Englishwoman and wondered why he hadn't insisted she miss her flight, so that he could have taken her on board his plane and made love to her. Most women couldn't resist sex on a private jet, and there was no reason she would be any different.

His mouth dried as he remembered the way she had jumped up from the bar stool like a scalded cat and run off to catch her flight as if she couldn't wait to get away from him. Had that ever happened to him before? He thought not.

She hadn't even asked for his business card!

Pushing her stubbornly persistent image from his mind, he decided to check on his grandfather's precious tiara, reaching for his bag and wondering why the old man wanted the valuable and mysterious piece of jewellery so much. Because time was fast running out for him? Dante felt the sudden painful twist of his heart as he tried to imagine a future without Giovanni, but he couldn't get his head around it. It was almost impossible to envisage a life without the once strong but still powerful figure who had stepped in to look after him and his siblings after fate had dealt them all the cruellest of blows.

Distracted by the turbulent nature of his thoughts, he tugged at the zip of the bag and frowned. He couldn't remember it being so full because he liked to travel light. He tugged again and the zip slid open. But instead of a small leather case surrounded by boxer shorts, an unread novel and some photos of a Spanish castle he really needed to look at for a client before his next meeting—it was stuffed full of what looked suspiciously like...

Dante's brows knitted together in disbelief.

Swimwear?

He looked at the bag more closely and saw that instead of softest brown leather embossed with *his* initials, this carry-on was older and more battered and had clearly seen better days.

Disbelievingly, he began to burrow through the bikinis and swimsuits, throwing them aside with a growing sense of urgency, but instantly he knew he was just going through the motions and that his search was going to be fruitless. His heart gave a leap in his chest as a series of disastrous possibilities occurred to him. How ironic it would be if he'd flown halfway across the globe to purchase a piece of jewellery which had cost a king's ransom, only to find that he'd been hoodwinked by the man who had sold it to him.

But no. He remembered packing the tiara himself, and although he was no gem expert, Dante had bought enough trinkets as pay-offs for women over the years to know when something was genuine. And the tiara *had* been genuine—of that he'd been certain. A complex and intricate weaving of diamonds and emeralds which had dazzled even him—a man usually far too cynical to be dazzled.

So where the hell was it now?

And suddenly Dante realised what must have happened. Willow—*what the hell had been her surname?*—must have picked up his bag by mistake. The blonde he'd been so busy flirting with at the airport, that he'd completely forgotten that he was carrying hundreds of thousands of dollars' worth of precious stones in his hand luggage. He'd been distracted by her misty eyes. He'd read in them a strange kind of longing and he'd fed her fantasy—and his own—by kissing her. It had been one of those instant-chemistry moments, when the combustion of sexual attraction had been impossible to ignore, until the last call for her flight had sounded over the loudspeaker and broken the spell. She'd jumped up and grabbed her bag. Only she hadn't, had she? She'd grabbed *his* bag!

He drummed his fingers on the armrest as he considered his options. Should he ask his pilot to divert the plane to London? He thought about his meeting with the Italian billionaire scheduled for later that evening and knew it would be both insulting and damaging to cancel it.

He scowled as he rang for a stewardess, one of whom almost fell over herself in her eagerness to reach him first.

'What can I get for you, sir?' she questioned, her eyes nearly popping out of her head as she looked at the haphazard collection of swimwear piled in the centre of the table.

Dante quickly shoved all the bikinis back into the bag, but as he did so, his finger hooked on to a particularly tiny pair of bottoms. He felt his body grow hard as he felt the soft silk of the gusset and thought about Willow wearing it. His voice grew husky. 'I want you to get hold of my assistant and ask him to track down a woman for me.'

The stewardess did her best to conceal it, but the look of disappointment on her face was almost comical.

'Certainly, sir,' she said gamely. 'And the woman is?'

'Her name is Willow Hamilton,' Dante ground out. 'I need her number and her address. And I need that information by the time this plane lands.'

There were four missed calls on her phone by the time Willow left the Tube station in central London, blinking as she emerged into the bright July sunshine. She stepped into the shadow of a doorway and looked at the screen. All from the same unknown number and whoever it was hadn't bothered to leave a voicemail. But she knew who the caller must be. *The sexy stranger. The man she'd kissed. The blue-eyed man whose carry-on she had picked up by mistake.*

She felt the race of her heart. She would go home first and then she would ring him. She wasn't going to have a complicated conversation on a busy pavement on a hot day when she was tired and jet-lagged.

She had already made a tentative foray inside, but the bag contained no contact number, just some photos of an amazing Spanish castle, a book which had won a big literary prize last year and—rather distractingly—several pairs of silk boxer shorts which were wrapped around a leather box. She'd found her fingertips sliding over the slippery black material of the shorts and had imagined them clinging to Dante Di Sione's flesh and that's when her cheeks had started doing that Scarlet Pimpernel thing again, and she'd hastily stuffed them back before anyone on the Heathrow Express started wondering why she was ogling a pair of men's underpants.

She let herself into her apartment, which felt blessedly cool and quiet after the heat of the busy London day. She rented the basement from a friend of her father's—a diplomat in some far-flung region whose return visits to the UK were brief and infrequent. Unfortunately one of the conditions of Willow being there was that she wasn't allowed to change the decor, which meant she was stuck with lots of very masculine colour. The walls were painted bottle-green and dark red and there was lots of heavy-looking furniture dotted around the place. But it was affordable, close to work and—more importantly—it got her away from the cloying grip of her family.

She picked up some mail from the mat and went

straight over to the computer where she tapped in Dante Di Sione's name, reeling a little to discover that her search had yielded over two hundred thousand entries.

She squinted at the screen, her heart beginning to pound as she stared into an image which showed his haunting blue eyes to perfection. It seemed he was some sort of mega entrepreneur, heading up a company which catered exclusively for the super-rich. She looked at the company's website.

We don't believe in the word impossible.
Whatever it is you want—we can deliver.

Quite a big promise to make, she thought as she stared dreamily at photos of a circus tent set up in somebody's huge garden, and some flower-decked gondolas which had been provided to celebrate a tenth wedding anniversary party in Venice.

She scrolled down. There was quite a lot of stuff about his family. Lots of siblings. *Snap*, she thought. And there was money. Lots of that. A big estate somewhere in America. Property in Manhattan. Although according to this, Dante Di Sione lived in Paris—which might explain why his accent was an intriguing mix of transatlantic and Mediterranean. And yet some of the detail about his life was vague—though she couldn't quite put her finger on why. She hadn't realised precisely what she'd been looking for until the word *single* flashed up on the screen and a feeling of satisfaction washed over her.

She sat back and stared out at the pavement, where from this basement-level window she could see the bottom halves of people's legs as they walked by. A pair of stilettos tapped into view, followed by some bare feet in a pair of flip-flops. Was she really imagining that she was in with a chance with a sexy billionaire like Dante Di Sione, just because he'd briefly kissed her in a foreign airport terminal? Surely she couldn't be *that* naive?

She was startled from her daydream by the sound of her mobile phone and her heart started beating out a primitive tattoo as she saw it was the same number as before. She picked it up with fingers which were shaking so much that she almost declined the call instead of accepting it.

Stay calm, she told herself. *This is the new you. The person who kisses strangers at airports and is about to start embracing life, instead of letting it pass her by.*

'Hello?'

'Is that you, Willow?'

Her heart raced and her skin felt clammy. On the phone, his transatlantic/Mediterranean twang sounded even more sexy, if such a thing was possible. 'Yes,' she said, a little breathlessly. 'It's me.'

'You've got my bag,' he clipped out.

'I know.'

The tone of his voice seemed to change. 'So how the hell did that happen?'

'How do you think it happened?' Stung into defence by the note of irritation in his voice, Willow gripped the phone tightly. 'I picked it up by mistake... *obviously.*'

There was a split-second pause. 'So it wasn't deliberate?'

'Deliberate?' Willow frowned. 'Are you serious? Do you think I'm some sort of thief who hangs around airports targeting rich men?'

There was another pause and this time when he spoke the irritation had completely vanished and his voice sounded almost unnaturally composed. 'Have you opened it?'

A little uncomfortably, Willow rubbed her espadrille toe over the ancient Persian rug beneath the desk. 'Obviously I had to open it, to see if there was any address or phone number inside.'

His voice sounded strained now. 'And you found, what?'

Years of sparring with her sisters made Willow's response automatic. 'Don't you even remember what you were carrying in your own bag?'

'You found, *what*?' he repeated dangerously.

'A book. Some glossy photos of a Spanish castle. And some underpants,' she added on a mumble.

'But nothing else?'

'There's a leather case. But it's locked.'

At the other end of the phone, Dante stared at the imposing iron structure of the Eiffel Tower and breathed out a slow sigh of relief. Of course it was locked—and he doubted she would have had time to get someone to force it open for her even if she'd had the inclination, which he suspected she didn't. There had been something almost *otherworldly* about her... and she seemed the kind of woman who wouldn't be interested in possessions—even if the possession in question happened to be a stunning diadem, worth hundreds of thousands of dollars.

He could feel the strain bunching up the muscles

in his shoulders and he moved them slowly to release some of the tension, realising just how lucky he'd been. Or rather, how lucky *she* had been. Because he'd been travelling on a private jet with all the protection which came with owning your own plane, but Willow had not. He tried to imagine what could have happened if she'd been stopped going through customs, with an undeclared item like that in her possession.

Beads of sweat broke out on his forehead and for a moment he cursed this mission he'd been sent on—but it was too late to question its legitimacy now. He needed to retrieve the tiara as soon as possible and to get it to the old man, so that he could forget all about it.

'I need that bag back,' he said steadily.

'I'm sure you do.'

'And you probably want your swimwear.' He thought about the way his finger had trailed over the gusset of that tiny scarlet bikini bottom and was rewarded with another violent jerk of lust as he thought about her blond hair and grey eyes and the faint taste of champagne on her lips. 'So why don't I send someone round to swap bags?'

There was a pause. 'But you don't know where I live,' she said, and then, before he had a chance to reply, she started talking in the thoughtful tone of someone who had just missed a glaringly obvious fact. 'Come to think of it—how come you're ringing me? I didn't give you my phone number.'

Dante thought quickly. Was she naive enough not to realise that someone like him could find out pretty much anything he wanted? He injected a reassuring note into his voice. 'I had someone who works for me track you down,' he said smoothly. 'I was worried that you'd want your bag back.'

'Actually, you seem to be the one who's worried, Mr Di Sione.'

Her accurate tease stopped him in his tracks and Dante scowled, curling his free hand into a tight fist before slowly releasing his fingers, one by one. This wasn't going as he had intended. 'Am I missing something here?' he questioned coolly. 'Are you playing games with me, Willow, or are you prepared to do a bag-swap so that we can just forget all about it and move on?'

In the muted light of the basement apartment, Willow turned to catch a glimpse of her shadowed features in an antique oval mirror and was suddenly filled with a determination she hadn't felt for a long time. Not since she'd battled illness and defied all the doctors' gloomy expectations. Not since she'd fought to get herself a job, despite her family's reluctance to let her start living an independent life in London. She thought about her sister Clover's wedding, which was due to take place in a few days' time, when she would be kitted out in the hideous pale peach satin which had been chosen for the bridesmaids and which managed to make her look completely washed out and colourless.

But it wasn't just that which was bothering her. Her vanity could easily take a knock because she'd never really had the energy or the inclination to make her looks the main focus of her attention. It was all the questions which would inevitably come her way and which would get worse as the day progressed.

So when are we going to see you walking down the aisle, Willow?

And, of course, the old favourite: *Still no boyfriend, Willow?*

And because she would have been warned to be on her best behaviour, Willow would have to bite back the obvious logic that you couldn't have one without the other, and that since she'd never had a proper boyfriend, it was unlikely that she would be heading down the aisle any time soon.

Unless...

She stared at her computer screen, which was dominated by the rugged features of Dante Di Sione. And although he might have been toying with her—because perhaps kissing random women turned him on—he had managed to make it feel *convincing*. As if he'd really *wanted* to kiss her. And that was all she needed, wasn't it? A creditable performance from a man who would be perfectly capable of delivering one. Dante Di Sione didn't have to be her real boyfriend—he just had to look as if he was.

'Don't I get a reward for keeping your bag safe?' she questioned sweetly.

'I'll buy you a big bunch of flowers.'

'Flowers make me sneeze.'

'Chocolates, then.'

'I'm allergic to cocoa.'

'Stop playing games with me, Willow,' he snapped. 'And tell me what it is you're angling for.'

Willow stared at the piercing blue eyes on the computer screen. His thick black hair looked as if he had been running his fingers through it and she remembered how it had felt to have his lips brushing over hers. It was now or never. It was all about seizing the moment and doing something you wouldn't normally do. Because what was the point of sitting back and moaning about your fate as if it was set in stone, instead of trying to hammer out something new for yourself?

And here was a chance staring her straight in the face.

She drew in a deep breath. 'What I want won't cost you anything but your time. I'm being a bridesmaid at my sister's wedding next weekend and I'm fed up with people asking me why I don't have a boyfriend. All you have to do is pretend to be that man. For one day only, you will be my fictitious but very convincing boyfriend, Mr Di Sione. Do you think you could manage that?'

CHAPTER THREE

HE SHOULD HAVE told her no. Should have told her that he hated weddings. Because marriage stood for everything he despised and distrusted. Lies and deception and manipulation.

Dante straightened the silver-grey tie which complemented his formal charcoal suit and stared at his reflection in the hotel mirror.

So why *hadn't* he said no? Why *had* he agreed to accompany Willow Hamilton to her sister's wedding, where she was being a bridesmaid? It was true that she had his grandfather's tiara in her possession and she had been demonstrating a not-very-subtle form of blackmail to get him to be her plus one. But Dante was not a man who could be manipulated—and certainly not by a woman. If he'd really wanted that tiara back he would have gone straight round to her apartment and *taken* it—either by reason or seduction or quiet threat—because he nearly always got what he wanted.

So why hadn't he?

He gave his tie one final tug and watched as his reflected face gave a grim kind of smile.

Because he wanted her? Because she'd interested

and intrigued him and awoken in him a sexual hunger he'd been neglecting these past weeks?

The reflected smile intensified.

Well, why not?

He picked up his car keys and went outside to the front of the hotel, where the valet was opening the door of the car he'd hired for the weekend. It was an outrageously fast car—a completely over-the-top machine which would inevitably attract the attention of both men and women. And while it wouldn't have been Dante's first choice, if Willow wanted him to play the part of a very rich and super-keen lover, then it followed that he ought to drive something which looked like everyone's idea of a phallic substitute.

He drove through the streets of central London and tooted the horn as he drew up outside Willow's basement apartment. She appeared almost immediately and he watched her walk towards him, narrowing his eyes with instinctive appraisal—because she looked... He swallowed. She looked *incredible*. Gone was the big pashmina which had shielded her from the airport's overzealous air conditioning and hidden most of her body. In its place was a pale dress which skimmed the tiniest waist he'd ever seen, its flouncy skirt swirling provocatively around her narrow knees. Her blond hair was plaited and Dante felt his mouth dry. As she grew closer he could see that the collar of her dress was embroidered with tiny daisies, and it made her look as if she'd been picked fresh from a meadow that morning. She looked ethereal and fragile and he couldn't seem to tear his eyes away from her.

He shook his head slightly as once again he acknowledged her fey beauty and the realisation that she didn't seem quite part of this world. Certainly not *his* world. And then he noticed that she was carrying nothing but a small suitcase.

'Where's my carry-on?' he demanded as he got out of the car to take the case from her.

There was a pause as she met his gaze. 'It will be returned to you after the deal is done.'

'After the deal is done?' he echoed softly.

'When the wedding is over.'

He raised his eyebrows at her mockingly, but made no attempt to conceal the sudden flicker of irritation in his voice. 'And if I insist on taking it now? What then?'

He saw a momentary hesitation cross her fragile features, as if she had suddenly realised just who it was she was dealing with. But bravado won the day and she shot him an almost defiant look which made him want to pin her over the bonnet of the car and kiss her senseless.

'You're not in a position to insist, Dante,' she said, sliding inside with a graceful movement which made him wish she could do it again, in slow motion. 'I have something you want and you have to pay for it.'

He switched on the engine and wondered if she was aware that she had something else *he* wanted, and that by the end of the day he would have taken it... 'So where are we going?' he said.

'My family home. It's in Sussex. I'll direct you.'

'Women are notoriously bad at directions, Willow—we both know that. So why don't you just give me the postcode and I can program it into the satnav?'

She turned to look at him, a frown creasing her

brow. 'Are you for real, or did you just complete a crash course in being patronising? I think I can just about find my way to my family home without needing a robot to guide me.'

'Just don't fall asleep,' he warned.

'I'll do my best. But you're not exactly an aid to relaxation, are you?' Settling back in her seat, she gave him a clear list of instructions, then waited until he had negotiated his way out of London towards the south, before she asked, 'So what's in the bag which makes you want it so much?'

'Boxer shorts.' He shot her a look. 'But you already know that.'

Willow didn't react, even though the mention of his boxer shorts was threatening her with embarrassment, which she suspected was his intention. Because this was the new Willow, wasn't it? The woman who had decided to take control of her own destiny instead of having it decided by other people. The woman who was going to live dangerously. She studied his rugged profile as he stared at the road ahead. 'A few items of underwear wouldn't usually be enough to get a man like you to take a complete stranger to a family wedding and pretend to be her boyfriend.'

'Let's get a couple of things straight, shall we, Willow? Firstly, I have no intention of discussing the contents of that bag with you,' he said as he powered the car into the fast lane. 'And secondly, I intend to play your *lover*—not your damned *boyfriend*—unless your looks are deceiving and you happen to be fifteen.'

'I'm twenty-six,' she said stiffly.

'You look much younger.'

'That's what everyone says.'

There was a pause. 'Is that a roundabout way of telling me I'm unoriginal?'

She shrugged. 'Well, you know what they say... if the cap fits...'

A reluctant smile curved the edges of his lips. 'You need to tell me something about yourself before we get there,' he said. 'If you're hoping to convince people we're an item.'

Willow stared out of the car window as they drove through the sun-dappled lanes, and as more and more trees appeared, she thought about how much she loved the English countryside. The hedgerows were thick with greenery and in the fields she could see yellow and white ox-eye daisies and the purple of snake's head fritillary. And suddenly she found herself wishing that this was all for real and that Dante Di Sione was here because he wanted to be, not because she was holding him to ransom over some mystery package.

She wondered how much to tell him. She didn't want him getting scared. She didn't want him to start treating her as if she was made of glass. She was worried he'd suddenly start being *kind* to her if he learned the truth, and she couldn't stand that. He was rude and arrogant and judgemental, but she rather liked that. He wasn't bending over backwards to please her—or running as fast as he could in the opposite direction, which was the usual effect she had on people once they knew her history.

His words interrupted her silent reverie.

'We could start with you explaining why you need an escort like me in the first place,' he said. 'You're a pretty woman. Surely there must be other men who could have been your date? Men who know you better than I do and could have carried off a far more convincing performance.'

She shrugged, staring at the toenails which were peeping through her open-toed sandals—toenails which had been painted a hideous shade of peach to match the equally hideous bridesmaid dresses, because Clover had said that she wanted her sisters to look like 'a team.'

'Maybe I wanted to take someone who nobody else knew,' she said.

'True,' he agreed. 'Or you could—and I know this is controversial—you could always have chosen to attend the wedding on your own. Don't they say that weddings are notoriously fertile places for meeting someone new? You might have got lucky. Or are you one of those women who believes she isn't a complete person unless she has a man in tow?'

Willow couldn't believe what he'd just said. Had she really thought his rudeness was charming? Well, scrub that. She found herself wishing she'd asked around at the magazine to see if anyone there could have been her guest. But most of the men she worked with were gay—and the place was a hotbed of gossip. It wouldn't have done her image much good if she'd had to trawl around for a suitable escort, because the biggest sin you could commit in the fashion industry was to admit to being lonely.

She sneaked a glance at Dante. Whatever his shortcomings in the charm department he was certainly a very suitable escort—in every sense of the word. The formality of his pristine two-piece looked just as good against his glowing olive skin as the faded denim jeans had done. Perhaps even more so. The made-to-measure suit hugged his powerful body and emphasised its muscularity to perfection—making her shockingly aware of his broad shoulders and powerful thighs. The slightly too long black hair appeared more tamed than it had done the other day and suddenly she found herself longing to run her fingers through it and to muss it up.

She felt a rush of something molten tugging at the pit of her belly—something which was making her wriggle her bottom restlessly against the seat. Did she imagine the quick sideways glance he gave her, or the infuriatingly smug smile which followed—as if he was perfectly aware of the sudden aching deep inside her which was making it difficult for her to think straight.

She licked her lips. 'I'm not really like my sisters,' she began. 'You remember I'm one of four?'

'I remember.'

'They've always had millions of boyfriends, and I haven't.'

'Why not?'

He shot the question at her and Willow wondered if now was the time for the big reveal. To tell him how ill she'd been as a child. To tell him that there had been times when nobody had been sure if she would make it. Or to mention that there were residual aspects of that illness which made her a bad long-term choice as a girlfriend.

But suddenly her attention was distracted by the powerful interplay of muscles as he tensed one taut thigh in order to change gear and her mouth dried with longing. No, she was not going to tell him. Why peddle stories of her various woes and make herself look like an inevitable victim in his eyes? Today she was going to be a different Willow. The kind of Willow she'd always wanted to be. She was going to embrace the way he was making her feel, and the way he was making her feel was...*sexy*.

Carelessly, she wriggled her shoulders. 'I've been too wrapped up in my career. The fashion world can be very demanding—and competitive. I've been working at the magazine since I left uni, and they work you very hard. The swimwear shoot I was doing in the Caribbean was my first big break and everyone is very pleased with it. I guess that means I'll have more time to spend on my social life from now on. Take the next turning on the right. We're nearly there. Look. Only seven more miles.' She pointed at a signpost. 'So you'd better tell me a bit about you.'

Dante slowed the car down as he turned into a narrow lane and thought how differently he might have answered this question a few years back. The first thing he would have said was that he was a twin, because being a twin had felt like a fundamental part of his existence—like they were two parts of the same person. But not any more. He and Dario hadn't spoken in years. Six years, to be precise—after an episode when anger and resentment had exploded into misunderstanding and turned into a cold and unforgiving rift. He'd discovered that it was easier to act like his brother no longer existed, rather than acknowledge the fact that they no longer communicated. And that it hurt. It hurt like hell.

'But surely you must have looked me up on the internet,' he murmured.

She quickly turned her head to look at him, and for the first time, she seemed uncertain. 'Well, yes. I did.'

'And didn't that tell you everything you wanted to know?'

'Not really. Bits of it were very vague.'

'I pay people a lot of money to keep my profile vague.'

'Why?'

'To avoid the kind of questions you seem intent on asking.'

'It's just down that long drive. The entrance is just past that big tree on the right.' She leaned forward to point her finger, before settling back against the leather car seat. 'It said you had lots of siblings, and there was something about you having a twin brother and I was wondering what it was like to have a twin. If the two of you are psychic, like people say twins can be. And…'

'And what?' he shot out as her words trailed off.

She shrugged. 'There wasn't much information about your parents,' she said quietly.

Dante's fingers tightened around the steering wheel as he drew up outside a huge old house, whose beauty was slightly diminished by shabby paintwork and a general sense of tiredness. Bad enough that Willow Hamilton should have made breezy assumptions about his estranged twin, but worse that she had touched on the one fact which had ruthlessly been eliminated from his history. Didn't she realise that there was a good reason why there was scant mention of his parents in his personal profile?

He felt a slow anger begin to build inside him, and if it hadn't been for the damned tiara, he would have dropped her off there and then, and driven away so fast that you wouldn't have seen him for smoke. Because personal questions about his family were forbidden; it was one of the ground rules he laid down at the beginning of any date.

But this wasn't a normal date, was it? It was a means to an end. He stared down at her bare knees and felt a whisper of desire. And perhaps it was time he started taking advantage of some of the very obvious compensations available to drive these unwanted irritations from his head.

'I doubt whether knowing about my parentage or siblings is going to be particularly relevant in the circumstances,' he said coolly. 'Of far greater importance is finding out what turns each other on. Because, as lovers, we need to send out the vibe that we've had more than a little...*intimacy*. And in order to convey that to some degree of satisfaction, then I really need to explore you a little more, Willow.'

And before Willow could properly appreciate what was happening, he had undone their seat belts and was pulling her into his arms, as if it was something he had done countless times before. His cold blue eyes swept over her like a searchlight but there was something in their depths which disturbed her. Something which sent foreboding whispering over her spine. Was it the realisation that this man was way too complicated for her to handle and she shouldn't even try? Instinctively, she tried to pull away but he was having none of it, because he gave a silky laugh as he lowered his head to kiss her.

Willow sucked in a disbelieving breath as their lips met, because this wasn't like that lazy kiss at the airport. This was a completely different animal—an unashamed display of potent sensuality. This was Dante Di Sione being outrageously macho and showing her exactly who was in charge. It was a stamp and an unmistakable sexual boast and something told Willow that this emotionless kiss meant nothing to him.

But that didn't stop from her reacting, did it?

It didn't stop her from feeling as if she'd just stepped from the darkest shadows into the brightest sunlight.

His seeking lips coaxed her own apart and she felt the tips of her breasts harden as he deepened the kiss with his tongue. Did he know she was helpless to resist from the moment he'd first touched her? Was that why he splayed his fingers over her dress and began to caress her aching breast? She gave a whimper of pleasure as she lifted her arms to curl them around his neck and felt a rush of heat between her legs— a honeyed throb of need which drove every other thought and feeling straight from her body. It felt so good. Unimaginably good. She felt exultant. Hungry for more. Hungry for him.

Softly, Willow moaned with pleasure and he drew his head away, his blue eyes smoky with desire and an unmistakeable trace of mockery glinting in their lapis lazuli depths.

'Do you want me to stop, Willow?' he taunted softly, his words a delicious caress which whispered over her skin, making her want him to talk to her that way all day long. 'Or do you want me to touch you a little more?'

His hand was now moving beneath the hem of her dress and she held her breath. She could feel the tiptoeing of his fingertips against the bare skin and the heat between her legs was increasing as he started to kiss her again. His words were muffled against her mouth as he repeated that same sensual, taunting question—and all the while he was inching his fingers further and further up her thigh.

'Do you?'

Her heart pounded as she opened her mouth to reply when the sound of footsteps crunching over gravel broke into the kiss like a rock smashing through a thin sheet of ice. Reluctantly Willow opened her eyes and pulled away from him, in time to see her sister's astonished face looking at them through the car window.

CHAPTER FOUR

'FLORA!' SOMEHOW WILLOW managed to stumble her sister's name out through lips which were swollen by the pressure of Dante's kiss. She tried to pull away from him but he wasn't having any of it—keeping his arm anchored tightly around her shoulders. Her voice trembled a little as his fingertips started stroking at the base of her neck, as if he couldn't bear not to be touching her. 'What...what are you doing here?'

But Flora wasn't looking at her. She was staring at Dante as if she couldn't quite believe her eyes. Willow watched as her sister surreptitiously touched her blond hair as if to check that it was pristine—which naturally, it was—and then spread her fingers out over her breastbone, as if to emphasise that at least one of the Hamilton sisters had breasts.

'And just who is *this*, Willow?' she said in a voice which didn't quite manage to hide her disbelief. 'You really must introduce me.'

'He's...' Willow's voice faltered. *He's the man I've bribed to be here. The man who made me feel I was almost going to explode with pleasure, and that was only from a single kiss.*

'My name is Dante Di Sione and I'm Willow's

guest for the wedding,' interjected Dante, and Willow saw Flora almost melt as his sensual lips curved into a lazy smile. 'Didn't she tell you I was coming?'

'No,' said Flora crisply. 'No, she did not. We weren't...well, we weren't expecting her to bring anyone—and as a consequence we've made no special allowances. Which means you'll be in Willow's old bedroom, I'm afraid.'

'And is there a problem with Willow's old bedroom?' he questioned.

'I would say there is, especially for a man of your dimensions.' Flora looked Dante up and down, as if shamelessly assessing his height. 'There's only a single bed.'

Willow wanted to curl up and die, and that was before Dante moved his hand from her neck to place it proprietarily over her thigh. He smiled up at her sister as he pressed his fingers into her flesh. 'Great,' he murmured. 'I do love a good squeeze.'

This clearly wasn't the reaction Flora had expected and the sight of Dante with his hand on her sister's leg must have confused the life out of her. But a lifetime of social training meant that her irritation didn't last long and she made an instant recovery. 'If you'd like to park over by the stables, Dante.' She flashed him a glossy smile. 'Once you've settled in we'll be serving coffee in the drawing room and you'll be able to meet my mother. Oh, and you'll have to try on your bridesmaid dress again, Willow—though I warn you that Clover is going to go ballistic if you've lost any more weight! And don't you think you ought to put a cardigan on? Your arms are covered in goose bumps.'

Dante started up the engine as they watched Flora walk into the main entrance of the grand house. Her blond hair swung down her back in a glossy curtain and she walked with the confident wiggle of a beautiful woman who knew she was being watched.

'So that's one of your sisters,' he said slowly as she disappeared through the open front door.

'Yes.' Willow nodded her head. *So get in first*, she thought. *Say all the stuff he must be thinking and that way you won't come over as vulnerable.* 'I told you my siblings were gorgeous, didn't I? And Flora especially so. Every man she meets falls in love with her. I...I think maybe she's single at the moment, though you can never be...'

'Willow.' He halted her flow of words by placing his finger firmly over her lips. 'Will you please shut up? I may have something of a reputation where women are concerned but even I would draw the line at going to a wedding with one sister, and then making out with another.'

'Not taking into account the fact that she might not be interested in you,' she said indignantly.

'No, of course not,' he murmured as he started up the engine. 'She was looking at me with nothing but cool indifference in her eyes.'

Willow couldn't decide whether to pull him up for his arrogance or simply acknowledge that he was telling the truth, because Flora *had* been looking at him as if she'd like to eat him up for breakfast, lunch and dinner and then maybe go back for a midnight snack. And yet he had been kissing *her*, hadn't he? Kissing her in a way she'd never been kissed before. She could still recall the fizzing excitement in her blood and the way she'd wanted to dissolve beneath his seeking fingers. She'd wanted him to carry on burrowing his fingers beneath her dress and to touch her where she was all hot and aching. Would he laugh or be horrified if he knew she'd never felt like that before? Would he be horrified to discover that she'd never actually had sex before?

They parked the car and she led Dante through the house by one of the back doors, beginning to realise what a big gamble she'd taken by bringing him here. Was he really a good enough actor to pretend to be interested in her when there was going to be so much Grade One crumpet sashaying around the place in their killer heels?

She pushed open the door of her old bedroom, the room where she had spent so much of her childhood—and immediately it felt like stepping back in time. It always did. It made her feel weird and it made her feel small. Little had changed since she'd left home, and whenever she came here, it felt as if her past had been preserved in aspic—and for the first time, she began to question why. Had her parents' refusal to redecorate been based on a longstanding wish not to tempt fate by changing things around?

Willow looked around. There was the portrait done of her when she was six—years before the illness had taken hold—with a blue sparkly clip in her blond hair. How innocent she looked. How totally oblivious to what lay ahead. Next to it was the first embroidery she'd ever done—a sweet, framed cross-stitch saying *Home Sweet Home*. And there were her books—row upon row of them—her beloved connection to the outside world and her only real escape from the sickroom, apart from her sewing. Later on, she'd discovered films—and the more slushy and happy-ever-after, the better. Because fantasy had been a whole lot better than reality.

Sometimes it had felt as if she'd been living in a gilded cage, even though she knew there had been good reasons for that—mainly to keep her away from any rogue infections. But her inevitable isolation and the corresponding protectiveness of her family had left her ill-equipped to deal with certain situations. Like now. She'd missed out on so much. Even at college she'd been watched over and protected by Flora and Clover, who had both been studying at the same university. For a long time she'd only had the energy to deal with maintaining her health and completing her studies and getting a decent degree—she hadn't had the confidence to add men into the mix, even if she'd found anyone attractive enough.

And she had never found anyone as attractive as Dante Di Sione.

She watched him put their bags down and walk over to the window to stare out at the wide green-grey sweep of the Sussex Downs, before turning to face her—his incredible lapis lazuli eyes narrowed. She waited for him to make some comment about the view, or to remark on the massive dimensions of her rather crumbling but beautiful old home, but to her surprise he did neither.

'So,' he said, beginning to walk towards her with stealthy grace. 'How long have we got?'

'Got?' she repeated blankly, not quite sure of his meaning even when he pulled her into his arms and started trailing his fingertips over her body so that she began to shiver beneath the filmy fabric of her delicate dress. 'For...for what?'

Dante smiled, but it was a smile edged with impatience and a danger that even Willow could recognise was sexual.

'That depends on you, and what you want.'

'What I want?' she said faintly.

'Forgive me if I'm mistaken, but I thought that you were as frustrated by your sister's interruption as I was. I was under the distinct impression that our fake relationship was about to get real, and in a very satisfying way. It would certainly be more convincing if we were properly intimate instead of just pretending to be. So are we going to play games with each other or are we going to give in to what we both clearly want?' he murmured as he began to stroke her breasts. 'And have sex?'

Willow quivered as her nipples tightened beneath his expert touch and even though his words were completely unromantic...even though they were the direct opposite of all those mushy rom-coms she used to watch—they were still making her *feel* something, weren't they? They were making her feel like a woman. A *real* woman—not some pale and bloodless creature who'd spent so much time being hooked up to an intravenous drip, while cocktails of drugs were pumped into her system.

Yet this hadn't been what she'd planned when she'd rashly demanded he accompany her here. She'd thought they were engaging in nothing more than an indifferent barter of things they both wanted. Unless she wasn't being honest with herself. *Face the truth, Willow.* And wasn't the truth that from the moment she'd seen him walk into the Caribbean airport terminal, her body had sprung into life with a feeling of lust like she'd never felt before? In which case—why was she hesitating? Wasn't this whole trip supposed to be about changing her life around? To start living like other women her age did.

She tipped up her face so that he could kiss her again. 'Have sex,' she said boldly, meeting the flicker of humour in his smoky blue gaze.

He smiled and then suddenly what was happening *did* feel like a fantasy. Like every one of those mushy films she'd watched. He picked her up and carried her across the room, placing her down on the bed and pausing only to remove the battered old teddy bear that used to accompany her everywhere. She felt a wave of embarrassment as he pushed the bear onto the floor, but then he was bending his lips to hers and suddenly he was kissing her.

It was everything a kiss ought to be. Passionate. Searching. Deep. It made Willow squirm restlessly beneath him, her fingers beginning to scrabble at his shirt as she felt the rush of molten heat between her legs. And maybe he had guessed what was happening—or maybe this was just the way he operated—but he slid his hand beneath her skirt and all the way up her leg, pushing aside the damp panel of her knickers and beginning to tease her there with his finger. Her eyes fluttered to a close and it felt so *perfect* that Willow wanted to cry out her pleasure—but maybe he anticipated that too, because he deepened the kiss. And suddenly it became different. It became hard and hungry and demanding and she was matching it with her own demands—arching her body up towards his, as if she couldn't get close enough.

She could feel the hardness at his groin—the unfamiliar rocky ridge nudging insistently against her—and to her surprise she wasn't daunted, or scared. Maybe it was just her poor starved body demanding what nature had intended it for, because suddenly she was writhing against him—moaning her eagerness and her impatience into his open mouth.

He reached for his belt and Willow heard the rasp of his zip as he began to lower it, when suddenly there was a loud knock on the door.

They both froze and Willow shrank back against the pillows, trying to get her ragged breath back, though it took several seconds before she could speak.

'Who is it?' she demanded in a strangled voice.

'Willow?'

Willow's heart sank. It was Clover's voice. Clover, the bride-to-be. Well-meaning and bossy Clover, the older sister who had protected her as fiercely as a lioness would protect one of her cubs. Just like the rest of her family.

'H-hi, Clover,' she said shakily.

'Can I come in?'

Before Willow could answer, Dante shook his head and mouthed, *No*, but she knew what would happen if she didn't comply. There would be an outraged family discussion downstairs. There would be talk of rudeness. They would view Dante with even more suspicion than she suspected he was already going to encounter. The atmosphere would be spoiled before the wedding celebrations had even begun.

She shook her head as she tugged her dress back down, her cheeks flaming bright red as she readjusted her knickers. 'Hang on a minute,' she called, wriggling out of Dante's arms and off the bed, mouthing, *Don't say a word.*

His responding look indicated that he didn't really have much choice but there was no disguising the flicker of fury sparking in his blue eyes.

Willow scuttled over to the door and pulled it open by a crack to see Clover outside, her hair in rollers and an expression on her face which couldn't seem to make up its mind whether to be cross or curious.

'What the hell are you doing?' Clover asked sharply.

For a minute Willow was tempted to tell her to mind her own business, or at least to use her imagination. To snap back that she had just been enjoying a glorious initiation to the mysteries of sex when she had been so rudely interrupted. What was it with her sisters that they kept bursting in on her at the most inopportune moments? But then she reminded herself of everything that Clover had done for her. All those nights she'd sat beside her, holding her hand and helping her keep the nightmares at bay.

Telling herself that her sister was only acting with the best intentions, Willow gave a helpless kind of smile. 'I was just showing Dante the amazing view of the Sussex Downs.'

Clover slanted her a *who-do-you-think-you're-kidding?* look. 'Ah, yes,' she said, loud enough for the entire first floor corridor to hear. 'Dante. The mystery man who drove you here.'

'My guest,' said Willow indignantly.

'Why didn't you tell us you were bringing him?' said Clover.

'Maybe she wanted it to be a surprise,' came a drawling voice, and Willow didn't need to turn round to know that Dante had walked up behind her. She could tell from her sister's goggle-eyed expression even before he placed his hand on her shoulder and started massaging it, the way she'd seen people do in films when they were trying to help their partner relax. *So why did the tight tension inside her body suddenly feel as if it was spiralling out of control?*

'This is...this is Dante,' she said, hearing the hesitance of her words. 'Dante Di Sione.'

'I'm very pleased to meet you, Dante.' Clover's face took on the judgemental expression for which she was famous within the family. 'Perhaps Willow could bear to share you enough to bring you downstairs for coffee, so that everyone can meet you. My mother is particularly keen to make your acquaintance.'

'I can hardly wait,' murmured Dante, increasing the pressure of his impromptu massage by a fraction.

Willow had barely shut the door on her sister before Dante turned her round to face him, his hands on her upper arms, his lapis lazuli gaze boring into her.

'Why do you let her speak to you like that?' he demanded. 'Why didn't you just ignore her, or tell her you were busy? Surely she has enough imagination to realise we were making out?'

Willow gave a half-hearted shrug. 'She's very persistent. They all are.'

He frowned. 'What usually happens when you bring a man home with you?'

Willow licked her lips. Now they were on dangerous territory, and if she told him the truth, she suspected he'd run a mile. Instead, she shot him a challenging look. 'Why, are you afraid of my sisters, Dante?'

'I don't give a damn about your sisters.' He pulled her close against him. 'I'd just like to continue what we were doing a few minutes ago. Now...' His hand cupped her aching breast once more. 'Where were we, can you remember?'

For a minute Willow let him caress her nipple and her eyes fluttered to a close as he began to nuzzle at her neck. She could feel the renewed rush of heat to her body and she wondered how long it would take. Whether they would have time to do it properly. But what if it hurt? What if she *bled*? Pulling away from him, she met the frustration in his eyes.

Was she about to lose her mind? *Of course they wouldn't have time.* She'd waited a long time to have sex—years and years, to be precise—so why rush it and then have to go downstairs in an embarrassing walk of shame, to face her judgemental family who would be assembled in the drawing room like a circle of vultures?

'We've got to go downstairs,' she said. 'For...for coffee.'

'I don't want coffee,' he growled. 'I want you.'

There was a pause before she could summon up the courage to say it and when she did it came out in a breathless rush. 'And I want you.'

'So?'

'So I'm going to be a bridesmaid and I have to get my hair and make-up done before the ceremony.'

She swallowed. 'And there'll be plenty of time for that...later.'

Knowing he was fighting a losing battle—something he always went out of his way to avoid—Dante walked over to the window, trying to calm his acutely aroused body before having to go downstairs to face her frightful family.

He wondered what had made her so surprisingly compliant when her sister had come up here snooping around. He wondered what had happened to the woman who had flirted so boldly with him at the airport. The one who had demanded he be her escort as the price for returning his bag. He'd had her down as one of those independent free spirits who would give great sex—and her going-up-in-flames reaction every time he laid a finger on her had only reinforced that theory.

Yet from the moment he'd driven up the long drive to her impressive but rather faded country house, she had become ridiculously docile. He stared out at the breathtaking view. The magnificence of the distant landscape reminded him of his own family home, back in the States. Somewhere he'd left when he'd gone away to boarding school at the age of eight, and to which he had never really returned. Certainly not for any great length of time. His mouth twisted. Because wasn't it something of a travesty to call the Long Island place a *family home*? It was nothing but a grand house built on some very expensive real estate—with a magnificent facade which concealed all kinds of dirty secrets.

He turned back to find Willow watching him, her grey gaze wary and her manner slightly hesitant—

as if she expected him to say that he had changed his mind and was about to leave. He suddenly found himself thinking that she reminded him of a delicate gazelle.

'Why are you suddenly so uptight?' he questioned. 'Is something wrong?'

Willow stilled and if she hadn't fancied him so much she might have told him the whole story. But it was precisely *because* she fancied him so much that she couldn't. He'd start treating her differently. He'd be overcautious when he touched her. He might not even *want* to touch her. Because that was the thing with illness—it did more than affect the person it struck; it affected everyone around you. People who were mature and sensible might try to deny it, but didn't they sometimes behave as if the illness she'd once had was in some way contagious?

And why *shouldn't* she forget about that period in her life? She'd been given the all-clear ages ago and now was her chance to get something she'd wanted for a very long time. Something as powerful and as uncomplicated as sexual fulfilment, with a man she suspected would be perfect for the purpose, as long as she reminded herself not to read too much into it. For the first time in her life, she had to reach out for what she wanted. Not the things that other women wanted—because she wasn't asking for the impossible. She wasn't clamouring for marriage and babies— just a brief and heady sexual relationship with Dante Di Sione. But she had to be proactive.

She smiled into his hard blue eyes. 'I think it's because I'm the youngest, and they've always been a little protective of me. You know how it is.' She began to walk across the room towards him, plucking up the courage to put her arms around his neck. This close she could see into his eyes perfectly. And although she was short on experience, she recognised the desire which was making them grow so smoky.

And if she detected a flicker of suspicion lurking in their depths, then surely it was up to her to keep those suspicions at bay.

'I don't want to do it in a rush. I want to savour every single moment,' she whispered, trying to sound as if she made sexual assignations with men every day of the week. 'And don't they say that the best things in life are worth waiting for?'

He framed her face in his hands and there was a split second when she thought he was about to bend his head and kiss her, but he didn't. He just stared at her for a very long time, with the kind of look in his eyes which made a shiver trickle down her spine.

'I hear what you're saying and I am prepared to take it on board. But be very clear that I am not a patient man, Willow—and I have a very low boredom threshold. Better not keep me waiting too long,' he said roughly as he levered her away from him, in the direction of the door.

CHAPTER FIVE

DANTE GLANCED AROUND at the guests who were standing on the newly mown lawn drinking champagne. He risked another glance at his watch and wondered how soon this would be over and he could get Willow into bed—but like all weddings, this one seemed never-ending.

The place had been a hive of activity all afternoon. The faded grandeur of Willow's vast home had been transformed by legions of adoring locals, who had carried armfuls of flowers from the nearby village to decorate the house and gardens. Hedges had been trimmed and Chinese lanterns strung high in the trees. Rough wooden trestle tables had been covered with white cloths before being decked with grapes and roses and tiny flickering tealights.

It quickly dawned on him that the Hamiltons were the kind of aristocratic family with plenty of cachet but very little cash. The ceremony had taken place in *their own church*—he found that quite hard to believe—a small but freezing building situated within the extensive grounds. The bride looked okay—but then, all brides looked the same, in Dante's opinion. She wore a white dress and a veil and the service had been interminable. No change there. But he'd found himself unable to tear his eyes away from Willow as she'd made her way up the aisle. He thought how beautiful she looked, despite a deeply unflattering dress and a smile which suggested that, like him, she'd rather be somewhere else.

Before the ceremony he had endured a meet-and-greet with her family over some unspeakable coffee, drunk in a room hung with dusty old paintings. Flora and Clover he'd already met and the remaining sibling was called Poppy—a startlingly pretty girl with grey eyes like Willow's, who seemed as keen to question him as her sisters had been. Their attitude towards him had been one of unrestrained suspicion. They were curious about where he and Willow had met and how long they'd been an item. They seemed surprised to hear he lived in Paris and they wondered how often he was seeing their sister. And because Dante didn't like being interrogated and because he wasn't sure what Willow had told them, he was deliberately vague.

Her parents had appeared at one point. Her mother was tall and still beautiful, with cheekbones as high as Willow's own. She was wearing what looked like her husband's old smoking jacket over a dress and a pair of wellington boots and smiled rather distractedly when Dante shook her hand.

But her attitude changed the instant she caught sight of Willow, who had been over on the other side of the room, finding him a cup of coffee. 'Are you okay, darling? You're not tiring yourself out?'

Just what *was* it with these people? Dante wondered. Was that a warning look from Sister Number Three being slanted in his direction? He *got* that Willow probably didn't bring a lot of men home and he *got* that as the youngest daughter she would be a little overprotected. But they seemed to be fussing around her as if she was some kind of teenager, rather than a woman in her mid-twenties. And she seemed to be letting them.

But now the wedding was over, the photo session was finished and he was standing on a warm summer's evening with a growing sense of sexual anticipation. He felt his mouth dry as he glanced across the lawn, to where Willow was listening to something her mother was saying, obediently nodding her blond head, which was woven with blooms and making her look even more ethereal than before. Her dress emphasised the razor-sharp slant of her collarbones and the slenderness of her bare arms.

Maybe her intrinsic delicacy was the reason why everyone seemed to treat her with kid gloves. And why her gaggle of interfering sisters seemed to boss her around so much.

Her mother walked off and Dante put his untouched drink onto a table, walking through the growing dusk until he was standing in front of her. He watched as her expression underwent a series of changes. He saw shyness as well as that now-familiar wariness in her eyes, but he saw desire too—and that desire lit something inside him and made him want to touch her again.

'Dance with me,' he said.

With a quick bite of her lip, she shook her head. 'I'd better not. I have masses of things I need to do.'

'It wasn't a question, Willow,' he said, pulling her into his arms. 'It was a command and I won't tolerate anyone who disobeys my commands.'

'That's an outrageous thing to say.'

'So outrageous it's made you shiver with desire?'

'I'm not.'

'Yes, you are.' Pulling her against his body, he breathed in the scent of flowers which made him long to remove that fussy dress and have her naked in his arms. He'd had enough of behaving like a teenager—only getting so far before another of her damned sisters interrupted them. He slid his hand over her ribcage, his heart thundering as his fingertips stroked the slippery satin. 'So how long does this damned wedding go on for?'

'Oh, ages,' she said, but the sudden breathlessness in her voice coincided with his thumb casually beginning to circle the area beneath her breast. 'We haven't even had the speeches yet.'

'That's what's worrying me,' he said, swinging her round and thinking how slight she was. He remembered how feather-light she'd felt when he'd carried her over to that ridiculously tiny bed and he wished he was on that bed right now with his mouth on her breast and his fingers between her legs. 'I don't know how much longer I can wait,' he said huskily.

'Wait?' She drew her head back and it was as if she had suddenly recognised her power over him, because her grey eyes were dancing with mischief. 'Yes, I suppose you must be hungry. Well, don't worry—supper won't be long. Just as soon as my father and the best man have spoken.'

In answer, he pressed his hardness against her with a sudden calculated stamp of sexual mastery and watched as her pupils dilated in response. 'I want you,' he said, very deliberately. 'And I'm tempted to take you by the hand and get us lost in these enormous grounds. I'd like to find somewhere sheltered, like the shade of a big tree, so that I could explore what you're wearing underneath that monstrosity of a dress. I'd like to make you come very quickly. In fact, I think I could make myself come right now, just by thinking about it.'

'Dante!'

'Yes, Willow?'

She drew away from him, trembling slightly, and once again he was confused, because wasn't she just a mass of contradictions? One minute she was so hot that he almost scorched his fingers when he touched her—and the next she was looking up at him with reproachful grey eyes, like some delicate flower he was in danger of crushing beneath the full force of his desire. And that was how her family treated her, wasn't it? Like she couldn't be trusted to make her own judgements and look after herself.

'You're very...'

'Very what?' He stalled her sentence with the brush of his lips against her cheek and felt her shiver again.

'D-demanding,' she managed.

'Don't you like me being demanding?'

Willow closed her eyes as he tightened his arms around her, distracted by the heat of his body and acutely aware that they were being watched. *Of course they were being watched.* Dante Di Sione was easily the most watchable man here—and hadn't that been one of the reasons she'd demanded his company? To show people that she was capable of attracting such a man? But suddenly it felt like much more than just *pretending* to be his lover; she wanted to *be* his lover. She wanted it to be real. She wanted to be like everyone else, but she couldn't. So she was just going to have to make the best of what she was capable of, wasn't she?

'Yes,' she whispered. 'I like it very much. It's just not very appropriate right now. We're in the middle of a crowd of people and there are things I'm supposed to be doing.'

'Like what?'

'Checking that everyone's got a drink so they can make a toast once the speeches start. And introducing people who don't know each other—that sort of thing.'

'All this hanging around and waiting is very dull,' he observed.

'Then circulate,' she said lightly. 'That's what people do.'

'I've done nothing *but* circulate,' he growled. 'I think I'll go crazy if I have to endure yet another society matron trying to calculate what my net worth is.'

She tilted her head back and studied him. 'So how do you usually cope with weddings?'

'By avoiding them whenever possible.'

'But you were unable to avoid this one?'

'It seems I was.'

She narrowed her eyes at him. 'There must be something very valuable in that bag to make you want it so much.'

'Right now, I want you far more than anything in that damned bag.'

Willow giggled, feeling a sudden heady rush of excitement which had more to do with the way he was making her feel than the glass of punch she'd drunk. 'Which was a very neat way of avoiding my question.'

'I don't remember you actually asking a question and it's the only answer you're going to get. So when can we leave?'

'After the cake has been cut,' she said breathlessly. 'Look, there are the main players getting ready to speak and I'm supposed to be up at the top table. I'll see you in a while.'

She tore herself away from his arms, aware of his gaze burning into her as she walked across the garden, but at that moment she was on such a high that she felt as if she could have floated over the candlelit lawn.

It didn't take Flora long to bring her right back down to earth as she joined her in the throng of Hamiltons at the top table.

'I've looked him up on the internet,' she said as soon as Willow was in earshot.

'Who?'

'Who do you think? The man who drove you here today in his flashy red sports car,' replied her sister. 'Mr Macho.'

Willow reached for a glass of champagne from a passing waitress and took a sip as her gaze drifted over towards Dante's statuesque form, which seemed to stand out from the milling crowd. 'He's gorgeous, isn't he?' she said, without really thinking.

'Nobody's denying that,' said Flora slowly. 'And I'm guessing that if you've brought him here, it must be serious?'

'Well, I suppose so,' said Willow evasively.

Flora lowered her voice. 'So you're aware that he's

an *international playboy* with lovers in every major city in the world who is also known as a complete maverick in the world of business?'

Willow took a mouthful of fizz. 'So what? I'm not planning some kind of corporate takeover with him.'

'He's way out of your league, love,' said Flora gently. 'He's a wolf and you're an innocent little lamb. You haven't exactly had a lot of experience with the opposite sex, have you?'

'Only because my family is too busy mounting an armed guard around me!'

Flora frowned. 'So what exactly is going on between you?'

There was a pause. 'I like him,' said Willow truthfully. 'I like him a lot.'

It was perhaps unfortunate that Great-aunt Maud should have chosen just that moment to drift past in a cloud of magenta chiffon and gardenia perfume, blinking rapidly as she caught the tail end of their conversation. 'So does that mean you're going to be next up the aisle, Willow?' She beamed, without waiting for an answer. 'I must say I'm not surprised. He is quite something, that young man of yours. Quite something.'

Dante listened to the formal speeches which always bored the hell out of him and steadfastly ignored the redhead who was flashing him an eager smile. But for once the sentiments expressed went beyond the usual gags about mothers-in-law and shotguns. The groom thanked all the bridesmaids and told them how beautiful they looked, but he left Willow until last, and suddenly his voice grew serious.

'I'd just like to say how much it meant to Clover, having Willow's support. But much more than that is having her here today, looking so lovely. It means... well, it means everything to us.'

Dante frowned as people began to cheer, wondering why the atmosphere had grown distinctly *poignant* and why Willow's mother was suddenly groping in her bag for a handkerchief.

But then Willow's father began speaking and after he had waxed long and lyrical about the bride, he paused before resuming—his eyes resting affectionately on the slender blonde in the bridesmaid dress who was twisting the peachy satin around her fingers and looking slightly awkward.

'I just want to echo Dominic's words and say how happy we are to see Willow here today looking, if I might add, positively radiant. We just want her to know how proud we are of her, and the way she handled her illness, when all her peers were running around without a care in the world. And how her recovery has made us all feel very, very grateful.'

The applause which followed was deafening and Dante's lips froze as suddenly it all made sense.

Of *course*.

That's why she looked so fragile and that's why her family fussed around her and were so protective of her.

She'd been ill.

How ill? It must have been bad for it to warrant a mention in not one but *two* of the wedding speeches.

He felt momentarily winded. Like that time when a tennis ball hit by his twin had slammed straight into his solar plexus. He had been itching to take Willow away from here as soon as the speeches were over, but suddenly he needed time. And distance. Because how could he now take her to bed in the light of what he had learned?

Did Willow sense where he was in the throng of people? Was that why her grey eyes suddenly turned to meet his? Only this time it was more than desire which pumped through his veins as his gaze connected with hers. It was a cocktail of emotions he was unfamiliar with. He felt sympathy and a flare of something which clenched his heart with a sensation close to pain. The sense that life was unfair. And yet why should that come as a surprise, when he'd learnt the lesson of life's unfairness at the age of eight, when his entire world had changed for ever?

Why the hell hadn't she told him?

He watched as the smile she was directing at him became slightly uncertain and she picked up her glass and took a mouthful of champagne. And part of him wanted to run. To get into his car and drive back to London. To fly on to Paris as soon as possible and put this whole incident behind him. Yet he couldn't do that—and not just because she still had his grandfather's precious tiara. He couldn't just turn his back on her and walk away. If she'd known real suffering, then she deserved his compassion and his respect.

He saw all the women lining up and giggling and wondered what was happening, when he realised that the bride was about to throw her bouquet. And he wondered why it came as no real sense of surprise when Willow caught it, to the accompaniment of more loud cheers.

He couldn't stay here. He could see some of her

relatives smiling at him, almost—*God forbid*—as if they were preparing to welcome him into the fold and he knew that he had to act. Ignoring the redhead with the cleavage who had been edging closer and closer, he walked straight up to Willow and took the empty champagne glass from her hand.

'Let's get out of here.'

He couldn't miss the look of relief on her face.

'I thought you'd never ask,' she said, sounding a little unsteady.

On her high-heeled shoes she was tottering as they walked across the darkening grass as if she'd had a little too much to drink—but for once Dante wasn't about to take the moral high ground.

He waited for her to mention the speeches, but she didn't. She was too busy weaving her fingers into his and squeezing them. He thought again about her father's words and how her experience had affected her. It meant she'd probably learnt in the hardest way possible about the fragility of life and the random way that trouble could strike. He wondered if she'd plumped for recklessness as a result of that. Was that why she would have had sex with him before the wedding had even started, if her damned sister hadn't interrupted them? He wondered if she was this free with everyone—an aristocratic wild child who'd learned to be liberal with her body. And he was unprepared for the sudden dark shaft of anger which slammed into him.

They reached her room without meeting anyone and the sounds of celebration drifted up through the open windows as she shut the bedroom door behind them and switched on a small lamp. He could hear music and laughter and the rising lull of snatched conversation, but there was no joy in Dante's heart right then.

She leaned against the door, her shiny ruffled dress gleaming and her grey eyes looking very bright. 'So,' she said, darting a rather embarrassed glance at the bride's bouquet she was still holding, before quickly putting it down on a nearby table. 'Now what?'

He wished he could wipe what he'd heard from his mind, leaving his conscience free to do what he really wanted—which was to walk over there and remove her dress. To take off her bra and her panties and strip himself bare, before entering that pale and slim body with one slow and exquisite thrust.

He went to stand by the window, with his back to the strings of Chinese lanterns which gleamed in the trees.

'Did you enjoy the wedding, Willow?' he asked carefully.

She walked across the room, pulling the wilting crown of flowers from her head and placing it on the dressing table, and a clip which clattered onto the wooden floor sounded unnaturally loud.

'It was okay,' she said, taking out another clip, and then another, before putting them down. She turned around then, her hair spilling over her shoulders, and there was a faint look of anxiety in her eyes, as if she had just picked up from his tone that something was different. She licked her lips. 'Did you?'

He shook his head. 'No, not really. But then, I'm not really a big fan of weddings.'

Her smile became a little brittle. 'Oh, well, at least

it's over now,' she said. 'So why don't we just take our minds off it?'

She began to walk unsteadily towards him and Dante knew he had to stop this before it went any further. Before he did something he might later regret. But it was hard to resist her when she looked so damned lovely. There was something so compelling about her. Something pure and untouched which contrasted with the hungry look in her eyes and the wanton spill of her half-pinned hair. She looked like a little girl playing the part of vamp.

He shook his head. 'No, Willow.'

But she kept on walking towards him until she was standing in front of him in her long dress. And now she was winding her arms around his neck and clinging on to him like a tender vine and the desire to kiss her was like a fever raging in his blood.

Briefly, he closed his eyes as if that would help him resist temptation, but it didn't—because the feel of her was just as distracting as the sight of her. And maybe she took that as an invitation—because she brushed her mouth over his with a tentative exploration which made him shiver. With an angry little groan he succumbed to the spiralling of desire as he deepened the kiss. He felt the kick of his heart as her hands began to move rather frantically over him, and what could he do but respond?

She was tugging at his tie as he started to caress the slender lines of her body, his fingers sliding helplessly over the slippery material. He felt her sway and picked her up, carrying her over to the bed, like a man acting on autopilot. She lay there, almost swamped by the silky folds of her bridesmaid dress, and as his hand reached out to stroke its way over her satin-covered breast, he felt a savage jerk of lust.

'Oh, Dante,' she breathed—and that heartfelt little note of wonder was almost his undoing.

Would it be so wrong to take her? To have her gasp out her pleasure and him do the same, especially when they both wanted it so badly? Surely it would be a *good* thing to end this rather bizarre day with some uncomplicated and mindless sex.

Except that it wouldn't be uncomplicated. Or mindless. Not in the light of what he'd learned. Because she was vulnerable. Of course she was. And he couldn't treat her as he would treat any other woman. He couldn't just strip her naked and pleasure her and take what he wanted for himself before walking away. She had gone through too much to be treated as something disposable.

With an effort which tore at him like a physical pain, he moved away from the bed and went to stand by the window, where the darkness of the garden was broken by the flickering gleam of candlelight. Tiny pinpricks of light glittered on every surface, like fallen stars. Beneath the open window he could hear a couple talking in low voices which then abruptly stopped and something told him they were kissing. Was that envy he felt? Envy that he couldn't just forget everything he knew and block out his reservations with a kiss?

It took several moments for the hunger to leave him, and when he had composed himself sufficiently, he turned back to find her sitting up on the bed looking at him—confusion alternating with the desire which was skating across her fine-boned features.

He drew in a deep breath. 'Why didn't you tell me you'd been so ill?'

Willow's first reaction was one of rage as his words fired into her skin like sharp little arrows. Rage that her father and Dominic should have seen fit to include the information *in their speeches* and rage that he should suddenly have started talking to her in that new and gentle voice. She didn't want him to be *gentle* with her—she wanted him hot and hungry. She wanted him tugging impatiently at her clothes like he'd been before, as if he couldn't wait to strip her bare.

'What does that have to do with anything?' she demanded. 'I had leukaemia as a child. What's the big deal?'

'It's a pretty big deal, Willow.'

'Only if people choose to make it one,' she gritted out. 'Especially since I've had the all-clear, which makes me as disease-free as you or the rest of the general population. What did you want me to do, Dante? Tell you all about the drugs and the side effects and the way my hair fell out, or how difficult it was to actually keep food down? When it comes to interacting with men, it's not exactly what they want to hear as a chat-up line. It doesn't really make you attractive towards the opposite sex.' She glared. 'Why the hell did Dom and my father have to say anything?'

'I think I might have worked it out for myself,' he said slowly. 'Because I'd had my suspicions ever since we arrived.'

'You had your *suspicions*?' she echoed angrily.

'Sure. I wondered why your sisters were acting as

if I was the big, bad ogre and I wondered why everyone was so protective of you. It took me a while to work out why that might be, but now I think I have.'

'So once I was very sick and now I'm not,' she said flippantly. 'End of subject, surely?'

'But it's a little bit more complicated than that, Willow?' he said slowly. 'Isn't it?'

For a minute she stiffened as she thought he might have learned about her biggest fear and secret, before she told herself he couldn't know. He wasn't *that* perceptive and she'd certainly never discussed it with anyone else. 'What are you talking about?' she questioned.

His eyes narrowed. 'Something tells me you've never brought a man back here before. Have you?'

Willow felt humiliation wash over her and in that moment she hated Dante Di Sione's perception and that concerned way he was looking at her. She didn't want him looking at her with *concern*—she wanted him looking at her with *lust*. *So brazen it out*, she told herself. *You've come this far. You've dismissed your illness, so deal with the rest.* She had him here with her—a captive audience—and judging by his body language, he still wanted her just as much as she wanted him.

'And how did you manage to work that out?' she questioned.

His eyes were boring into her, still with that horrible, unwanted perception.

'Just that every time I was introduced as your partner, people expressed a kind of barely concealed astonishment. I mean, I know I have something of a reputation where women are concerned, but they were acting like I was the devil incarnate.'

For a second Willow thought about lying to him. About telling him that his was just another anonymous face in a sea of men she'd brought here. But why tell him something she'd be unable to carry off? She didn't think she was *that* good a liar. And all she wanted was for that warm feeling to come back. She wanted him to kiss her again. She wasn't asking for commitment—she knew she could never be in a position to ask for that. All she wanted was to be in his arms again.

She thought about the person she'd been when he'd met her at the airport—that bold and flirtatious Willow she'd never dared be before—and Dante had seemed to like that Willow, hadn't he? She was certainly a more attractive proposition than the woman sitting huddled on the bed, meekly listening to him berate her.

'I thought you would be the kind of man who wouldn't particularly want a woman to burden you with every second of her past.'

'That much is true,' he conceded reluctantly.

'So, what's your beef?'

Rather unsteadily, she got off the bed, and before he could stop her she'd reached behind her to slide down the zip of her bridesmaid dress, so that it pooled around her ankles in a shimmering circle.

Willow had never stood in front of a man in her underwear before and she'd always wondered what it would feel like—whether she would feel shy or uninhibited or just plain self-conscious. But she could still feel the effect of the champagne she'd drunk and, more than that, the look on his face was powerful enough to drive every inhibition from her mind. Because Dante looked almost *tortured* as she stepped out from the circle of satin and stood before him wearing nothing but her underwear and a pair of high-heeled shoes.

And although people often told her she looked as if she could do with a decent meal, Willow knew from her time working in the fashion industry that slenderness worked in your favour when you were wearing nothing but a bra and a pair of pants. She could see his gaze lingering on the swell of her breasts in the ivory-coloured lace bra which was embroidered with tiny roses. Reluctantly, it travelled down to her bare stomach before seeming to caress the matching thong, lingering longest on the flimsy triangle and making her ache there.

Feeling as if she was playing out a part she'd seen in a film, she lifted her fingers to her breast and cupped the slight curve. As she ran her finger along a twist of leaves, she thought she saw him move, as if he was about to cross the room and take her in his arms after all, and she held her breath in anticipation.

But he didn't.

Instead a little nerve began working furiously at his temple as he patted his pocket, until he'd found his car keys.

'And I think that's my cue to leave,' he said harshly.

'No!' The word came out in a rush. 'Please, Dante. I don't want you to go.'

'I'm sorry. I'm out of here.'

'Dante...'

'No. Listen to me, Willow.' There was a pause

while he seemed to be composing himself, and when he started speaking, his words sounded very controlled. 'For what it's worth, I think you're lovely. Very lovely. A beautiful butterfly of a woman. But I'm not going to have sex with you.'

She swallowed. 'Because you don't want me?'

His voice grew rough. 'You know damned well I want you.'

She lifted her eyes to his. 'Then why?'

He seemed to hesitate and Willow got the distinct feeling that he was going to say something dismissive, or tell her that he didn't owe her any kind of explanation. But to her surprise, he didn't. His expression took on that almost gentle look again and she found herself wanting to hurl something at him...preferably herself. To tell him not to wrap her up in cotton wool the way everyone else did. To treat her like she was made of flesh and blood instead of something fragile and breakable. To make her feel like that passionate woman he'd brought to life in his arms.

'Because I'm the kind of man who brings women pain, and you've probably had enough of that in your life. Don't make yourself the willing recipient of any more.' He met the question in her eyes. 'I'm incapable of giving women what they want and I'm not talking about sex. I don't do emotion, or love, or commitment, because I don't really know how those things work. When people tell me that I'm cold and unfeeling, I don't get offended—because I know it's true. There's nothing deep about me, Willow—and there never will be.'

Willow drew in a breath. It was now or never. It was a huge risk—but so what? What did she have to lose when the alternative of not having him suddenly seemed unbearable? 'But that's all I want from you,' she whispered. 'Sex.'

His face hardened as he shook his head.

'And I certainly don't have sex with virgins,' he finished flatly.

She stared at him in disbelief. 'But…how on earth could you tell I was a virgin?' she whispered, her voice quivering with disappointment, before realising from his brief, hard smile that she had just walked into some sort of trap.

'Call it an informed guess,' he said drily. 'And it's the reason why I have to leave.'

The hurt and the rejection Willow was feeling was now replaced by a far more real concern as she realised he meant it. He was going to leave her there, aching and alone and having to face everyone in the morning.

Reaching down to the bed, she grabbed at the duvet which was lying on the bed and wrapped it around herself, so that it covered her in an unflattering white cloud. And then she looked into the icy glitter of his eyes, willing him not to walk away. 'If you go now, it will just cause a big scene. It will make people gossip and stir up all kinds of questions. And I don't think I can face them. Or rather, I don't want to face them. Please don't make me. Don't go,' she said urgently. 'At least, not tonight. Let's pretend that you're my lover, even if it's not true. Let me show my sisters and my family that I'm a grown-up woman who doesn't need their protection any more. I want to break free from their well-meaning intervention, and you're the person who can help me. So help me, Dante. Don't make me face them alone in the morning.'

Dante heard the raw appeal in her voice and realised how difficult that must have been for her to say. She seemed so vulnerable that part of him wanted to go over there and comfort her. To cradle her in his arms and tell her everything was going to be all right. But he couldn't do that with any degree of certainty, could he? He didn't even trust himself to touch her without going back on his word and it was vital he kept to his self-imposed promise.

'This is a crazy situation,' he growled. 'Which is going to get even crazier if I stay. I'm sorry, Willow—but I can't do it.'

In the distance, the music suddenly came to a halt and the sound of clapping drifted in through the open windows.

'But I still have your bag,' she said quietly. 'And I thought you badly wanted it back.'

There was a pause.

'Are you...*threatening* me?' he questioned.

She shrugged. 'I thought we had a deal.'

He met her grey gaze and an unwilling feeling of admiration flooded through him as he realised that she meant it. And even though she wouldn't have had a leg to stand on if he had decided to offer *real* resistance, he knew he couldn't do it. Because there were only so many setbacks a person could take—and she'd had more than her fair share of them.

'Okay,' he said at last. 'The deal still stands, though the terms have changed. And this is what we're going to do. You are going to get ready for bed in the bathroom and you're going to wear something—anything—I don't care what it is as long as it covers you up. You are then going to get into bed and I don't want to hear another word from you until morning, when we will leave for London before anyone else is awake, because I have no intention of facing your family first thing and having to continue with this ridiculous farce.'

'But...where will you sleep?'

With a faint feeling of disbelief that he should be consigning himself to a celibate night, he pointed to a faded velvet chaise longue on the opposite side of the room. 'Over there,' he said.

'Dante...'

'No,' he said, his patience dwindling as he moved away from her, because despite the fact that she was swaddled beneath that fat, white duvet, the image of her slender body wearing nothing but her bra and pants was seared into his memory. He swallowed. 'I want you to do that right now, or the deal is off—and if I have to drive myself back to London and break into your apartment in order to retrieve what is rightfully mine, then I will do it. Do you understand, Willow?'

She met his eyes and nodded with an obedience which somehow made his heart twist.

'Yes, Dante,' she said. 'I understand.'

CHAPTER SIX

THE STRONG SMELL of coffee filtered into her senses, waking Willow from her restless night. Slowly, her eyelids flickered open to see Dante standing by her bed with a steaming mug in his hand. He was already dressed, though looked as if he could do with a shave, because his jaw was dark and shadowed.

So were his eyes.

'Where did you find the coffee?' she asked.

'Where do you think I found it? In the kitchen. And before you ask, the answer is no. Everyone else in the house must be sleeping off their hangover because I didn't bump into anyone else along the way.'

Willow nodded. It was like a bad dream. Actually, it was more like a nightmare. She'd spent the night alone in her childhood bed, covered up in a baggy T-shirt and a pair of pants, while Dante slept on the chaise longue on the other side of the room.

Pushing her hair away from her face, she sat up and stared out of the windows. Neither of them had drawn the drapes last night and the pale blue of the morning sky was edged with puffy little white clouds. The birds were singing fit to burst and the powerful scent of roses drifted in on the still-cool air. It was an English morning at its loveliest and yet its beauty seemed to mock her. It reminded her of all the things she didn't have. All the things she probably never *would* have. It made her think about the disaster of the wedding the day before. She thought about her sister laughing up at her new husband with love shining from her eyes. About the youngest flower girl, clutching her posy with dimpled fists. About the tiny wail of a baby in the church, and the shushing noises of her mother as she'd carried the crying infant outside, to the understanding smiles of the other women present, like they were all members of that exclusive club called *Mothers*.

A twist of pain like a knife in her heart momentarily caught Willow off-guard and it took a moment before she had composed herself enough to turn to look into Dante's bright blue eyes.

'What time is it?' she asked.

'Still early.' His iced gaze swept over her. 'How long will it take you to get ready?'

'Not long.'

'Good,' he said, putting the coffee down on the bedside table and then walking over to the other side of the room to stare out of the window. 'Then just do it, and let's get going as soon as possible, shall we?'

It was couched as a question but there was no disguising the fact that it was another command.

'What about my parents?'

'Leave them a note.'

She wanted to tell him that her mother would hit the roof if she just slunk away without even having breakfast, but she guessed what his response would be. He would shrug and tell her she was welcome to stay. And she didn't *want* to stay here, without him. She wanted to keep her pathetic fantasy alive for a while longer. She wanted people to see what wasn't really true. Willow with her boyfriend. Willow who'd just spent the night with a devastatingly attractive man. Lucky Willow.

Only she wasn't lucky at all, was she?

Sliding out of bed, she grabbed her clothes and took the quickest shower on record as she tried very hard not to think about the way she'd pleaded with Dante to have sex with her the night before. Or the way he'd turned her down. He'd told her it was because he was cold and sometimes cruel. He'd told her he didn't want to hurt her and maybe that was thoughtfulness on his part—how ironic, then, that he had ended up by hurting her anyway.

Dressing in jeans and a T-shirt and twisting her hair into a single plait, Willow returned to the bedroom, drank her cooled coffee and then walked with Dante through the blessedly quiet corridors towards the back of the house.

She should have realised it was too good to be true, because there, standing by the kitchen door wearing a silky dressing gown and a pair of flip-flops, stood her mother. Willow stared at her in dismay. Had she heard her and Dante creeping through the house, or was this yet another example of the finely tuned antennae her mother always seemed able to call upon whenever she was around?

'M-Mum,' stumbled Willow awkwardly.

A pair of eyebrows were arched in her direction. 'Going somewhere?'

Willow felt her cheeks grow pink and was racking her brains about what to say, when Dante intercepted.

'You must forgive us for slipping away so early after such a fabulous day yesterday, Mrs Hamilton—but I have a pile of work I need to get through before I go back to Paris and Willow has promised to help me.' He smiled. 'Haven't you?'

Willow had never seen her mother look quite so flustered—but how could she possibly object in the face of all that undeniable charm and charisma Dante was directing at her? She saw the quick flare of hope in her mother's eyes. Was she in danger of projecting into the future, just as Great-aunt Maud had done last night?

Kissing her mother goodbye she and Dante went outside, but during the short time she'd spent getting ready, the puffy white clouds had accumulated and spread across the sky like foam on a cup of macchiato. Suddenly, the air had a distinct chill and Willow shivered as Dante put the car roof up and she slid onto the passenger seat.

It wasn't like the outward journey, when the wind had rushed through their hair and the sun had shone and she had been filled with a distinct sensation of hope and excitement. Enclosed beneath the soft roof, the atmosphere felt claustrophobic and tense and the roar of his powerful car sounded loud as it broke the early-morning Sunday silence.

They drove for a little way without saying anything, and once out on the narrow, leafy lanes, Willow risked a glance at him. His dark hair curled very slightly over the collar of his shirt and his olive skin glowed. Despite his obvious lack of sleep and being in need of a shave, he looked healthy and glowing—like a man at the very peak of his powers, but his profile was set and unmoving.

She cleared her throat. 'Are you angry with me?'

Dante stared straight ahead as the hedgerows passed in a blur of green. He'd spent an unendurable night. Not just because his six-foot-plus frame had dwarfed the antique piece of furniture on which he'd been attempting to sleep, but because he'd felt bad. And it hadn't got any better. He'd been forced to listen to Willow tossing and turning while she slept. To imagine that pale and slender body moving restlessly against the sheet. He'd remembered how she'd felt. How she'd tasted. How she'd begged him to make love to her. He had been filled with a heady sexual hunger which had made him want to explode. He'd wanted her, and yet rejecting her had been his only honourable choice. Because what he'd said had been true. He *did* hurt women. He'd never found one who was capable of chipping her way through the stony walls he'd erected around his heart, and sometimes he didn't think he ever would. And in the meantime, Willow Hamilton needed protection from a man like him.

'I'm angry with myself,' he said.

'Because?'

'Because I should have chosen a less controversial way of getting my bag back. I shouldn't have agreed to be your plus one.' He gave a short laugh. 'But you were very persuasive.'

She didn't answer immediately. He could see her finger drawing little circles over one of the peacocks which adorned her denim-covered thigh.

'There must be something in that bag you want very badly.'

'There is.'

'But I don't suppose you're going to tell me what it is?'

The car had slowed down to allow a stray sheep to pick its way laboriously across the road, giving them a slightly dazed glance as it did so. Dante's instinct was to tell her that her guess was correct, but suddenly he found himself wanting to tell her. Was that because so far he hadn't discussed it with anyone? Because he and his twin brother were estranged and he wasn't particularly close to any of his other siblings? That all their dark secrets and their heartache seemed to have pushed them all apart, rather than bringing them closer together...

'The bag contains a diamond and emerald tiara,' he said. 'Worth hundreds of thousands of dollars.'

Her finger stopped moving. 'You're kidding?'

'No, I'm not. My grandfather specifically asked me to get it for him and it took me weeks to track the damned thing down. He calls it one of his Lost Mistresses, for reasons he's reluctant to explain. He sold it a long time ago and now he wants it back.'

'Do you know why?'

He shrugged. 'Maybe because he's dying.'

'I'm sorry,' she said softly, and he wondered if she'd heard the slight break in his voice.

'Yeah,' he said gruffly, his tightened lips intended to show her that the topic was now closed.

They drove for a while in silence and had just hit the outskirts of greater London, when her voice broke into his thoughts.

'Your name is Italian,' she commented quietly. 'But your accent isn't. Sometimes you sound American, but at other times your accent could almost be Italian, or French. How come?'

Dante thought how women always wanted to do things the wrong way round. Shouldn't she have made chatty little enquiries about his background *before* he'd had his hand inside her panties yesterday? And yet wasn't he grateful that she'd moved from the subject of his family?

'Because I was born in the States,' he said. 'And spent the first eight years of my life there—until I was sent away to boarding school in Europe.'

She nodded and he half expected the usual squeak of indignation. Because women invariably thought they were showcasing their caring side by professing horror at the thought of a little boy being sent away from home so young. But he remembered that the English were different and her aristocratic class in particular had always sent young boys away to school.

'And did you like it?' she questioned.

Dante nodded, knowing his reaction had been unusual—the supposition being that any child would hate being removed from the heart of their family. Except in his case there hadn't been a heart. That had been torn out one dark and drug-fuelled night—shattered and smashed—leaving behind nothing but emptiness, anger and guilt.

'As it happens, I liked it very much,' he drawled, deliberately pushing the bitter thoughts away. 'It was in the Swiss mountains—pure and white and unbelievably beautiful.' He paused as he remembered how the soft white flakes used to swarm down from the sky, blanketing the world in a pure silence—and how he had eagerly retreated into that cold space where nothing or nobody could touch him. 'We used to ski every day, which wore us out so much that there wasn't really time to think. And there were kids from all over the world, so it was kind of anonymous—and I liked that.'

'You must speak another language.'

'I speak three others,' he said. 'French, Italian and German.'

'And that's why you live in Paris?'

His mouth hardened. 'I don't remember mentioning that I lived in Paris.'

Out of the corner of his eye he saw her shoulders slump a little.

'I must have read that on the internet too. You can't blame me,' she said, her words leaving her mouth in a sudden rush.

'No, I don't blame you,' he said. Just as he couldn't blame her for the sudden sexual tension which seemed to have sprung up between them again, which was making it difficult for him to concentrate. Maybe that was inevitable. They were two people who'd been interrupted while making out, leaving them both aching and frustrated. And even though his head was telling him that was the best thing which could have happened, his body seemed to have other ideas.

Because right now all he could think about was how soft her skin had felt as he had skated his fingertips all the way up beneath that flouncy little dress she'd been wearing. He remembered the slenderness of her hips and breasts as she'd stood before him in her bra and panties—defiant yet innocent as she'd stripped off her bridesmaid dress and let it pool around her feet. He'd resisted her then, even though the scent of her arousal had called out to his hungry body on a primitive level which had made resistance almost unendurable. Was that what was happening now? Why he wanted to stop the car and take her somewhere—anywhere—so that he could be alone with her? Free to pull aside her clothes. To unzip her jeans and tease her until she was writhing in helpless appeal.

He wondered if he'd been out of his mind to say no. He could easily have introduced her to limitless pleasures in his arms—and what better initiation for a virgin than lovemaking with someone like him? But it wasn't his technique which was in question, but his inbuilt emotional distance. He couldn't connect. He didn't know how.

'So why Paris?' she was asking.

Make her get the message, he thought. *Make her realise that she's had a lucky escape from a man like you.*

'It's well placed for central Europe,' he said. 'I like the city and the food and the culture. And, of course, the women,' he added deliberately. 'French women are very easy to like.'

'I can imagine they must be,' she said, her voice sounding unnaturally bright.

The car was soon swallowed up by the heavier London traffic and he noticed she was staring fixedly out of the window.

'We're nearly here,' he said, forcing himself to make some conversational remark. To try to draw a line under this as neatly as possible. 'So...have you got any plans for the rest of the day?'

Willow gazed at the familiar wide streets close to her apartment and realised he was preparing to say goodbye to her. What she would like to do more than anything else was to rail against the unfairness of it all. Not only had he turned her down, but he'd deliberately started talking about other women—*French women*—as if to drive home just how forgettable she really was. And he had done it just as she'd been speculating about his fast, international lifestyle. Thinking that he didn't seem like the sort of man who would ever embrace the role of husband and father...the sort of man who really would have been a perfect lover for a woman like her.

Well, she was just going to have to forget her stupid daydreams. Just tick it off and put it down to experience. She would get over it, as she had got over so much else. No way was she going to leave him with an enduring memory of her behaving like a victim. *Remember how he moaned in your arms when he kissed you*, she reminded herself fiercely as she slanted him a smile. *Remember that* you *have some power here, too.*

'I'll probably go for a walk in Regent's Park,' she said. 'The flowers are gorgeous at this time of the year. And I might meet a friend later and catch a film. How about you?'

'I'll pick up my bag from you and then fly straight back to France.' He stifled a yawn. 'It's been an eventful few days.'

And that, thought Willow, was that.

She was glad of all the times when her mother

had drummed in the importance of posture because it meant that she was able to walk into her apartment with her head held very proud and her shoulders as stiff as a ramrod, as Dante followed her inside.

She pulled out the leather case from the bottom of her wardrobe, her fingers closing around it just before she handed it to him.

'I'd love to see the tiara,' she said.

He shook his head. 'Better not.'

'Even though I inadvertently carried a priceless piece of jewellery through customs without declaring it?'

'You shouldn't have picked up the wrong bag.'

You shouldn't have been distracting me. 'And I could now be languishing in some jail somewhere,' she continued.

He gave a slow smile. 'I would have bailed you out.'

'I only have your word for that,' she said.

'And you don't trust my word?'

She shrugged. 'I don't know you well enough to answer that. Besides, oughtn't you to check that the piece is intact? That I haven't substituted something fake in its place—or stolen one of the stones. That this Lost Mistress is in a decent state to give to your grandfather and...'

But her words died away as he began to unlock the leather case and slowly drew out a jewelled tiara—a glittering coronet of white diamonds and almond-size emeralds as green as new leaves. Against Dante's olive skin they sparked their bright fire and it was impossible for Willow to look anywhere else but at them.

'Oh, but they're beautiful,' she breathed. 'Just beautiful.'

Her eyes were shining as she said it and something about her unselfconscious appreciation touched something inside him. And Dante felt a funny twist of regret as he said goodbye. As if he was walking away from something unfinished. It seemed inappropriate to shake her hand, yet he didn't trust himself to kiss her cheek, for he suspected that even the lightest touch would rekindle his desire. He would send her flowers as a thank-you, he decided. Maybe even a diamond on a fine gold chain—you couldn't go wrong with something like that. She'd be able to show it off to her sisters and pretend that their relationship had been real. And one day she would be grateful to him for his restraint. She would accept the truth of what he'd said and realise that someone like him would bring her nothing but heartache. She would find herself some suitable English aristocrat and move to a big house in the country where she could live a life not unlike that of her parents.

He didn't turn on his phone until he was at the airfield because he despised people who allowed themselves to get distracted on the road. But he wished afterwards that he'd checked his messages while he was closer to Willow's apartment. Close enough to go back for a showdown.

As it was, he drove to the airfield in a state of blissful ignorance, and the first he knew about the disruption was when his assistant, René, rushed up to him brandishing a newspaper—a look of astonishment contorting his Gallic features.

'*C'est impossible!* Why didn't you tell me, boss?'

he accused. 'I have been trying to get hold of you all morning, wondering what you want me to say to the press...'

'Why should I want you to say anything to the press?' demanded Dante impatiently. 'When you know how much I hate them.'

His assistant gave a flamboyant shake of his head. 'I think their sudden interest is understandable, in the circumstances.'

Dante frowned. 'What the hell are you talking about?'

'It is everywhere!' declared René. 'Absolutely everywhere! All of Paris is buzzing with the news that the bad-boy American playboy has fallen in love at last—and that you are engaged to an English aristocrat called Willow Anoushka Hamilton.'

CHAPTER SEVEN

WILLOW FELT RESTLESS after Dante had left, unable to settle to anything. Distractedly, she wandered around her apartment—except that never had it felt more like living in someone else's space than it did right then. It seemed as if the charismatic American had invaded the quiet rooms and left something of himself behind. She couldn't seem to stop thinking about his bright blue eyes and hard body and the plummeting of her heart as he'd said goodbye.

She slipped on a pair of sneakers and let herself outside, but for once the bright colours of the immaculate flower beds in the nearby park were wasted on her. It was funny how your thoughts could keep buzzing and buzzing around your head, just like the pollen-laden bees which were clinging like crazy to stop themselves from toppling off the delicate blooms.

She thought about the chaste night she'd spent with Dante. She thought about the way he'd kissed her and the way she'd been kissed in the past. But up until now she'd always clammed up whenever a man touched her. She'd started to believe that she wasn't capable of real passion. That maybe she was incapable of reacting like a normal woman. But Dante Di Sione had awoken something in her the moment he'd touched her. *And then walked away just because she'd been ill as a kid.*

She bought a pint of milk on her way home from the park and was in the kitchen making coffee when the loud shrill of the doorbell penetrated the uncomfortable swirl of her thoughts. She wasn't really concentrating when she went into the hall to see who it was, startled to see Dante standing on her doorstep with a look on his face she couldn't quite work out.

She blinked at him, aware of the thunder of her heart and the need to keep her reaction hidden. To try to hide the sudden flash of hope inside her. Had he changed his mind? Did he realise that he only had to say the word and she would be sliding between the sheets with him—right now, if he wanted her?

'Did you forget something?' she said, but the dark expression on his face quickly put paid to any lingering hope. And then he was brushing past her, that brief contact only adding to her sense of disorientation. 'What do you think you're doing?'

'Shut the door,' he said tersely.

'You can't just walk in here and start telling me what to do.'

'Shut the door, Willow,' he repeated grimly. 'Unless you want your neighbours to hear what I have to say.'

Part of her wanted to challenge him. To tell him to go right ahead and that she didn't care what her neighbours thought. Because he didn't want her, did he? He'd rejected her—so what right did he have to start throwing his weight around like this?

Yet he looked so golden and gorgeous as he towered over her, dominating the shaded entrance hall of the basement apartment, that it was difficult for her to think straight. And suddenly she couldn't bear to be this close without wanting to reach out and touch him. To trace her finger along the dark graze of his jaw and drift it upwards to his lips. *So start taking control*, she told herself fiercely. *This is* your *home and* he's *the trespasser. Don't let him tell you what you should or shouldn't do.*

'I was just making coffee,' she said with an airiness which belied her pounding heart as she headed off towards the kitchen, aware that he was very close behind her. She willed her hand to stay steady as she poured herself a mug and then flicked him an enquiring gaze. 'Would you like one?'

'I haven't come for coffee.'

'Then why *have* you come here, with a look on your face which would turn the milk sour?'

His fists clenched by the faded denim of his powerful thighs and his features darkened. 'What did you hope to achieve by this, Willow?' he hissed. 'Did you imagine that your petulant display would be enough to get you what you wanted, and that I'd take you to bed despite my better judgement?'

She stared at him. 'I don't know what you're talking about.'

'Oh, really?'

'Yes. *Really.*'

'So you have no idea why it's all over the internet that you and I are engaged to be married?'

Willow could feel all the blood drain from her face.

'No, of course I didn't!' And then her hand flew to her lips. 'Unless...'

'So you do know?' he demanded, firing the words at her like bullets.

Please let me wake up, Willow thought. *Let me close my eyes, and when I open them again he will have disappeared and this will have been nothing but a bad dream.*

But it wasn't and he hadn't. He was still standing there glaring at her, only now his expression had changed from being a potential milk-curdler, to looking as if he would like to put his hands on her shoulders and throttle her.

'I may have...' She took a deep breath. 'I was talking to my sister about you—or rather, she was interrogating me about you. She asked if we were serious and I tried to be vague—and my aunt overheard us, and started getting carried away with talking about weddings and I didn't...well, I didn't bother to correct her.'

His eyes narrowed. 'And why would you do something like that?' he questioned dangerously.

Why?

Willow met his accusing gaze and something inside her flared like a small and painful flame. Couldn't he see? Didn't he realise that the reasons were heartbreakingly simple. Because for once she'd felt like she was part of the real world, instead of someone just watching from the sidelines. Because she'd allowed herself to start believing in her own fantasy.

'I didn't realise it was going to get out of hand like this,' she said. 'And I'm sorry.'

'You're *sorry*?' he repeated incredulously. 'You think a couple of mumbled words of apology and everything's going to go back to normal?' His face darkened again. 'My assistant has been fielding phone calls all morning and my Paris office has been inundated with reporters asking for a comment. I'm in the process of brokering a deal with a man who is fiercely private and yet it seems as if I am about to be surrounded by my own personal press pack. How do you think that's going to look?'

'Can't you just…issue a denial?'

Dante stared into her soft grey eyes and felt close to exploding. 'You think it's that simple?'

'We could say that I was…I don't know…' Helplessly, Willow shrugged. *'Joking?'*

His mouth hardened, and now there was something new in his eyes. Something dark. Something bleak.

'A denial might have worked, were it not for the fact that some enterprising journalist was alerted to the Di Sione name and decided to telephone my grandfather's house on Long Island to ask him for his reaction.' His blue eyes sparked with fury as they captured hers with their shuttered gaze. 'And despite the time difference between here and New York, it just so happened that my grandfather was suffering from insomnia and boredom and pain, and was more than willing to accept the call. Which is why…'

He paused, as if he was only just hanging on to his temper by a shred.

'Why I received a call from the old man, telling me how pleased he is that I'm settling down at last. Telling me how lovely you are—and what a good family you come from. I was trying to find the right moment to tell him that there is nothing going on between us, only the right moment didn't seem to come—or rather, my grandfather didn't give me a chance to say what I wanted to.'

'Dante...'

'Don't you *dare* interrupt me when I haven't finished,' he ground out. 'Because using the kind of shameless emotional blackmail he has always used to ensure he gets his own way, my grandfather then told me how much *better* he'd felt when he heard the news. He said he hadn't felt this good in a long time and that it was high time I took myself a wife.'

'I'm sorry.' She gave him a beseeching look. 'What else can I say?'

Dante felt a feeling of pure rage flood through him and wondered how he could have been stupid enough to take his eye off the ball. Or had he forgotten what women were really like—had he completely wiped Lucy from his memory? Had it conveniently slipped his mind that the so-called *fairer sex* were manipulative and devious and would stop at nothing to get what it was they wanted? How easy it was to forget the past when you had been bewitched by a supposedly shy blonde and a sob story about needing a temporary date which had convinced him to go to the damned wedding in the first place.

He stared at the slight quiver of Willow's lips and at that moment he understood for the first time in his life the meaning of the term *a punishing kiss*, because that was what he wanted to do to her right now. He wanted to punish her for screwing up his plans with her thoughtlessness and her careless tongue. He watched as a slow colour crept up to inject her creamy skin with a faint blush, and felt his body harden. Come to think of it, he'd like to punish her every which way. He'd like to lay her down and flatten her against the floor and...and...

'Are you one of those habitual fantasists?' he demanded hotly. 'One of those women who goes around pretending to be something she isn't, to make herself seem more interesting?'

She put her coffee cup down so suddenly that some of it slopped over the side, but she didn't even seem to notice. Her hands gripped the edge of the table, as if she needed its weathered wooden surface for support.

'That's an unfair thing to say,' she breathed.

'Why? Because you're so delicate and precious that I'm not allowed to tell the truth?' He gave a short laugh. 'I thought you despised being given special treatment just because you'd been ill. Well, you can't have it both ways, Willow. You can't play the shrinking violet whenever it suits you—and a feisty modern woman the next. You need to decide who you really are.'

She met his eyes in the silence which followed. 'You certainly don't pull your punches, do you?'

'I'm treating you the same as I would any other woman.'

'Oh, but that's where you're wrong, because you're not!' she said with a shake of her head. 'If I was any other woman, you would have had sex with me last night. You know you would.'

Dante felt the heavy beat of a pulse at his temple and silently cursed her for bringing that up again. Did she think she would wear him down with her persistence? That what Willow wanted, Willow would get. His mouth hardened, but unfortunately, so did his groin. 'Like I told you. I don't sleep with virgins.'

She turned away, but not before he noticed the dark flare of colour which washed over her cheekbones and he felt his anger morph inconveniently into lust. How easy it would be to vent his feelings by giving her what she wanted. What he wanted. Even now. Despite the accusations he'd hurled at her and the still-unsettled question of how her indiscretion was going to be resolved, it was sexual tension which dominated the air so powerfully that he couldn't hardly breathe without choking on it. He couldn't seem to tear his gaze away from her. She looked as brittle as glass as she held her shoulders stiffly, and although she was staring out of the small basement window, he was willing to lay a bet she didn't see a thing.

But he did. He saw plenty. He could see the slender swell of her bottom beneath the dark denim. He could see the silken cascade of her blond hair as it spilled down her back. Would it make him feel better if he went right over there and slid down her jeans, and laid her down on the kitchen table and straddled her, before feasting on her?

He swallowed as an aching image of her pale, parted thighs flashed vividly into his mind and he felt another powerful tug of desire. On one level, of *course* it would make them both feel better, but on another—what? He would be stirring up yet more consequences, and weren't there more than enough to be going on with?

She turned back again to face him and he saw that the flush had gone, as if her pale skin had absorbed it, like blotting paper. 'Like I said, I'm sorry, but there's nothing I can do about it now.'

He shook his head. 'But that's where you're wrong, little Miss Hamilton. There *is*.'

Did something alert her to the determination which had hardened his voice? Was that why her eyes had grown so wary?

'What? You want me to write to your grandfather and apologise? And then to give some kind of statement to the press, telling them that it was all a misunderstanding? I'll do all that, if that's what it takes.'

'No. That's not what's going to happen,' he said. 'It's a little more complicated than that. My grandfather wants to meet the woman he thinks I'm going to marry. And you, my dear Willow, are going to embrace that role.'

The grey of her eyes was darker now, as if someone had smudged them with charcoal and a faint frown was criss-crossing over her brow. 'I don't understand.'

'Then let me explain it clearly, so there can be no mistake,' he said. 'My grandfather is a sick man and anything which makes him feel better is fine with me. He wants me to bring you to the family home to meet him and that's exactly what's going to happen. You can play the fantasist for a little while longer because you are coming with me to Long Island. As my fiancée.'

CHAPTER EIGHT

A SOFT BREEZE wafted in through the open windows, making the filmy drapes at the window shiver like a bridal veil and the mocking significance of *that* didn't escape Willow. She drew her hand over her clammy brow and looked around the luxurious room. She could hardly believe she was here, on Dante's estate, or that he had persuaded her to come here for a long weekend, despite the many objections she'd raised.

But he'd made her feel guilty—and guilt was a powerful motivator. He'd said that her lies about being his fiancée had given his grandfather hope, and it was in her power to ensure that a dying man's hopes were not dashed.

'You seemed to want to let your family believe that you were going to be my bride,' were his exact, silken words. 'Well, now this is your chance to play the role for real.'

Except that it wasn't real, because a real bride-to-be would be cherished and caressed by her fiancé, wouldn't she? Not kept at a chilly distance as if she was something unwanted but necessary—like a bandage you might be forced to wrap around an injured arm.

They were installed in an unbelievably cute cottage in the extensive grounds, but in a way that was worse than staying in the main house. Because in here there was the illusion of intimacy, while in reality they were two people who couldn't have been further apart. She was closeted alone with a man who clearly despised her. And there was only one bed. Willow swallowed. This time it was a king-size bed, but the principle of where to sleep remained the same. Was he really willing to repeat what had happened at the wedding—sharing a bedroom, while keeping his distance from her?

Dante had telephoned ahead to tell the housekeeper that they wished to be guaranteed privacy. She remembered the look on his face as he'd finished the call. 'They'll think it's because we're crazy about each other and can't keep our hands off each other,' he'd said mockingly.

But Willow knew the real reason. It meant that they wouldn't be forced to continue with the farce for any longer than necessary. There would be no reason for Dante to hide his undeniable hostility towards her. When they were with other people they would be sweetness and light together, while in private...

She bit her lip, trying hard to block out the sound of the powerful shower jets from the en-suite bathroom and not to think about Dante standing naked beneath them, but it wasn't easy. Their enforced proximity had made her achingly aware of him—whether he was in the same room, or not.

They had flown in by helicopter an hour earlier and Willow's first sight of the Di Sione family home had taken her breath away. She'd grown up in a big home, yes—but this was nothing like the crumbling house in which she'd spent her own formative years. This, she'd realised, was what real wealth looked like. It was solid and real, and clearly money was no object. The white marble of the Long Island mansion was gleaming and so pristine that she couldn't imagine anyone actually *living* in it. She had been aware of the endless sweep of emerald lawns, the turquoise flash of a swimming pool and the distant glitter of a huge lake as their helicopter had landed.

A housekeeper named Alma had welcomed them and told Dante that his grandfather was sleeping but looking forward to seeing them both at dinner.

'And your sister is here, of course,' she said.

'Talia?' questioned Dante as the housekeeper nodded.

'That's right. She's out making sketches for a new painting.' Alma had given Willow a friendly smile. 'You'll meet Miss Natalia at dinner.'

And Willow had nodded and tried to look as she thought a newly engaged woman *should* look—and not like someone who had recently been handed a diamond ring by Dante, with all the emotion of someone producing a cheap trinket from the remains of a Christmas cracker.

'What's this?' she'd asked as he had deposited a small velvet box on her lap.

'Your number one prop,' came his mocking response as their helicopter had hovered over the Di Sione landing pad. 'The bling. That thing which women love to flash as a symbol of success—the outward sign that they've *got their man*.'

'What an unbelievably cynical thing to say.'

'You think it's cynical to tell the truth?' he'd demanded. 'Or are you denying that women view the acquisition of diamonds as if it's some new kind of competitive sport?'

The awful thing was that Willow secretly agreed with him. Her sisters were crazy about diamonds—and so were plenty of the women she worked with—yet she'd always found them a cold and emotionless stone. The giant solitaire winked at her now like some malevolent foe, splashing rainbow fire over her pale fingers as Dante emerged from the bathroom.

Quickly, she looked up, her heart beginning to pound. She'd been half expecting him to emerge wearing nothing but a towel slung around his hips, and guessed she should be pleased that he must have dressed in the bathroom. But her overriding sensation was one of disappointment. Had she secretly been hoping to catch a glimpse of that magnificent olive body as he patted himself dry? Was there some masochistic urge lurking inside her which wanted to taunt her with what she hadn't got?

Yet the dark trousers and silk shirt he wore did little to disguise his muscular physique and his fully dressed state did nothing to dim his powerful air of allure. His black hair was still damp and his eyes looked intensely blue, and suddenly Willow felt her heart lurch with a dizzying yet wasted sense of desire. Because since that interrupted seduction at her sister's wedding, he hadn't touched her. Not once. He had avoided all physical contact with the studied exaggeration of someone in the military walking through a field studded with landmines.

His gaze flickered to where she'd been studying

her hand and his eyes gleamed with mockery. As if he'd caught her gloating. 'Do you like your ring?'

'It looks way too big on my hand,' she said truthfully. 'And huge solitaire diamonds aren't really my thing.'

He raised his dark brows mockingly, as if he didn't quite believe her.

'But they have a much better resale value than something bespoke,' he drawled.

'Of course,' she said, and then a rush of nerves washed over her as she thought about the reality of going to dinner that evening and playing the part of his intended bride. 'You know, if we're planning to convince your grandfather that we really are a couple, then I'm going to need to know something about you. And if you could try being a little less hostile towards me that might help.'

He slipped a pair of heavy gold cufflinks in place and clipped them closed before answering. 'What exactly do you want to know?'

She wanted to know why he was so cynical. And why his face had darkened as soon as the helicopter had landed here today.

'You told me about being sent away to boarding school in Switzerland, but you didn't say why.'

'Does there have to be a reason?'

She hesitated. 'I'm thinking that maybe there was. And if there was, then I would probably know about it.'

Dante's instinct was to snap out some terse response—the familiar blocking technique he used whenever questions strayed into the territory of *personal*. Because he didn't trust personal. He didn't trust anyone or anything, and Willow Hamilton was no exception in the trust stakes, with her manipulation and evasion. But suddenly her face had become soft with what looked like genuine concern and he felt a tug of something unfamiliar deep inside him. An inexplicable urge to colour in some of the blank spaces of his past. Was that because he wanted his grandfather to die happy by convincing him that he'd found true love at last? Or because—despite her careless tongue landing them in this ridiculous situation—she possessed a curious sense of vulnerability which somehow managed to burrow beneath his defences.

His lips tightened as he reminded himself how clever Giovanni was. How he would see through a fake engagement in the blinking of an eye if he wasn't careful. So tell her, he thought. She was right. He should tell her the stuff which any fiancée would expect to know.

'I'm one of seven children,' he said, shooting out the facts like bullets. 'And my grandfather stepped in to care for us when my parents died very suddenly.'

'And...how did they die?'

'Violently,' he answered succinctly.

Her eyes clouded and Dante saw comprehension written in their soft, grey depths. As if she understood pain. And he didn't want her to *understand*. He wanted her to nod as he presented her with the bare facts—not look at him as if he was some kind of problem she could solve.

Yet there had been times when he'd longed for someone to work their magic on him. He stared out at the distant glitter of the lake. To find a woman he'd be happy to go to bed with, night after night—instead of suffering from chronic boredom as soon as anyone tried to get close to him. To find some kind of *peace* with another human being—the kind of peace which seemed almost unimaginable to him. Was that how his twin had felt about Anais? he wondered.

He thought about Dario and felt the bitter twist of remorse as he remembered what he had done to his brother.

'What exactly happened?' Willow was asking.

Her gentle tone threatened to undermine his resolve. Making him want to show her what his life had been like. To show her that she didn't have the monopoly on difficult childhoods. And suddenly, it was like a dam breaking through and flooding him.

'My father was a screwed-up hedonist,' he said bluntly. 'A kid with too much money who saw salvation in the bottom of a bottle, or in the little pile of white dust he snorted through a hundred dollar bill.' His lips tightened. 'He blamed his addictions on the fact that my grandfather had never been there for him when he was growing up—but plenty of people have absent parents and don't end up having to live their lives on a constant high.'

'And what about your mother?' she questioned as calmly as if he'd just been telling her that his father had been president of the Union.

He shook his head. 'She was cut from the same cloth. Or maybe he taught her to be that way—I don't know. All I do know is that she liked the feeling of being out of her head as well. Or maybe she needed to blot out the reality, because my father wasn't exactly known for his fidelity. Their parties were legendary. I remember I used to creep downstairs to find it looking like some kind of Roman orgy, with people lying around among the empty bottles and glasses and the sounds of women gasping in the pool house. And then one day my mother just stopped. She started seeing a therapist and went into rehab, and although she replaced the drink and the drugs with a shopping addiction, for a while everything was...' He shrugged as he struggled to find a word which would sum up the chaos of his family life.

'Normal?'

He gave a short and bitter laugh. 'No, Willow. It was never normal, but it was better. In fact, for a while it was great. We felt we'd got our mother back. And then...'

'Then?' she prompted again.

He wasn't even angry with her for her persistence because now it felt like some rank poison was throbbing beneath his skin and he needed to cut through the surface to let that poison out.

'One night there was some big row. I don't know what it was about—all I do know is that my father was completely loaded and my mother was shouting at him. I heard him yell back that he was going out and then I heard her going after him. I knew he was in no state to drive and I tried to stop her. I...'

He'd done more than try. He'd begged her not to go. He'd run over and clung to her with all the strength his eight-year-old body could muster, but she hadn't listened. She'd got in the car anyway and the next time he'd seen his mother was when she'd been laid out in her coffin, with white lilies in her hands and that waxy look on her cold, cold cheeks.

'She wouldn't listen to me,' he bit out. 'He crashed

the car and killed them both. And I didn't manage to stop her. Even though deep down I knew what a state my father was in, I let her go.'

He stared out at the grounds of the house he'd moved into soon afterwards when his grandfather had brought them all here. A place where he'd been unable to shake off his sorrow and his guilt. He'd run wild until his grandfather had sent him and Dario away to school. And he'd just kept on running, hadn't he? He wondered now if the failure of his attempt to stop his mother had been the beginning of his fierce need to control. The reason why he always felt compelled to step in and influence what was happening around him. Was that why he'd done what he'd done to his twin brother?

'But maybe you couldn't stop her.'

Willow's voice—suddenly so strong and sure—broke into his thoughts.

'What are you talking about?' he demanded.

'Children can't always make adults behave the way they want them to, Dante,' she said, her words washing over him like balm. 'No matter how hard they try.'

Dante turned round, still unable to believe how much she'd got out of him. She looked like some kind of angel sitting there, with her pale English skin and that waterfall of silky hair. In her simple cotton dress she looked so pure—hell, she *was* pure. But it was more than just about sex. She looked as if she could take all the darkness away from him and wash away the stain of guilt from his heart. And her grey eyes were fixed on him, quite calmly—as if she knew exactly what was going on inside his head and was silently urging him to go right ahead and do it.

He wasn't thinking as he walked across the room to where she sat at an antique writing desk with the oil painting of Sicily which hung on the wall behind it. The hot, scorched brushstrokes and cerulean blue of the sky contrasted vividly with her coolness. Her lips looked soft and inviting. Some warning bell was sounding inside his head, telling him that this was wrong. But some of the poison had left him now. Left him feeling empty and aching and wanting her. Wanting to lose himself in her.

She didn't object when he pulled her out of the chair and onto her feet. In fact, the sudden yearning in her eyes suggested that she'd wanted him to touch her just as badly as he needed to.

His hands were in her hair and his mouth was hovering over hers, their lips not quite touching, as if he'd had a last-minute moment of sanity and this was his chance to pull back from her. Was that why she stood up on tiptoe and anchored her hands to his shoulders? Why she flickered the tip of her tongue inside his mouth?

'Willow,' he whispered as his heart began to pound.

'Yes,' she whispered back. 'I'm right here.'

He groaned as he tasted her—his senses tantalised by the faint drift of her scent. Dropping his hands from her hair, he gripped her waist and he thought how incredibly *light* she felt. As light as those drifts of swansdown you sometimes saw floating across hazy summer lawns. He deepened the kiss, and as she sucked in a breath, it felt like she was sucking him right inside her. For a moment he thought about the very obvious place where he would like to *be* sucked and his hand reached down to cup her breast. He heard the urgent little sigh of delight she made. He felt the restless circle of her narrow hips, and he could feel control leaving him as she kissed him back. He tried to remember where he'd put his condoms and just how long they had before they were expected up at the main house. And all the time he could feel himself going under—as if he was being consumed by a tide of rich, dark honey.

But along with the sweet, sharp kick of desire came the reminder of all the things he'd told himself he wasn't going to do. He'd messed up enough in his life. He'd failed to save his mother. He'd ruptured his relationship with his twin brother. In business he'd achieved outstanding success, but his personal relationships were not the same. Everything he touched turned to dust. He was incapable of experiencing the emotions which other men seemed to feel. And even though Willow Hamilton had allowed her stupid fantasies to manipulate events... Even though she had dragged him into her fantasy and made it impossible for him to walk away from her—that gave him no right to hurt her.

It would be too easy to take her innocence. To be the first man to claim her body for his own. To introduce her to the powerful but ultimately fleeting pleasures of sex. He closed his eyes because imagining her sweet tightness encasing him was almost too much to bear. He thought about easing into her molten heat, with his mouth clamped to one of her tiny nipples. He thought about how good it would feel to be able to come inside her. To pump his seed into her until he was empty and replete. To kiss her and kiss her until she fell asleep in his arms.

But a woman's virginity was a big deal, and someone who had suffered as Willow had suffered deserved more than he could ever give her. Because he was programmed not to trust and never to stay. He would take pleasure and give pleasure and then close the door and leave without a backwards glance.

Dragging his mouth away from hers and dropping his hand from her breast as if it was on fire, he stepped away, trying to quieten down the fierce sexual hunger which was burning inside him. But when he saw the confusion clouding her beautiful eyes, he felt a moment of unfamiliar doubt which he couldn't seem to block out.

His mouth twisted.

'I meant what I said back in England,' he gritted. 'You aren't somebody I intend to get intimate with, Willow. Did you think that because I've just told you something about my *deeply troubled* past...' His voice took on a harsh and mocking tone. 'That I would want you? Did you think any of this was for real? Because if you do, you're making a big mistake. For the sake of my grandfather and his romantic ideals, we will play the part of the happily engaged couple whenever we find ourselves in his company. But when we're alone, the reality will be very different. Just so you know, I'll be sleeping on the couch.' He gave a tight smile. 'And I'll do my best not to disturb you.'

CHAPTER NINE

THE DARK SHAPE was moving almost silently around the room but it was enough to disturb Willow from her troubled sleep. Pushing the hair back from her face, she sat up in bed and snapped on the light to see Dante standing fully dressed, his face shadowed and unfriendly.

'What are you doing?' she whispered.

'Going out for a drive.'

'But it's only...' She picked up her watch and blinked at it. 'Just after five in the morning!'

'I know what the time is,' he growled back as he grabbed a clutch of car keys.

'So...why?' Her voice was full of bewilderment as she looked at him. 'Why in heaven's name are you going out before the sun is even up?'

'Why do you think?' He turned to look at her properly and all his dark and restless energy seemed to wash over her. 'Because I can't sleep.'

Willow swallowed. 'That couch *does* look very uncomfortable,' she agreed carefully. 'It can't be doing your back any good.'

'It's got nothing to do with the damned couch, Willow, and we both know it.'

She leaned back against the pillows, wishing that

he would stop snapping at her, and just end this impasse. Wishing he'd just take off those jeans and that stupid jacket and come and get in bed with her and do what was almost driving her out of her mind with longing. How many nights had they spent here now? And still her virginity was intact. Nothing had changed—at least, not in him—though her desire for him was as strong as ever. She wanted to kiss him. She wanted to hold him. Yet he acted as if she was contaminated.

'It was a mistake to come to this damned cottage,' he bit out. 'And an even bigger mistake to agree to stay on until after Natalia's opening.'

'So why *did* you agree to it?'

'You know damned well why,' he growled. 'Because you managed to make yourself completely irresistible to my grandfather, didn't you? So that I could hardly refuse his suggestion that we hang around for a few more days.' His fingers tightened around his car keys as he glared at her. 'Was this just more of the same kind of behaviour you demonstrated so perfectly at your sister's wedding? Manipulating events so they'd turn out the way you wanted them to?'

'That is an outrageous thing to say,' she retorted, wrapping the duvet more tightly around herself and trying very hard to keep the sight of her tightening nipples away from his accusing eyes. 'Unless you're suggesting that I deliberately went out of my way to be nice to your grandfather, just because I had some sort of hidden agenda to trap you in this cottage?'

He gave an impatient shake of his head. 'That wasn't what I meant.'

'Because, believe me, no one would deliberately angle to have more time alone with you, when you're in *this* kind of mood!'

His eyes narrowed. 'I guess not,' he said.

'And to be honest, I don't know how much longer I can go on like this,' she said. 'Maintaining this crazy fiction of presenting ourselves as the happy couple whenever we're with Giovanni or Natalia—and yet the moment we're alone, we're…we're…'

Dante stilled as he heard the unmistakable break in her voice, which only added to his growing sense of confusion and frustration. Because he hated it when she acted vulnerable—something which was surprisingly rare. When her voice wobbled or she got that puppy-dog look in her eyes, it started making all kinds of unwanted ideas flood into his head. Was it possible that duplicity didn't come as easily to her as he'd originally thought? That the sweet and uncomplicated Willow he'd seen here in his Long Island home—being endlessly patient with his grandfather and lovely towards his sister—was actually the real Willow? His mouth hardened. Or was she trying and managing very successfully to twist him around her little finger?

'We what, Willow?' he questioned silkily.

'We circle each other like two wary animals whenever we're together!'

'Well, let me ease the burden by going out and making sure we're alone for as little time as possible,' he said. 'Like I said, I'm going out for a drive. I'll see you later.'

Walking across the room, he clicked the door shut behind him, and as Willow listened to the sound of his retreating footsteps, she slumped dejectedly back into the pillows.

A heavy sigh escaped from her lips. She was living in a prison. A gilded prison where everything she wanted was right in front of her. The only man she'd ever wanted was constantly within touching distance—only she wasn't allowed to touch. And the fiction of the happy front they presented to the outside world was cancelled out by the spiralling tension whenever they were alone together.

She'd thought she'd been getting close to him. She *had* been getting close to him. On the day they'd arrived, he'd dropped his formidable guard and told her things about his past—things about his childhood and his family which had made her want to reach out to him. She'd seen the bitter sadness distorting his features and had wanted more than anything else to comfort him.

And for a while he had let her. For a few moments he had held her tight and kissed her and something deep and strong had flickered into life as they'd stood, locked in each other's arms. Her experience of men was tiny, but she had *known* that kiss was about more than sexual desire. It had been about understanding and solace. She'd thought it had been about hope.

But then he had pushed her away almost coldly, and since then he hadn't come close. Only when they were being observed by other people did he soften his attitude towards her.

She'd met one of his sisters, Natalia—a talented artist who lived at the house. With her wavy brown hair tied back in a ponytail and tomboyish clothes, she wasn't a bit how Willow had imagined Dante's sister to be. She had recently returned from a trip to Greece, but her clear hazel eyes became shuttered whenever anyone asked about it.

And Willow had at last met the legendary Giovanni, Dante's grandfather. She'd felt a punch of painful recognition after being shown into his room and seeing the pills which the attendant nurse was tipping into a small plastic container. A sense of sadness had curled itself around her heart as she saw the unmistakable signs of sickness. She thought how the Di Sione family had so many of the things which society lusted after. With their lavish wealth and a sprawling mansion in one of the world's most expensive areas of real estate, they were a force to be reckoned with...but nobody could avoid the inevitability of death, no matter how rich they were. And Dante's grandfather's eyes held within them a pain which Willow suspected was caused by more than his illness. Was he trying to get his affairs in order before the end? Was that why he'd asked Dante to trace the costly tiara and bring it to him?

On the first of what became twice daily visits, Willow would perch on a chair beside the bed and chat to the old man. She told him all about her life in England, because she knew better than anyone how being housebound made the dimensions of your world shrink. She was less enthusiastic about her fictitious future with his beloved grandson, even though the old man's eyes softened with obvious emotion when he reached out to examine her sparkling engagement ring. And she hoped she'd done her best to hide her guilt and her pain—and to bite back the urge to confess to him that none of this was real.

After Dante had gone she lay in bed until the light came up, then walked over to the main house for breakfast. The dining room was empty but Alma must have heard her because she came in with a pot of camomile tea, just as Willow was helping herself to a slice of toast.

'Where is everyone?' asked Willow as she reached for a dish of jam.

'Signor Giovanni is resting and Miss Natalia's upstairs, trying on dresses for her exhibition,' replied Alma. 'Would you like Cook to fix you some eggs?'

Willow shook her head. 'I'm good, thanks, Alma. This jam is amazing.'

Alma smiled. 'Thank you. I made it myself.'

Slowly, Willow ate her breakfast and afterwards went for a wander around the house where there was always something new to discover. And it was a relief to be able to distract herself from her endless frustration about Dante by admiring the fabulous views over the Di Sione estate, and the priceless artwork which studded each and every wall of the mansion. She was lost in thought as she studied a beautiful oil painting of Venice when suddenly she heard a small crash on the first floor, followed by the unmistakable sound of Natalia's voice exclaiming something.

Curiosity getting the better of her, she walked up the curving staircase and along a wide corridor, past an open door where she could see Natalia standing in front of a mirror, a heavy silver hairbrush lying by her bare feet. She was wearing a green shift dress—one of the most shapeless garments Willow had ever seen—which did absolutely nothing for her athletic physique.

Instinctively, she winced and the words were out of her mouth before she could stop them. 'You're not wearing that, surely?'

'What?' Natalia looked down at the garment before glancing up again and blinking. 'This is one of my best dresses.'

'Okay,' said Willow doubtfully, going into the room and walking around behind Natalia to see if it looked any better from the back. It didn't.

'So what's wrong with this dress?' Natalia asked.

Willow shrugged as she looked at Dante's sister. 'Honestly? It looks like a green bin bag. Admittedly a very nice shade of green, but still…' She narrowed her eyes in assessment. 'Did Dante tell you that I work in fashion?'

Natalia shook her head. 'Nope. He's been characteristically cagey about you. If you want the truth, I was pretty surprised to meet you. He once told me that he didn't think that marriage was for him, and I believed him.' Her voice softened. 'That's why I'm so happy for him, Willow. Sometimes he seems so… alone…despite all the planes and the parties and the money he's made. I'm so glad he's found you.'

Willow's heart clenched with a guilt even though she felt a perverse kind of pride that their farce of togetherness was working so effectively. She turned her attention to Natalia again.

'You have a knockout figure and gorgeous hair and you don't do much with either.'

'I've never had to.'

'But today is different, isn't it?' persisted Willow. 'I mean, it's meant to be special.'

There was silence for a moment before Natalia answered. 'Yes.'

Willow glanced over at the clock on the mantelpiece. 'Look, we have plenty of time. I can see what you have in your wardrobe or we could raid mine. And I'm a dab hand with a needle and thread. Will you let me give you a bit of a makeover? Only if you want to, of course.'

There was a moment of hesitation before Natalia gave Willow the sweetest smile she'd ever seen. 'Sure,' she said. 'Why not?'

Dante parked the car and walked slowly to the house, his dark glasses shading his eyes against the bright golden glitter of the day. It was a beautiful day and he should have felt invigorated by the air and the drive he'd just had. He should have felt all kinds of things, but he didn't.

Because none of this was turning out the way it was supposed to. He'd thought that maintaining a fake relationship with Willow would be easy. He just hadn't anticipated the reality.

He hadn't thought through what it would be like, being with her day in and day out, because he had no experience of what it *would* be like. Because he didn't do *proximity*. He slept with women, yes. He *loved* sleeping with women and occasionally taking them out to dinner or the theatre—but any time he spent with them was doled out in very manageable slots and always on *his* terms. Yet now he found himself stuck with her in a cottage which seemed way too small and claustrophobic, and with no means of escape. His throat dried. She was there, but not there.

She was tantalisingly close, yet he had forbidden himself to touch her, for reasons which seemed less important as each day passed. And now a terrible sexual hunger raged somewhere deep inside him and it was driving him crazy.

For the first time in a long time, he found himself thinking about his twin. Was it being back here, and seeing the great sweep of lawns where they used to climb trees and throw balls, which had made the pain suddenly feel so raw again? He thought about what he'd done to Dario, and how he'd tried to make amends, and the taste in his mouth grew bitter. Because Dario hadn't wanted amends, had he? There was no forgiveness in his brother's heart.

Deciding to have some coffee before he faced Willow, Dante walked into the house to hear laughter floating down the curving staircase from one of the upstairs bedrooms. His eyes narrowed—the carefree quality of the sound impacting powerfully on his troubled thoughts. Frowning a little, he followed the unfamiliar sound until he reached his sister's bedroom, unprepared for the sight which awaited him.

Talia was standing on a chair, and Willow was kneeling on the floor beside it, with pins in her mouth as she tugged at the hem of a beautiful floaty dress quite unlike anything he'd ever seen his sister wear before. And it wasn't just the dress. He'd never seen Natalia with her hair like that either, or her eyes looking so big. He caught the milky lustre of pearls at her ears—they glowed gently against her skin—and suddenly felt a surge of protectiveness, because this was his baby sister, looking all grown up.

'What's going on?' he said.

Natalia looked up. 'Hi, Dante.' She smiled. 'I'm deciding what to wear to the exhibition of my work.'

He raised an eyebrow. 'But you never go to the exhibition.'

'Not in the past. But tomorrow night I do,' she said softly. 'And Willow has helped me choose what to wear. Isn't she clever?'

Willow.

For the first time, Dante allowed his gaze to linger on the slim blonde scrambling to her feet, her cheeks slightly pink as she removed a pin from her mouth and dropped it into a little pewter box. Her dress was creased and her legs were bare and he was hit by a wave of lust so powerful that he could feel all the blood drain from his head, to go straight to where his body was demanding it.

He'd left their suite early because he'd felt as if he would *explode* if he didn't touch her, and suddenly he began to wonder just what he was doing to himself. Whether pain was such an integral part of his life that he felt duty-bound to inflict it on himself, even when it wasn't necessary. Was he trying to punish himself by denying himself the pleasure which he knew could be his, if only he reached out and took it? Because Willow hungered for him, just as much as he did for her. He could read it in every movement of her body. The way her eyes darkened whenever she looked at him.

Her carelessness had led to that crazy announcement about them being engaged, but hadn't he committed far graver sins than that? Hadn't he once told the biggest lie in the world to his twin brother—a lie by omission. He had stood silent when Dario had accused him of sleeping with his wife, and hadn't their relationship been in tatters ever since?

Pushing away the regret which he'd buried so deep, he thought instead about what his grandfather had said, soon after he'd given him the tiara. That Willow was caring and thoughtful, and that he liked her. And Giovanni wouldn't say something like that unless he meant it. His sister seemed to like her too—and Talia could be notoriously prickly with new people, after all the bad stuff which had happened in *her* life.

He realised that Natalia was waiting for an answer to a question he'd forgotten. Something about Willow, he thought—which was kind of appropriate because it was difficult to concentrate on anything other than a pair of grey eyes and a soft pair of lips he badly needed to kiss.

'Yes, she is,' he said slowly. 'Very clever.'

A funny kind of silence descended as Willow's cheeks grew pink.

'Well, I think that's everything,' she said, brushing her hand down over the creases in her dress. 'You look gorgeous, Natalia.'

'Gorgeous,' Dante agreed steadily. 'And now I'd like to talk to you, Willow. That is, if Natalia has finished with you.'

'Sure.' Natalia gave a quick smile. 'We're all done here.'

In silence Dante followed Willow from Natalia's room, and once he had closed the door, she turned to him, her eyes filled with question.

'What is it?' she asked. 'Has something happened?'

But he shook his head. He didn't want whispered explanations in the corridors of this great house, with Natalia suddenly emerging from the bedroom or Alma or another member of staff stumbling upon them. He badly wanted to kiss her, and once he'd started, he wasn't sure that he'd be able to stop.

'I need to talk to you,' he said. 'In private.'

The journey to their cottage seemed to take for ever, and Willow's heart was pounding as she followed Dante through the grounds because she was aware that something about him was different. When he'd walked into the room and seen her and Natalia giggling together, there had been something in his eyes which had made her want to melt. He'd looked at her in a way which had made goose bumps whisper all over her skin and her heart start thumping with an urgent kind of hope. She'd seen a new tension in his body and hoped she hadn't imagined the hunger she'd seen in his blue eyes, but even if it was true, she wasn't sure she trusted it. Was he going to take her in his arms and run his hands over her body like he'd done before? Was he going to kiss her passionately—to the point where she was gasping with hunger and frustration—only to push her away again and add to that frustration?

In tense silence they walked down an avenue of tall trees, whose leaves were brushed with the first hints of gold, and when finally they reached the cottage, she turned to face him as he closed the door.

'What is it?' she questioned again. 'Why are you acting like this?'

'I'm not acting,' he said unsteadily. 'Up until now, maybe—but not any more. I've wanted you for so long and I've reached a point where I can't go on like this any longer because it's driving me insane. I've tried to resist you, but it seems I can't resist any more. And now I'm through with trying. I want you, Willow. I want you so badly I can hardly breathe.'

Her heart was performing somersaults as she looked at him, scarcely able to believe what she was hearing. 'You make it sound as if you're doing something you don't want to do.'

'Oh, I want to do it, all right,' he said simply. 'I can't remember ever wanting a woman as much as I do right now. Maybe because you've been off-limits for so long that it's stirred my appetite until I can think of little else but you. I don't know. All I know is that I don't want to hurt you.'

'Dante…' she said.

'No. Hear me out, because it's important that you do.' His gaze was very intense—his eyes like blue flames which burned right through her. 'I'm afraid your innocence will make you read too much into this and so I'm flagging it up before that happens. To make sure it doesn't happen. Because the act of sex can be deceptive, Willow. The words spoken during intimacy can often mimic the words of love and it's important you recognise that.'

She dug her teeth into her bottom lip. 'And you're afraid that if I have sex with you, I'll fall hopelessly in love with you?'

His face became shuttered. 'Will you?'

Willow wondered if it was arrogance which had made him ask that—or simply a remarkable honesty. She wondered if she should listen to the voice inside her head which was telling her to heed his warning.

That maybe she was setting herself up for a hurt bigger than any she'd ever known.

But it wasn't as easy as that. She wanted Dante in a way she'd never wanted anyone—a way she suspected she never would again. Even if she met someone else like him—which was doubtful—her fate was always going to be different from other women her age.

Because a normal life and marriage had never been on the cards for her and it never could.

But none of that was relevant now.

She wasn't asking the impossible. She wasn't demanding that he *love* her—all she needed to do was to keep her own emotions in check. *She had to.* Because anything else would frighten him away—instinct told her that. She gave a little shrug.

'I'll try my very hardest not to fall in love with you,' she said lightly.

'Good. Because there isn't going to be some fairytale ending to this. This fake engagement of ours isn't suddenly going to become real.'

'I don't care.'

And suddenly neither did he. He didn't care about anything except touching her like he'd wanted to do for so long.

Dante peeled the dress from her body and then couldn't stop staring—as if it was the first time he'd ever undressed a woman. She was all sweetness and delicacy. All blond hair and floral scent and pure white lingerie. He wrapped his arms around her. He wanted to ravish her and protect her. He wanted to spill his seed inside her—and yet surely a virgin of her stature could not take him when he was already this big and this hard.

He brushed a lock of hair away from the smoothness of her cheek. 'I'm afraid I might break you.'

'You won't break me, Dante. I'm a woman, not a piece of glass.' Her voice trembled a little as she lifted her chin and he saw the sudden light of determination in her eyes. 'Don't be different towards me just because I've never done this before, or because once I was sick. Be the same as you always are.'

'Be careful what you wish for.' With a little growl, he picked her up and carried her into the bedroom. Carefully, he laid her down on the bed before moving away and beginning to unbutton his shirt, telling himself that if she looked in any way daunted as he stripped off, then he would stop.

But she was watching him like a kid in a candy store and her widened eyes and parted lips were only adding to his desire—if such a thing was possible. He eased the zip down over his straining hardness and carefully watched her reaction as he stood before her naked—but her face was full of nothing but wonder, and hunger.

'Oh, Dante,' she said, very softly.

It was the sweetest thing he'd ever heard. He went over to the bed and bent over her, tracing the pad of his thumb over her trembling lips and following it with the slowest, deepest kiss imaginable. It made his heart kick and his groin throb, and when he drew back he could see she looked dazed. *You and me both, sweetheart*, he thought, his fingertip stroking along the delicate lace of the bra which edged her creamy skin, and he felt her tremble.

'Scared?' he said.

She gave a little shrug. 'Scared I might not meet your expectations.'

He unclipped the front clasp of her bra, so that her delicious little breasts sprang free and he smiled as he bent his head to trace each budding nipple with his tongue.

'You already have,' he murmured throatily. 'You're perfect.'

Willow didn't react to that because she knew she wasn't. Nobody was and in her time she had felt more imperfect than most. But the look on his face was making her feel pretty close to perfect and she would be grateful to him for ever for that.

And now his thumbs were hooking into the sides of her knickers and he was sliding them all the way down her legs.

'Mmm...' he said, his gaze pausing to linger on her groin. 'A natural blonde.'

And Willow did something she'd never imagined she'd do on her long-anticipated initiation into sex. She burst out laughing.

'You are outrageous,' she said as he dropped the discarded underwear over the edge of the bed.

'But you like me being outrageous, don't you, Willow?'

And that was the thing. She did. Dante Di Sione was both arrogant and outrageous, yes. She could understand why they called him a maverick. But he was a lot of other things too. Most men in his position, she suspected, would have bedded her before now—but Dante had not. He had tried to do the right thing, even though it had gone against all his macho instincts. He had resisted and resisted until he could resist no more. He was strong and masterful, yet he had a conscience which made her feel safe. And safety had always been a big deal for her.

'I think you know the answer to that question,' she murmured as she tipped her head back so that he could kiss her neck.

And Dante did know. He gave a groan of satisfaction as he explored her. He touched her wetness until she was trembling uncontrollably—until she had begun to make distracted little pleas beneath her breath. She was so ready, he thought, his heart giving a thunder of expectation as his hand groped blindly towards the bedside locker.

Thank God for condoms, he thought—though as he rolled the contraceptive on, it was the only time she seemed uncertain. He saw her biting down on her lip and he raised his eyebrows, forcing himself to ask the question, even though he could barely get the words out.

'It won't be easy and I can't promise that it won't half kill me to do it, but if you want to change your mind...'

'No,' she said fiercely, her eager kisses raining over his eyelids, his jaw and his mouth. 'Never! Never, never, never.'

Her eagerness made him smile and when finally he entered her there was only the briefest moment of hesitation as he broke through her hymen, and he was filled with a powerful sense of possession.

'Does it hurt?' he said indistinctly, fighting against every instinct in his body as he forced himself to grow still inside her.

But she shook her head. 'It feels like heaven,' she said simply.

Dante closed his eyes and finally gave himself up to the rhythm which both their bodies seemed to be crying out for, though already he could sense she was very close to the edge.

Gripping her narrow hips he brought himself deeper inside her, bending his head to let his tongue flicker over her peaking nipples while she twisted like some pale and beautiful flower beneath him.

'Dante,' she gasped, but she didn't need to tell him what he already knew.

He had watched with rapt fascination the build-up of tension in her slender frame. The darkening of those wintry eyes. The way her head moved distractedly from side to side so that her hair fanned the pillow like a silky blond cloud. Her back began to arch and her legs to stiffen, and just as her body began to convulse helplessly around him, he saw the rosy darkening of her skin above her tiny breasts.

'Dante,' she gasped again, and mumbled something else, but he didn't know what it was, and frankly, he didn't care. Because he'd been holding off for so long that he couldn't endure it for a second longer, so that when eventually his orgasm came, he felt the rush of blood and pleasure as his senses began to dissolve—and he felt like he was floating.

CHAPTER TEN

To Willow, it felt like living in a dream.

Dante Di Sione was her lover and he couldn't seem to get enough of her. And the feeling was mutual.

But it wasn't a dream. It was real. She needed to remember that. To remind herself that this was temporary. That it meant nothing. It meant nothing but sex. *He'd told her that himself.*

She pulled the rumpled sheet over her and listened to the sound of running water coming from the en-suite bathroom.

The trouble was that when you really wanted something it was easy to start constructing fantasies—the kind of fantasies which had got her into trouble in the first place. She started thinking about Dante's lifestyle. About his dislike of weddings and expressed distaste of settling down and doing the 'normal' stuff. What would he say if she told him she didn't care about all that stuff either? And that they might actually be a lot more compatible than he thought.

But thinking that way could lead to madness. It could make you start hoping for the impossible—and hope was such a random and unfair emotion. Hadn't she watched her young friends die in hospital and vowed that she would never waste her time on useless hope?

So just enjoy what you have, she told herself fiercely. *Store it all up in your mind and your heart—so that you can pull it out and remember it when you're back in England and Dante Di Sione is nothing but a fast-fading memory.*

It started to feel like a real holiday as he showed her around his home territory and introduced her to places he'd grown up with. He took her to tiny restaurants in New York's Little Italy, where the maître d' would enquire after his grandfather's health and where Willow ate the best pasta of her life. They spent a day at a gorgeous place in Suffolk County called Water Mill, where a friend of Dante's had the most beautiful house, surrounded by trees. They visited Sag Harbor and spent the night having sex in a stunning hotel overlooking the water, and the following day took a trip out on the Di Sione boat, which was anchored offshore. But when she told him she wanted to see the guidebook stuff as well, he took her to Manhattan and Staten Island, to Greenwich Village and Gramercy Park—where the beautiful gardens reminded her of England. And when he teased her about being such a *tourist*, he couldn't seem to stop kissing her, even though the wind blowing off the Hudson River had felt icy cold that day.

'What are you smiling about?' questioned Dante as he came in from the shower, rubbing his hair dry.

Willow shifted a little on the bed. It was weird how your life could change so suddenly. One minute she'd been someone who knew practically nothing about men—and the next she was someone watching as one headed towards her, completely naked.

Don't get used to it, she thought. *Don't ever get used to it.*

'My thoughts are my own,' she said primly.

'I suspect you were thinking about me,' he drawled. 'Weren't you?'

'That's a very...' His shadow fell over the bed and she looked up into the glint of his blue eyes. 'A very arrogant assumption to make.'

He bent to trace a light fingertip from nipple to belly button, weaving a sensual path which made her shiver. 'But you like my arrogance,' he observed.

Willow shrugged as guilty pleasure washed over her. 'Sometimes,' she murmured. 'I know I shouldn't, but I do.'

I like pretty much everything about you.

He smiled as he sat down on the edge of the bed and slid his hand between her legs.

'What are you doing?' she said.

'I think you know the answer to that question very well, Willow Hamilton.'

She tried telling herself not to succumb as he began to move his fingers against her, because surely it would be good to turn him down once in a while? But she was fighting a losing battle. She couldn't resist him when he started to touch her like that. Or when he brushed his lips against her neck. And suddenly it was not enough. It was never enough. 'Come back to bed,' she whispered.

'I can't. I'm expecting a call from Paris. There isn't time.'

'Then make time.'

'And if I say no?'

'You'll say yes in the end, you know you will.'

Dante laughed softly as he lay down beside her, smoothing his hands over her body as he drew her close. He stroked her breasts and her belly. He brushed his lips over her thrusting nipples and the soft pelt of hair between her thighs. For a while the room was filled with the sounds of breathing and kissing and those disbelieving little gasps she always gave when she came and then in the background the sound of his work phone ringing.

'I'll call them back later,' he murmured.

Afterwards he fought sleep and dressed, though he had to resolutely turn his back on her, for fear she would delay him further. He pulled on a shirt and began to button it, but his thoughts were full of her and he didn't want them to be. He'd told himself time and time again that now Talia's show was over, he needed to finish this. To let Willow go as gently as possible and to move on. It would be better for her. Better for both of them. He frowned. So what was stopping him?

He kept trying to work out what her particular magic was, and suddenly the answer came to him. Why he couldn't seem to get enough of her.

It was because she made him feel special.

And he was not.

He was not the man she thought him to be.

He stared out of the window at the lake and felt the swell of something unfamiliar in his heart. Was this how his twin had felt when he'd met Anais—the sense of being poised on the brink of something significant, something so big that it threatened to take over your whole life?

'Dante, what is it?' Willow was whispering from over on the bed, her brow creased. 'You look as if you've seen a ghost.'

He turned around to face her. Perhaps he had. The ghost of his stupid mistake, which had led to the severing of relations with his twin brother.

He shook his head. 'It's nothing.'

But she was rising from the rumpled sheets like a very slender Venus, her blond hair tumbling all the way down her back as she walked unselfconsciously across the room and looped her arms around his neck.

'It's clearly something,' she said.

And although she was naked and perfectly poised for kissing, in that moment all Dante could see was compassion in her eyes and his instinct was to turn away from her. Because all his life he'd run from compassion...a quality he'd always associated with pity, and he was much too proud to tolerate *pity*—he'd had enough of that to last a lifetime. He'd seen it on the faces of those well-meaning psychologists his grandfather had employed after the fatal crash which had left them all orphaned. He'd seen it etched on the features of those matrons at boarding school, where they'd been sent when Giovanni had finally admitted he couldn't cope any more. They'd all tried to get him to *talk* about stuff and to tell them how he *felt*. But he had clammed up, like those mussels he sometimes ate with frites in France—the ones with the tight shells you weren't supposed to touch.

Yet something about Willow made him want to talk. Made him want to tell her everything.

'You know I have a twin brother?' he said suddenly.

Cautiously, she nodded. 'But you don't talk about him.'

'That's because we are estranged. We haven't spoken in years.'

He untangled her arms from his neck and walked over to the bed, picking up a flimsy silk wrap and throwing it to her, disappointed yet relieved when she slipped it on because he couldn't really think straight when she was naked like that.

He drew in a deep breath as he met the unspoken question in her eyes. 'The two of us were sent away to a fancy boarding school in Europe,' he said slowly. 'And after we left, we started up a business together—catering for the desires of the super-rich. Our motto was *"Nothing's impossible,"* and for a while nothing was. It was successful beyond our wildest dreams...and then my brother met a woman called Anais and married her.'

There was a pause. 'And was that so bad?'

Dante looked into her clear grey eyes and it was as if he'd never really considered the matter dispassionately before. 'I thought it was,' he said slowly. 'I was convinced that she wanted Dario's ring on her finger for all the wrong reasons. Women have always been attracted to the Di Sione name in pursuit of power and privilege. But in Anais's case, I thought it was for the sake of a green card. More than that, I could see that she had her hooks into my brother. I could tell he really cared about her—and I'd never seen him that way before.'

'So what happened?' she said, breaking the brittle silence which followed.

Dante met her eyes. He had done what he had done for a reason and at the time it had seemed like a good reason, only now he was starting to see clearly the havoc he had wrought. He suddenly realised that his dislike of his twin's wife went much deeper than suspecting she just wanted a green card.

'I didn't trust her,' he said. 'But then, I didn't trust any woman.'

'Why not?'

'It's complicated.'

'Life is complicated, Dante.'

His mouth twisted. 'It's not a story I'm particularly proud of, but when we were at college, I was sleeping with a woman called Lucy. She was quite something. Or at least, so I thought—until I discovered she'd been sleeping with my twin brother as well.'

Willow stared at him. 'That's terrible,' she whispered.

He shrugged. 'I laughed it off and made out like it didn't matter. But it did. Maybe it turned her on to have sex with two men who looked identical. Or maybe she was just after the family name and didn't care which brother should be the one to give her that name.' He hesitated. 'All I know is that, afterwards, things were never quite the same between me and Dario. Something had come between us, though neither of us acknowledged it at the time. And after that, I always viewed women with suspicion.'

'I suppose so,' said Willow, and her hand reached up to touch his jaw. 'But after what had happened, it was natural you would be suspicious and examine the motives of the woman he eventually married. You were obviously looking out for him—you shouldn't beat yourself up about it.'

But Dante shook his head, forcing himself to look at the situation squarely for the first time. To see things as they were and not how he'd wanted them to be. And Willow needed to hear this. He didn't want her building up fantasies about him being the kind of caring brother who was just looking out for his twin. She needed to hear the truth.

'It wasn't just that,' he admitted slowly. 'The truth was that I wasn't crazy about Dario's new wife. I didn't like the power she had once she had his ring on her finger. She was so damned...*opinionated* and I hated the way Dario started listening to her, instead of me. Maybe I was just plain jealous.' He gave a ragged sigh. 'When he was out one morning I went round to confront Anais about her real motives in marrying him. I accused her of using him to get herself a green card and we had one hell of a row, which ended up with her throwing a glass of water over me. I guess I deserved it. We both backed down and that might have been the end of it—in fact, we'd both started talking—had Dario not walked in and found me walking out of *his* bedroom, buttoning up one of *his* shirts. He thought we'd been having sex.' He looked into Willow's widened eyes. 'He asked whether we'd been having sex.'

'And what...what did you say?'

'I didn't,' said Dante slowly. 'I didn't say anything. I used my silence to allow him come to his own conclusions, only they were the wrong conclusions. Because even though we'd both slept with Lucy, there was no way I would have ever touched his wife. But that didn't matter. All that mattered was that I felt this fierce kind of anger that he had accused me of such a thing. I thought that their relationship couldn't be so great if he thought his wife would jump straight into bed with his brother at the first opportunity. I thought the only way for things to get back to normal would be for them to break up—and they did. The marriage imploded and Dario cut all ties with me. He held me responsible and I couldn't blame him for that.'

'And did you...did you ever try to make amends?'

He nodded. 'At first I did. I was eaten up with guilt and remorse. But no matter how many times I tried to contact him, his mind was made up and he wouldn't see me, or speak to me. It was like trying to smash my way through a concrete wall with nothing but my bare hands, and in the end I gave up trying.'

He waited for her judgement. For the shock and outrage he would expect from a woman whose innocence he had taken and whose total tally of sexual partners was just one. Wouldn't she be disgusted by what he had done? Wouldn't she want to walk away from him, no matter how good he was between the sheets?

But there was no judgement there. The concern had not left her eyes. And for the first time in his life he was finding compassion tolerable.

'Why don't you go to him?' she asked.

'Because he won't see me.'

'Couldn't you at least...*try*? Because...' She sucked in a deep breath. 'The thing is, Dante...one thing I learnt when I was so ill was just how important family are. They should be the people you can depend on, no matter what. And you never, ever know what's around the corner. If something happened to Dario and you were still estranged, you'd never forgive yourself. Would you? And it's not too late to try again.' Her words became urgent. 'It's *never* too late.'

He shook his head, because hadn't he grown weary with being stonewalled? And all these years down the line, surely rejection would be all the harder to take. But as Dante looked into Willow's face, he realised he needed to be bigger than his pride and his ego. He thought about all the things she'd been through—things she hadn't wanted to tell him but which eventually he'd managed to prise from her. He thought about how she'd minimised her sickness with a few flippant sentences, making it sound no more inconvenient than a temporary power cut. Despite her slight frame and ethereal appearance, she was brave and resilient and he admired her for those strengths.

Walking over to the writing desk, he picked up his phone, but when he saw the name which had flashed onto the screen, he felt a sense of disbelief as he scrolled down to read the message. He looked up, to where Willow hadn't moved, a question darkening her grey eyes.

'What's wrong?'

'It's from Dario,' he said incredulously. 'And he wants to meet me.'

Her expression echoed his own disbelief. 'Just like that? Right out of the blue? Just after we'd been talking about him?'

'He says he heard I was at the house and decided to contact me.'

She gave a slightly nervous laugh. 'So it's just coincidence.'

'Yeah. Just coincidence.' But Dante found himself thinking about something he hadn't allowed himself to think about for a long time. About the intuition which had always existed between Dario and him—that mythical twin intuition which used to drive everyone crazy with frustration. They'd used it to play tricks on people. They'd loved making their teachers guess which twin they were talking to. But there had been another side too. The internal side which had nothing to do with playacting. His pain had been his brother's pain. Their joy and dreams had been equally shared, until a woman had come between them.

And maybe that was how it was supposed to be. Maybe he had wasted all that energy fighting against the inevitable. For now he could see that not only had he been jealous of Anais, he'd been angry that for once in his life he'd been unable to control the outcome of something he wanted. Because the little boy who'd been unable to save his mother had grown into a man with a need to orchestrate the world and the way it worked. A man who wanted to control people and places and things. And life wasn't like that. It never could be.

He looked at Willow and once again felt that strange kick to his heart. And even though part of him wanted to act like it wasn't happening, something was stubbornly refusing to let him off the hook so easily. Was it so bad to acknowledge the truth? To admit that she made him feel stuff he'd never felt before—stuff he hadn't imagined himself *capable* of feeling. That she had given him a flicker of hope in a future which before had always seemed so unremittingly dark?

'What does your brother say?' she was asking.

'That he wants to meet me.'

'When?'

'As soon as possible. He lives in New York. I could leave right away.'

'Then shouldn't you get going?'

The words were soft, and the way she said them curled over his skin, like warm smoke. Smoky like her eyes. He wanted to take her back to bed. To forget all about the damned text and touch her until he was drowning in her body and feeling that strange kind of peace he felt whenever they were together, but he knew he couldn't. Because this meeting with Dario was long overdue. The rift was as deep as a canyon, and he needed to address it. To face it and accept the outcome, whatever that might be, and then go forward.

'I shouldn't be more than a few hours,' he said.

'Take as long as you like.'

His eyes narrowed. She was giving him a permission he hadn't asked for and his default setting would usually have kicked against her interference. Because he hated the idea of a woman closing in on him…trapping him…trying to get her claws hooked right into him. Yet he would have welcomed Willow clawing him—raking those neatly filed fingernails all the way down his back and making him buck with pleasure.

He wondered when it was that his opinion of her had changed so radically. When he'd realised she wasn't some overprivileged aristocrat who wanted the world to jump whenever she snapped her pretty fingers—but someone who had quietly overcome her illness? Or when she'd offered him her body and her enduring comfort, despite his arrogance and his hard, black heart?

He walked across to her. The morning sun was gilding her skin and the silky nightgown she wore was that faded pink colour you sometimes found on the inside of a shell. She looked as pink and golden as a sunrise and he put his arms around her and drew her close.

'Have I told you that every time I look at you, I want you?' he said unevenly.

'I believe you said something along those lines last night.'

He tilted up her chin with the tip of his finger. 'Well, I'm telling you again, now—only this time it's not because I'm deep inside your body and about to explode with pleasure.'

Her lips parted. 'Dante...'

He nuzzled his mouth against her neck, before drawing back to stare into her clear eyes, knowing now of all the things he wanted to say to her. But not now. Not yet. Not with so much unfinished business to attend to. 'Now kiss me, Willow,' he said softly. 'Kiss me and give me strength, to help get me through what is going to be a difficult meeting.'

CHAPTER ELEVEN

AFTER DANTE HAD gone Willow tried to keep herself busy—because it was in those quiet moments when he wasn't around that doubts began to crowd into her mind like dark shadows. But she wasn't going to think about the future, or wonder how his Manhattan meeting with his twin brother was going. She was trying to do something she'd been taught a long time ago. To live in the day. To realise that this day was all any of them knew for sure they had.

She set off for a long walk around the grounds, watching the light bouncing off the smooth surface of the lake. The leaves were already on the turn and the whispering canopies above her head hinted at the glorious shades of gold and bronze to come. She watched a squirrel bounding along a path ahead of her and she listened to the sound of birdsong, thinking how incredibly peaceful it was here and how unbelievable it was to think that the buzzing metropolis of the city was only a short distance away.

Later she went to the library and studied row upon row of beautifully bound books, wondering just how many of them had actually been read. She found a copy of *The Adventures of Huckleberry Finn* and settled down to read it, soon finding herself engrossed in the famous story and unable to believe that she'd never read it before.

The hours slid by and she watched the slanting sunlight melt into dusk and shadows fall across the manicured lawns. As evening approached, Alma came to find Willow to tell her that Giovanni was feeling well enough to join her downstairs for dinner.

It was strangely peaceful with just her and Dante's grandfather sitting there in the candlelight, eating the delicious meal which had been brought to them. The old man ate very little, though he told Willow that the tagliatelle with truffle sauce was a meal he had enjoyed in his youth, long before he'd set foot on the shores of America.

They took coffee in one of the smaller reception rooms overlooking the darkened grounds, silhouetted with tall trees and plump bushes. Against the bruised darkness of the sky, the moon was high and it glittered a shining silver path over the surface of the lake. All around her, Willow could feel space and beauty—but she felt there was something unspoken simmering away too. Some deep sadness at Giovanni's core. She wondered what was it with these Di Sione men who, despite all their wealth and very obvious success, had souls which seemed so troubled.

Quietly drinking her espresso, Willow perched on a small stool beside his chair, listening to the sweet strains of the music which he'd requested Alma put on for them. The haunting sound of violins shimmered through the air and Willow felt a glorious sense of happiness. As if there was no place in the world she'd rather be, though it would have been made perfect if Dante had returned home in time to join them.

She thought about the way he'd kissed her goodbye that morning and she could do absolutely nothing about the sudden leap of her heart. Because you could tell yourself over and over that nothing was ever going to come of this strange affair of theirs, but knowing something wasn't always enough to kill off hope.

And once again she found herself wondering if she came clean and told Dante the truth about *her* situation, whether this affair of theirs might last beyond their flight back to Europe.

Giovanni's accented voice filtered into her thoughts.

'You are not saying very much this evening, Willow,' he observed.

Willow looked up into his lined face, into eyes which were dull with age and lined with the struggle of sickness, but which must once have burned as brightly blue as Dante's own.

And I will never know Dante as an old man like this, she thought. *I will never see the passage of time leave its mark on his beautiful face.*

Briefly, she felt the painful clench of her heart and it was a few seconds before she could bring herself to speak.

'I thought you might be enjoying the music,' she said. 'And that you might prefer me not to chatter over something so beautiful.'

'Indeed. Then I must applaud your consideration as well as your taste in music.' He smiled as he put down his delicate coffee cup with a little clatter. 'But time is of the essence, and I suspect that mine is fast running out. I am delighted that my grandson has at last found someone he wishes to marry, but as yet I know little about the woman he has chosen to be his bride.'

Somehow Willow kept her smile intact, hoping her face didn't look clown-like as a result. She'd had been so busy having sex with Dante that she'd almost forgotten about the fake engagement which had brought them here in the first place. And while she didn't want to deceive Giovanni, how could she possibly tell him the truth? She opened her mouth to try to change the subject, but it seemed Giovanni hadn't finished.

'I am something of an expert in the twists and complexities of a relationship between a man and a woman and I know that things are rarely as they seem,' he continued, the slight waver in his voice taking on a stronger note of reflection. 'But I do know one thing...'

Willow felt the punch of fear to her heart as she looked at him. 'What?' she whispered.

He smiled. 'Which is to witness the way you are when you look at Dante or speak of him.' He paused. 'For I can see for myself that your heart is full of love.'

For a moment Willow felt so choked that she couldn't speak. Yes, she'd once told her sister that she liked Dante and that had been true. But love? She thought about his anguish as he'd recounted the story of his childhood and her desire to protect him—weak as she was—from any further pain. She thought about the way he made her laugh. The way he made her feel good about herself, so that she seemed to have a permanently warm glow about her. He made her feel complete—even though, for her, such a feeling could never be more than an illusion.

So could those feelings be defined as love? Could they?

Yes.

The knowledge hit her like a rogue wave which had suddenly raced up out of the sea. Yes, they could.

And even if Dante never loved her back, surely they could still be a couple until he tired of her.

Couldn't they?

'Your grandson is very difficult to resist,' she said with a smile. 'But he is a very complex man.'

Giovanni laughed. 'But of course he is. All Di Sione men are complex—it is written into our DNA. That complexity has been our attraction and our downfall—although pride has played a big part in our actions. Sometimes we make decisions which are the wrong decisions and that is part of life. We must accept the shadows in order to experience light.' His voice suddenly hardened. 'But I know as an old man who has seen much of the world that regret is one of the hardest things to live with. Don't ever risk regret, Willow.'

She nodded as she leaned forward to tuck a corner of the blanket around his knees. 'I'll try not to.'

'And let me tell you something else.' His voice had softened now, shot through with a trace of something which sounded like wistfulness. 'That I long to see the bloodline of my offspring continue before I die, and to know there is another generation of Di Siones on the way.' He smiled. 'I know deep down that Dante would make a wonderful father, even though he might not yet realise that himself. Don't wait too long before giving him a baby, my dear.'

It felt like a knife ripping through her heart as Giovanni's blessing brought all her secret fears bubbling to a head. Willow tried hard not to let her distress show, but she was grateful when the nurse came to help the patriarch to bed. And as she made her way back to the cottage, she couldn't stop Giovanni's unwittingly cruel words from echoing round and round in her head.

Don't wait too long before giving him a baby, my dear.

Stumbling inside, it took a few moments before she could compose herself enough to get ready for bed and to register from the quick glance at her cell phone that there was no missed call or text from Dante. With trembling fingers she put on her silk nightdress, slithering beneath the duvet and staring sightlessly up at the ceiling, as she reminded herself that he hadn't promised to ring.

She had to stop relying on him emotionally. She had to learn to separate from him.

This wasn't going anywhere.

It *couldn't* go anywhere, she reminded herself fiercely. And sooner or later she had to address that fact, instead of existing in la-la land.

She fell asleep—her sleep peppered with heartbreaking dreams of empty cribs—and when she awoke, the pale light of dawn was filtering through the windows, bringing Dante's still and silhouetted form into stark relief.

Brushing the hair from her eyes, Willow sat up.

'How long have you been there?' she questioned sleepily.

He turned round slowly. So slowly that for a minute she was scared of what she might see in his face. Distress, perhaps—if his reconciliation with Dario had come to nothing.

But she couldn't tell what he was thinking because his eyes gave nothing away. They were shadowed, yes, but there was no apparent joy or sorrow in their lapis lazuli depths.

'I got back about an hour ago.'

'You didn't come to bed?'

She could have kicked herself for coming out with something so trite. Obviously he hadn't come to bed, or he wouldn't be standing at the window fully dressed, would he?

But he didn't seem irritated as he walked towards her and sat down on the edge of the mattress.

'No,' he said. 'I thought if I came to bed, then I'd have sex with you, and…'

'And you don't want sex?'

He laughed. 'I always want sex with you, Willow, but it's very distracting and right now I don't want any form of distraction.'

She nodded, staring very hard at the needlepoint bedspread before lifting her eyes to his. 'Do you want to talk about what happened?'

Dante considered her question and thought that of all the women he'd ever known, no one else would have asked it in quite that way. It was curious, yes—but it wasn't intrusive. She was making it plain that she could take it or leave it—it was entirely up to him what he chose to tell her. She didn't want to give him a hard time, he realised. And wasn't her kindness one of the things which kept drawing him back to her, time after time?

He sighed and the sound seemed to come from somewhere very deep in his lungs. It hadn't been an easy meeting with his twin, but it had been necessary. And cathartic. The pain of his remorse had hurt, but not nearly as badly as the realisation of how badly he had hurt his brother. And now that it was over he was aware of feeling lighter as a result.

'Not really. I'm done with talking about it,' he said, taking her hand within the palm of his own and wrapping his fingers around it. 'Would it be enough to tell you that Dario and I are no longer estranged?'

Willow nodded. 'Of course it's enough.' Her fingertips strayed to his shadowed jaw, where she felt the rasp of new growth against her skin.

'Willow, I need to talk to you.'

'I thought you just said you were done with talking.'

'That was about family rifts. This is something else.'

She bit her lip because now he sounded like she'd never heard him sound before. All serious and...*different*. Did he want to end it now? *Already?* 'What is it?' she questioned nervously.

Almost reflectively he began to trace a little circle over her palm before lifting his gaze to hers. And Willow didn't know if it was the fact that the sun was higher in the sky, but suddenly his eyes seemed clearer and bluer than she'd ever seen them before, and that was saying something.

'I'm in love with you,' he said.

Willow froze.

'With me?' she whispered, her voice choking a little.

He reached out his other hand—the one which wasn't holding hers—and touched her hair, as if he was testing how slowly he could slide his fingers over it.

'Yes, with you,' he said. 'The woman who has me twisted up in knots. Who made me do what I told myself I didn't want to do. Who gave herself to me—the sweetest gift I've ever had, as well as the best sex of my life. Who taught me how to forgive myself and to seek forgiveness in others, because that has helped me repair the bitter rift with my brother. You are the strongest and bravest woman I've ever met.'

'Dante...'

'Shh. Who has withstood more than the average person will ever know,' he continued. 'And then just shrugged it off, like the average person would shrug off rain from a shower. But you are not an average person, Willow. You're the most extraordinary person I've ever met—and I want to marry you and have babies with you.'

Her voice was more urgent now. 'Dante...'

'No. Just let me finish, because I need to say this,' he said, his fingers moving from their slow exploration of her hair to alight on her lips, to silence her. And when he next spoke, his words seemed to have taken on a deeper significance and his face had grown thoughtful—as if he'd just discovered something which had taken him by surprise. 'I never thought I wanted marriage or a family because I didn't know what a happy family was, and I wasn't sure I could ever create one of my own. The only thing I did know was that I never wanted to exist in an unhappy family. Not ever again.' His mouth twisted. 'But somehow I believe I can do it with you, because I believe—with you—that anything is possible. And I want you by my side for the rest of my life, Miss Willow Anoushka Hamilton.'

Willow blinked her eyes, trying furiously to hold back the spring of tears as she tried to take in words she'd never expected to hear him say. Beautiful, heartfelt words which made her heart want to melt. Wasn't it funny how you could long for something—even though you tried to tell yourself that it was the wrong thing to long for—and then when it happened, it didn't feel quite real.

It seemed inconceivable that Dante Di Sione should be sitting there holding her hand, with all the restraint and decorum of an old-fashioned suitor and telling her he'd fallen in love with her and wanted her to have his babies. She should have been jumping up and down with excitement, like a child on Christmas morning. She should have been flinging her arms around his neck and whooping with joy, because wasn't this the culmination of all the hopes and dreams which had been building inside her, despite all her efforts to keep them under control?

So why was she sitting there, her heart sinking with dismay as she looked into his beautiful eyes and a feeling of dread making her skin grow cold and clammy?

Because she couldn't do it. She couldn't. She could never be the woman he wanted.

She thought about something else his grandfather

had said to her last night and the wistful expression on his face as he'd said them. *Regret is one of the hardest things to live with. Don't ever risk regret, Willow.*

He was right. She couldn't risk regret—not for her sake, but for Dante's. Because if he married her, he would have a lifetime of regret.

Yet how could she possibly convey that? She didn't want to disclose her own dark secret and have him kiss away her fears and tell her it didn't matter. Because it did. Maybe not now, when they were in the first flush of this powerful feeling which seemed to have crept up on them both—but later, almost certainly it would matter. When the gloss and the lust had worn off and they were faced with the reality of looking at the future. Would Dante still want her then? Wouldn't he long for his heart's desire, knowing she could never give it to him?

She couldn't give him the choice and have him decide to do something out of some misplaced sense of selflessness, or kindness. She had to make the choice for him, because it was easier this way. She drew in a deep breath and knew she had to dig deep into the past, to remember how best to do this. To recall the way she'd managed to convince her weeping parents that no, of course the treatment didn't hurt. She'd worked hard on her acting ability when she'd been sick and realised it was the people around her who needed comfort more than she did. Because in a funny way, what she had been going through had been all-consuming. It was the people who had to stand and watch helplessly from the sidelines who suffered the most.

So use some of that acting talent now. Play the big-

gest part of your life by convincing Dante Di Sione that you don't want to marry him.

'I can't marry you, Dante,' she said, aware that his blue eyes had narrowed. Was that in surprise, or disbelief? Both, probably. He may have just made the most romantic declaration in the world but that hadn't eradicated the natural arrogance which was so much a part of him.

He nodded, but not before she had seen that look of darkness cross over his face, and Willow had to concentrate very hard to tell herself it was better this way. That it might hurt him a bit now—and it would certainly wound his ego—but in the long run it would be better. Much better.

She knew he was waiting for an explanation and she knew she owed him one, but wouldn't all the explanations in the world sound flimsy? She couldn't say that she thought their lifestyles were incompatible, or that she'd never want to live in Paris, or even New York—because she suspected he would be able to talk her out of every single one.

There was only one way to guarantee Dante Di Sione's permanent exit from her life and it was the hardest thing to say. Hard to say it like she really meant it, but she knew she had to try.

So she made her features grow wooden and her voice quiet. Because, for some reason, quiet always worked best. It made people strain towards you to listen. It made them believe what you said.

'I can't marry you because I don't love you, Dante.'

CHAPTER TWELVE

DANTE'S EYES WERE shards of blue so cold that Willow could feel her skin freezing beneath that icy gaze. 'You don't love me?' he repeated slowly.

Willow nodded, hanging on to her composure only by a shred. 'No,' she said. 'I don't.'

She began to babble, as if adding speed to her words would somehow add conviction. 'It was just a part we were both playing for the sake of your grandfather,' she said. 'You know it was. It was the sex which made it start to seem real. Amazing and beautiful sex—although I've got nothing to compare it to, of course. But I'm guessing from your reaction that it was pretty special, and I guess that's what made us get carried away.'

He gave a short laugh. 'Made *me* get carried away, you mean?'

Keep going, she told herself. *Not much longer now. Make him think you're a cold hard bitch, if that helps.* 'Yes,' she said with a shrug of her shoulders. 'I guess.'

A strange note had entered his voice and now his eyes had grown more thoughtful. 'So it's only ever really been about sex, is that what you're saying, Willow? You decided early on that I was to be the man who took your virginity, and you were prepared to do pretty much anything to get that to happen, were you?'

All she had to do was agree with him and very soon it would be finished. Except that something in the way he was looking at her was making her throat grow dry. Because the softness had left his face and her breasts were beginning to prickle under that new, hard look in his eyes. Willow licked her lips. 'That's right.'

Dante stared at her, wondering how he could have got it so wrong. Had he been so bewitched by her proximity that he had started believing the fantasy which they'd both created? Had his reconciliation with his brother made him overly sentimental—making him want to grab at something which up until recently hadn't even been on his agenda? Perhaps his grandfather's illness had stirred up a primitive need inside him and he had made a bad judgement call. She didn't want him, or his babies. She didn't love him. She didn't care.

A smile twisted his lips. Ironic, really. He could think of a hundred women who would fight to wear his ring for real. Just not Willow Hamilton. And just because she'd never had sex with anyone before him didn't make her a saint, did it? He'd turned her on in a big way and it seemed he had liberated her enough to want to go out there and find her pleasure with other men. He felt a savage spear of something else which was new to him. Something he automatically despised because deep down he knew it would weaken him. Something he instinctively recognised as jealousy.

And suddenly he knew that in order to let her go,

he had to have her one last time. To remind himself of how good she felt. To lick every inch of her soft, pale skin and touch every sinew of her slender body. To rid himself of this hateful need which was making his groin throb, even though he told himself he should be fighting it. But he couldn't. For the first time in his life, he couldn't. His sexual self-control was legendary and he had walked away from women when they'd been begging him to take them. Willow was not begging—not any more. His bitter smile returned. But pretty soon she would be.

'Well, if it's only ever been about sex, then maybe we ought to go out with a bang.' He smiled as her head jerked back, her shock palpable. 'If you'll pardon the pun.'

Willow's heart pounded as she looked into his eyes and saw the smoulder of intent there. She told herself that this was dangerous. Very dangerous. That she needed to get out of here before anything happened.

'Dante,' she whispered. But the words she'd been about to say had died on her lips because he was walking towards her with an expression on his face which was making her blood alternatively grow hot and cold. She could *see* the tension hardening his powerful body as he reached her. She could *smell* the raw scent of his arousal in the air. As he stroked a finger down over her arm, she began to shiver uncontrollably. This was wrong. It was wrong and dangerous and would lead to nowhere but pain and she knew she had to stop it. She *had* to. 'Dante,' she whispered again.

'One for the road,' he said in a cruel voice.

And then he kissed her in a way which shocked her

almost as much as it turned her on. It was hard and it was masterful—an unashamed assertion of sexual power. It was all about technique and dominance—but there was no affection there.

So why did she kiss him back with a hunger which was escalating by the second? Why didn't she just press her hands against that broad chest and push him away, instead of clinging on to him like some sort of limpet? He was strong enough and proud enough to accept her refusal. To just turn and walk away. They could end this strange relationship without stoking up any more emotional turmoil and then try to put the whole affair behind them.

But she couldn't. She wanted him too much. She always had and she always would. She wanted—how had he put it?—*one for the road.*

Did he see the sudden softening of her body, or did her face betray her change of feelings? Was that why he reached down to her delicate silk nightdress and ripped it open so that it flapped about her in tatters? His eyes were fixed on hers and she wanted to turn her head away, but she was like a starving dog sitting outside a butcher's shop as he swiftly bared his magnificent body and carelessly dropped his clothes to the floor.

Naked now, he was pressing her down against the mattress as he moved over her, his fingertips whispering expertly over her skin, making her writhe with hungry impatience. His big body was fiercely aroused, and even though his face looked dark and forbidding, Willow didn't care. Because how could she care about anything when he was making her feel like *this*?

She shuddered as he palmed her breasts and then bent his head to lick them in turn, his breath warm against her skin as she arched against his tongue. She could feel the rough rasp of his unshaved jaw rubbing against her skin and knew that it would be reddened by the time he had finished. And when he drew his head back she almost gasped when she saw the intense look of hunger on his face, his cheekbones flushed and his blue eyes smoky.

'Ride me,' he said deliberately.

She wanted to say no. She wanted him to kiss her deeply and passionately, the way he usually did—but she recognised that she had forfeited that luxury by telling him she didn't love him. All she had left was sex—and this was the very last time she would have even that. So make it raunchy, she told herself fiercely. Make him believe that this was what the whole thing had been about.

She slid out from underneath him to position herself on top, taking his moist and swollen tip and groping on the nearby bedside table for the condoms he always kept there. He had taught her to do this as he had taught her so much else, and she had worked on her condom application skills as diligently as a novice pianist practising her scales. So now she teased him with her fingertips as she slid the rubber over his erect shaft, enjoying his moan of satisfaction—even though it was breaking her heart to realise she would never hear it again. And when she took him deep inside her and began to move slowly up and down, he felt so big that she was certain he would split her in two. But he didn't. Her body quickly adapted to him, slickly tightening around him until she saw his fingers claw desperately at the rucked sheet on which they lay.

For a while she played the part expected of her and for a while it came so easily. Her fingers were tangled in her hair and her head was thrown back in mindless ecstasy as she rode him, glad she didn't have to stare into his beautiful face, scared that she might falter and give away her true feelings. Blurt out something stupid, and very loving. But suddenly he caught hold of her hips and levered her off him. Ignoring her murmur of protest, he laid her down flat against the mattress and moved over her again.

'No,' he said, his voice very intent as he made that first renewed thrust deep inside her. 'I want to dominate you, Willow. I want to remind myself that everything you know you have learned from me. I want to watch your face as you come, and I want you to realise that never again will you feel me doing this... and this...and *this*...'

She cried out then, because the pleasure was so intense it was close to pain. And if the first time they'd ever made love she had begged him not to be gentle with her—not to treat her as if she was made of glass—he certainly wasn't gentle now. It was as if he was determined to show her everything he was capable of, as he drove into her with a power which had her nails digging helplessly into his shoulders.

She almost didn't *want* to come—as if her orgasm would be a sign of weakness and by holding it back she could retain some control over what was happening—but already it was too late. Her back was beginning to arch, her body spasming around him as she opened her mouth to cry out her satisfaction.

But for once he didn't kiss the sound away and blot it into silence with his lips. Instead he just watched her as she screamed, as cold-bloodedly as a scientist might observe an experiment which was taking place in the laboratory. Only then did he give in to his own orgasm and she thought it seemed brief and almost perfunctory. He didn't collapse against her, whispering the soft words in French or Italian which turned her on so much. He simply pumped his seed efficiently into the condom before withdrawing from her and rolling away to the other side of the bed.

Several agonisingly long minutes passed before he turned to look at her and something about the coldness of his blue gaze made her want to shiver again.

'Time to get on that road,' he said softly.

And he walked straight towards the bathroom without a backward glance.

Willow's hands were trembling as she gathered up the tattered fragments of her torn nightdress and stuffed them into her suitcase, terrified that one of the staff would find them. She had composed herself a little by the time Dante emerged, freshly showered and shaved and wearing a dark and immaculate suit which made him seem even more distant than the look in his eyes suggested he was.

'Are you…are you going somewhere?' she said.

'I am.' He gave a cold smile. 'I'm leaving. And obviously, you'll be coming with me. We will drive to the airport—only we'll be going our separate ways from now on. You'll be heading for London, while my destination is Paris. But first, I need to speak to my grandfather.'

'Dante…'

'Save your breath, Willow,' he said coolly. 'I think we've said everything which needs to be said. I guess I should thank you for playing such a convincing fiancée. But I'm going to sit down with Giovanni and tell him that our relationship is over, and to remind him that he knows better than anyone that marriages simply don't work if there is no love involved.' His eyes glittered. 'If you're willing to sign a confidentiality clause, you can keep the ring. You should be able to get a decent amount of money for it.'

'I don't need to sign a confidentiality clause. And I won't talk about this to anyone. Why would I? It's not exactly something I'm very proud of.' Her voice was trembling as she stared at the huge diamond and thought about how much it must be worth. Shouldn't she keep it and sell it, and use the money to do some real good—for people who badly needed it? And wouldn't it help if he thought of her as greedy and grasping? If she could give him yet another reason to hate her? She curved her mouth into a speculative smile. 'But yes, I will keep the ring.'

The look of contempt on his lips was unmistakable as he turned away. 'Be my guest. And now pack your case and get dressed,' he said harshly. 'And let's get out of here.'

CHAPTER THIRTEEN

BEHIND THE FLASHING blue and gold illuminations of the Eiffel Tower, the Parisian sky was dark and starless and the streets were quiet. Far below the windows of his offices, the river Seine looked cold and uninviting and Dante was lost in thought when he heard the door open behind him and someone walk in. He swivelled round in his chair to see his assistant standing there, a pointed expression on his face.

'Yes, what is it, René?' he questioned impatiently.

'You are due at a drinks party at the Ritz...' René looked down at his watch. 'Ten minutes ago actually.'

Dante scowled. 'Ring them. Tell them that I've been held up and unlikely to make it in time.'

'I could do that, of course,' said René carefully. 'But it is the birthday party of the countess—and you know how much she wants you there.'

Dante leaned back. Yes, he knew. The whole world always wanted him, women especially. Except for one woman. His mouth hardened as he stared into space.

One woman. One infernal, infuriating woman who had made it clear that wanting him was the last thing on her particular wish list.

'Is there...is there something wrong, boss?'

Dante glanced across the room, tempted to confide in his loyal assistant—not something he ever did usually. But then, he didn't *usually* feel as if a heavy weight was pressing down hard on his heart, did he? Or his life seem as if there was something fundamental missing which made him feel only half complete. He shut his eyes. Had he imagined that the heartless way that the beautiful blonde had rejected him would have been enough to make him see sense? And that it would somehow be easy to forget her? Because if that was the case then it seemed that yet again he had been wrong, and he didn't like being wrong.

He thought about the contradiction she'd been. The tender and passionate woman in his arms who had rapturously embraced the joys of sex. He remembered her childlike delight when he'd taken her to Shelter Island for breakfast. The way she'd charmed his grandfather and made his tomboy sister look like a million dollars. He thought about the crazy hope she'd awoken in his heart, along with the realisation that, suddenly, all the things he'd never dared dream of felt as if they could be possible with her. He remembered the trembling expression on her face when he'd asked her to marry him. The way she'd tried to blink back the sudden tears of joy as she looked at him.

And then?

Then...nothing. In a voice which was deathly quiet and a face devoid of emotion, she had told him she couldn't marry him. She'd told him she didn't love him when those words belied her every action. It didn't make sense. He shook his head. None of it made sense. If she hadn't been so innocent, he might have suspected the presence of another man. Though maybe that wasn't such a crazy idea? She'd grabbed at the diamond ring quickly enough, hadn't she? So maybe she wasn't quite as naive as she seemed.

He watched as the lights on the tower turned to red, and then to gold. Perhaps he had been nothing but her *stud*—an alpha male chosen as the ideal candidate for her sexual initiation. Maybe the fact that he was a foreigner had allowed her to shed all her inhibitions—he knew some women were like that—when all along she'd intended to marry an English aristocrat of the same class as herself.

Once again, an unwanted streak of jealousy flooded through his veins like dark poison and he opened his eyes to find René looking at him with that same expression of concern. He thought about his assistant's question and he realised that yes, something was *very* wrong and it was more to do with his own behaviour. Because since when had he taken to asking himself questions, without bothering to seek out the answers?

'I need some information about a woman.'

'Same woman as before?' asked René innocently. 'It wouldn't happen to be a Miss Willow Hamilton, would it?'

'As quickly as possible,' said Dante impatiently.

'Bien sûr.' René's lips twitched. 'This is getting to be a bit of a habit if you don't mind my saying so, boss.'

'Well, I do mind.' Dante glowered as he stood up and pulled off his tie. 'I don't pay you to give your opinion when it isn't wanted. Have the car brought round and I will call at the countess's party for a while. And will you please wipe that smug expression from your face, because it is starting to infuriate me.'

Dante was driven to the first *arrondissement*, to the glittering cocktail party being held in one of the famous hotel's penthouse suites, but his heart wasn't in it—nor in any of the stellar guests who were present. The countess was delectable, but she left him cold—as did the other women who smiled at him with open invitation in their eyes. He endured it for a while, then slipped away—and when he arrived at work early the following morning, it was to find René already in the office, with a look of triumph on his face.

'I have the information you require,' he said.

'Go on.'

'She is living in London…'

'I already know that,' interrupted Dante impatiently.

'And she will be attending a fundraiser for the Leukaemia Society being held at the Granchester Hotel in London this Saturday.' René paused, his dark eyes hooded. 'You might also be interested to know that she has put her diamond engagement ring up for the charity auction.'

And for the first time in his life, Dante was speechless.

Willow looked up from behind the podium and for a moment there was complete silence in the large ballroom, before she spoke again. 'And that is why I consider it such an honour to be your new patron.'

An expectant hush fell over the assembled throng and she drew in a deep breath, knowing that she had to get this right. 'I wanted to give fellow sufferers hope, as well as supporting the fantastic new research which is taking place all over the world. I'm prepared to step out of the shadows and talk openly about what happened to me, instead of hiding it away. Because I'm better. And because, every day, there are more and more people like me, getting better. And I...'

Her words tailed off because, for a moment there, a trick of the light made her think she saw Dante standing at the back of the ballroom. She blinked, slightly impatient with herself. Was she now beginning to conjure him up from nowhere, so that he was about to become a constant presence in her daytime as well as her night-time thoughts?

'I...' She couldn't remember what she had been saying and someone held a glass of water towards her, but she shook her head. She stared to where the man stood, her eyes drinking him in—registering every pore of his sensual face. It *was* him. Very definitely him. Because nobody in the world looked quite like Dante Di Sione. Tall and broad and strong and magnificent and somehow managing to dominate the entire room.

And she couldn't allow herself to go to pieces at this point. Too many people were relying on her.

She fumbled around for the words which had been on the tip of her tongue and somehow managed to produce them. 'I just want to say that I think you are all wonderful, and I'm delighted to be able to tell you that the silent auction has raised almost half a million pounds.' She swallowed, and then smiled—a big smile which just grew and grew. 'So thank you again from the bottom of my heart—for allowing me to give something back.'

The sound of clapping began and swelled, echoing loudly throughout the vast room as Willow stepped carefully down from the stage, her narrow silver dress not the easiest of garments to move around in. Now what did she do? She risked a glance to where Dante had stood, but he was no longer there and she felt her heart plummet. Of course he wasn't there! She had dreamt him up. It had been a fantasy—nothing more. Why would he be here when he'd flown straight back to Paris and they hadn't spoken since he had boarded his jet in New York, all those weeks ago?

'Willow.'

The sound of his voice was unmistakable and her knees buckled, but even though his hand was instantly on her elbow and his strength seemed to flow straight into her, she shook herself free. Because she had to learn to live without him. She had to.

'Dante,' she said, but her voice sounded faint. 'What are you doing here?'

His eyes were curious, but his tone was dry. 'No ideas?'

She licked her lips. 'You were in London?'

'And happened to be passing? Yeah, you could say that.' He gave a mirthless smile. 'Is there anywhere quieter we can go to talk?'

She knew she should tell him that no, there wasn't. She knew she ought to fetch her wrap and go outside to find a cab. Go home and forget she'd ever seen him. Her gaze travelled over his face and stayed fixed on the features she'd missed so much. His blue eyes. His sensual lips. The faint darkness which always lingered around his jaw. 'There's the hotel's Garden Room,' she croaked.

In silence they walked to the plant-filled bar, with its white baby grand piano tucked away in the corner. Dante immediately managed to commandeer a quiet table at the back of the room but Willow knew instantly that she'd made a mistake in her choice of venue. A big mistake. Because the air was filled with the scent of jasmine and gardenia—heady scent which seemed unbearably romantic, as did the soft music which the pianist was playing. And the flickering candlelight didn't help. Maybe she could concentrate on her drink. Order some complicated cocktail with a cherry and an umbrella and give it her full attention.

But Dante waved the hovering waiter away and she guessed it was an indication of his charisma that he should be allowed to occupy the best table in the place without even ordering a drink.

She waited to hear what he would say and she tried to second-guess him, desperately trying to work out the right answers to whatever he was going to say. Trouble was, he asked the last question she wanted to hear. The one question she didn't want to answer. She'd lied about this once before, but she had been stronger then. She'd been so certain it had been the right thing to do and she hadn't been starved of his presence for almost five weeks, so that she could barely stop herself from reaching out to touch him.

'Do you love me, Willow?'

She looked into his eyes—which were the colour of midnight in this candlelit room—and she opened her mouth to tell him no. But a rush of stupid tears filled her own eyes and prevented her from saying anything, and mutely, she found herself shaking her head.

'Do you?' he said again. 'Just tell me, Willow. Say it out loud. That's all I'm asking. Tell me you don't love me and I'll walk out of here and you'll never see me again.'

She tried. For almost a minute she tried. Tried to force the words out of her mouth in the same way that you sometimes had to prise a stubborn Brazil nut from its shell. But the words wouldn't come. They just wouldn't come. At least, not the words she knew she should say. The other ones—the eager, greedy ones—they suddenly came pouring from her lips as if she had no control over them.

'Yes,' she burst out. 'Yes, I love you. Of course I do. I didn't want to. I still don't want to. And I'm sorry. I don't want to mess you around and I certainly don't want to send out mixed messages. So it's probably better if you forget everything I've just said. Because...because it can't lead anywhere, Dante—it just *can't.*'

His eyes narrowed, like someone who had just been presented with a locked room and was working out how best to open it without a key. 'Do you want to tell me why?'

'Because I can't give you what you want,' she whispered. 'You told me you wanted marriage. And babies. Your grandfather told me that he longed for nothing more than to see the next generation of Di Siones.'

'And?'

'And I can't promise you that. I had...' She swallowed and licked her lips. 'I had treatment for my illness before I started my periods and they said it's possible—even likely—that I may not be able to have children.'

'But you didn't ever find out for sure?'

She shook her head. 'No. I know it's stupid, but I preferred to live in a state of not knowing. I guess I was too scared to confront it and I didn't want yet another negative thing to define me. It seemed much easier to just bury my head in the sand.' She shrugged and bit her lip. 'But I suppose that's difficult for you to understand.'

She didn't know what she had expected but it hadn't been for Dante to pick up her hand—her left hand—and to turn it over and study her palm as if he was able to read her future, before lifting his solemn gaze to hers.

'No,' he said. 'It's not difficult at all, because all of us are sometimes guilty of not facing a truth which is too hard to take. I did it with my own brother—refused to accept that my reluctance to share him was what lay at the root of our rift. But listen to me very carefully, Willow—because you're not thinking logically.'

Her blurry gaze fixed on his stern features. 'What do you mean?'

'There is *always* the chance that you or I can't have a baby. That applies to every couple in the world until they try themselves. Unless you're advocating putting all prospective brides and grooms through some kind of fertility test before they're allowed to marry?' He raised his eyebrows. 'I don't think even royal families adopt that strategy any more.'

'Dante…'

'No,' he said. 'You've had your say and now I'm having mine. Understand?'

Pressing her lips in on themselves, she nodded.

'I love you,' he said simply. 'And the past few weeks have made me realise how much. Time spent away from you has only increased the certainty that I want to spend the rest of my life with you, and only you.' He placed a warning finger over her lips as they began to open. 'With or without children of our own. Because children aren't a deal-breaker. You not loving me would be the only deal-breaker. That's the only thing which would stop me from wanting to marry you, and I'm afraid you've just signed your own fate by telling me that you *do* love me.'

Dazed, she stared at him. 'Am I allowed to say anything yet?'

'Only if you're prepared to see sense and accept my proposal—unless you want me to go down on one knee in this very public place and ask you all over again, despite the fact that you've already auctioned off the first ring I gave you?'

'No! No, please don't do that. Don't you *dare* do that.'

'So you will marry me?'

'It seems I have no choice!'

She was laughing but somehow she seemed to be crying at the same time and Dante was standing up and pulling her into his arms and wiping her tears away with his fingers, before kissing her in a way that made the last of her reservations melt away.

And when the picture of that ecstatic kiss made its way into the gossip columns of next day's newspapers—with the headline *Society Girl to Wed No-*

torious Playboy—Willow didn't care. Because now she realised what mattered—the only thing which mattered. She was going to focus on what was truly important, and that was yet another thing Dante had taught her.

He'd taught her that love made you strong enough to overcome anything.

So she threw the newspaper down onto the carpet and turned to look at him, running her fingers over his olive skin and thinking how magnificent he looked in *her* bed.

Sleepily, he opened his eyes and gave a huge yawn as he glanced down at the bare hand which was currently inching its way up his thigh. 'I guess we'd better go out and buy you another ring. Would you like that?'

'I'd like that very much.'

'But not a diamond.' He smiled. 'A rare grey pearl, I think.'

'Mmm... That sounds perfect.' She moved over him, skin against skin, mouth against mouth—and ripples of desire shivered over her as she felt his hardness pressing against her. 'Just not now,' she whispered indistinctly. 'The ring can wait. But this can't.'

EPILOGUE

'Come and sit in the shade,' Dante said lazily. 'I don't want you getting burned.'

Willow pushed her straw hat back and smiled up into her husband's face. 'I'm unlikely to burn when you insist on applying factor fifty to my skin at every opportunity, am I?'

'True. In fact, I think you need another application right now,' he murmured, rising to his feet and standing over her. 'Come here.'

'That sounds like another excuse for you to start rubbing cream into my body.'

'You really think I need an excuse, Mrs Di Sione?' he growled, lifting her off the sun lounger and leading her inside to the air-conditioned cool of their beachside house.

Willow bit her lip with sheer pleasure as she felt his lips whisper over her throat, thinking she couldn't remember ever feeling so happy. Or lucky. So very lucky. For the past month they'd been honeymooning in a Caribbean beach house, while nearby the crystal waters lapped contentedly against sugar-fine sands. They swam in the mornings, napped in the afternoons and took lazy days out on the Di Sione boat, which had been sailed from New York and was now anchored off the island.

They had married quietly in the small church built in the grounds of her parents' house and the building had been transformed for the occasion, discreetly bankrolled by her future husband. The badly repaired hole in the ceiling had been miraculously fixed and the air was scented with gardenias and jasmine similar to those which had perfumed the Garden Room at the Granchester on the night Dante had asked her to marry him.

'Did you like our wedding?' she questioned softly.

'I loved it. Every second.'

'You didn't think it was too quiet?'

'No. It was perfect. Just like you.' Dante unclipped her bikini top and began to skate his fingertips over her nipples. He had wanted a quiet wedding. There had still been so much *stuff* going on about Giovanni's Lost Mistresses—with his brothers and his sisters all over the place trying to find random pieces of jewellery and other stuff which had once belonged to his grandfather, and nothing completely resolved. The uncertainty about who would be able to attend and who wouldn't had made Dante decide to have the smallest of weddings, with only his brother Dario in attendance as his best man. He told Willow he planned for them to visit the Long Island estate during the forthcoming holidays, where they would have a big post-wedding party.

But he'd known all along that he didn't need pomp, or ceremony. If it could have been just him and Willow, he wouldn't have complained. In the end, he was the one who badly wanted to place a gold ring on her finger and make her his. He'd wanted to marry her more than he could ever remember wanting anything. Because she gave him everything he needed—and more.

And if she'd questioned him over and over about his need for children, he had reassured her with a certainty which went bone-deep. He'd told her that there were lots of possibilities open to them if they couldn't conceive. Like he'd said, it wasn't a deal-breaker. Until one day she'd started believing him and never mentioned it again. And if either of them had been able to see into the future, they would have seen Willow Di Sione holding two baby girls—beautiful, blue-eyed twins, just like their daddy.

Dante gave a contented sigh as he remembered back to their wedding day. Without a doubt she had made the most exquisite bride in the history of the world—with a veil which had been worn by her grandmother, held in place with the glittering tiara of white diamonds and emeralds as green as new leaves. Dario had offered her use of the matching earrings, but although Willow had been very grateful, she had declined the offer. 'A woman can wear *too* much jewellery, you know,' she'd whispered to her prospective husband—and Dante had laughed with a feeling of pure pleasure.

Her slender figure had been showcased by a pale, gauzy dress, beneath which she'd sported a garter embroidered with dramatic flames of yellow and red. And when slowly he'd been removing it on their wedding night, his hand had lingered on the raised surface of vibrant hues, which she'd so lovingly stitched.

'Flames?' he questioned with a frown.

'As a kind of homage to an earlier Dante and his famous inferno.' She smiled. 'But mainly because my life would be hell without you.'

He smiled back. 'Interesting. But I thought brides were traditionally supposed to have something blue?'

And that was when her fingertips reached up to trace over his cheeks with the most gentle touch he had ever known. A touch which had made him shiver with pleasure and count his blessings.

'Your eyes are the bluest thing I've ever seen, Dante Di Sione.' Her voice had been low and trembling. 'I'll settle for those.'

* * * * *

COMING SOON!

We really hope you enjoyed reading this book. If you're looking for more romance be sure to head to the shops when new books are available on

Thursday 25th September

To see which titles are coming soon, please visit
millsandboon.co.uk/nextmonth

MILLS & BOON

FOUR BRAND NEW BOOKS FROM MILLS & BOON MODERN

Indulge in desire, drama, and breathtaking romance – where passion knows no bounds!

OUT NOW

Eight Modern stories published every month, find them all at:

millsandboon.co.uk

MILLS & BOON TRUE LOVE IS HAVING A MAKEOVER!

Introducing

Love Always

Swoon-worthy romances, where love takes center stage. Same heartwarming stories, stylish new look!

Look out for our brand new look
COMING SEPTEMBER 2025
MILLS & BOON

afterglow BOOKS

Afterglow Books is a trend-led, trope-filled list of books with diverse, authentic and relatable characters, a wide array of voices and representations, plus real world trials and tribulations. Featuring all the tropes you could possibly want (think small-town settings, fake relationships, grumpy vs sunshine, enemies to lovers) and all with a generous dose of spice in every story.

@millsandboonuk
@millsandboonuk
afterglowbooks.co.uk

#AfterglowBooks

For all the latest book news, exclusive content and giveaways scan the QR code below to sign up to the Afterglow newsletter:

afterglow BOOKS

Let's Give 'Em Pumpkin to Talk About
She's grumpy. He's sunshine. Will love grow?
ISABELLE POPP

The Secret Crush Book Club
Could this be the start of a new chapter?
KARMEN LEE

- Grumpy/sunshine
- Small-town romance
- Spicy

- LGBTQ+
- Small-town romance
- Spicy

OUT NOW

Two stories published every month. Discover more at:
Afterglowbooks.co.uk

OUT NOW!

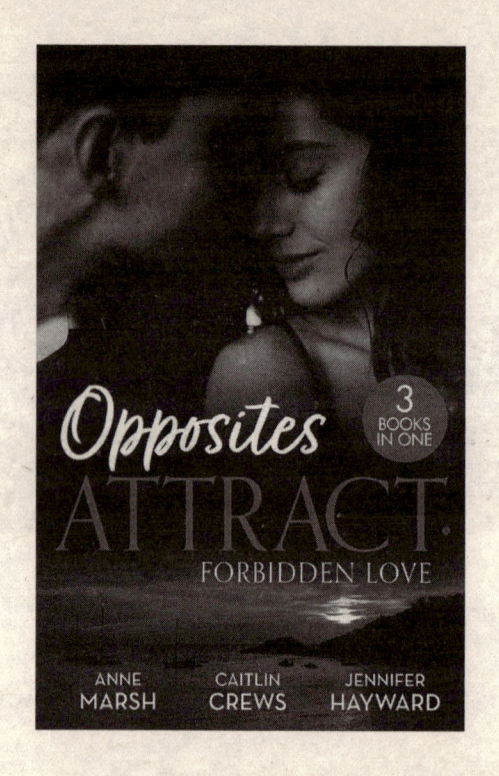

Opposites Attract: Forbidden Love

3 BOOKS IN ONE

ANNE MARSH · CAITLIN CREWS · JENNIFER HAYWARD

Available at
millsandboon.co.uk

MILLS & BOON

OUT NOW!

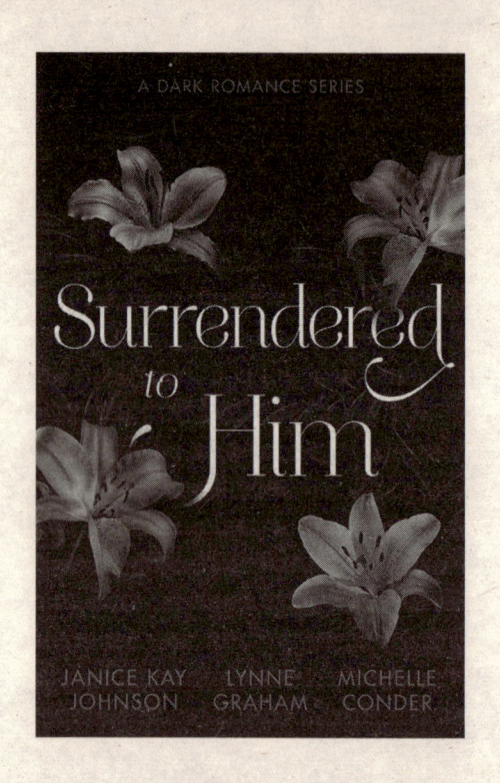

Surrendered to Him

A DARK ROMANCE SERIES

JANICE KAY JOHNSON · LYNNE GRAHAM · MICHELLE CONDER

Available at
millsandboon.co.uk

MILLS & BOON

LET'S TALK
Romance

For exclusive extracts, competitions and special offers, find us online:

- **f** MillsandBoon
- **X** @MillsandBoon
- **◉** @MillsandBoonUK
- **♪** @MillsandBoonUK

Get in touch on 01413 063 232

For all the latest titles coming soon, visit
millsandboon.co.uk/nextmonth

MILLS & BOON

THE HEART OF ROMANCE

A ROMANCE FOR EVERY READER

MODERN — Prepare to be swept off your feet by sophisticated, sexy and seductive heroes, in some of the world's most glamourous and romantic locations, where power and passion collide.

HISTORICAL — Escape with historical heroes from time gone by. Whether your passion is for wicked Regency Rakes, muscled Vikings or rugged Highlanders, awaken the romance of the past.

MEDICAL — Set your pulse racing with dedicated, delectable doctors in the high-pressure world of medicine, where emotions run high and passion, comfort and love are the best medicine.

True Love — Celebrate true love with tender stories of heartfelt romance, from the rush of falling in love to the joy a new baby can bring, and a focus on the emotional heart of a relationship.

HEROES — The excitement of a gripping thriller, with intense romance at its heart. Resourceful, true-to-life women and strong, fearless men face danger and desire - a killer combination!

afterglow BOOKS — From showing up to glowing up, these characters are on the path to leading their best lives and finding romance along the way – with plenty of sizzling spice!

To see which titles are coming soon, please visit

millsandboon.co.uk/nextmonth